TRANSLATED BY

THE DEVILS' DANCE

HAMID ISMAILOV

DONALD RAYFIELD

TILTED AXIS PRESS

POEMS TRANSLATED BY JOHN FARNDON

جينلر بازمي   The Devils' Dance

The *jinn* (often spelled *djinn*) are demonic creatures (the word means 'hidden from the senses'), imagined by the Arabs to exist long before the emergence of Islam, as a supernatural pre-human race which still interferes with, and sometimes destroys human lives, although magicians and fortunate adventurers, such as Aladdin, may be able to control them. Together with angels and humans, the jinn are the sapient creatures of the world. The jinn entered Iranian mythology (they may even stem from Old Iranian *jaini*, wicked female demons, or Aramaic *ginaye*, who were degraded pagan gods). In any case, the jinn enthralled Uzbek imagination. In the 1930s, Stalin's secret police, inveigling, torturing and then executing Uzbekistan's writers and scholars, seemed to their victims to be the latest incarnation of the jinn. The word *bazm*, however, has different origins: an old Iranian word, found in pre-Islamic Manichaean texts, and even in what little we know of the language of the Parthians, it originally meant 'a meal'. Then it expanded to 'festivities', and now, in Iran, Pakistan and Uzbekistan, it implies a riotous party with food, drink, song, poetry and, above all, dance, as unfettered and enjoyable as Islam permits.

I buried inside me the spark of love,
Deep in the canyons of my brain.
Yet the spark burned fiercely on
And inflicted endless pain.

When I heard 'Be happy' in calls to prayer
It struck me as an evil lure.
So I told the angel my personal myths;
They seemed to me more pure.

But playing with her hair, the angel said:
'Your legends are needed no more!'
Her words buzzed noisily in my ears:
'You're swimming in blood and gore.'

The king of lies told me to swim on:
'Your fortune's waiting there.'
But my soul arrayed in funeral black
Is already awaiting there.

Leave now, Satan; I am afraid.
Go! My sword's smashed, my shield holed.
Don't you see? I am lying underneath
A mountain of troubles, crushed and cold?

Oh angel, one last breath, the last of all:
One last look, then may the skies fall!

Cho'lpon

CHAPTER 1

POLO

Autumn was particularly fine that year.

Wherever you happened to be – walking home down the empty streets from the new tram stop, casting an eye over the clay walls of Tashkent's Samarkand Darvoza district, or going out into your own garden after a long day – every imaginable colour was visible under a bright blue sky. In autumns like this, the yellow and red leaves linger on the branches of trees and shrubs, as if they mean to remain there right until winter, quivering and shining in the pure, translucent air. But this motionless air and the tired sun's cooling rays already hint at grief and melancholy. Could this bitterness emanate from the smoke of dry leaves, burning some distance away? Perhaps.

Abdulla had planned to prune his vines that day and prepare them for the winter. He had already cut and dried a stack of reeds to wrap round the vines; his children, playing with fire, had nearly burnt the stack down. But for the grace of God, there would have been a disaster. Walking about with his secateurs, Abdulla noticed that some of the ties holding the vines to the stakes were torn, leaving the vines limp. He couldn't work out how this had happened: had the harvest been too plentiful, or had the plants not been cared for properly? Probably the latter: this summer and early autumn, he hadn't managed to give them the attention they needed, and the vines had had a bad time of it. He was uneasy. He had the impression that some devilish tricks had been at play ever since he freed the vines from their wrappings in early spring. Almost daily, you could hear bands playing loud music, and endless cheering in the streets. Enormous portraits hung everywhere from the building on Xadra Square as far as Urda. Every pole stuck into the earth had a bright red banner on its end. As for the nights, his friends were being snatched away: it was like a field being weeded.

Not long ago, the mullah's son G'ozi Yunus turned up – dishevelled and unwashed from constantly having to run and hide – and asked Abdulla to lend him some money, pledging his father's gold watch as a token of his trustworthiness. Then Cho'lpon's wife Katya came, distraught, bursting into tears and begging Abdulla to write a letter of support. 'They'll trust you,' she said. But who would trust anyone these days? These were vicious, unpredictable times; clearly, they hadn't finished weeding the field. As the great poet Navoi wrote, 'Fire has broken out in the Mozandaron forests'. And in the conflagration everything is burnt, regardless of whether it is dry or wet. Well, if it were up to him, he would have been like a saddled horse, raring to go. Just say 'Chuh' and he'd be off.

With these gloomy thoughts in mind, Abdulla bent down to the ground to prune the thin, lower shoots of the vines. He systematically got rid of any crooked branches. If only his children would come running up in a noisy throng to help. Sadly, the eldest had fallen ill some time ago and was still in bed; otherwise he would have joined his father and the job would have been a pleasure. The youngest, Ma'sud, his father's pampered favourite, might not know the difference between a rake and a bill-hook, but he was an amusing chatterbox. The thought made Abdulla smile. The toddler found everything fun: if you put a ladder against a vine stake he would clamber to the top like a monkey, chattering, 'Dad, Dad, let me prune the top of the vine...' 'Of course you can!' Abdulla would say.

Possibly, Abdulla wouldn't have time to prune, tie back and cover all the vines with reeds today. But there was always tomorrow and, if God was willing, the day after that. Soon after he'd protected his vines, the cold weather would pass, the spring rains would bring forth new shoots from the earth, and the cuttings he had planted in winter would come into bud. It was always like that: first you pack and wrap each vine for the winter; the next thing you know, everything unfurls in the sun and in no time at all it's green again. Just like literature, Abdulla thought, as he wiped a drop of sweat from the bridge of his nose.

The flashes of sunlight coming through the leaves must have dazzled him, for it was only now, when he tugged at a vine shoot bearing an enormous, palm-shaped leaf, that he discovered a small bunch of grapes underneath it: the qirmizka which he'd managed to get hold of and plant last year with great difficulty. The little bunch of fruit hiding under a gigantic leaf had ripened fully and, true to its name, produced round, bright-red berries, as tiny as dewdrops, so that they looked more like a pretty toy than fruit. Abdulla's heart pounded with excitement. He had been nurturing an idea for a book: the story of a beautiful slave-girl who became the wife of three khans. The autumn discovery of a bunch of berries as red as the maiden's blushing cheek, hidden among the vine's bare branches, had brought on a sudden clarity and harmony. Turning towards the house, he called out joyfully, 'Ma'sud, child, come here quick!' *But suppose the first fruit is too bitter?* He plucked a berry from the bunch that he meant to give the toddler, and put

it in his own mouth. Ramadan had just ended: he had forgotten the feel of food in daylight. The large pip crunched
between Abdulla's teeth, and its sweet flesh dissolved like
honey through his entire body.

And suddenly he had a revelation: he knew how to
begin his book. It would be a terrific story, surpassing both
Past Days and *The Scorpion from the Altar*. Ahmad Qori,
who lived at the top of Abdulla's street, had lent him a
stack of books by the classic historians, and he had already
researched the fine details. If he could get the supplies in
quickly he could then be on his own, sitting in front of
the warm coal fire of his *sandal*. Surely the three months
of cold would be long enough for him to finish his novel.

Abdulla didn't wait for his youngest child to toddle out
from the ancestral house: he picked one more berry of the
unexpected gift, tucked the tiny bunch of grapes behind
his ear and got down to work.

On 31 December, 1937, a freezing winter's day, Abdulla was
taken from his home and put in prison, neither charged
nor tried. So he did not begin his narrative with that
early-ripening bunch of grapes in the shade of a broad leaf.
Instead, Abdulla began his novel by describing a typical
game of bozkashi, where players fight for a goat carcass...

—

Nasrullo-xon, ruler of Qarshi, was very fond of bozkashi,
though as a spectator rather than a participant. Today,
mounted on a bay racehorse which had only just been
brought out from the stables, he rode onto the boundless meadow that lay outside the city. He preferred bay
horses to those of any other colour, possibly because
he could whip the horse's croup or slash its leg with his

sword and the blood would barely be noticeable against its copper coat. When they saw their ruler and his courtiers, the people raised their voices in welcome. Nasrullo glanced at his lively mount with satisfaction: tiny golden bells were attached to its mane, and it quivered nervously each time it caught the faint sound of their ringing. The soft leather bridle was decorated with mother-of-pearl, the saddle edged in red gold, while the saddle-cloth was made of white baby camel wool felt. 'Damn you,' the corpulent ruler barked at his horse every time he was jolted. And what a wonderful gold-embroidered gown he wore! It shone so bright that it dazzled the eyes. But even more bewitching was his belt with its pure gold buckle and a jewel the size of a horse's eye. A scabbard and sword were attached by a strap to the belt. Nobody would doubt that the khan's horse alone was worth more than all the possessions of the crowd that had gathered here. Ah, what a treasure, Nasrullo thought, bursting with pride as he gave his horse a slap on the croup.

As he rode up to a spacious open marquee, one of his eager guards immediately seized the reins of his horse and deftly hobbled it, while two servant boys worked the fans on either side: the applause was immediately replaced by silence. The khan's chef and the city mufti stepped out. The mufti made a long speech in praise of the holy city of Bukhara and the dynasty of the Mangits who had brought Islam to their world, and also in praise of this dynasty's precious jewel, Prince Nasrullo. He stepped aside only when the ruler waved his riding whip, after which the court chef came forward. Today he spoke as the master of the games: he shouted out orders to the riders while their horses stamped their hooves and snorted. 'Firstly,' the chef roared, 'don't pull each other off your horses, and don't hit each other with your whips. Secondly,' his throat straining a little with the effort, 'don't let your horses bite or kick. Thirdly, don't let anyone who falls off his horse be trampled.' 'Quite right! Quite right!' the people shouted in approval, punctuating these announcements. Just then, two horsemen came rushing up on black steeds, clutching to their thighs the carcass of a goat, the size of a calf. The horsemen pulled up about ten yards from the ruler's marquee, just long enough to let the carcass thud to the ground. Then they wheeled around and galloped off, shoulder to shoulder, towards the crowd.

'The goat's been lifted!' the master of the games cried out, disappearing all of a sudden behind the cloud of dust left behind by the riders rushing into the fray. It was like the Last Judgement: the wild horses barely controlled by their riders; the sound of hooves hitting the ground, of riders urging their mounts on, and of the spectators roaring; it was as if tight reins had been loosened, everything had leapt into motion and been drowned in noise. In the distance a flock of crows, tempted by the carcass, soared into the air.

'Grab it,' one man yelled. 'Hold it,' another said. The thousands who had assembled to watch echoed such cries. There was such confusion that it was hard to work out what was happening. A dog wouldn't have been able to recognise its own master.

The snorting of the horses as they joined battle either frightened or excited Nasrullo's bay – it too tried to rush forwards, despite its fetters. It managed to keep its balance, but lashed out furiously with its hind hooves. The Prince gripped the reins hard to hold the horse back, and two guards clung to the stirrups on either side. The horse twisted its head and foam spattered from its mouth while Nasrullo's whip rained down blows. How could the ruler see the game like this?

All he could make out was brief glimpses of necks colliding against necks. His heart was pounding. He wanted to push his guards aside and ride into the thick of the game, using his sword to clear a path if necessary, then bend down and pick up the dead goat, his whip poised between his teeth... As if it had guessed what its master was thinking, the bay horse rushed forward again. If a piercing, heart-stopping cry had not just then come from the crush of circling horses, then who knows? Perhaps Nasrullo would have overlooked his royal status and thrown himself into the skirmish.

The flanks of the horses on the outer edge shifted and he caught a glimpse between their hooves of a carcass, not a goat's but a man's, being picked up by the ankle and flung onto the back of a horse.

'He's been trampled, trampled!' the people clamoured, and the court chamberlain hurried over to the scrum, which stopped moving. Then a rider burst forth from the mass of horse flesh: the body of his fellow contestant hung lifelessly from his horse's back. The riderless horse, a young dun not much more than a colt, followed: its reins were grabbed and passed along until they reached the chamberlain, who bowed and looked enquiringly at the Prince. Nasrullo nodded. Two servants brought a brocade gown from the marquee and threw it over the dun horse's back. The chamberlain handed the reins to the rider who had brought the contestant's body out of the crush, and the man trotted off, leading both horses towards the lamenting spectators.

Despite the hysterical tears of the dead man's relatives, the game resumed, the goat's carcass thrown back to be torn apart. This time the horsemen who had been waiting at the edge of the meadow galloped to the centre.

A week earlier, Haydar, Emir of Bukhara and Nasrullo's

father, had visited Qarshi. Today the Emir's vizier, Chief Minister Hakim, had sent a courier with the following message, 'Your father and noble benefactor fell ill on his return: despite the doctor's efforts, His Majesty's condition worsens with each day.' The Chief Minister also added an oral message: 'Make your preparations.'

Nasrullo's father was devoted to intellectual pursuits, and the Mangit dynasty had weakened with him; the Emirate was swamped with intrigues and betrayal spread like a contagion. Recently, a group of armed men from the Chinese-Kipchak district had raided the viceroy of Samarkand and Umar, Emir of Kokand, had taken advantage of the situation by besieging Jizzax castle.

Meanwhile Nasrullo's father's condition was worsening. Could that plotting chef have put something in the food during his visit to his Majesty? He had been boasting that he had a stock of arsenic which could kill a horse with a single drop. Could he have snuck it into some dish of plov? The man would have to be interrogated... But never mind that now. First, Nasrullo had his duties to carry out.

There was more whooping from the riders, then uproar and a deafening cry. 'The goat, the goat's been lifted!' As the goat was held up, one man tried to grab it, only to have his arm violently knocked away by another rider's knee. There was a general clamour while the second rider snatched the carcass and galloped away at great speed. This rider was very young, his horse the same bay colour as the prince's. He was pursued by other horses of every conceivable colour and breed: chestnuts, blacks, greys and browns, whites and piebalds, Akhal-Teke and Karabair, duns and light bays. There was no chance of the chamberlain's orders – 'Don't hit, kick, bite or unhorse!' – being observed now. Men lashed out with their whips wherever they could, at faces or heads; horses harrumphed as they knocked each other over; fallen riders, trampled by hooves, lay on the turf.

The bay horse had barely made fifty yards when it stumbled and came to a sudden halt. Immediately, two other riders came galloping up on both sides and the battle broke out again. At full tilt, the bay horse's rider hit one of his competitors in the side with the handle of his whip, then veered off to the left. He directed his knee at the hand of the second – who had just managed to clutch the goat – and threw him from his saddle, dragging his victim a few yards.

'What a rider!' Nasrullo exclaimed. He couldn't help comparing himself with this youth who had not only managed to snatch the goat from someone else's firm grip, but to carry it off, too, out of the scrum. If his father, the sovereign, had been present now, Nasrullo would certainly have summoned the master of the games to his presence and reprimanded him for allowing the rules to be breached; but now, in thrall to his own private thoughts, he merely expressed his admiration for the horseman. If anything happened to his father, then Nasrullo's brothers, the eldest Husein, the younger Umar, Zabair, Hamza and Sardar, would each try to take the throne, just as these horsemen had scuffled over the goat carcass. But that prize would not go to anyone like these dolts on their clumsy nags; it would of course be him, Emir Nasrullo, dominating all on his lively bay steed.

Not sparing even a glance for his bewildered courtiers, the ruler left just when the game was at its nail-biting peak and – his horse no longer hobbled – he rode off towards the palace.

—

It was significant that Abdulla's novel began not with the

miraculous discovery of the bunch of grapes, but with the game of bozkashi over the carcass of a goat.

On 31 December, they had broken into his house, ignoring the shrieks and cries of his children and wife who had gathered round the dinner-table for the New Year's feast. The NKVD men overturned the dinner table and stormed through the house, ransacking everything, rummaging through Abdulla's books and papers: just then, the spectacle of that game of bozkashi passed through Abdulla's mind. *Just as I was imagining myself to be a horse ready and saddled, waiting to be told 'Chuh', these 'riders' seem to be grabbing me as they would a goat's carcass,* Abdulla was thinking, when the men handcuffed him, dragged him out into the yard and bundled him into the sleek car parked by his gates, as his weeping household looked on.

While crossing Xadra square, Abdulla heard the explosions of fireworks, and fragments of a celebratory speech booming from a loudspeaker. What a pity: the New Year presents which he'd brought back after a cultural evening at the Railway Workers' Palace were tucked away at home. There were packets of confectionery from Moscow and oranges, the colour of the setting sun, fruit for each child. Would his wife, Rahbar, hand them out once the children had calmed down, or would she be too upset to remember?

Abdulla had been arrested once before, eleven years ago, so he was not particularly bewildered or aghast on this occasion. Then, his soul had rebelled against the injustice; now he felt nothing much. His only regret was that his children were being deprived of the joys of New Year's, and that the work he had planned for the winter had been interrupted.

He could hear the festive clamour of trumpets, chalumeaux, drums: each time the car bumped over a pothole, his handcuffs rattled, turning his mind to quite a different occasion, a scene from the novel his handcuffed hands should have been writing...

Early one morning at the end of summer, in the year 1235 by the Muslim calendar, a burst of shawms rent the air of the city of Kokand. Town criers loudly proclaimed to citizens and to visitors that the Muslim Emir Umar was to wed the daughter of the revered G'ozi-xo'ja. Doleful music and Hafiz songs could be heard coming from the palace. Plov was dished out for the people in the square, while the palace's guests and courtiers were to be entertained to a banquet lasting three continuous days.

This was not the Emir's first marriage feast: on this occasion the Emir and his people were beginning a three-day celebration, instead of the customary longer celebrations. Florists were staggering to the palace with armfuls of flowers; the confectioners stood over their cauldrons, conjuring up halva, sheep-lard pastries, boiled sweets and candy on sticks; two Russian soldiers, prisoners of war, removed the covers from the cannon barrels, which they cleaned with wooden brass-tipped rods in preparation for a spectacular salvo.

Meanwhile the Emir, for whom entire towns and fortresses were not plunder enough, sat enchanted with the prospect of yet another conquest: an eighteen-year-old beauty, whose equal could not be found in eighteen thousand worlds, and who that night was to become his third wife! As the revered poet Navoi said:

> Eighteen thousand worlds yet never once seen:
> This girl, slim as a cypress, and barely eighteen.

Alas, a number of intrigues were put into place for the

Emir to get her. A new stanza was composed:

> Oh angel nymph, grief has weakened my soul:
> The sword of exile has drained my blood whole.

While Umar was in Shahrixon to see his younger sister Oftob, he also encountered the clever and virtuous wife of the Khan of Shahrixon, who offhandedly told the Emir: 'Sire, you may remember being angry with G'ozi-xo'ja and expelling him from his home. This man now lives in a cottage very close by, just behind my house, and he is very poor. But he has a daughter called Oyxon, a girl of indescribable beauty – words simply can't capture her, tongues become numb, pens break. As the couplet says:

> The moment I see her, my eyes run with tears
> As the stars only shine when the sun disappears.

This wise woman described the girl so vividly that the Emir suspected it could not be true. When the other guests had left, he questioned Oftob, and the cunning princess replied, 'My lord, I have been lucky enough to see this girl: her face is as smooth as porcelain, her eyes are like two evening stars when night falls, her waist is as small as a wasp's, her buttocks are as heavy as rounded sacks of sand...' Oftob resorted to the language of *A Thousand and One Nights*, which she and the Emir had so loved to listen to when they were children: Umar's heart was conquered.

Several times he sent matchmakers to G'ozi-xo'ja's house, but the reply was always 'no'. The pretext was that Oyxon was betrothed to a relative, that their marriage was imminent, after which G'ozi-xo'ja gave a detailed account of his poverty and complained that he was being unjustly punished and that Umar's actions contradicted the laws of Islam; but, if his Lordship wished to force a marriage, then that was in his power and on his conscience. G'ozi-xo'ja added that his wife hadn't stopped weeping since the matchmakers started pestering their household. Then he sent the matchmakers away. And yet…

———

It was dark when the car came to a sudden halt and Abdulla lost the thread of his thoughts. They must have arrived at the prison. What had he been thinking about? Oh yes, the five bright-red oranges he hadn't been able to give his children, now left in a house where the lights were out. When he was still very young, he'd written a story called 'Devils' Dance' about something terrible that had happened to his father. Could Abdulla have been taken captive by devils, as his father was?

The doors of the vehicle were wrenched open. The snow fell quietly, but in big flakes: a shout rang through this lacework: 'Qodiriy, out!' The courtyard was a shade of white tinged with blue, a pure covering still untouched by human feet and surrounded on all four sides by dark brown buildings.

———

Hands cuffed, elbows gripped, Abdulla was taken down a dark staircase into the building's basement. In one of the niches, by the dim light of the caged paraffin lamp, a swarthy Russian stuck his hands under Abdulla's gown and poked in all his pockets, pulling out everything to the last penny, and then, after feeling his trousers, removed his thick leather belt. 'Sign this!' he barked, holding out a piece of paper. Abdulla gestured to his handcuffed wrists. 'Well, scribbler,' the guard laughed, 'you've had your itchy little hands put out of action!' He kicked Abdulla in the knee so hard that the latter curled up in agony. 'Hold the pen with your teeth,' the Russian demanded.

'Hold on, Vinokurov,' said one of the men who had searched Abdulla's house. 'Watch you don't finish him straight away, we've only just brought him in! I've still got to interrogate the son of a bitch.' This man, evidently in charge, wished Vinokurov a Happy New Year before he left, presumably to celebrate with his own family.

Whether out of annoyance at having to work on New Year's eve, or because he'd started the festive drinking early, Vinokurov kicked, cursed and beat Abdulla before throwing him into the solitary cell. Abdulla wanted to strangle his tormenter, but his hands were shackled and he hadn't the courage to use his teeth. He could only bite his lips till they bled.

You get used to physical pain: you synchronise your breathing to its throbbing waves, you are ready for the waves to surge up and you can wait for the waves to die down. But the pains of humiliation are unbearable, and it is impossible to endure the suffering caused by your own helplessness. At first Abdulla attributed Vinokurov's brutality to the fact that he was a Russian, but he then recalled that among the men who searched his house there had been an interrogator who spoke Uzbek like a Tatar, replacing all his 'j's with 'y's.

In prison you can't avoid getting a kicking. In 1926, too, Abdulla had been beaten within an inch of his life. What made his blood boil was not the physical pain so much as the treachery of his own people, black-eyed blood relatives whom he had trusted and considered to be friends. Back then he'd begged for death's release: that would have been easier to bear than the company of his own black-eyed friends. He'd been too young then: he hadn't thought of his children, nor of Rahbar.

Had Rahbar given the children the oranges he'd meant for them? Tomorrow (but wasn't it tomorrow already?)

Abdulla had planned to take them to see the New Year fir at the Railway Workers' Palace, where the biggest and best celebrations were supposed to take place. Last year the children's favourites had been the trained dogs which answered questions and took turns pulling each other round on sleighs. Would Rahbar take them this time, and would they be allowed in if she did? Might they find themselves turned away at the doors, as the family of an arrested man? His heart sank at the thought.

Abdulla recalled a day from his own childhood, when he had dressed up in new trousers and an Uzbek gown to go to the Christmas tree celebrations. The caretaker at his Russian-language school stopped him at the school gates. 'Have you become a kaffir now?' the man grumbled, raising his stick to deal Abdulla a terrific blow on the thigh. The literature teacher, seeing this, hurried over and rebuked him: 'This is a celebration of the birth of Jesus son of Mary, and Jesus is a prophet of yours!' Abdulla's leg was bleeding and his new trousers were stained; he ended up visiting the hospital instead of the Christmas tree. The teacher drove him all the way home, in his own carriage: a Russian, who had defended him from an Uzbek. No, generosity or meanness had nothing to do with nationality.

After all, now the whole country was run by a Georgian, and the result? Everyone was eating each other's flesh.

—

Less than a week after the bozkashi game, another message came from Chief Minister Hakim in Bukhara to Nasrullo in Qarshi. 'Your father, our benefactor, has ended his journey on earth and set off for the true world. We keep the fortress's high gates locked, and we have not yet announced this news to anyone else. Take this opportunity: bring your troops at a gallop to holy Bukhara and occupy the place that befits you.' Since all the preparations for this outcome had been made, Nasrullo set off for Bukhara that same day with three hundred warriors.

But the cat had to be let out of the bag. The news of the grief that had overcome Emir Haydar's harem spread like wildfire through the Bukhara markets and then the whole city. When the Emir's eldest son Husayn heard the news, he too gathered his troops and dashed off to the fortress.

Chief Minister Hakim kept the gates shut, as he had promised Nasrullo. Nasrullo moved with his elite troops towards Bukhara, but Husayn fired on the rebel army with artillery and rifles. They got as far as the fortress walls, and Husayn fought them at the mint next to the fortress, where they had taken cover.

Then Chief Minister Hakim ordered rocks and beams to be hurled down from the fortress walls onto Husayn's troops. One of these missiles struck Husayn's head: he was bleeding badly, but would not retreat. Instead, his men – enraged at the sight of their injured prince – climbed over the barriers and rushed to the fortress gates, smashing them down with the same rocks that had been hurled at them.

As a drop becomes a rivulet, and a rivulet a river, and a river a torrent, so the men broke into the fortress in a matter of hours, pouring in until they had flooded it. The wounded prince Husayn rode through the open gates as the new Emir. Despite extensive searches, the rebellious vizier Hakim was nowhere to be found. Shortly afterwards he appeared before the Emir of his own accord, carrying the severed head of his chief of artillery. 'Forgive your servant: I was in the grip of ignorance, when this ungrateful dog started firing cannon instead of opening the gates to Your Majesty,' he said, bowing and scraping at length. Husayn forgave him his sins, appointing Hakim as his vizier as his father had done before him.

The next day Husayn was crowned Emir, but he did not hold power for long; a mysterious illness forced him off the throne in less than three months. The doctors failed to conjure one of their miracles, and Emir Husayn left this world of sorrows. When Nasrullo heard what had happened, his thoughts turned to his master chef, who he had only recently sent to serve his brother Husayn as a peace-offering: 'Seems the bastard took his arsenic with him'. Then he gathered his army and set off for Bukhara once again.

—

Thoughts have strange paths. Where had all this come from? The injuries to his body, Vinokurov's threats, the immortal Georgian Leader? After all, Abdulla had been thinking only about his children, left to weep on New Year's eve.

His father was right when he said that a man can be in thrall to devils, especially if he is a writer. You have only to set to work to be gripped by your plans and inventions, and everything else seems vanity, triviality, a distraction. Over the last month Abdulla had covered reams of paper, having told himself: If I can sit down on my own this winter, I will finish writing the novel. And now all those hopes had been dashed. The Tatar NKVD man had found the manuscript, stuffed it in the only suitcase in the house, and taken it away with him. And he was hardly going to read it, was he? Could he even decipher the old Arabic script of Uzbek? Or would he hire some black-eyed locals to read it for him?

Why hadn't Abdulla begun his story with a description of the bunch of grapes? He might have got away with saying that this was just a little sketch of a fictitious gardener.

But now his pieces would certainly damn him. Thoughts have strange paths, indeed.

He had only recently been thinking about Umar's first marriage in 1220 to Nodira, daughter of the governor of Andijan. Abdulla had carefully worked out all the details of the matchmaking, the wedding ceremony obligatory for any marriage in the East. So why had his thoughts switched from one marriage to the other? Why does it happen that you get carried away writing about something and suddenly a single word or sentence makes you deviate from your original idea?

Take now, for instance: is Abdulla trying to lull his sense of pain and humiliation? Or are the habits of many years taking over so that even here, lying in this God-forsaken place, after letting his head fall on the pillow and saying his evening prayer, he lets his thoughts roam free of whatever was shackling them, free of anything that has nothing to do with the task in hand: writing? But he hadn't yet pronounced the words of the prayer, 'I lie down in peace'…

Abdulla had described every detail of Khan Umar's first wedding: the ceremony in the state palace, the dancing and the games, the laughter and the joyful voices. The drumbeats that shook the sky's blue dome when the people heard that the newly-weds had retired. The intoxicating joy which foamed in chalices while the sound of music filled hearts with delight and ecstasy.

That's why he sought to describe the second marriage in a different key.

For a third time Umar sent a matchmaker to G'ozi-xo'ja's house: this time it was the talkative Hakim, Umar's sister's son, a relation which made him a *mahram*, a man entitled to enter the harem. The Emir was wary of letting an outsider see his future bride's beauty, but he could allow his nephew to behold her. Only the matchmakers and the girl's father, whose white brows were wet with sweat, knew what was said during the negotiations. Realising that it was impossible to play with fire, G'ozi-xo'ja reluctantly nodded his agreement.

That same morning Hakim brought the girl home with him, entrusting her to the care of his mother Oftob. Delighted by the bride's beauty, the young matchmaker recited a Persian couplet to his mother:

> A miracle of beauty! On seeing her figure and movement
> Even a hundred-year old hermit will gird his belt!

The poor girl arrived wearing an old dress: Emir Umar was in a hurry to marry, so he dressed her in silk and ordered the old gown be given to his concubines, since it was too sacred to be thrown away. The concubines spurned the offer...

But no sooner had Abdulla composed this scene than the idea flew away like a spark. What was going on?

Breaking the cell's silence, bouncing off the walls and the bars, Vinokurov's thunderous voice slurred the words: 'Happy New Year, you pricks!'

For a moment, Abdulla didn't know whether to laugh or to weep. Was there nobody left to keep that monster company, so that he had to remind people, if only the prisoners, that he still existed? Or had he got drunk with the soldiers on guard and was yelling this at them?

It was now New Year. Happy New Year to you, Abdulla! You said that if you could sit down for one winter, you would finish your novel. Clearly, you didn't say *inshallah* at the time. But you had sensed the danger. Writers as well-known as you had already been arrested – Fitrat and Cho'lpon, G'ozi Yunus and Anqaboy – hadn't they? Were you really likely to be left alone? When you tell a horse to 'Chuh', you have given it a bit more rope. He can go on writing for a bit, they would have thought, we'll squash him when the time is ripe.

You'll spend the new year wherever you spent New Year's day, as the Russian proverb goes. So, Abdulla, it looks as if you'll be spending this year in prison. Last time you were let out after six months, but now... Fitrat and Cho'lpon have been languishing here for longer than that time already, and who knows when they'll be released? There might just be a few walls separating them from you, Abdulla. If you were to yell out like Vinokurov, might you get an answer?

Ah, he now remembered the spark that had just flashed in his head: Umar's nephew Hakim waiting for the newly-weds, who were concealed behind a curtain on the first night of their wedding. Abdulla remembered Hakim's book *Selected Histories*, almost by heart.

> Because of his youth and naughtiness, your humble servant continued sitting by the curtain and, following the path of disrespect, raised a corner of the cover to hide under it so that he could enjoy the spectacle of the Sun meeting the Moon. The wine of desire foamed in the throat of Emir Umar-xon, and the moisture of shame appeared on the face of the beauty, like drops of dew on a rose. Moments of tenderness and elegant caresses were becoming more and more wild: the buyer's desire grew, while the mistress of the goods gave ever greater concessions. For rain, ready to show the cloud's final aim, was now about to pour down on the field of desire. The flower bud, submitting to the playful brazenness of the wind, was forced to unfurl its petals and turn itself bright red. And since the innate urge of the flower bud was to bear fruit, it opened fully under the force of the wind, so that a pearly drop now fell on its pollen.

Would it have been at that precise moment that your humble servant was overcome by laughter? By whispering these words as if they were a prayer, Abdulla found that he could order his thoughts and see everything clearly. Hadn't he just responded to Vinokurov's roar with a burst of laughter? That was why he had recalled Hakim hiding behind a curtain. For a second, he felt as if he were Emir Umar's nephew, except the curtain was now a stone wall and enclosed not a love scene but a death act. Wait, wait! This was no time to drop the reins. Watch out, don't let a torrent of flighty thoughts sweep you away! If you ignored the superfluous florid style, the scene was described splendidly, especially the beginning and the end. Yet it seemed to have propelled Abdulla in an entirely different direction.

—

Oyxon was the eldest daughter of a revered hereditary *sayid*, G'ozi-xo'ja. She was not yet eighteen, but her many worries made her so serious that she was often mistaken for a younger sister of her mother Qantak. In the first days of the winter of 1232, their city O'ratepa was seized by Umar; all the *sayids*, including G'ozi-xo'ja, were arrested and shackled. Their property confiscated, they were driven out of their houses into the thick winter snow, crowded into wagons and packed off to Kokand. Oyxon was then fifteen. When they reached Kokand, cold and hungry, they found Umar still angry: he sent them even further, to Shahrixon. The family was so destitute that a flat loaf of bread seemed a gift from heaven, a set of old clothes a precious luxury. When they arrived at their place of exile, G'ozi-xo'ja's family somehow built themselves a hovel to protect themselves from the fearful cold. They now had to live on what their father could earn by teaching children of the local poor to read and write, while Qandak and

Oyxon made embroidered skull-caps. They embroidered in silk, but wore coarse calico dresses. All their earnings were spent on food. To relieve her father, Oyxon taught her younger siblings herself, putting them to bed at night, telling them fairy stories and writing verses for them.

The sufferings Qantak endured gave her a swollen goitre the following winter, and she developed a cough which she could not shake. G'ozi-xo'ja managed to get some deergrass to make an extract, which he gave her to drink. But nothing was of any use: by spring Qantak had departed this treacherous world, leaving behind five motherless children. There was a great deal of mourning and lamenting. The eldest daughter became her father's sole support, a substitute mother to her siblings. Oyxon had been embroidering ten skull-caps a week; now she had to embroider twenty. Her doe-like eyes became as sharp as a blade and she herself as quick and nimble as a panther. She bathed, fed, nursed and taught the children, attending, also, to her prematurely aged father: her voice became as sweet as honey served in porcelain.

Her cousin Qosim was the first to notice the changes in her. He would come to Shahrixon to help his uncle's family tend the vegetable plot. This time, with his uncle's blessing, he put off going home, instead finding more jobs to do around the house: repairing shoes, patching up the mud-brick wall, setting up the bread-baking oven – there was no lack of things to do – any excuse to stay on.

G'ozi-xo'ja's children grew fond of Qosim and lent a hand when he was working, or clung to his side and begged him to make them a clay toy. One of the girls – the youngest but one – insisted that she would be his wife when she grew up. Only Oyxon was reserved in her cousin's presence, doing no more than what duty obliged of her: preparing tea, serving dinner, making up a spare bed on the floor.

At the beginning of spring, when everything else had been taken care of, Qosim stayed on to remove the winter covering from the vines and tie them to their stakes. He was so carried away by his task that he failed to accompany the elderly G'ozi-xo'ja, as he had intended, on his way to pay respects at the graves of the holy men in Eski-Novqat. At the time, Oyxon's two younger sisters were staying with a neighbour to study more advanced reading and writing. The older boy was with his father; only the youngest, Nozim, was still at home. And, early in the morning, Nozim was still asleep.

Qosim fixed the loose cross-ties on the vine stakes and drove in new ones, before starting to rake over the dry reeds. He lifted the reeds carefully and saw that mercifully the frost hadn't got at the vines: they could be tied to the stakes. The vine buds were already about to burst open: any day now the green shoots would break through.

'Your good health, cousin!' Oyxon greeted him, spreading a cloth on the ground and laying some flatbread on it. 'Come and have some tea!'

'As you wish,' he replied. He moved to where she had laid out breakfast. Watching the girl get up to return to the house, her slender figure supple as a vine, he surprised himself by calling out, 'I need your help!'

Oyxon looked around. 'What for, cousin?'

She said the word 'cousin' so gently that Qosim couldn't help missing a breath at the implications. He could barely whisper: 'Would you mind holding the ladder? The cross-beams on the stakes are too thin, and I need to tie the vine branches firmly...'

Oyxon spun round to face him. 'As you wish...'

The tea was left undrunk. His hands trembling with excitement, his breath quickening, Qosim picked up the ladder which lay near the vineyard and placed it against a strong supporting pillar. 'If you hold it from this side, I'll have the branches tied to the crossbeams in no time,' he said.

Oyxon tensed her slim figure and gripped the ladder with all her strength. Imagining himself a tightrope walker, Qosim flew effortlessly up to the top. The spring breeze tickled his cheeks and hair; he felt he was flying not just over the vineyard, but the expanse of the whole world.

He used the reeds he had prepared to tie one branch and then another, but the third proved intractable, and had bent too far out. Qosim leaned out towards it, and while he swung out in one direction, the ladder went the other way: there was a high-pitched shriek and this time Qosim really did fly, only downwards, all the way to the ground.

'Help!' Oyxon cried as she rushed up to him and slapped his face, grabbing him by the collar and shaking him to see if there were any signs of life. A torrent of tears bathed Qosim's face, but when her grieving lips touched his sweaty brow, a groan escaped the young man's throat. Gripped by fear for what she had done, the girl cried out.

'I saw it, I saw it, I saw the kiss,' a small voice threatened her.

That night, putting Nozim to bed next to her, she stroked his head and whispered in a conspiratorial tone, 'Don't tell anyone what you saw this morning.'

Qosim was in bed in the next room. His entire body ached from the bruising, but his heart was intoxicated, like new green shoots in the wind.

At some point in the night, Abdulla raised himself up, dragged himself to a corner and slumped onto a black shape there. His body ached, but for some reason he felt at ease. How could that be?

—

Whether because Nozim had let slip the secret after all, or because G'ozi-xo'ja had spoken to his relatives in Eski-Novqat in the course of his brief pilgrimage, Qosim left for home as soon as he was able to. In the afternoon, G'ozi-xo'ja summoned his eldest daughter, intending to disclose his heart's secret desire: to do so, he went back all the way to Adam and Eve, alluding to every Old Testament story there was.

'Qosim is a good lad. He's hard-working, good in the garden and the orchard, and he knows how to build things. Look at the extra space he built in our yard. He's educated, too: his father has plans for him to study further in the Kokand madrasa. But I'm old now, my eyes don't see as well as they used to, my hands have lost their strength, and I've lost my better half: there's nobody to help run the household. If only your mother could have seen how you've grown up.'

Oyxon didn't understand all this beating around the bush. At first she thought her father was rebuking her; she wept: 'Father, forgive your unhappy daughter. It's my fault, I've haven't looked after you well. I've been too busy all the time, embroidering, or cooking, or laundering. I'll give you more of my attention now. I can see I didn't learn much from my mother...'

'No, daughter, don't talk like that: you've been both mother and father in this house, while I've been an old fool to express myself so badly. In the Qur'an, in the Surat *Al-Hujur'at* it says "O people! Verily, we have created you men and women, we have made you nations and tribes, so that you should know one another..." Marriage between a man and a woman is a directive of the Prophet: you've reached the marriageable age, so I have decided...'

Oyxon's trembling lips didn't dare form the response, 'As you command!' She merely nodded and bowed her head.

At the end of spring it was decided that Oyxon and her young brothers would stay for a week with their uncle in Eski-Novqat. Qosim came in his cart to fetch them. At dawn, after morning prayers and their father's blessing, they set off. The cart had three thick rugs spread over a bed of reeds and hay. They jolted along a road, and towards noon they reached a Kyrgyz village. Here they broke for refreshment and, getting back into the cart after a bowl of real, icy Kyrgyz kumys both Oyxon's brothers fell into a deep, sated sleep. The road passed through foothills, then mountains, following the course of a rushing stream. Sitting up front to drive the horses, Qosim broke the silence, speaking as if to himself:

'How fresh the mountain breeze is!' It could have been a question, or an exclamation by someone whose soul was brimming over with emotion.

Since the road they were travelling along was deserted, Oyxon removed her horse-hair veil, and, weary of the prolonged silence, responded: 'Yes, the spring air is special, it's different somehow...'

'That's what I felt when I was at the top of the ladder, standing over the vineyard.' Qosim said quite without thinking, and immediately bit his tongue, for he could sense, even without turning round, that Oyxon's heavy silence was one of embarrassment.

'I was so clumsy,' she apologised, 'I couldn't hold the ladder up...'

Qosim had the sense to change the subject: 'Somehow, these mountains always make me want to sing.'

The bright greenery of the hills, the roar of the clear mountain torrent beneath them, the icy air and the after-effect of the kumys combined to relax Oxyon's guard: she nodded in agreement and added, overcome by reticence,

'Perhaps you'll sing something, cousin?'

Qosim didn't wait to be asked twice. He filled his lungs, swelled his chest and began to sing:

> Let the morning breeze hear my plea
> Let the morning breeze hear my plea
> Her eyes bright as Venus, her hair wild and free
> The grace of a cypress, brows black as can be!
> Let my prayers be heard by this shimmering beauty.
> She vanished from me like some mischievous fairy
> And left me to live with nothing but misery.
> We made to each other an unbreakable vow
> So if one of us breaks it, it's in God's hands now.

The young man's voice rose higher and higher, as if competing with the winds that blew over the peaks. The high notes made his voice resonate, and the girl could not stop herself from quietly joining in.

They joined forces for a second song. Oyxon's voice sounded less constrained in the open air. When Qosim sensed this change, he broke off and insisted jokingly, 'Now let's hear you, cousin Oyxon!'

She cast a glance at her brothers: seeing that they were still fast asleep, tipsy from the kumys, she sang verses which Qosim had never heard before.

> If my voice starts to quaver, let strength come into it
> If the flower is half-coloured, let blood fill it up.
>
> If tears overwhelm me, flowing night and day
> And Venus burns my eye, let the sun rise with a sigh.

The girl's voice was as full of tenderness and shyness as the red poppies on the mountain slopes, as nimble and youthful as a vine, and as strong as the intoxicating sap of the earth. Apparently guessing what Qosim was thinking, Oyxon suddenly started singing *sotto voce*:

> Though someone sets the ladder, don't brush muck from the roof:
> Let the leaves drop in autumn, or let your gardener lend a hand.

Every beat of his heart clearly confirmed to Qosim the authorship of this verse.

> When you look at me, it means death in two worlds.
> If I come alive in one, I die in the other.

Qosim nearly dropped the reins. Looking behind him, he saw that the evening sun, setting over the humped peaks, shone on the girl's unveiled face, and that face seemed to him like a moon, shining desperately in the glare of the sun.

> I tried to nail down today, and fix it forever
> But it rips my heart – let it go now in peace.

Those words should have been sung by Qosim, not by her. The sun had half disappeared behind a mountain, leaving only a dim semi-circle behind. The girl seemed also to have waned, and she finished her song in a barely audible voice:

> If my heart is full of holes, patched with repairs –
> Let the sky be like Oyxon, and the breeze fly the kite.

The warmth of the sun and the song's emotions kept the young people from feeling the chill now in the air, as they climbed onto the alpine pastures. Qosim recited the fourth prayer of the day crouching in a yurt, while a young Kyrgyz fed their horses. They took another young man along as a guide and set off again, so as to arrive before darkness fell. 'There's one small pass we still have to climb,' said Qosim, translating for Oyxon and the children what his Kyrgyz friend had said. Oyxon found the pass terrifying. The road climbed very steeply, the horses fought for breath as they pulled the cart; Qosim and the young Kyrgyz dismounted, took the horses by the bridles and began pulling them up, while a third helper pushed the cart from behind.

As Oyxon had predicted in her song, the sun dropped behind the mountain and then seemed to freeze for a while. It couldn't set fully, for their cart was climbing higher and higher, chasing the sun. Qosim pressed on as fast as he could, as if trying to hold back the sun, so that it would light up his cousin's radiant face for longer, though that face was now concealed by the horse-hair veil. Wrapped in her black garments, Oyxon hunched fearfully. When they reached the top of the pass, the young man again felt the same soaring feeling that he had experienced in the vineyard. 'Oh God, don't let the cart collapse now as the ladder did then,' he thought with a shudder, spitting for luck on his damp chest under his shirt. The mountain peak was still sunlit, but the first shadows of darkness had fallen over the lush valleys which flanked the pass.

Who knows what terrified Oyxon most, the descent from these mountains, or the start of the journey, but it was already getting dark when they reached a place where the numerous rivulets of a mountain torrent streamed everywhere like a young girl's braids. It took only another hour to reach Eski-Novqat, where the magnificent night sky glimmered with stars.

Oyxon was never as happy as she was in the week she spent there.

But less than a month later her father's humble house was pestered by Umar's matchmakers, and by the end of summer Oyxon found herself the third wife in the Emir's harem: caught in a palace, like a bird in a golden cage.

After filling his mind with these thoughts, Abdulla could not tell what he was groaning over: whether it was the pain of young Qosim's fall – not just off the ladder, or the mountain pass, but from the star-spangled heavens – or Oyxon's agonised heart, which was reflected in the eyes of Abdulla's children, standing aghast in the snow as he was taken away. Where was he? What was going on in this world, in this endless darkness? Was there anything other than pain?

Dropping down behind the mountains, the sun suddenly fell away, like five sunset-coloured oranges, and Abdulla fell into an oblivious sleep.

———

In the morning the prison door scraped open. Opening his eyes to see the duty soldier, who had brought him a bowl of gruel and a mug of tea, it took Abdulla a few moments to recall where he was. The first time you wake up in a prison is unique. Abdulla could never forget it. At night, as you fall into a heavy, dreamless slumber, you feel you are in prison, but in the morning, when you wake up, your first thought is: might yesterday's nightmare have been merely a dream? And then you realise that it was neither a dream nor a nightmare, and that you really are in prison. You realise that on the night of 31 December, three men really had burst into your house, called in the neighbours as witnesses, started searching the premises, handcuffed you while your Rahbar and your children, who ran out in the snow in their night clothes, wept. 'Pick me up,' said Ma'sud, who was used to being held. 'Daddy!' he called, stretching his hands out to his handcuffed father.

It was true: he had been beaten and kicked. Even raising himself up to a sitting position, Abdulla's body ached so much that he stretched out again where he had lain. No, what next? He'd missed his morning prayers: he must gently get to his feet, shuffle over to the water bucket in the corner, wash his face, hands and feet, and recite – however late – the morning prayer. Fighting his pain, Abdulla got up, washed, then went back to bed where – not knowing which direction Mecca was – he prayed facing the wall. He couldn't stomach the bowl of gruel, but took a sip of the bitter tea.

The tea sent his thoughts down another circuitous path.

It occurred to him that these walls might possibly be housing the scholar G'ozi Yunus, the teacher Fitrat, perhaps, even Cho'lpon, yes, perhaps. Hadn't Cho'lpon written about a girl singing in a cart: who could portray Shahrixon and Eski-Novqat better than Cho'lpon, a native of the region? Abdulla longed to see him. There was an enormous amount to talk about, all stored up in his mind. How likely was it that their paths would cross here? Could he tell Cho'lpon about his wife's troubles? The first day in prison is always peculiar. Abdulla's mind was constantly alert, listening to every scrabbling sound on the other side of the door. But for a very long time nothing happened. This dullness made him return to his idle, pointless thoughts. Again, you remember things; again, your soul is ground down between the heavy millstones of the mind. And all that results are conjectures. Guesses turn to dust if you blow on them.

—

It was like a heavy stone. But wasn't the first time Oyxon awoke in her golden cage a hundred times worse? The girl had been raped, yet in the morning she came out to greet everyone – bowing to her own father G'ozi-xo'ja, and smiling at the other women, the aunts and wives of the Emir, the Emir who had raped her and left her with cramps in her throat and stomach. Momentarily pierced by the idea of this pain, Abdulla forgot his own grievances and directed his thoughts to the name of Allah.

A certain amount of time passed before the cell door opened again and a soldier barked an order in Russian: 'Prisoner Qodiriy! Out, with your hands behind your back!' Abdulla was taken to another tiny room in the basement, where they thrust a board with a number on it into his hand and photographed him, first full-face, then in profile. In a neighbouring cell an elderly Jewish man shaved Abdulla's head and chin with a razor. The barber was clearly forbidden to open his mouth in front of the soldier standing by, or perhaps he was a mute: he hissed and whispered the whole time, made wordless shushing and whooshing sounds, waving his arms to satisfy his craving for communication. Now and again he tapped Abdulla's cheek; when it was shaved and free of foam, he tugged at his shirt collar, bent down to his ear and whispered again.

Abdulla was reminded of Oyxon affectionately fussing over Qosim, and again he almost laughed. No, he had to behave seriously while the razor was shaving his head, and now his face, under the soldier's icy gaze. And he didn't want his laughter to get the unfortunate barber into trouble: wasn't the barber just another prisoner? Or did he do this job precisely so as to keep his freedom? Having your hair cut is usually relaxing, but to lose all the hair on your head and your face in one fell swoop is disagreeable. Abdulla's upper lip was swollen. It was a good thing that he hadn't been photographed in this state. Either because he was now hairless, or because he was looking at the Russian soldier, a narrative strand occurred to him, which he would use to full effect in the novel he had planned.

In the early nineteenth century, in the Polish province of Szawel, then part of the Russian empire, a son was born to the aristocratic Witkiewicz family. His father named him Jan, but his mother, who was a Francophile, called him Jean. The boy grew up to be clever and quick-witted. Apart from Polish, he had a fluent command of Russian, English, French and German. At the age of fourteen, when he was a pupil at the grammar school in Kroży, Jan Witkiewicz created a secret society called the Black Brotherhood, but was caught by the Russian gendarmerie while publicly distributing poems and leaflets attacking Russians and Russian autocracy. Despite his youth, the boy was deprived of all his property, his rights and his freedom, and sent into exile.

In the steppes around Orenburg, among Tatars and Kazakhs, the young Polish nobleman began studying local languages, and his mastery led the Tatars to call him not Jan or Jean, but Halimdzian, the Scholar.

From the occasional merchants who set off from Bukhara to Moscow, he acquired Farsi. So he spent six years wandering about, acquiring ever more knowledge. The famous German orientalist Wilhelm Humboldt, returning from his Siberian expedition, stopped at Orenburg and happened to meet the twenty-year-old Jan Witkiewicz. Delighted by the young man's knowledge, Humboldt introduced him to Colonel Petrovsky, newly appointed governor of Orenburg.

The Tsar's government had given Petrovsky the task of conquering Central Asia: he had great need for men like Witkiewicz. In 1835 he sent 'Halimdzian' to Bukhara as a secret agent. Jan took only a year to ingratiate himself with the Emir's viziers and favourites, and brought important information back to Petrovsky. Numerous secretive missions followed, to Turkmenistan and Afghanistan.

For his service to the Russian government he was made an officer, and his rights and property were restored. In 1839 this thirty-year-old officer with brilliant prospects was summoned to the capital, St. Petersburg. In a hotel there he met, by chance, a childhood friend, the poet Konstantin Tyszkiewicz. The friends locked themselves in the hotel room, recalling stories of their shared youth and regaling each other with their recent experiences.

As Tyszkiewicz listened to Jan's adventures – his transformation to Halimdjan, his travels to Bukhara, Nishapur, Kabul – he became paler and paler; when Witkiewicz told him about his officer's promotion and the restoration of his rights, Tyszkiewicz could hold back no longer.

'Do you know what you've done? You've sold out! You're a traitor! Didn't we swear to one another that we'd fight the Russians unto death ? You're playing up to their Tsar!' Tyszkiewicz leapt to his feet and stormed out of the room, slamming the door behind him.

The next day Witkiewicz was found in his hotel room, a revolver in his hand and a bullet hole in his head.

—

Abdulla left this episode as a draft to work on later when he had time, perhaps, to include in his book as a separate chapter, 'Russian Roulette'. If, God willing, he got out of here alive, he would go back to Witkiewicz's adventures in Bukhara. The story needed one or two extra subtleties to give it shape. And the language needed to be refined a great deal. For now, could he tell the story to the young Russian soldier? Would he be able to understand it? Like his hair, Abdulla's thoughts had left his head and scattered. He had to focus his mind. Especially in this place.

The barber had finally finished his work. Abdulla was again led down a long corridor, past identical steel doors, back to his cell. He had to concentrate his mind, reign in these wild fantasies. What was he going to be asked if he was interrogated? He ought to have his answers ready. What was he accused of? The Tatar interrogator's paper, if he wasn't mistaken, mentioned Articles 58 and 67. That morning Abdulla had noticed a battered book, *The Criminal Code*, by the door of his cell. He picked it up and searched through it for the relevant articles. The 58th.

> A counter-revolutionary action is any action aimed at overthrowing, undermining or weakening the power of workers' and peasants' Soviets and of governments of the USSR and Soviet and autonomous republics, elected by them under the Constitution of the USSR and the constitutions of the union republics, or at the undermining or weakening of the external security of the USSR and the main economical, political and national achievements of the proletariat's revolution.

> Given the international solidarity of interests of all workers, such actions are considered counter-revolutionary also when they are directed against any other workers' state, even though this state may not be part of the USSR.

Abdulla re-read the article several times, but could not understand what action of his could fall under these charges. Still, if the cap fits, wear it!

He turned a few pages to article 67:

> Any kind of organisational activity directed at preparing or committing counter-revolutionary crimes, as well as participation in an organisation formed for preparing or committing any such crime, is punishable as a crime in accordance with the appropriate articles of this section.

However hard he tried, this article left Abdulla equally stumped. On the one hand, the fact that he couldn't understand it depressed him; on the other, reason told him that he'd never been involved in any such crimes, a thought that gave him relief.

For want of anything else to do, he started reading other articles. The one on 'Hooliganism' made him think of the troublemaker Toshp'olat; when he came to 'Theft', he remembered Namoz-the-Thief, both characters in his own stories. After reading the book from beginning to end, he had still failed to find an article that applied to him; so he began inventing new articles, comic ones which he might well be charged under – 'Dreaming', 'Reflecting', 'Taciturnity', and so on. But none of those activities were listed in the Code.

—

Early in the spring of 1242, Nasrullo gathered an army and again set off to attack Bukhara. The first time, he had returned empty-handed. Then, less than three months later, when Emir Husayn also passed away and the throne was hurriedly taken by their younger brother Umar, a second mission had also proved in vain. But this journey was going to be victorious: it was going to get Nasrullo his quarry.

Now, according to reports sent by courier from his faithful vizier Hakim, Umar spent his time not on matters of state, but drinking and making merry. At a time of crisis, when the emirate was on the verge of collapse, all he wanted to hear about was wine and concubines. His viziers and lords, displeased by this, encouraged Hakim to send messengers to Nasrullo.

This time there would be no false delicacy. Nasrullo was not going to back down: you get a throne not by asking for it, but by snatching it, just as in bozkashi. On his way to Bukhara, Nasrullo paid a visit to the tomb of Xo'ja Bahoviddin and asked the venerable saint to support his cause. After a few weeks' siege, on the twentieth of Shaaban, the first month of autumn in 1826, the nobility, led by vizier Hakim, betrayed the acting ruler Umar, opened the gates of the castle to Nasrullo, imprisoned the younger brother and put the elder on the throne.

Whether our venerable saint had a hand in this, or

whether Nasrullo's strong will was sufficient, the disgraced Umar was bundled onto a horse and driven out of the city. As he rode away, a commoner raised his hand to snatch off the former Emir's gold-embroidered hat; someone else tore off his silk gown and cummerbund, so that yesterday's Emir left the streets of Bukhara bare-headed and naked. Oh treacherous and disappointing world!

Once Nasrullo had been crowned, and in accordance with the saintly Bahoviddin's testament on magnanimity, he ordered that his younger brothers Zubayra, Hamza and Sardar be made joint governors of Narazim, a province of Bukhara. He reappointed Hakim as first vizier and treated the common people to a banquet of plov.

One day, however, when Hakim was closeted with his ruler, the vizier hinted in a jocular tone: 'Your grace, it's possible that appointing your younger brothers to stately positions might be interpreted negatively.'

'Why?' the Emir asked rather brusquely.

'I've heard that in the Ottoman sultanate there is a strange view that when someone inherits the throne, his brothers, even if they are babies, should be executed. So that they don't have any claim to the throne.'

'Do you agree? Then I'd have been martyred myself.' This time, there was discernible menace in Nasrullo's tone.

'God forbid!' said Hakim, hurriedly correcting his mistake. 'The aim is to keep this throne which has come into your august hands free from pretenders or protests.'

The ceiling candelabra was flickering, casting strange shadows on Hakim's face.

'Tell me something else,' Nasrullo asked casually, 'what sort of man is that chef of yours? Can he be trusted?'

'He hasn't forgotten what you taught him when he was in your service,' said the Chief Minister, confused, not knowing what attitude to take.

'The reason I'm asking is that our noble father fell ill so suddenly. And our brother Emir Husayn's life was destroyed when he was in his prime. Could your chef have had a hand in this?' Nasrullo's questions had taken the tone of an interrogation.

'Good God, no!' the vizier exclaimed, reining in the conversation again. 'He's a pious man, the only things he worries about are pastry and heaven.'

'Pastry, you say. I suggest we take precautions against my younger brothers.'

Anyone who happened to overhear this conversation would probably have understood little, but a vizier who had served five or six rulers had to be alert to all the implications, like a small porcelain bowl nesting inside a bigger one. Were these the final words of the unreliable Nasrullo, governor of the province of Qarshi, or the words of the newly enthroned Emir Nasrullo, now taking advice from Hakim his Chief Minister?

'The chef is here, and their lordships are in Narazim,' he said, testing out the ground.

'That's what I was saying.'

No, the old fox reflected, our Emir is still too fragile to conceal his thoughts and intentions: as the chef himself would put it, the syrup hasn't been distilled yet. When he spoke, his voice was firm. 'We'll get the Master of the Emir's horses to do what's necessary.'

Before the month was out Emir Nasrullo's three younger brothers had their handsome throats slit in the middle of the night. On Nasrullo's orders, three days' mourning was observed in Bukhara for the martyred princes.

Now that's what you call a crime, Abdulla thought to himself.

—

The even flow of Abdulla's thoughts was broken. Even when a man has been in prison before, he cannot get used to the tricks it plays on his mind. At midday a small mustard-coloured rissole was served with thick noodles. Abdulla was mulling over a question. 'Is this nightmare of mine going to go on much longer? If I can wake up now, let me do so, let me wake up now,' he said. The day dragged on relentlessly. Abdulla recited his midday prayers sitting down. Were they going to give him any news of Rahbar and the children? Instead of going to the Railway Workers' Palace for the New Year celebrations, were they on Leningrad Street, freezing in the January cold as they tried to find out what had happened to him? What was the thread of his thoughts before this one? It was impossible to think straight in such a situation. When your life had been razed to the ground, could your thoughts make sense or form a response? He didn't know which one to fixate on, which one to allow, which might give comfort or an answer to the quandary that had befallen him. Or was he now truly in thrall to mania? Had the devil which had taken control of his thoughts likewise taken hold of his life? When Abdulla was a child, the moment he told a story about the devils' dance, his late father had joked, 'Turn your thoughts to something good; can't you think about more constructive things?'

True, wasn't it high time he directed his thoughts to worthier subjects? Mightn't he then turn this novel into something material like his previous one, *Past Days*?

He recalled the poet Nodira. He recalled a female reciter, who wrote under the name Uvaysiy, and the Emir Umar, who used the pseudonym Amiriy.

Nodira was jealous of Umar from the day she married

him, when he was still a prince. Initially, she was jealous
of his princely title; later, when his father Emir Olim suddenly died and the emirate was inherited by the son, her
jealousy extended to the endless tasks of the ruler: the state
council, the hunts, the invitations to banquets.

Nodira imagined that the world was trying to take him
away from her embraces:

> The fire of jealousy has burned flowers in the meadow,
> Together with her smile's buds and the open seed-pods, its fine
>   narcissus eyes...

On the eve of her wedding, Nodira's father gave his daughter the following advice: 'Be attentive to your husband,
always take care of him. A man is a ruler outside the house;
but when he comes home, he is ruled by his wife. Lead by
your mother's example!' Of course, her mother may have
slipped these words in her husband's ears to further her
own noble interests, but Nodira seemed to have taken this
good advice to heart: from time to time, examining her
doubts and suspicions, she would reflect further.

One day, Umar went hunting on the reed-covered
banks of the Syr-Darya river with his male courtiers. To
stave off boredom, Nodira invited the womenfolk to the
palace. After a feast and a banquet with much amusement
and dancing, Uvaysiy recited some riddles:

> What is this dome, whose door has no sign of an opening,
> How many fair maids stroll around the place?
> If I cared for the girls and broke the dome by force,
> Their faces veiled, their livers would bleed...

Someone guessed, 'The Emir's harem'; someone said
'Bread in the oven'. Only the clever Nodira grasped the
underlying meaning: a palace with no doors or windows
had to be dealt with by breaking it down, how else could

the girls be freed? 'Smashing the dome' clearly referred to the hymen. 'Hiding from blood', red juice, that was… 'Pomegranate juice' exclaimed Nodira. Uvaysiy showed her admiration for Nodira by punning on her pseudonym: '"Precious" doesn't do you justice!'

The day before, the royal lady had risen from her blessed bed rather belatedly: her husband had left early for a meeting of his council, the smell of his royal body still lingered on the pillow, and his gown lay on the blanket. Picking it up, she spotted a piece of paper sticking out from the cuff. Nodira unfolded the paper to find a stanza in the Emir's hand.

> My darling's cheeks were ruby red, ripened pomegranate red
> And pomegranate red the liver's blood that rose in every tear I
>   shed.

Having read the first two lines of this refrain, Nodira's face flushed bright red, as red as pomegranate juice. Her eyes ran over more of the verses.

> My dear one teased the luscious fruits, and for them her lips did
>   part:
> 'My lips are ripe and juicy figs, my throat a pomegranate's heart.'
>
> If a garden plays with flowers and with pomegranate fruit –
> For my love my face is the rose, my smile pomegranates suit.

Nodira moved her lips as she read on, and thousands of heart-breaking suspicions began to form within her mind, as densely packed as pomegranate seeds. She knew what 'figs' meant in love's language, and it made her apprehensive.

> I'm drawn to your peach lips, oh gardener, I simply cannot
>   choose
> But do not let my blood spill out like pomegranate juice.

> If my juice flows out then take it to the dance under the moon
> Let my love know my soul will bleed like the pomegranate soon.

Her eyes anxiously perused the lines, she whispered as she examined them: 'My Emir never compared my lips to a peach. He never likened them to a pomegranate.' Her heart ached as if withered and squeezed.

> I tried to mend my broken heart, with every tear I shed
> Who's my sultan in this garden but the pomegranate red?

> Parted from the apple of your throat, my flesh pales as yellow pear
> I swallow my own blood – my teeth the pomegranate's snare.

When she read the phrase 'the apple of your throat', it was clear that the mysterious pomegranate dome had been smashed; no, this was no young girl, not a young woman. Scattered seeds had been crushed, threshed… surely not…

> Parted from your grape-like eyes, their seeds in my eyes sow
> Tears that drop by bloody drop fall to my hem below.

'"Grape-like",' remarked Nodira, her jealousy turning to anger at her husband's clumsy turn of phrase.

> There is no loyalty to be had anywhere in this wide world
> It is elusive as the wind, a rare and precious pearl.

Nodira recalled her own verse with tears in her eyes. A large drop fell on the piece of paper and the word "grape-like" was blotted, so that it was now illegible. Nodira quickly put the gown's cuff over the ink blot, but the paper was irrevocably stained. Her lacklustre eyes, blurred with tears, hurt feelings, anger and jealousy, looked at a couplet of the poem.

> In this bright garden the Emir longs to see your face within it:
> You are my one and only destiny, oh my dear pomegranate!

'One mistake after the other,' Nodira sighed vindictively. But what did she mean by that? Grammatical mistakes or misspellings of Arabic words, or clumsy expressions, or her husband's clumsy act of leaving his poems for her to find? Perhaps she was wrong to trust friends and relatives, and perhaps there was no faithfulness in this world; perhaps this life was just a series of accidents?

> Parted from your grape-ripe lips and your throat apple's sweet flower,
> This earthly garden's every fruit is tasteless now, or sour.

—

Though the dungeon lacked even a grille through which to glimpse a piece of the sky and its colours, Abdulla could tell intuitively that it was evening. After the evening prayers yesterday he had sat at his desk in his home, beneath the window which framed the twilit sky, and poured all his feelings onto paper: the tender and the melancholy. Cho'lpon had written a remarkable poem called 'Evening Falls', which Abdulla knew by heart.

> Little balconies, houses big and small,
> Roofs of red, of blue and green,
> And above, clouds, billowing and flowing
> Gathering in masses across the skies.
>
> The sun sinks and scatters as it falls
> Trampled tulips over the cloudy screen.
> But soon the fevered hues are fading
> And from the east the darkness flies.
>
> A quivering echo hangs in the air
> As the muezzin cries the evening prayer.
> Then comes the rain – briefly it seems –
> But the winding street's awash with streams.
>
> To seek their fortune, young and old

Spread into the world far and wide
But now they're coming back to the fold –
A sluggish, weary incoming tide.

And in the village, the children call
As they play together before bed,
But darkness soon embraces all
With its heavy wings outspread.

Lamps flicker, flicker listlessly,
Dull and sad as the eyes of a djinn –
And the rainwater spills on aimlessly
Over the ground like a silvery skin.

Yesterday, sitting by the window at his home in Samarkand, Abdulla looked at the roofs of the houses in Ko'kcha and fancied he heard the faint sound of a muezzin. Clouds, clouds, he had thought, where are you coming from, where are you going – you link the day to the night – what evidence are you whisking away to the past? If I can get through these blank hours, then I can write in the darkness, by candle-light. In the next room, the table was being laid for the New Year; Abdulla reckoned he could get two or three pages down before Rahbar called him in. But he had barely sat down when there was a knock at the door. 'Daddy,' he heard the children calling, 'someone's at the door.' Throwing a gown over his shoulders, Abdulla went to answer it.

Who could be visiting so late? he wondered. Surely everyone would be busy getting ready to celebrate, to sit down to feast with their families. Before sliding the wooden bar from across the door, he called out, 'Who is it?' From the other side a voice responded: 'It's me, sir, your concierge'. Even as he unbarred the door, Abdulla had misgivings. Why should the concierge, who never showed his face otherwise, have turned up then of all times? Then three men in black leather coats burst in, without a word of greeting or explanation.

Through the open door Abdulla saw the Black Maria, and everything became clear. His children saw it all. As he was dragged off to the car, one of his daughters, Anis or Adiba, ran after him and tripped: she fell and cried out. She lay there, watching him with tears in her eyes. The eyes of the Tatar secret policeman flashed behind his lenses as he threw the girl a contemptuous glance.

> Lamps flicker, flicker listlessly,
> Dull and sad as the eyes of a djinn –
> And the rainwater spills on aimlessly
> Over the ground like a silvery skin.

An entire day had passed.

—

Once it had passed, Nodira was ashamed of the doubts she had entertained the previous day. All that because of one or two words which seemed suspect? After all, it is possible that I myself recited Uvaysiy's pomegranate riddle to my sultan...

The same had happened not so long ago with the following couplet by Uvaysiy:

> To openly ask my beloved to meet me is like dying; not to ask is also death.
> If I build love's house for grief's people, that is death; not to ask is also death.

On hearing these lines, she had herself that very night feverishly recited it to Umar, 'the Emir of all Muslims' as he was now called, hoping to stir his jealousy.

She was even tempted, for a moment to swap the pen name 'Uvaysiy' for her own 'Nodira' in the following lines:

> Mine is shame, disgrace and suffering, this life departs from an

ephemeral world,
Poor Nodira, if I turn yellow, this is death; if I don't, I die.

All the same, these lines applied much more closely to Nodira than to Uvaysiy.

Uvaysiy's character, in any case, was odd in every way. Nodira had tried a thousand times to get close to her, singling her out in the palace harem, showing her respect, omitting to mention her own lyrics, making it clear that she regarded Uvaysiy's poems beyond compare. But she couldn't get to grips with the other woman's thoughts. She couldn't figure out what Uvaysiy's heart was hiding. Take her latest lyric:

> You who have come from Kokand city, my shoe's missing, do you have it?
> You know my soul's in jeopardy, my shoe's missing, do you have it?

What did that lyric say about her? What was it about?

> There's no comfort in this misery, my face is wet, I have lost it
> You're soul's balm Kukabibi, my shoe's missing, do you have it?

What shoe was she talking about?

> You're my soul, I'm a body, now my yearning's all that's left to me.
> God my judge, hear my plea, my shoe's missing, do you have it?

Nodira was intelligent enough not assume that every single word in the lyric referred to herself; but still, this was one enigma buried under another, as if mocking the sense of the poem. Unable to suppress her shrieks and sighs along the way, when Nodira got to the final couplet, she didn't know how to react:

> May the prince be aware, my wail's echoed through nine heavens.
> Errant Uvaysiy, say a prayer, my shoe's missing, do you have it?

No, no, she wasn't calling on any earthly Prince, Nodira had no cause for jealousy. Uvaysiy was appealing to the almighty King of Heaven. Could Nodira be jealous of something a beloved was forced to say to a heavenly King? Too overwrought to make her own pen compose a response, Nodira was forced to recall the poet Fuzuli:

> Show mercy, my lordly King,
> Now is the time for magnanimity.

—

For evening prayers Abdulla read aloud the Surats *As-Shams* and *Ad Dhuha*. Halfway through the prayer the door scraped open, and supper was brought in: pickled cabbage soup with a piece of black bread. The acrid smell of sour cabbage filled the cell. Interrupting his prayer, Abdulla took the food from the hands of the soldier-cook. He recalled his eldest son: whenever cabbage was served at home, Habibullo would start singing in a low voice, 'Please can I have some cabbage...' When he was arrested, the lad had been ill in bed. And Abdulla hadn't been able to say goodbye.

Something about the soldier who had brought in supper – a certain gentleness about the way he proffered the food in its metal bowl – put Abdulla at ease. If he hadn't been in the middle of his prayers, Abdulla would have talked to him, could have tried to get some news of Cho'lpon and G'ozi Yunus. Finishing his prayers, Abdulla tried the food. The taste of the sour pickled cabbage in his mouth was revolting. He set it aside, telling himself that he could eat it later, if need be, and turned to the bread. As evening fell, his bones started aching again. Every time he chewed, the pain in his jaws spread to both shoulder blades, then from his shoulder blades to his ribs, and from his ribs to his waist and his legs. Though it was agony to eat, the bread left a pleasant taste in his mouth. He wouldn't spoil that with the acrid cabbage.

Had he managed to remember what he had written down? Alas, had it all now merged into a meaningless mass? If he could set it down on paper he would never confuse Umar's Kokand palace with Nasrullo's fortress in Bukhara, especially as the events were not one year apart, but ten. If he wanted to draw out the parallels, then he needed to think more about Emir Haydar and his story. Why had he jumped straight to Nasrullo? And wasn't his interpretation of Nodira's actions somewhat unusual? What was happening in Abdulla's brain? Had a so-called devil managed to worm its way inside?

He made an effort to try and forget all these things. Cho'lpon had written:

> Night is fear, night is torment,
> At night, old or new,
> All thoughts are a mirage.

Now he would have happily exchanged all his dark thoughts to finish reading the *Book of Fables,* which he had been enjoying so much before he was taken away. He hadn't yet figured out how to work it into his novel.

'Storytellers tell the tale as follows: for time immemorial there have been in the lands of Fergana the ruins of an ancient city founded by the horseman king Kaykubod. The air there was fresh and pleasant. In early spring, when the greenery came to life and the wild flowers bloomed, everything was as brightly coloured as a peacock's tail. Near the city, in a dense wood, the Screech Owl lived in its ancestral home. And his neighbour the Tawny Owl had a daughter of indescribable beauty.

Her face make the sun and the moon abashed,
Her words make the Shah's sugar tasteless,
Her harvest and life are so rich,
This moon-like creature's name? Gunashbon.

But this was just like the story of Emir Umar's marriage to Oyxon! Why hadn't Abdulla seen the parallel before now? Excellent!

Repeating each word with pleasure, Abdulla triumphantly confirmed his discovery. Remembering how the Screech Owl had sent the Scops Owl as a matchmaker, he couldn't help likening this episode to a similar historical event described by Hakim-to'ra – the same Hakim who went to win Oyxon for his uncle Umar – in his *History of the Elect*:

"'The Tawny Owl has a beautiful daughter. Go and ask for her hand on my behalf. No matter how great the bride price."

'But the Scops Owl quoted a popular proverb: "Boasts from haves are accepted, boasts from have-nots are dismissed." The Tawny Owl's response came: "My daughter's bride price is a thousand houses". For in the reign and times of our king his Majesty Sayid Umar-xon, Emir of the Muslims, the rulers and the ruled alike are joyful. All the family households are made of coral, we would be ashamed if there were a single deserted house. People say, "A lying fable doesn't last long", "Disgrace is more cruel than death". Again it is said: "Once bent, a wormwood bush is broken; once disgraced, a young man is dead".'

Didn't Abdulla know that the original author of this fable was the poet Gulxaniy, who had also lived in the Tajik part of the Fergana valley? What a pity he hadn't investigated further. Gulxaniy may have been a relative or at least a pupil of G'ozi-xo'ja. Those lines about Emir Umar were surely sarcastic.

Furthermore, it is known that Gulxaniy was a soldier in Umar's service. Who knows: the Emir may have sent this well-built man together with Hakim to ask G'ozi-xo'ja for his daughter's hand. True, Hakim never wrote about what passed between father and daughter, but in his *Book of Fables* Gulxaniy gave a very full account indeed!

'Then the Tawny Owl said, "Shame on me, my daughter is grown up. Before I give you an answer I have to ask her if she agrees." He went to her and said, "My child, the son of the Screech Owl, the king of the birds, is so excited by your beauty that he has sent matchmakers. What is your answer?"

'So the young lady, being an exemplary well-brought up girl, rises to the occasion: in accordance with the saying "Silence is a sign of consent," she merely sat there, head bowed. The Tawny Owl understood his daughter's secret wishes, and said, "This child seems to want to get married". No sooner had he said this, than the girl suddenly spoke up: "Hey, you ridiculous old man, is saying nothing an answer? Does someone who speaks of doing something good shout about it?'

A key creaked in the lock, the door banged open, and Vinokurov came into the cell. 'Did you think you'd dig yourself in here to celebrate New Year, you bourgeois-nationalist rat?' Just as Gulxaniy said, 'What came of the trumpeter's blast? A puff of wind,' Vinokurov managed to give Abdulla's whole face a beating and a kicking before leaving.

—

Covered in blood, regaining consciousness with great pain, Abdulla bitterly regretted this episode. Why had he let himself be carried away by pointless thoughts instead of steeling himself for a likely attack? Although his hand wasn't strong enough to grab Vinokurov by the throat, he could at least have sunk his teeth into him; even if he'd been shot on the spot for doing so, wouldn't that be a thousand times better than lying there? There was no going back now. If he got his strength back, the moment he set eyes on that creature, he'd leap at him, bite him, strangle him, kill him.

He spent the whole night obsessed with vain thoughts, thinking only of avenging himself. He felt no pain, the clots of blood didn't bother him: vengeance burned in his heart. He forgot about the night-time prayer. Only after midnight did he fleetingly remember it, but the word for prayer, namaz, recalled in some corner of his brain a historical figure with a similar name: Namoz the Robber. At the beginning of the twentieth century, Namoz had escaped from a Russian prison and started robbing the rich in the Samarkand province. Betrayed by his rich victims, Namoz the Bold was thrown back into prison, where he murdered five or six soldiers who tried to assault him. After that nobody dared enter his murky cell alone: soldiers went in only in groups of ten or a dozen, their rifles at the ready.

Namoz's men seem to have been very enterprising: two or three committed petty thefts and got themselves put into the same prison as their leader. They found out which cell Namoz was in, and communicated with him by tapping the bars with a stone, or singing a song in which they inserted the words of their message. In the end, some of them took their punishment of about fifty lashes and started digging as soon as they were out of prison, all the way into Namoz's cell. But merely escaping would have been too easy for Namoz. Concealing the hole, he banged on his cell door early one morning. He woke the soldiers and ten of them rushed in, rifles cocked. In the murk they could not see their prisoner: they fired a couple of times into the air, and ran about the cell. It was sheer chaos. But Namoz was clinging by his elbows and knees to a ceiling joist all that time: he then leapt down straight onto one of the soldiers, knocked him to the ground, grabbed his rifle and vanished down the tunnel…

About fifteen or so other prisoners then took the opportunity to escape.

Having recalled this scene, Abdulla intended to work it into his novel. But what had made it come to him just then? Wasn't this incident an event for a different novel, about different times? If Abdulla wanted to repeat Namoz's actions, he had neither the men to do it, nor any way of smashing the concrete floor of his cell. There weren't even any joists in the ceiling, only a metal grid around the lamp, but Abdulla had nothing to attach to it, since they'd taken away his belt, his waistband and his shoelaces.

All the same, he would grab Vinokurov by the throat! Whatever happened.

No sooner had he made that wish than Abdulla fell into a deep pit of dreamless sleep.

—

Awoken early by the creak of the door, Abdulla was in just as much pain as when he had fallen asleep. Alert to the prospect of another attack, he clenched his fists, but the man entering the cell was the same awkward Uzbek soldier as the day before. God has preserved me, Abdulla told himself. As a Muslim, he didn't want to show his face to this young man before he had washed, so he moved aside and hurriedly started cleaning the congealed blood from his forehead, his swollen cheeks and eyelids, his aching chin.

The young soldier was the first to make a greeting, albeit in a whisper. His words 'Good morning, boss,' were in the Tashkent style. Drying his face on the hem of his gown, Abdulla responded in kind.

'I've brought you bread and tea, boss.'

As he had the day before, Abdulla accepted the gruel and the mug of tea with a bow; he then asked quietly: 'Are you from Tashkent? Which district are you from?'

The soldier rattled the crockery to drown out his voice: 'From Qumloq. My name is Sunnat. If there's anything you need, let me know.'

Abdulla likewise rattled the mug against his plate as he spoke, 'All right, I'll see.' Then he turned round to face the little soldier, who was now leaving, and said: 'Cho'lpon and the man they call G'ozi Yunus: which cell might they be in?'

Who knows if the soldier from Qumloq had heard the question? The door was slammed shut and Abdulla was left alone with his gruel and his thoughts.

What could he ask the soldier for? What was the man able to do? Could he be asked to bring a knife? Would that really be possible? Or would it be easier to ask him to bring paper and pencil, so Abdulla could write a letter to his family? But what could he write about? If he wrote that everything was fine, that would be a lie; that he'd be free any day now, would be an idle dream: he couldn't write that he was being beaten and kicked. Or suppose he wrote, 'I'm going to kill that scoundrel Vinokurov, forgive me and farewell'. That would be absolutely idiotic. All the same, Abdulla decided to ask for paper and pencil first.

At least he could write and ask Rahbar, 'Did you take the children to the Railway Workers' Palace?' Or should he say, 'I hid the manuscript of the novel about the slave in the Sultan's harem in the stove under the summer porch in the yard. Keep it, and hide it where nobody will find it.' At least he'd managed to conceal the manuscript in a place where the secret policemen, naturally, hadn't thought of looking. They'd ransacked the whole house, even taken away the torn shreds of his manuscripts, but they'd over-looked the yard stove.

Chewing his tasteless millet porridge, Abdulla recalled the secret policemen, the treacherous concierge. When would the interrogations begin? The interrogators would need to take a break for the New Year holiday, but only for a couple of days; after that he would be put on Vinokurov's list and would become the Russian's lawful hostage.

He had to ask the young man from Qumloq for a knife.

———

Oyxon lay behind the white wedding curtains, wrecked and desolate. She didn't have the strength to cry for help, nor to weep bitter tears, nor to hang herself. The night was endless for the violated girl… The monster that had raped her pushed the curtains aside and went out to wash his body. As she watched him, hatred weighed on Oyxon's breast as heavily as a millstone. She had kicked, she had scratched and bitten, but this had only served to inflame him more. The girl lay there, sticky with blood, seized by pain. 'The moment he comes back, I'll sink my teeth in his throat,' she thought as she lay there, clenching her pearly teeth.

When Oyxon was put into a cart to be brought here, she had spotted a tall, slightly ruddy man among the bod-yguards. This courtier had guarded Umar almost as far as the wedding-bed curtains, and he seemed familiar to her. Of course, the handsome Gulxaniy, who had studied under her father at O'ratepa! Her father had given him that nickname himself, 'Fiery', because of his reddish beard… the men had been fond of each other. Could she not, by begging and fawning on him, persuade him to give her a dagger?

—

To think that that Nodira had once been jealous of Umar's state duties, even of the word 'pomegranate' – what a joke that had turned out to be! Once she had borne a couple of children and was occupied in looking after them, the Emir took a second wife, a rather squat Kipchak girl. But that was just the beginning. Destructive jealousy, deep suspicions, furious envy were yet to come.

Who had led her lord and master astray? One summer, he went to visit his younger sister in Shahrixon and returned utterly changed. Could Nodira's poetic heart have deceived her?

> The tulips are blooming – where has my beloved fled?
> Has she vanished from my sight, who inspired the words I said.
>
> Everyone seeks their prey, in this worldly hunting land.
> What am I to do? My sweet hawk has flown my hand.

Nodira could tell that she was going to be flooded with misery. As Mashrab said:

> With a thousand shrieks of woe, calamity made us stagger.
> The soul cries out to be alone, disaster is a dagger.

Nodira was taking measures, but before that she found in a pocket of his lordship's gown a poem written on Kokand paper:

> My heart yearns to meet you, oh my beloved, welcome
> You have made my eyes shine, my dear beloved, welcome!
>
> I was sick from the feast – hey bring some wine here!
> You filled my glass right up, yes my beloved, welcome!
>
> With your forms and shapes, you teased the tedious banquet –
> Skewered their shadows on the wall, ah my beloved, welcome!
>
> Last night the moon came in secret, and the Emir said quietly:
> 'Don't tell our rivals of your kindness, yes, you are welcome!'

Even if it was merely a rumour that this moon-like creature was a rival, the shadows on the wall were troubling for the lady of the castle. She set reliable plotters to work, and found out that the wife of the ruler of Shahrixon was the source of this intrigue, that the disaster was already in full swing: it had taken root, and was now too late for any remedy. Some time ago two of Umar's courtiers had gone to Shahrixon and visited the exiled G'ozi-xo'ja to ask for his daughter's hand in marriage.

Nodira burned with resentment. 'Who is this moon-faced girl?' she demanded to know. The young Hakim took her to see his mother Oftob, the Emir's sister, in Shahrixon. There she was unable to see this fine figure, 'the shadow on the wall', who had become a beautifully arrayed pea-hen hidden behind a curtain. When she did see the maiden, all her former jealousies were cast aside as trivial: this girl became the sole object of her obsession. Now Nodira knew what real jealousy meant; lacking the strength to express it in her own words, her enfeebled lips again whispered Mashrab's fiery verses:

> With a thousand shrieks of woe, calamity made us stagger.
> The soul cries out to be alone, disaster is a dagger.
>
> Gripping his steel, the executioner's come for my head.
> He's snuffed out my life with his blade: I am dead.

—

To wash down his tasteless millet porridge, Abdulla sipped a mouthful of bitter tea: it had been made from used tea-leaves, dried in the sun. Cho'lpon and Fitrat must by now be used to the prison regime, as well as to the smell of chlorine and sweat, to the foul food, the smoking ceiling lamp, the attacks at night: as Abdulla knew from his first incarceration, it was surprising how quickly you got accustomed to such things. From time to time the days were disturbed by interrogations and confrontations with witnesses, which were a kind of contact with the outside world – though a false, distorted version of it.

In any case, the New Year holiday meant there was still no investigation: were they planning to simply beat him up first and ask questions later? The recent visit by Sunnat from Qumloq had given Abdulla hope, and in doing so weakened his resolve: his obsession was fading – perhaps he wouldn't kill Vinokurov after all. But now it remained to be seen if Abdulla would really let him get away with his actions. He'd drunk all the tea: it left a bitter taste in his mouth.

It would be wonderful if he could get the young soldier on his side! Might the boy have read any of his books? He looked rather simple-minded, but there must be more to him than that. The NKVD wouldn't take just anyone on. And he was the only Uzbek Abdulla had come across among all the guards and interrogators here… He could write a note to Rahbar; it would be good if she could take care of his manuscripts, assuming the worst forty days of winter hadn't started, and she hadn't used the manuscripts to stoke the stove… The thought made Abdulla very nervous. To a certain extent, the scenes he had written were still there in his memory, but the point was not just sketching out the scenes, it was a matter of finding the right tone, putting the words together, placing a full stop at just the right point.

Some artistic works are like buildings constructed from carefully placed bricks, with no cracks you can put a finger through. The walls of such buildings ring like a bell. Other works are mere hovels, their crooked walls are jerry-built with lumps of clay; the slightest tremor is enough to finish them off.

—

Oyxon emerged for the bride's morning greeting: her face was made up, but her loins and her legs hurt unbearably. When she walked, her legs refused to obey her. The women of the harem praised her beauty with ululations, while she felt like a cat that had fallen into the water, or a cockroach that had been flayed… no, like a lifeless kid goat, thrown into the bozkashi scrum. The elderly harem guests were fussing and bustling around her, gabbling verses:

> Girl as slender and graceful as a cypress, you are welcome.
> With all the beauty of a peacock, you are welcome.
>
> Take pleasure in your bride-time, you are welcome.
> Light of my eyes, my crown and bride, you are welcome.
>
> May your life be long and happy, you are welcome.
> Live long and well with your bridegroom, you are welcome.

Oyxon found this constant babble agonising. Who had composed such a clumsy, ugly poem? It didn't rhyme, it made no sense. This was the very opposite of art or grace: amateurish, overfamiliar word-play. From under her fine silk veil Oyxon looked discreetly out at her surroundings. On her right, she was surrounded by old women, all expecting gifts of clothing in honour of the bride.

The reciter was getting carried away, leaping from

poem to poem. First she called on Oyxon to bow to the senior members of the family, but the gifts of rubies and pearls that she received from them didn't brighten her dulled eyes. Then the reciter called upon Oyxon to stand to the right of the Emir's senior wives, paying especial deference to Nodira, the palace's chief wife, whom she likened to a nightingale:

> This day presents are given out,
> While hems are raised magnificently,
> Let us give to all the poor and destitute…

From behind her veil, Oyxon stole a glance at this incomparable, extraordinary woman: she saw not two eyes, but two daggers pointed at her. Her heart missed a beat. After all, she had read the anthologies: she knew by heart all the poems that had been written under the pen-name Nodira.

> Separated in the evening from my beloved, I have not failed to
>   suffer agony.
> Have mercy, now, it is impossible not to suffer…

With her two adolescent sons standing behind her, Nodira handed Oyxon her gift of soft crimson silk. Bewildered and horrified, unable to straighten her aching back, the new young wife retrieved from somewhere deep down another opening couplet which she spoke to her own heart:

> Blood is shed all over the town square, if she moves elegantly
>   everywhere,
> Like a river, blood ebbs over the town square and flows
>   everywhere.

CHAPTER 2

KNUCKLEBONES

On the fourth night of January, using a bit of powder to cover up the bruises and the black eyes inflicted by Vinokurov – who appeared to be lying low – someone led Abdulla to the same room where his belt and cummerbund had been removed. There they showed him the rifle they had taken from his house, and made him confirm in writing that it belonged to him. Abdulla signed: if he was going to be kicked and trampled on now, he wouldn't fire the rifle, but he'd go for them with the butt and smash their heads open. But no, there was no beating: as soon as he had signed to confirm that the rifle was his, they thrust his padded sleeping mat into his hands and led him off, not to his old cell, but to a different one.

It was now midnight. Given that he'd had his face powdered, Abdulla assumed that he was going to be taken to see one of the higher-ups or interrogators. He was mistaken. A door was opened, and he was flung inside. A filthy stench struck him: the sweat of dozens of men, the stench of urine, farts and unwashed male bodies. There were five barred lamps hanging from the ceiling, so Abdulla guessed that this cell was three or four times bigger than the previous, which had had only one. His eyes needed time to get used to the darkness, but even from the threshold he could sense that there were many rows of objects lying there. Then, retching from the foul stench, he bent down and saw that these were human beings lying on their sides.

In the corner by the entrance one man awoke, raised himself to a sitting position, and stared long and hard at Abdulla. When he finally appeared to have convinced himself of something, he shook the man lying next to him.

'Muborak, get up, they've brought another one in!'

'Tell the chief to find a place for him,' Muborak grumbled.

The first man, however, gestured to Abdulla. 'Come over here, you look like a decent man.' Then he jostled Muborak again: 'Move over, make a space for him between us!'

His neighbour's persistence meant Muborak was now fully awake; he looked at Abdulla with surprise. 'You're not Abdulla Qodiriy, are you?' he said, rubbing his eyes.

His nostrils flaring from the stench, Abdulla repressed his desire to retch, and nodded.

'What are you doing in this place?' Muborak asked, but then seemed to find an immediate answer to this question. 'Well, never mind that now: just come over here,' he said, and made room between himself and his neighbour for the quilt that Abdulla was holding.

'Sodiq, didn't you recognize him?' Muborak whispered as Abdulla unrolled his narrow quilt between them. 'This man is the greatest writer in Uzbekistan!'

'I recognised him by his red gown!' Sodiq insisted. And then, to Abdulla: 'Lie down, sir! Let's get some rest. Tomorrow we can have a proper talk.'

'Only, here we lie half the night on one side, then turn over on to the other side,' Muborak explained. He turned over onto his left side, and Abdulla followed his lead.

Whether it was the stench, or what he had just seen,

or the snoring on either side of him, Abdulla couldn't get to sleep. After four cold nights in isolation, at least he was back among people like himself.

—

In the Emir's harem, was it better to be a senior or a junior wife? Let someone who's been in that situation say. Nodira was in her quarters with Uvaysiy, listening to the latter reading; but her thoughts were elsewhere.

Uvaysiy was reciting a fable chosen from somewhere in the anthologies. Nodira wondered whether certain aspects of the fable were directed deliberately at her, or were merely accidental reminders of her life.

'In days of yore there lived two doves, one called Bazanda, the other Navozanda. They were together day and night in an idyllic place, they lived harmoniously in the same luxurious chambers. One day Navozanda looked Bazanda in the face: she could read the anguish on the other's forehead, itself a thing of beauty. She said, "Listen, light of my eyes and moon, bliss of my melancholy heart, dim mirror of secret thought, your face bodes ill: what did you see, what has affected your ill-fated days?"

'Bazanda said, "As the ancients say, 'Cheap transport from the town just causes trouble.' I have neither a man nor a pack animal. The terrors of making this journey weigh heavily on my mind. A parrot, after leaving the cage, must soar.'

Uvaysiy carried on with the story of the two sad doves, but Nodira applied the last words to herself. In fact, her spirits were downcast: it was all so like her own situation... In her recital, Uvaysiy switched between prose and verse. Nodira's confused thoughts prevented her from under-standing fully: the same two lines kept running through her mind:

> The evil rival who hates me
> Is an infidel, her mind denies God

Uvaysiy easily picked up on Nodira's distracted state; the older woman raised her voice and articulated each word as she recited:

'Then Navozanda said, "When setting off on a journey you mustn't be frugal, but if you have one thing too many, it is hell. You need a friend on a journey… With a good friend a journey may be a pleasure, with a bad friend it will be disastrous. The proof of this is the journey a scorpion made with a tortoise."

'Then Bazanda said, "How did that go? Tell me."

'Navozanda said, "According to what I've heard, a tortoise was on its way from Iraq to the Hejaz. It took up with an exhausted scorpion it met by the side of the road. The two of them were obliged to go together. Now, this tortoise was very sharp-witted, having been on many journeys and having acquired a great deal of valuable experience. Still, it put its trust in the scorpion. They crossed deserts and came to a wayside inn. Eventually they found themselves facing a big river. They looked both ways along its banks, but could see no bridges or ferries. Finally, the tortoise, being near its desired goal, went down to the water's edge, thinking to swim across. It shook itself like a goose or a duck. But then it looked around and saw that its companion was hanging back, its sting raised up over its shoulder. "Hey, friend," the tortoise said, "why won't you come here?"

"'You'll have to forgive me," the scorpion said, "even a tear-drop of water is a drop too much for me." The tortoise said to itself, Isn't it the duty of travelling companions to tackle such problems together? This isn't so difficult a task. It will be best if I carry him across. I'll follow the ancient sages' advice, 'Do a good deed, tell it to the water; if the water doesn't take it in, let the fish know; if the fish don't take it in, the Creator will know'.

'To cut a long story short, the tortoise took up a paddle. "Hey, friend," it said. "I've decided to take you across the river. Get on my back. Don't move, or it will be dangerous for you."

'The scorpion said, "Every person knows what is right for them," and climbed onto the tortoise's back. They set off across the river. After a while the scorpion started swaying about, and said to the tortoise, "Today I've found a wide enough battlefield. The sages used to say, 'A donkey plays once in forty years.' Today I'll stick my steel sting neatly into your flat back."

'The tortoise said, "That nasty sting of yours is too weak to harm my back."

'Then the scorpion said, "You know that it's all the same to me; a scorpion's urge is to sting, whether it's a friend's breast or an enemy's back.

> Everyone has their own habits,
> Therefore we have no will.
> There is no scorpion without a sting of stone,
> So you have no cause to be amazed."

'The tortoise said, "I have heard a saying of the sages: Don't trust a friend, he'll flay you alive. And now, my friend, you must walk like straw on the water. I myself must take a look at the precious stones on this seabed." Saying this, the tortoise plunged down like a pearl-diver, and the scorpion gave up the ghost. The moral of the fable is this: "You can't mistake a genuine friend; and a false person has no friends". These words stay in the mind, but the goal slips from the hand. We've left these words to have their effect...'

Uvaysiy set the book down on the table, next to a

burning candle. Privately, Nodira wondered: What did Navozanda have in mind when she told that fable? Was it a hint that two hands are stronger than one, or was she warning herself to be on guard against a rival, a senior wife? Who wrote that fable? It can't have been Uvaysiy, the language is too simple and crude, more like the language of the street…'

Her thoughts once more revolved around her own verse: giving voice to them, like a flickering candle. Nodira sang:

> If there were any quarry, hearts would hunt in pairs,
> Keep your state single, save your locks of hair as a trap and a net…

—

From time to time, Umar, Emir of all Muslims, liked to fling some well-worn garment over his shoulder and wander the streets, pretending to be a dervish. Tucked into a leather bag hanging from his belt he always kept some much-used knucklebone dice and five or six gold coins, while by his side was his most reliable guard, the handsome strongman known by the name Gulxaniy. Unarmed, they set off for markets, tea-houses, merchants' inns and gambling dens. The Emir's pretext was that he wanted to study what the people really thought of their government; despite Islam's prohibitions, he loved to spend his time on wild pleasures.

Umar could have stayed in the palace to smoke a hookah or drink opium syrup, but he felt the urge to go to a gambling house for a game of knucklebones. With his guard by his side, Umar saw no need for restraint: if the mood took him, he was as ready for a fight as for a game.

But on this particular day, he was just about to change his clothes when the chief mulla happened to come to his council chamber. The matter was this: the inhabitants of Kokand, too fond of trade, had stopped visiting the mosques, especially for afternoon and evening prayers, which were now attended only by the imam, the muezzin and the charity heads. Running out of patience, Umar hastily dictated a decree to his clerk: 'As for anyone who fails to attend prayers for our Prophet Mohammed the Messenger, peace be upon him, especially the afternoon and evening prayers, let them be given fifty strokes of the lash.' After dealing with this, Umar changed his clothes and, accompanied by Gulxaniy, headed straight for the gambling den.

Umar threw his well-worn knucklebone with a cry 'to Lady Luck!', but the die refused to fall concave side up; at best it landed concave side down, and at least managed to avoid hitting another die. His hand was out of luck; he lost all but a single gold coin. As his fingers felt in his purse for the coin, he suddenly exclaimed, 'Let's play a different game!' Some of the players looked at him with disapproval, others with eager anticipation. 'Let's go on with this game,' some said, 'we're enjoying it.' But Umar had Gulxaniy by his side: the strongman's arms, crossed over his chest like two big weights from a set of scales, made the gamblers reconsider.

'What kind of game?' they asked.

'I'll spread out my satin waistband here in the middle, then each of us will line up behind it and put two knuckle-bones down. Then we stand back five paces and take turns to throw a knucklebone. If you knock a knucklebone off the waist-band, you win it and can throw another one; any-one who knocks off two knucklebones, gets both, the one he first hit, and the one he threw.' The players scratched their heads, convinced that this was a child's game, but after one or two more questions they started playing. With a shout of 'Lady Luck' a man stepped forward to throw a polished knucklebone. It landed six inches short of the row of knucklebones on the waistband, bounced off, touching one of the others, then settled down in the middle. Biting his dirty fingernails, the man moved away.

The next player to throw gave a cry of 'Help me, saint!' His knucklebone struck the first, then rolled away off the cloth.

'As much use as a fan for an orphan girl,' Gulxaniy laughed.

It was the cobbler's turn. This thickly bearded man, before taking his knucklebone, stepped back and asked Gulxaniy: 'Do I throw it flat side down, or concave up?'

'Do I look like an expert in bones? Would you ask a butcher "Will this boot fit my wife?"' Laughter shook the ceiling of the gambling den.

Embarrassed, the cobbler threw his knucklebone, but it didn't get anywhere near the other bones: it even fell short of the waistband itself.

'No wonder he can't reach a waistband,' Gulxaniy commented, 'he's a cobbler, after all'; the gamblers' laughter was like a marsh full of croaking frogs. Two more players took their turns. The second had some cunning and knocked out two knucklebones, but his next throw ended badly, for it struck the remaining bones too hard, ending up in a pile with the others.

Then Umar had his turn: he brought out of his pocket not a small sheep's knucklebone but a bull's ankle bone, the size of a man's fist. 'Cheat!' somebody hissed. 'Crook!' another growled. 'Why shouldn't I take advantage?' Umar said, grimacing nastily as his strongman quietened everybody down by raising his ten-kilo hands and saying, 'Is my fist as big as your father's grave, or a courtroom? One of you, come up and see me!' And he called upon Niyozcha the Councillor.

'Say something,' he told Niyozcha, as he pointed to his boots. 'If I chuck this boot of mine, will it fall heel first, or top first? If you get it right, you win; if not, my pal here does.'

The gamblers argued amongst themselves, some saying 'top first', others 'heel first'. Niyozcha inspected the boots very carefully before giving his verdict: 'The boot has a heavy heel, so it will fall with the heel furthest away'. The Tajik strongman kicked his boot up to the ceiling; as it fell, it span round two and a half times and landed neatly heel first. Gulxaniy then instructed Umar, 'Throw your bone!' Crying 'Lady Luck!', the disguised Emir hefted his bone by its side. The mud-brick sized missile scattered the other knucklebones like sparks in all directions. The big ankle bone turned over once before settling on the waist-band. First of all Umar got it into his head to crush the cunning player's knucklebone, then he finished up by knocking off the others, two by two. When only one bone was left on the satin cloth, the call to evening prayers came.

Some heard it, others were too busy throwing knucklebones. But the bang with which the gambling den's doors were thrown open dwarfed the clatter of the bones, as did the voices of the dozen guards who rushed in with their whips flailing.

Thus, Umar barely escaped the fifty strokes he himself had ordered that morning. Gulxaniy, living up to his role as strongman, had managed to get him out of trouble after wounding four or five of the guards.

Now he was sitting in his library, still wearing his old dervish garments, and with Gulxaniy still with him. 'Tell me a story,' Umar said.

'This is one I've heard,' Gulxaniy began, in his rather rough Tajik accent, 'a man smoked a bit of opium syrup, and when it was time for evening prayers he came to someone's living-room, where they were eating a meal. The table was laid and people were sitting around it, then the call for prayers sounded out. The people said, "Let's pray first, and afterwards go on with the feast. Anyone who doesn't pray doesn't get any dinner." The man felt that he had done nothing wrong as far as prayers were concerned. He got up, performed his religious ablutions, said his prayers, then looked reproachful, and said crossly: "Oh, this damned desire to eat! Despite my having smoked opium, you've made me dip my hands, as decency demands, in cold water, made me turn the colour of resin, and finally you've told me to pray". You are like him. Do the decent thing: renounce either your passions, or the ruler's power. "Two liquids can't mix in one heart," they say. And another thing the sages used to say, "If you board two ships, you drown; to cross the sea safely you have to take only one.'"

The Emir didn't know whether to laugh or to curse.

———

The bride's first forty days of marriage had passed and Oyxon was getting ready to visit her father in Shahrixon. It was a convenient coincidence: Umar was preparing to go hunting nearby, on the Syr-Darya river. Umar's sister Oftob had visited for the wedding ceremony, but that visit, too, had run its course, and she was returning to her house in Shahrixon. Umar had her accompany his young bride and appointed to go with them a few old maidservants plus his eldest son Madali, his nephew Hakim, and his most reliable guard, Gulxaniy.

The weather had turned cold; there was a touch of frost in the air, and hoar-frost lay on either side of the roads; the men were wearing leather coats, the women fur-lined gowns and woollen headscarves. Everyone's breath was visible, except for that of the usually talkative Gulxaniy, for whom the cold had dampened the desire for speech. The snorting horses couldn't yet go slow enough for the cart; they were pulling hard so as to warm up more quickly. The ladies and the elderly maidservants had arranged themselves in a circle as if sitting around a table, their legs covered with one big quilted blanket; the men were on horseback on either side of the cart, adjusting the pace of their wild mounts to that of Gulxaniy's draft horses.

The weather was so harsh that under her veil Oyxon's two cheeks turned bright red, like apples; she remembered with affection and with bitterness an earlier cart journey. At times it seemed as if it was her beloved Qosim, not Gulxaniy, in the driver's seat, and her loving young brothers, not strange old women, who were sitting pressed against her. The cart wheels creaked, like two heavy millstones grinding her sweet dreams into flour...

> Day and night I see shadows, I spy something behind me,
> Haunting my solitude, they follow me like day follows night.
>
> My horror and fear are as shallow as a sigh,
> Every step on my path heads towards the grave's abyss.

Oyxon composed this poem, but didn't set it down on paper, for she was wary of her rebellious thoughts. Like threaded pearls under a high-necked dress, she kept her verses away from other people's eyes, reserving them for her burning heart. Dreams, dreams, dreams... if only there were an end to you, or some good could come of you. You are like a road that goes straight from early spring to autumn. I see a field of stubble instead of a bed of tulips, an apricot grove now gutted by autumn, the boundless sky tumbling down, its blue darkened by thick clouds. The cart wheels go screeching on without end.

> Like arrows of wood, like the blades of mountains and rocks
> In sight of the emptiness, fear of light stabs me in the back.

There was another difference from the cart journey of Oyxon's melancholy memory: Gulxaniy didn't sing, as Qosim had. Instead, his deep voice was employed in stories to amuse the women, stories as miserable as the mood of the day:

> There was a drover down Fergana way
> Well, his old she-camel gave birth one day.
>
> The drover's wife was very pretty
> But their house was a hovel, mean and dirty.

'The camel and the baby camel were the drover's only possessions. One day, he saddled the camel, loaded it up with heavy bags and set off. The camel calf was upset by being separated from its mother; it trotted off after her. Some distance away, in the desert, in the shade of a solitary tree, the drover made the camel kneel down.

> That young calf trailed far behind its mum
> Panting with the heat and overcome.
>
> "Hey, mum," it said, "Give me a break!
> I've had as much of this heat as I can take."
>
> "If you moved slower then I'd be happy
> You could just give me milk on tap."
>
> The mum turned and looked at her daughter
> And soon was shedding tears like water.
>
> "See – this man holds my muzzled head
> And his eyes are fixed one way – ahead."
>
> "But if he let me just a little bit free,
> For dust, he wouldn't see you and me!"

When she heard these words, Oyxon felt so humiliated that she could not freeze the tears in her eyes: they almost splashed through her veil.

By noon they reached Marg'ilon, where everyone knew Gulxaniy and was eager to invite him in. 'Wouldn't you like to sit down and have a bowl of tea?' Choosing the most respectable house, they halted, performed noonday prayers and had a bite to eat before setting off again, not waiting for the dish of plov that had been cooked for them.

They had covered about ten miles when they realised that the weather had turned quite bad. Madali dismounted, tied his horse's reins to the cart and declared that he was 'frozen stiff' before promptly climbing up into the women's cart and getting under their blanket.

Oyxon noticed that under the blanket he was constantly touching her legs with his own, but avoiding meeting her eyes. At first she thought he might simply be showing affection to her as his stepmother, but there was something sensual in the way he intertwined their legs. She asked Gulxaniy to stop the cart and let her ride one of the horses instead. Hakim helped her mount Madali's riding horse. The horse was apparently bored of hauling the cart: kicking up its front legs, it now cantered ahead. Hakim whipped his own horse to follow. The daylight was fading as the two riders quickly vanished out of sight. Gulxaniy followed them, driving the cart at a cautious gallop, but no sooner had they reached the next settlement than two spokes on the right-hand wheel broke.

Fortunately, Gulxaniy was well-known here too. While the travellers drank tea the wheel was repaired, but Oyxon and Hakim seemed to have disappeared. 'Before the twilight fades, we can get as far as a place called Nayman and stop there overnight,' said Gulxaniy. But when they reached Nayman, there was neither news nor sighting of the two riders. 'Well then, God is great; even if they do get lost, there's only one road, they'll end up here,' the others decided; they spent the night with the village elder.

Now for what happened to Oyxon and Hakim. Once they had left the cart behind they made their horses gallop ahead, one after the other without looking back. Oyxon felt free at last, having emerged from the dark; she was drunk with freedom, rushing like a fire in the cold air. Chasing after the girl intoxicated Hakim, and he didn't lag behind his sister-in-law. As they galloped together, thick clouds unexpectedly covered the sky, a squall started and the world turned dark. In this pitch-black darkness only the horses' flowing manes were still visible. Snow began to fall, the wind howled. They found themselves in the middle of thorny scrub, the path had now become hard to make out. Who panicked? Young Hakim. 'Let's turn back,' he pleaded, but his sister-in-law wouldn't listen: she urged her horse into a gallop.

But their mounts had come to the end of their endurance, and could no longer bear the cold air that filled their lungs: panting hard, they pulled up. Hakim tethered both horses by their legs to the handle of his sword. Oyxon was the first to find a way into a gap that cut between two flat rocks. Fearing for their lives, expecting death, they huddled there. Then their ears were struck by a noise that came out of the icy darkness, the grunting and ferocious roars of wild animals. Right by the lair where they were crouching, a herd of wild boars passed by. As soon as they saw the horses, the boars broke into a run, so that everything under their hooves was trampled down and destroyed. Frightened out of his mind, Hakim clung to Oyxon and prayed, '*La hawla*... There is no power and no strength except with Allah...' Then, when the horses regained their breath, Oyxon again rode hers at a gallop towards the light of distant lamps: it was the settlement of Nayman, where their cart had halted…

It was these lamps that Abdulla's sleepless eyes saw when the cell elder ordered everybody to turn over onto the other side. He had been considering for some time which of these three scenes to include in his narrative; still unable to decide, he turned over like the others, and fell asleep.

———

In the morning the order came in Russian, 'Get up!': everyone rose at once, and Abdulla saw that there were roughly fifty men there. In the years when he had been a gardener, he had kept a bee-hive; now he had the impression that there were as many men in the cell as bees in that hive. When he was arrested the first time, there hadn't been so many in the cell with him, only about twenty, and if there hadn't been an elder among them, there would have been nowhere to wash or urinate, no food to eat, and no arrangement for sleeping. Here, the elder was a fat red-bearded man, who let the prisoners know in a menacing way whose turn it was to go to the bucket in the corner to urinate and wash. After Muborak had taken his turn, the elder glared at Abdulla: 'Who are you? Why don't I know about you?' he roared.

Abdulla had an answer on the tip of his tongue, but little Sodiq spoke up for him, 'He's the greatest Uzbek writer!' he said, parroting Muborak from the day before. 'They brought him in at midnight, ' he added. 'We didn't dare wake you, Mr Jur'at, sir.'

'What's your name?' Jur'at demanded of Abdulla, just as overbearing, but a little gentler.

Somewhat awed by the elder's imposing figure and booming voice, embarrassed to have so many pairs of eyes on him, Abdulla spoke shyly: 'Abdulla…'

'Hey, it's Abdulla Qodiriy!' a couple of prisoners exclaimed.

'We already have a poet with us, he's called Cho'lpon; they're sending you lot here to improve your minds.' Jur'at's tone could have indicated either pity or sarcasm. 'All right, you can tell your fairy stories later; for now, go and relieve yourself.'

Everyone watched while Abdulla went to the corner. Once he got to the bucket he felt the pressure on his neck of other men's gazes, and at first couldn't unbutton his trousers; when he thought about the queue of desperate men, however, his fingers quickened. But he couldn't urinate, and had to try and distract himself by looking at the ceiling. Later, when he recalled this moment, he sensed that the cell elder had guessed what was happening and had rounded on a prisoner whom he had spotted wiping his face and hands on someone else's shirt. Everyone's attention was drawn to another corner of the cell, and so Abdulla relieved his bladder. Washing his body seemed impossible, so he made do with washing his face and hands as thoroughly as he could. Instead of washing his feet, he symbolically ran his wet fingers over his slippers, praying 'May God forgive me!'

Returning to his place, he greeted Muborak. To judge by the latter's accent, he was a native of Bukhara, but there was also a trace – just a nuance – of another dialect, which Abdulla didn't recognise. Abdulla racked his memory, but didn't think it right to ask questions. By now Sodiq had washed and come back. After greeting him, Abdulla asked what had happened to Cho'lpon. Both his neighbours shrugged their shoulders. 'I wouldn't know, he must have been locked up before we came.' Discreetly, because of the darkness all around, Abdulla moved away, but whether it was because the cell was so dark, because of the recent confusion, or the constant seething in this wasp's nest, he couldn't find a single familiar face. Which of them had called out 'Abdulla Qodiriy'? Could they have recognised him or have read any of his books? Abdulla's crowded thoughts had again dispersed, like a nest of bees. No, this was not a market or a crowd; the cacophony was reminiscent of a poetry-reading, the kind which Abdulla and Cho'lpon used to attend together.

—

Poetry readings in Umar's palace were occasions for pomp and ceremony. The ruler was very fond of hunting, of the pursuit of a quarry, and poetry gatherings were, for him, no different. First, he was like the hunter who hides in wait, relying only on his eyes and ears, reaping a sort of modest satisfaction if someone shot a wild sheep or a pheasant, because he himself was holding out for a rather bigger beast. While waiting for a poem that could be considered a lion, or even just a hyena, Umar would from time to time amuse himself by inciting the gathering of poets and scholars to outdo each other in their praises.

Husayn, the younger brother of Haydar, Emir of Bukhara, abandoned Persian speech and recited an ode in pure Turkic.

> After we, destitute and homeless, had roamed the world,
> Finally we found a home with his Majesty Emir Umar.
> We have girded ourselves with the belt of bonds of devotion,
> The sight of generous sympathy has made us give thanks to God.
> The king is our king, the ruler is our ruler,
> The times are our times, the epoch is our epoch.

Umar took the fur gown off his own shoulders, a gown worth five hundred gold coins, and draped it over Husayn's shoulders. The odes of praise continued to sound out, gifts and offerings were distributed to the eloquent writers. Waiters and servants served delicious dishes, the cup-bearers poured out wines and sherbets. Soloists sang and instrumentalists played with subtle skill.

At the height of the festivities, the palace's chief poet Mavlono Fazliy whispered something in Umar's ear then loudly clapped his hands. The gathering instantly fell silent, and, pointing to a screened-off corner, Fazliy said, 'The contest now continues between the poet Fazliy and the poetess Mahzuna.' Fazliy started with his own impromptu:

> A hundred times I praise your words, without seeing to the heart of things,
> Unless the mirror is silvered, it won't reflect the clothing.

Some shouted their admiration, some clapped, some guffawed. Once the noise had died down, a gently quivering woman's voice rang out from behind the screen:

> Unless the liver bleeds, who will speak any words,
> The pearl won't be revealed, unless you break the shell...

The noise aroused by these words was twice as loud. 'Bravo!' someone exclaimed; 'Brilliant!' someone else responded. Mavlono Fazliy bowed and continued:

> Chaste words need a modest covering,
> I will not see the sense of your syllables unless I see a veil.

A response came the moment this was said, before shouts could burst out:

> There is no blame if my words are not polite,
> As if grass can grow green without seeing sunlight...

Again, cries of delight came in response. 'What did she say? What did she say?' people asked one another, and, after a delay, the whole audience was in high spirits. In all this uproar not everyone could hear some of the verses, but those who heard them enjoyed them so much that they ignored the sense, so fired up were they by the festivities. Finally Mavlono Fazliy clapped his hands again to get attention:

> You are so refined, who was your teacher?
> The moon cannot give light without sight of the sun...

From behind the screen the silence was broken:

> As great value is gathered by a river of light,
> So this poor poet gets her learning, without a master for even a
>   single night...

Now you could see a real uproar. It was known to some, but not to everyone, that the girl whose pseudonym was Mahzuna was in fact Mavlono Fazliy's latest and best loved pupil. Could you hide the moon behind a skirt? The last verses that she had recited were drowned out in the enthusiastic applause; at this point, like a hunter stalking a large beast, Umar stood up and, watched by the amazed spectators, went to join Mavlono Fazliy. He gave the poet his bejewelled silver-buckled belt and in the general silence addressed the screen, asking in Persian:

> Assuage my suffering, saviour, with a glimpse of your clothing.

A rather teasing voice replied from the corner:

> A deer's eye is best perceived through a frame of autumn leaves.

All was quiet. Umar spoke:

> Throw a stone at me, so I can drive your image from my heart!

The girl responded from behind her curtain:

When the dew falls on the petals, the flower shuts its door.

Now the festive gathering had its day: Umar was drowning in a sea of ecstasy. He tore off his collar and shouted, 'I give you all everything that you can find here!' There was nothing left around the Emir: everything was stripped bare. 'Strip it,' said the Emir. 'Take it!'

'Take it!' This was Muborak and Sodiq offering Abdulla the morning millet gruel with a tea leaf stuck to the bowl.

'You're a strange sort of man,' said Sodiq. 'You really are in a dream world. You're not thinking straight, you're somewhere else…'

Abdulla was indeed like someone emerging from of a sea of wonder, looking around as if half-blinded.

———

After spending a few days in a solitary cell, Abdulla had got into the habit of giving his thoughts free rein. If he went on behaving that oddly in this cell, too, he would become a laughing stock. It might not be a bad idea for him to yank his head out of the clouds and study the people who were around him. Abdulla chewed the bread with his millet gruel as he sized them up. After all, the soldier who brought everyone their gruel had turned out, upon investigation, to be an Uzbek. Oh, you're being clever, comrade writer! Hadn't Cho'lpon spoken about failing to see the most important things?

> My thought goes on flying skywards,
> Now I am giving it free rein.
> How do I actually hold it back?
> It touches my tenderest cords…

Sunnat must have sensed Abdulla's gaze: making a furtive

gesture, he asked, 'Shall I give you another helping?' At any other time, Abdulla wouldn't have choked down even a single helping of this vile food, but he had caught the tone of the young man's remark, and, his heart pounding with anxiety, he quickly licked the steel spoon attached by a piece of wire to the metal plate, and stepped towards the soldier.

There was a lot of noise, as spoons were banged on plates: for the moment, nobody paid attention to the young soldier's whispers.

'Boss, I've brought what you asked for, it's between these two pieces of bread...' he said, and banging his ladle against the jerry-can of gruel, he offered Abdulla two pieces of bread.

Abdulla now deftly put the two pieces up the sleeves of his gown and went back to his place with half a ladle-full of gruel. His heart was pounding so hard that it seemed it would burst through his shirt and red gown. But neither Muborak nor the prisoners on either side of him had noticed anything. Somehow, Abdulla managed to eat his gruel and finish swallowing the bread crumbs, then, while the bowls were being handed back, put the sheet of paper and a pencil stub into his trouser pocket, and secretly gave the second piece of bread back to the Uzbek lad.

It worked. Bless your father, Muslim son! It worked! Abdulla had difficulty concealing his excitement as he returned to his place. So his manuscripts would now be safe. If, with God's help, he got out of here, it would take just one more summer, one more winter at his desk to get it all finished. And even if, God forbid, he was kept here longer, everything would remain intact.

Here the day had begun: some were taken off for interrogation, some were moved to a different cell, or were sent off with their possessions to Siberia. Some seemed engaged in purposeful discussion, others had nothing to do but engage in idle chitchat: in other words, the cell hummed just like a wasp's nest. Abdulla, however, was too distracted to answer Muborak and Sodiq's questions properly.

> It is flying… it is flying… It passes through
> A thousand layers, in close embrace.
> It goes on, never bored or idle,
> Sometimes perturbing an insane heart…

This evening he would write, if it could be sent, a guarded explanation to his wife Rahbar, then, God grant, the letter would reach her in a few days and she could hide the manuscripts. Who would she entrust them to? One of her relatives? Rahbar was sharp-witted, she would think it all through. When Abdulla thought about his wife, tears came to his eyes. Her memory was sheer torture to him in his unhappy state. The first time he was put in prison, she already had three small children to think of, and was pregnant with a fourth. Fortunately, that first term of imprisonment had been reduced. But how long would he be away this time? Once again, she had been left to fend for herself. Abdulla had a bit of money set aside, but he had been saving it for a rainy day, and hadn't told her where it was. Pain stung his heart. His mind had been wandering all over the place, back as far as the nineteenth century, yet he hadn't spared a thought for Rahbar's financial situation. Abdulla was ashamed of himself, he was burning with shame! 'A so-called writer can never be a human being,' he reproached himself.

The previous year his mother Josiyat had passed away. On the second day of the funeral, Abdulla and Cho'lpon had been sent by the Union of Writers to a congress of Tatar writers in Kazan. It was left to his neighbour to preside over the funeral rites. The night he came back from Kazan, Rahbar sobbed as she put the children to bed. 'God forbid,' she said to him, 'but suppose I die one day, and you can't get away from your writers' meeting: will you leave my corpse unwashed?' When he considered it, his unhappy wife was right. After all, would the heavens have fallen if he hadn't gone to Kazan? There it had been all wit and jokes, as they passed the time in pleasures, parties and indulgence... was that all he had gone there for?

Though if he had stayed at home and mourned, those with nothing better to do would have dropped by to bother him with their idle chat: 'This year we did farm work, nothing but trouble. Digging everywhere, ditching, grafting vines with grease, hay-making... you don't get time even to fart! Yesterday, my friend, I weeded the potatoes, then I only have to water them and it's time to unearth them...'

'Old man, it's after watering them that you should weed them. Anyway, do potatoes need watering?'

'None of your jokes! I'm knackered.'

'No, I'm not joking, you can ask anyone you like!'

Everyone would then nod their heads.

'All right then, what does it matter if I weed them or not?'

'If you don't, then you get a better harvest. If you do, you'll only get seed potatoes.'

'Oh dear, I've been wasting my time with all this vegetable growing: marvellous thing,' and with these words loud laughter burst out in a house in mourning.

More jokes, more witty remarks...

Abdulla pricked up his ears: the people around him were either telling jokes, or mocking others. In a word, they were passing the time, busting a gut laughing. Typical Uzbeks.

—

Once Nasrullo had exterminated all his close relatives and officials, he began to suspect his Chief Minister Hakim, who had put him on the throne. True, there were no flaws in his capabilities, no dark spots as far as the Emir could see, but could he expect anything good from that old fox, a vizier who had served four emirs? Although the Emir's mind was uneasy – might he fall into the man's nets? – he was softened by the vizier's sweet talk: flattery and ingenuity gradually undid the knot of suspicions. When Nasrullo asked him about the characters of the former emirs, he had a way of talking that made it impossible to determine whether he was inventing praise of their great eminence or simply laughing at them.

'One day, your distinguished father Haydar told this amusing story about Emir Sodiq-biy of Shahrisabz. "Sodiq-biy was returning to Kitob from Shahrisabz, and at the market he met an Uzbek leading a piebald ox; the emir asked him in Turkish 'What is your cow?' The simple-minded Uzbek didn't know what to say, and had to pretend he hadn't heard. The emir asked him again. The Uzbek really couldn't understand what the emir wanted, until finally the emir lost his temper and lashed out with his stick. The wretched Uzbek finally said, 'My ox's name is ox!' and tried to run away. One of the emir's friends guessed what he wanted and explained to the wretched Uzbek, 'The emir was asking what the price of the ox is!' The emir then realised he'd expressed himself in bad Turkish. The ox's owner said that he hadn't bought the ox, and so he didn't know what it cost, and that he regretted that he had been beaten with a stick when he had done nothing wrong...' Should Abdulla put this anecdote in his work? Would it be understood? Or would he sit there suspicious as any Uzbek would, wondering, much like Emir

Nasrullo, whether he was somehow the butt of the joke?

—

The women are what he should talk about, yes, the women. If four men are gathered together, doesn't the conversation automatically turn to them? He should talk about Umar's harem.

Nodira's peace of mind disappeared again when she found out about Umar's extravagance at the last poets' contest. She put all her female charm to work to ensure that any such contest should, in future, take place in the Emir's harem. She invited every well-born woman who had a claim to being a poet, both those who composed their own verses and those who simply recited, including Uvaysiy and her pupils. The older maidservants were ordered to bring female lute and viol players, whose music was not allowed to be heard outside the women's quarters of their houses.

Nodira had a secret wish. She told nobody about this wish, but the two women — Uvaysiy and Oyxon — who kept a constant eye on her were well aware of it. Nodira regretted that she hadn't been born when the Baburid dynasty ruled India. She was influenced by the books she had read in her youth: for her, the poetesses Dildor, Gulbadan, Arjuman, Zeb-un-Nissa, Nurjahan and Jahonaro lived not so much in her thoughts as in paradise, while Mumtaz, for whom Shah Jahan built the Taj Mahal, tugged at her heartstrings.

> If only I could see in my dreams my beloved Gulbadan,
> If only I could hear in my dreams her lips' sweet words…

At Nodira's poetry evening no one adorned themselves in the royal satin and patterned silk that was the usual style. Instead, they dressed in fabrics imported from India: brocades and fine silks. Fragrant breaths perfumed the air, while Nodira's two peacocks promenaded through the spacious hall, displaying their colourful tail feathers. The serving women were dancing; the peacocks, instead of being frightened, kept arrogantly pecking and upsetting the guests with their harsh cries. The poetesses' cheeks burned like embers, becoming as red as the pomegranate and grape juice they drank. Then poems of praise were recited in honour of the royal Nodira, the hostess of the festivities.

> There is no treasure so 'precious' in the world,
> My lady's soul is eternally generous.
> A shepherdess of wit and virtue,
> She has gathered every clan to her palace.
> She shows her mastery in her first poem,
> Every poet is to recite a lyric...

The panegyrists were presented with clothes and footwear brought from India by Andijan merchants. In one corner odes and lyrics were sung, drums began to play, and dances and part-songs started up.

> Nights of pale moonlight,
> Pure and silvery moonlight.
> Infused with rose and basil scent:
> The streets through which my true love went.

> And I will sweep with my own hair
> The cobbles that his feet trod there
> And if the dust swirls up and flies
> May dampening tears flow from my eyes.

The ebullient women left all inhibitions behind. After performing, they threw off their headscarves to wave them about as they danced and ululated; their laughter and clapping rose to the ceiling. The aromatic perfumes faded, there was an oppressive smell of sweat. The peacocks, huddled in a corner, had now ceased their cackling.

Oyxon, melancholic, was left on her own in the seat of honour. She spoke her thoughts:

> My life has passed in flagrant ignorance, what shame;
> What is left will now pass in repentance, o alas...

Without anyone noticing, she slipped away from the festivities and returned to her chambers. When she left, the feast was at its height; she had missed its climax. A moment or half a moment after Oyxon left, Nodira appeared from a corner door. The servants in that corner instantly blocked the door with a screen. Nodira was approaching the centre of the hall when Uvaysiy applauded loudly and cried out, 'Praise to Allah!' Willingly or not, the other women quietened down.

'The culmination of the contest will be between Nodira and...' Uvaysiy paused, then raised her voice: 'Emir Umar!'

'Oh!' the hall responded as one. That instant, Umar's royal voice sounded out from behind the screen:

> How much respect is there for her eminent reason and
> intelligence?

Nodira, standing in the middle of the hall, responded to him in her full, flirtatious and elegant voice:

> Do these fine minds belong only to those who wear padded
> tunics?

The women and girls desperately exclaimed 'Oh, alas!' Then Umar instantly picked up the theme:

> The falling dew showed the beauty of your flower-like face...
> All the talk is of the rosebud of your lips...

Again, there were gasps of amazement. Someone began to cry uncontrollably. The Emir said:

> Cup-bearer, make me merry for an hour with wine...

and one of the maidservants, lifting up a full bowl of wine, hurried past the screen. When she saw this, Nodira shook her head, uttering the line:

> My poor soul is hurt by the grief of separation...

Pausing for a minute or two to wipe his lips on the servant girl's hem, the Emir responded:

> Do not rebuke the bonds that hold me by the neck...

As if sensing something, the peacocks began chasing one another. In the middle of this uproar, Nodira, as if seeing her own hopes and dreams crystallised, said:

> In all this cruel path there is a Christian's hair belt round his neck...

The women asked one another what this meant, but nobody could understand; only Uvaysiy was quick-witted enough to grasp the sense behind those words. She smiled to herself. But she hadn't made sense of the secret that the last words might contain, because in the middle of this conversation the ingenious Emir Umar was in fact addressing somebody else:

> Just for a day, grace my ruined hovel with your angelic presence...

Excited by the wine, Umar had reacted to her words and couldn't have expected her response:

> If the time's shadow on the wall has vanished...

At one point Umar had devised a poem 'Welcome', a lyric with the recurring refrain 'shadow on the wall'. 'No, today I shan't darken your hovel's door; you can cast a shadow on her wall instead, this woman to whom you say "Welcome"!' – these were the words that Nodira had used as a loving reproach. As she said them again now, she looked in the direction of that third person, then bit her tongue: Oyxon had left the gathering... It was at that moment that the Emir said this astounding line:

How could my hospitable heart deny her welcome?

He waited and waited for her answer, but not receiving any response, he spoke from behind the screen:

As the king of love, Umar is a monument to justice...

This ending was his signature to the lyric, and leaving the ladies to get on with their celebrations, he left for his own chamber. Nodira was heart-broken:

Oh heavens, let your surface crack, your tyranny is unbounded,
Bereft is loving Nodira, parted now from her beloved.

—

Abdulla wondered if he should talk about such matters to the prisoners. Would they understand? Or should it mark the very start of his narrative, in the same way as *A Thousand and One Nights*? Might that not be a reason to work out the scenes he hadn't yet written? Muborak was observant enough to notice Abdulla taking an interest in the conversations taking shape around him:

'Abdulla, sir, what sins have you committed to be treated like a criminal?'

'How would I know?' Abdulla replied tartly. 'You'd need to ask the people in charge. When the time comes,

I'm sure they'll have something to say. How about you?'
But then Jur'at came up and interrupted.

'For a child slave even a shit is as good as a rest, they
say; you and I need to have a talk. You say you're a writer?
We haven't read anything of yours. I have read a book
called *The Naughty Child*. That man could really write!
I've also read a piece called *The Thief* by someone called
Abdulla – was that you?'

'No, that was Abdulla Qahhor...'

'I don't know about your writing, but that's a nice
gown you're wearing!'

Were these remarks of Jur'at's purposely casual, was he
trying to cheer Abdulla up, or had he genuinely taken a
shine to Abdulla's gown? In any case, it reminded Abdulla
of a story from Emir Nasrullo's era. Abdulla suddenly
laughed:

'In olden times, there was a king who was forced to
give up his throne. Absolutely destitute, he arrived one
day in Samarkand. He had no money, no horse: his only
possession was an old gown. Reluctantly, he went to sell
this gown in the market. He couldn't find a single buyer.
All anyone would give was a quarter of a dirham, which
he finally had to accept. The next day, when he was walking near the market, the man who had bought his gown
grabbed hold of him. "There was something wrong with
your gown," this man said, "yesterday's deal is off: I won't
have it!"

'"What's wrong with it?" asked the former king.

'The man replied, "All the lice in the world have got
into that gown. Last night they didn't leave an inch of me
untouched, you could say they ate me alive!"

'"My gown has the same drawback as that one,' said
Abdulla, ending his story with a smile.

'That's a good one! I must admit!' Jur'at laughed. 'If

you're ever bullied here, or you can't find anywhere to lie down, move to where I am. While we're gambling, you can entertain us with your stories.' As he said this, the elder rattled the knucklebones in his pocket and had Abdulla's bedding moved next to where he slept.

Then two prisoners in another corner started quarrelling over a share of something: Jur'at rushed over like lightning to pull them apart.

Muborak seized the opportunity to resume the conversation: 'Weren't you talking about Emir Nasrullo's times? I've read an awful lot of books about how it was back then. Especially about the English... about the spies,' he said.

'Really?' Abdulla exclaimed, unable to hide his amazement. 'I'm writing a book about exactly that!'

'Then you must have a chat with me,' Muborak said with a quick wink. 'Let me move your bedding, your heart can stay where it is. You asked me what I'm in for: I'm an English spy...'

Amazing the people you could meet in prison.

Abdulla had a game he had invented. When he was going by tram or bus to the city centre, or coming back home towards Xadra Square, he would study the other passengers' faces and imagine them living in different epochs. A short, thickset man, for instance, would be right for the job of Sharia judge in Nasrullo's castle. A frail, dishevelled woman would do as chief serving maid when there were guests in Nodira's harem. Abdulla rarely took his cue from their current profession: the tram driver with the gigantic moustache would be better as a butcher than a cart driver; the ticket inspector with the restless eyes, if he'd been in the Kokand market at the time, would have been a pickpocket, rather than a collector of taxes or land rents. Some unassuming passer-by would be promoted to poet; another, carrying a folder under his arm, would alight at the Market Mosque stop unaware that he was now an executioner.

Muborak tugged at his sleeve. 'Jur'at wants to see you!' he said, and before Abdulla could respond to the newly arrived mulla, he was taken to the far side of the cell.

Jur'at was lying back, with his elbows on two pillows. He gestured to Abdulla to sit down on his right, and then instructed Muborak: 'Everyone must be introduced to the writer. A writer should know his heroes. Bring your heroes in, one by one.'

Muborak began sending people over from the far side of the cell. Each one gave their name and reason for arrest, to which Jur'at always added a few words of explanation.

'So-and-so… such-and-such… Uzbek Criminal Code… article 150… complicity in bribery.' The elder told him, 'If a worthy man boasts, he gains; if an unworthy boasts, he loses.'

The great majority of those who came up to introduce themselves, however, named the same article, one that had been introduced to the Uzbek criminal code in 1926: article 66. Some were charged under paragraph 12 of article 66: failure to report a crime of a counter-revolutionary nature to the appropriate authorities; others were charged under paragraph 10: counter-revolutionary activity and propaganda. To these, Jur'at offered some words of sympathy: 'If you've got an untrustworthy friend, stick a straw in your skin', or 'Keep whatever's on your mind tucked away under your skirts.'

Altogether some fifty or sixty men passed before their eyes. Some bared their teeth in a smile: 'Who's this new right-hand man?' Others were annoyed by this strange puppeteer, frowning and muttering, 'Look what's turned up.' Because of their constant moving about, the foul air became even more stale, and there was a stink of rotting apples. There was now nobody new to meet. Muborak himself approached:

'Muborak Kukhanov, article 66, paragraph 6, espionage,' he announced.

'Ah, the ultimate cog in the machine, a spy,' Jur'at teased him. 'Article 66, did you say? Pretty good, eh! So we didn't see the sheep, but we did see the droppings? If you came to get the yoghurt, then don't hide the bucket! Spit it out, who were you spying for?'

'Mr Jur'at, sir, you know I'm no spy. We were looking for Moses's descendants, and we ended up in England. We Jews always end up getting the blame.'

'Did you at least find your relatives there?'

'I traced a few of them. There was one, a wise man, very well-respected. He'd written a lot of books about Bukhara. I read them myself...'

Abdulla listened to this exchange with interest, but because he couldn't stand the foul stench, or perhaps because he had been face-to-face with so many wretched men, or because they had been presented in such mocking tones, not as flesh-and-blood human characters, he suddenly began to feel nauseous.

'I'd feel better if I lay down by the door,' he said, I can't get enough air here.' Jur'at looked at the writer's pale face: 'Do a good deed, tell it to the water; if the water doesn't take it in, let the fish know; if the fish don't take it in, the Creator will know'. He ordered Muborak, 'Take him back to his old place.'

> 'A dragon-king has taken over the world's treasure
> And takes pleasure in angrily spreading fire.
> Anything in its maw that comes to life,
> Gets its payment in the dragon's maw...'

thought Abdulla, reciting Navoi, who himself was a vizier to one of those dragons. Abdulla went back to his old place, where he could feel the draught.

———

During this pleasant interlude, the midday meal was served. This time Vinokurov was in charge of distributing the food. The sight of the Russian made Abdulla's eyes blood-shot, and all his desire for vengeance – a feeling that had flooded his heart for some days – was concentrated in his clenched fists. If Vinokurov had so much as caught his eye, Abdulla would have summoned all his youthful sense of honour and gone for the Russian's throat. But Vinokurov didn't look at anyone: hanging back behind the two sol-diers who had wheeled in the trolley, he summoned Jur'at to him and the two conducted a whispered conversation. Then Vinokurov stepped abruptly back, like a wagging dog let off the leash, retreated to the door and left the cell. Abdulla's vindictiveness was now confined to his clenched fists and tense breathing.

What had the chat with Jur'at been about? Could he ask the elder about it? Or was some plot being hatched between them? Everyone knows that if two men are together, a third will only get in the way. And here there were sixty-two human beings, like scorpions in spring, packed into a single jar.

———

A plot... a plot... a plot... Umar was reclining on seven layers of quail feather quilts, chatting with Ernazar, the governor of Qurama province, about the land taxes col-lected: 'Your majesty, have mercy on me for a tiny error, but two days ago the tax collectors came back from a far part of the province: on their journey they came across two suspicious persons. When they were questioned, "Who are you, and what are you doing here?" both of them whipped their clapped-out horses and galloped off. The tax collectors showed their mettle, and caught them. We found this letter hidden in their clothes. With respect for your imperial majesty, I, as your tax collector, have not read the letter, but have brought it to you.'

The Emir took the proffered letter with no particular anxiety, but once his eyes had run over it, his eyebrows met in a menacing frown, and he clenched his fists.

'Sons of whores!' he exclaimed. Then he folded the letter in two, put it in his pocket and turned to Ernazar.

'Is that it?'

'Your majesty, I don't know anything about what is written in the letter, but when these men were tortured, they said that the writer had sent two other letters to the Kyrgyz, to the sons of Narbuta...'

'What have you done with the men you caught?' Umar demanded.

'Again I must beg for mercy, your majesty. I had them thrown into a dungeon, but when they tried to escape, my guards hacked them to pieces...'

'A pity!' Umar thrust his fist into a quail-feather pillow, crushing it out of shape. 'You can go. I'll deal with this mess myself! But don't drop your guard. Put someone better on the frontiers. Anyone you catch, send them to me!'

'Consider it done,' said Ernazar, stepping back without straightening his back. He then left the hall.

The Emir was worried; after a moment's thought he clapped his hands. One of his guards ran in from the next room.

'Send for Madali and Hakim,' Umar ordered.

The guard hurried off to find the Emir's son and nephew.

Very soon both young men presented themselves with a bow to the Emir.

'Read this!' said the Emir, handing the letter to Hakim. Hakim began, reading aloud,

> In the name of God, in the year 1232, in Rajab, on the first day
> of the seventh month. You should know, thanks be to Allah,
> we hope that as our true friend, always in our prayers, you are
> granted long life and well-being, just as our health is still without
> any shadow from providence or man's actions...

'Read the end,' Umar interrupted impatiently.

Hakim looked at the middle of the letter and then seemed to find the right place: he read further:

> Sunken in a mire of indulgence and depravity, sinfully hunting
> women and girls like a predatory bird, Emir Umar has stained his
> dagger with the black blood of our people...

'Vile!' the Emir yelled. Hakim was speechless for a moment, unsure whether this was a reaction to the letter, or to the person who had written it – he cautiously whispered a few more words, and then moved his eyes further down the letter.

> The time has come to strike in vengeance. Make the Kyrgyz
> of Jirg'atol rise up, prepare them. Let them know that the local
> population is ready for the Kipchaks and the Kyrgyz to rebel at
> the same time. Call on the Karateg people, too. Tell them that this
> winter they will have to pay land rent again. With Allah's help,
> we'll strike lucky: you will inherit the joys of royalty, that wretch
> will lose the throne of Kokand, and it will revert again to the
> possession of the descendants of Olim-khan.

> Your truly devoted Rajab Minister of Finance ...

'Swine!' Madali then exclaimed.

'Traitor!' Hakim said indignantly, as he reluctantly

handed the letter back to Umar.

'Bring me wine!' shouted Umar, turning away from them.

One of the guards brought in a jug of wine and poured out a bowlful. The Emir downed the wine in one.

'Go and get Rajab,' he ordered Madali, wiping his wet moustache on his sleeve. His son ran off to search for the vizier.

'Pour!' the Emir of the Faithful held out the bowl to Hakim. 'Let me know the moment that dog appears,' he added, and then noisily gulped down the wine.

Very quickly, Rajab appeared, kneeling and bowing in the Emir's presence. 'You ordered me to come, your majesty...'

Umar thrust the letter at him. 'Read this!' he roared.

As if totally surprised, Rajab started reading the document. When he got to the lines, 'Desert thorns are nasty; the loathsome Emir Umar has become a screech-owl on the ruins of vileness...' he stopped. 'No, I simply can't read out words as horrible as these, your Majesty!' he said.

'Look at the seal! Isn't it yours?' yelled Umar. Rajab looked at the bottom of the letter. The blood rushed to his face. 'This is a slanderous conspiracy!' he stuttered, and swore, 'God strike me dead if there's any truth in it.'

'It's your signature, isn't it?' asked Umar, unrelenting.

Rajab's reply to this was a couplet in Farsi:

Do not believe everyone when they talk about me or what
    they've heard,
There may be in it words of people who bear malice.

The dispute carried on for quite some time. Umar said one thing, the vizier another; Rajab said that he was innocent, the Emir that only the Creator was without sin. In the end the Emir seemed to believe his vizier: he took off his brocade gown and, in Madali's and Hakim's presence, placed it over Rajab's shoulders. The vizier was overjoyed, not so much by the gift itself, but by the forgiveness it signified. After receiving his Majesty's permission, he left.

As he saw Rajab off, Umar ordered his son and nephew to go to the caravanserai, find Ernazar immediately and bring him to the palace. He himself laid his heavy head down on the quilt.

We know not how long the Emir lay there in this drowsy state. The young men found Ernazar attending some feast at the caravanserai, and made him come to the palace. Umar then ordered his son and nephew to leave, and held some secret discussions with Ernazar.

What these discussions were, we do not know. What we do know is that, following the Emir's decree, Ernazar was relieved of the governorship of Qurama province, and was given instead the distant and less prosperous provinces of Turakurgan and Namangan, while Rajab the vizier was to assist the new governor in coping with these new responsibilities. The two of them set off: after crossing the River Saixun, they stopped for the night at a village. At midnight, four executioners strangled Rajab with a rifle fuse, put his body in a sack and threw it into the muddy waters of the river.

Abdulla's brain incorporated these scenes at such lightning speed that the thought of all the pruning and debris left in his mind – Vinokurov's whispering with Jur'at, and in his own home, the letter, alas, that he had mentally composed for his wife Rahbar – lost its sense as panic overwhelmed him.

In the background, the sound of the midday meal being guzzled rang in his ears.

—

Another day in his cell, anguished by the waste of a short winter's day, Abdulla was at the same time impatient for nightfall, when he could use the piece of paper and the pencil stub he had kept safe in his pocket.

Thankfully, Abdulla's thoughts were interrupted by Muborak's friend Sodiq, who clapped him on the shoulder. 'The man over there used to sleep next to the man you call Cho'lpon.' Abdulla looked to where Sodiq was pointing, and saw a rather grim and ill-tempered prisoner.

He greeted Sodiq's friend.

'Laziz,' the man introduced himself, somewhat stiffly. 'You were asking after Cho'lpon. We used to share the same bedding.'

With a marked lack of enthusiasm, Laziz chewed over the usual scenes of prison life; with a bitter pang of regret, Abdulla remembered how he had always intended to write about Cho'lpon's life in Moscow; intended, but never followed through. It was an unconscionable omission. Moscow, the centre of the world, a world that had flown off its axis, with revolution in every sphere. Botu and Fitrat had come to Moscow earlier, where Mayakovsky, Tatlin, Bakhtin and the Meyerholds were regular visitors at their apartments. Each one of those men had revolutionised their sphere of activity: they were geniuses who were doing everything anew. What Cho'lpon was doing in Uzbek poetry was just as original, but could any of these geniuses see the genius of the others?

Which of them did Abdulla make friends with? With the aristocratic nobleman Aleksei Tolstoy. What united them was a love of history. As for revolution, a poet had the right words:

From the old, formless

Chaos,
Creating the new,
This may perhaps come to life...

Both of them came to exactly the same conclusion
expressed in that idea. But Abdulla remembered Cho'lpon
as well as he did Tolstoy, as a poet missing his homeland:

I don't know what can comfort my heart,
The mountains, the rocks or the white-foaming waters...

Had Abdulla lost courage at the coming of the day?

If the seas should boil, if the waters should flood,
If the traveller's chosen paths should be cut,
If both right and left should swirl back to the sea,
Will tear-filled eyes be then consoled?

When Laziz mentioned Cho'lpon's pebble-lensed glasses,
Abdulla felt a fresh pang of shame.

When Abdulla was in Moscow as a student, someone
brought a copy of Cho'lpon's *Awakening* from Tashkent:
this book was immediately passed among the Uzbeks from
hand to hand. Abdulla had known Cho'lpon for a long
time. In 1919 the anthology *Young Uzbek Poets* had been
a sensation, and had made Cho'lpon's name. They met
each other a couple of times at Professor Fitrat's famous
evenings, the 'Chaghatai Symposiums', but Cho'lpon was
then already a famous poet, while Abdulla was merely a
little-known writer who had published a couple of stories.
Consequently, they settled on 'You go your way, I'll go
mine'.

But when Abdulla got his hands on a copy of *Awakening*,
his eyes were opened when he read two lines on the cover:
'Why have my eyes opened, where has my sleep disappeared to? / Into this awakening my griefs have burst their
banks.' Nobody had yet written in this language; compared

to it, literature hitherto was like faded rags, tattered and decrepit. When Abdulla looked at the Moscow sky, he was almost intoxicated as he quoted: 'Is it my thoughts that are so dark, or is it a cloud over the homeland?' He was struck by the urge to find the poet and express his heartfelt love and respect in person, his pride and his desire to emulate him.

He still remembered this Moscow encounter. Two 'red' poets, Ziyo Said and Ayn, came out with a proposal to hold a two-day seminar of young Uzbek prose-writers and poets at a dacha belonging to the Russian Association of Proletarian Writers. 'Let's make plov in the forest,' Cho'lpon, Abdulla and quite a few others suggested, eagerly joining forces. The seminar opened with an analysis of one of Cho'lpon's poems:

> The heart is quiet. In the cold night
> The haloed moon and stars overhead
> Looking down with icy light.
>
> From each direction, all around
> Loud cries of 'Bread!' and 'Gold!'
> From thieves and tired mongrels sound.
>
> The silent heart hearing the cries
> To the furthest distance is led,
> To the chill reaches of the skies.

One of the 'Reds' was the first to begin; practically foaming at the mouth, he laid into what he called the poem's 'ideological decrepitude and bourgeois individualism'. After reading the poem in a translation made by the second 'Red', the first denounced the poem's incompetence and lack of logic from the standpoint of Marxist ideas. 'To test the conclusion I have arrived at, I have turned the poem upside down. But nothing has changed: it's still hopelessly vague!'

To the chill reaches of the skies,
To the furthest distance, is led
The silent heart that hears the cries.

Thieving, troublemaking people
Noisy cries of 'Bread!' and 'Gold!'
From all around in each direction.

Looking down with icy light
The haloed men and stars overhead.
The heart is quiet. In the cold night.

After that, a couple of Russian proletarian groups joined in the attack. During the interval, Cho'lpon slipped away. In the second half of the seminar the experts praised Oltoy and encouraged Abdulla in his own efforts, but Cho'lpon's absence made the latter feel uneasy. Abdulla went to look for Cho'lpon in the next break, and found him lying on the iron bedstead in his room, with his hands behind his head. Only his spectacle lenses gleamed.

Abdulla went and sat on a corner of the bedstead. There was a silence. Then Cho'lpon spoke sadly: 'It wasn't me who wrote that poem,' he sighed heavily, 'I was translating Blok. I've had to pay for a pie I never even ate…'

Abdulla couldn't help bursting out laughing, then immediately reproached himself for his insensitivity. But then, to his surprise and relief, Cho'lpon laughed along with him.

Once the ice was broken, the two of them were able to have a frank conversation. Abdulla recited Cho'lpon's 'The Desire to Comfort':

Thoughts alone will not comfort the soul,
Thoughts alone will not sate its desire,
They say no candle will light up this darkness
If men of integrity do not strike a match…

'I was at Jumabozor station and desperately wanted to

smoke, but couldn't find a match,' Cho'lpon quipped, deftly puncturing the mood of impassioned solemnity. They both nearly bust a gut laughing again.

It was thanks to the intrigues of those proletarian writers that the two became dear friends.

—

It was not in Umar's council of ministers that the deepest intrigues surfaced, but in his harem. Oyxon's installation as a rival to Nodira had sparked a desire in the harem's first mistress to demonstrate how it felt when the boot was on the other foot. Had she not said in a poem:

> A ring of your curls, the turban's end on my neck,
> While I hunted for the moment of the dream.

Thus did quarry turn to hunter. Unlike Nodira, Oyxon was not the daughter of a Beg, but she ranked rather higher as a daughter of a Xo'ja, a fighter for Islam. None of the 'blue-blooded' aristocrats, even the descendants of the Caliphs, could be compared to her, except for Sayid or To'ra girls descended from the Prophet. The harem knew no lack of scheming old women, with time on their hands and minds sharpened by intrigue. Two of them were now put to work: they searched high and low for a girl unadulterated by any 'dark-faced' race, and they found her behind the immaculate curtains of the reverend Sultan Xo'ja. Descended on both her father's and mother's side from Sayids, the chaste Zubayda was silk woven from the purest thread. In addition, she was extraordinarily elegant, as beautiful as the moon. All in all, Nodira concluded, it was only fitting that news of this lovely offspring reach the ears of the Emir of all Muslims.

It was at this time that a descendant of the Prophet, Mahmud, threatened trouble if he wasn't made governor of O'ratepa: every other day he travelled to Kokand to present himself to Emir Umar. Nodira despatched one of the best female Qu'ran reciters to suggest to Mahmud, via his wife, that the rule of O'ratepa would only be his if he could arrange Umar's marriage to the Sayid Sultan's virgin daughter.

During his next audience with the Emir, Mahmud carefully expounded on the importance of an alliance with a family descended from the Prophet.

'In this world, our Creator has provided more than enough for you; but to become one of His most treasured creatures in the next, now is the time to make your preparations.'

A verbose man, and a persistent talker who spoke very forcefully, Mahmud seemed to say 'I wouldn't say this to anyone other than you…'

'Your high rank as Emir of all Muslims makes this a suitable goal.

Doesn't the garden's most beautiful flower automatically belong to the gardener? Our heavens have room for only one sun; how could the rose-bud's pearly dew not be its property? In the words of the poet:

> When 'if' is paired with 'whereas',
> Their child will be named 'probably'.

By putting forward one thing and another, he got Umar to agree. In no time at all, the matchmakers were beating down the very reverend Sultan Xo'ja's door. The Sayid family was thrown into confusion: the local people buzzed about the house like wasps. Noble Sayids and Xo'jas presented themselves to Umar: the Sheikh of Islam and his deputies, revered judges, begged him to renounce this depraved and unseemly enterprise. 'Rebellion!' said one judge, 'Mutiny!' said another, but the Emir of all Muslims dug his heels in. In rather bad taste, he recited to these 'blue-blooded' visitors verses which Nodira had composed the previous evening:

> The turban with a flap is granted as an honour
> To him who demonstrates himself a fine spiritual leader...

The furious Emir was then visited by Mahmud: the visit – mercifully – was like balsam to his heart. These were the words which Umar devised as a reply to the Sheikh of Islam:

> Aggrieved, I will silence him with an angry sigh,
> Though his speech be fast as fire, and blaze as high.

In short, the Emir of the Muslims' will was hardened. He sent Mahmud in person to Sultan-Xo'ja's house as a matchmaker. Once again, in his breathless, confiding tone, Mahmud lauded the match to the revered religious leader. At first Sultan-Xo'ja could not believe his ears, and was forced to doubt the distinguished visitor's good intentions: as the conversation proceeded, his bewilderment changed into wrath. Only the thought that Mahmud was a relative, and a Sayid like himself, kept the Sultan from speaking his mind.

'The Emir of all Muslims is God's shadow on earth. Sayid G'ozi-xo'ja, a relative of both of us, behaved in a sensible way, gave in to destiny and the needs of the times and lifted his daughter's veil of chastity...'

'What exactly did G'ozi-xo'ja do?' the Sultan asked sharply, refusing to let the discussion be mired in metaphors and fine phrases.

'He has had the pleasure of allying himself in marriage with the Thousand Noblemen, whose descendant is the revered Emir of all Muslims.'

'Everything you have said is highly improper,' the Sultan

interrupted, 'I don't care if it's a Thousand or a Hundred Thousand, I will only give my daughter to someone of blue blood, and that's my final word!'

He had dared to refuse Emir Umar and his relative Sayid Mahmud, but these fortifications of a repeated manly 'No!' would ultimately prove no match for the intrigues of the Khan's harem. Didn't Sultan Xo'ja also have wives? The fortifications collapsed due not to missiles from outside, but undermining from within.

In a month or so, according to the high-flown chronicles, 'Emir Umar-khan was presiding on the throne of happiness in his majestic wedding tent, at a celebration in honour of his marriage. And his merrymaking was shared by his worshipful Begs, whose foreheads shone in the radiance of his glory. Bowls of dark red wine and enchanting juices mingled with the lights reflected on guests' faces, dazzling their eyes. The silver-bodied cup-bearers with their radiant faces gave pleasure by lighting up the banqueting area. Sweet-voiced musicians sang enchanting songs, giving pleasure and enjoyment to the ears and hearts of the drunkards...'

In truth, Emir Umar had spurned his junior wife Oyxon in favour of a younger and more nobly born bride.

Who knows why Abdulla chose these particular scenes? Laziz was still droning on about things that had nothing to do with Cho'lpon. The two tufts of hair over his ears and the beginnings of a bald patch on his crown made him the caricature of a Party boss; his craggy face showed very well how irritable he was, and his fussy movements indicated a Party member's mindset.

'Didn't I myself pester him for news of Cho'lpon, then allow myself to be distracted by secret plots from a hundred years ago!' Abdulla reproached himself. 'Who knows what I might have missed?'

'It's the turn of our Sheherazade,' Jur'at interrupted. Rattling his knucklebones in one hand, he took Abdulla by the elbow and dragged him back to the other side of the stinking cell.

—

'Let's play knucklebones with Muborak the Jew until suppertime, and you tell us a story, something like Sinbad the Sailor,' Jur'at said, appending a proverb from his inexhaustible supply: 'You can sweet-talk a snake from its nest, but bitter words can make a Muslim renounce his faith.'

This rankled with Abdulla. Was he a radio loudspeaker, reading out fairy stories while two gamblers played knucklebones? But Jur'at was not bullying him. Rather, he was depressed and felt he needed to hear the written word. As the man himself would say, 'What does a horn-player have to do? Just puff!'

'As you wish,' Abdulla agreed after a little consideration. 'But you know the proverb, "If you want it hot, you may get burnt": writers like me are hot-tempered…'

'You say "down", we say "up". So let's not spoil our friendship. "The hat that was lost was too small anyway."' Jur'at threw his knucklebone onto the pile. The knucklebone span round and round, hit the ground and rolled first flat side up, then on its concave side, finally ending up on its winning convex side.

'Throw, Muborak!' the elder gestured. 'You can knock your father down, if you don't visit him.'

Abdulla began his fairy story:

'O blessed are the common people! The story goes that

in days of old an Emir called Umar-xon used to reign in
Kokand, and that he had three wives. The first was called
Nodira, the second was Oyxon, and the third was called...'

'Ah, you're telling us the story of Nodira!' said Muborak,
distracted for a moment from his unsuccessful gambling.

'Wait a bit,' Jur'at remarked brusquely. '"If you wait
long enough, green fruit will ripen."'

Abdulla continued:

'The Emir was fond of his wives, but he loved games
of knucklebones even more, and more than knucklebones
he loved hunting.'

Jur'at gave Abdulla an ironic glance. 'Sheherazade had
nothing on you. You've skewered us, right there in our
sore spot! All right, you can't put a stop to straight talking,
so carry on.'

'One spring, he offered to take his harem ladies on
an excursion to see the tulip fields, but the real reason
was to go off hunting with his gambling friends. The best
place for hunting was the reed beds on the banks of the
Syr-Darya. They left Kokand in a convoy of carts and cav-
alry: intoxicated by the soft spring breeze, the women in
the carts sang solo and choral songs, while the men darted
about on their horses, catching quails and shooting hares
with salt-shot.

'In the villages where they stopped, the people kissed
Umar's stirrups; in each place there was feasting, at each
staging post there was pleasure for the senses; the joys of
spring determined every step. In one town, the celebrations went on for four days in great splendour, and the
Emir treated his subjects to a feast of plov. In the next, they
made a pilgrimage to the graves of the great, distributed
alms to the people, and gave feasts.

'Then they made their way back along the river, pitched
camp and began a big hunt in the woods and reed-beds

all around. There were several thousand hunting falcons in all. The Emir himself owned more than three hundred falcons for his personal use, and nine gyrfalcons. There were forty goshawks, big hunting peregrine falcons, about forty saker falcons for hunting gazelles, and two hundred hounds, two of which were Phoenix-headed dogs, gifts from Kazakh khans. Each dog had a gold and silver collar, and each a velvet coat.

'The sortie into the reed-beds was magnificent. Umar sent in his hawks to flush out the game birds: so many soared up from the woods, the sky was blotted out. The hunt climaxed with calls of help from the reed beds. The Emir, his son Madali and nephew Hakim approached: they came face to face with a gigantic lion, the size of a calf, with two cubs. The lion's roar made the earth and the heavens tremble!

"'Don't you dare!' the Emir ordered the other hunters back. "Nobody touches the lion: anyone who does, forfeits all his property. I'll shoot this lion myself."

'Umar owned a splendid rifle, a gift from the Sultan of Turkey: he loaded it, lay down in ambush, and ordered the reed-beds around the lion to be set on fire. While the reeds were burning, the lion roared so loud that the heavens seemed to collapse. Running into flames on all sides, it killed three men and six horses, wounding several more. It had no option but to dash off into the steppe. It was then that the Emir fired his rifle. Struck squarely between the eyes, the king of beasts was flung into the air, and then collapsed with such a horrible roar that the hawks all flopped to the ground. It was as if an earthquake had shaken the area. Then there was bawling and jumping for joy.

'As the ground was strewn with the hawks and gyrfalcons, so the Emir was showered with paeans of praise. Umar then ordered two of the lion's canines to be pulled out: he hung them round his neck as an amulet.'

—

The next morning, after a breakfast of flaked rice gruel, Abdulla was pondering how to end his story. 'After that hunt, the Emir spent a few days enjoying himself with his wives before returning to Kokand.'

Seemingly bored with their game of knucklebones, Jur'at and Muborak were now not only listening to Abdulla, but staring him in the face.

'After covering a considerable distance, they entered the city of Namangan.'

'We've been to Namangan,' Muborak interrupted. This time, Jur'at said nothing, simply silenced his companion by tugging at his sleeve: Muborak bit his tongue and didn't utter another sound.

'In Namangan there were more celebrations and hunts, more singers and musicians, more beautiful women.' Abdulla played for time as he gathered his thoughts. Already, his mind was jumping ahead to his novel, and how he might incorporate Umar's pleasure party.

'Umar was a hunter to the marrow of his bones. He hunted not only game, big and small, but also women, as if they were quarry and he was a bird of prey. Apart from his three legitimate wives, he had dozens of pretty women, maidservants and slave-girls. Among them, whether he knew it or not, he had a nickname, 'the predator'.

'We have to say that Emir Umar's first wife was a poet, and his youngest was an aristocrat, while the middle wife was a beauty without peer in the world. Any living soul setting eyes on her couldn't help but be stunned by her beauty and enchanted by her elegance. Her eyes were especially magical: the sight of them made men's thoughts turn to adultery, left women stricken with pangs of jealousy. All wondered whether they were awake or truly dreaming.

'The predatory Emir had married them all by force, against their will. Their fathers had been a governor, a Xo'ja and a Sayid, respectively: each had submitted to the Emir's will and sacrificed their daughters.

'Umar had a son, Madali, by his first wife Nodira; Madali and Hakim, the Emir's nephew, were both allowed access to the harem, and Madali had fallen passionately in love with his stepmother Oyxon. When Hakim found out about this, he tried to make his cousin see sense; when reason failed to have the desired effect, he threatened to tell Umar of his son's incestuous passion. At this, Madali seemed to have dropped the idea, but appearances, as we know, can be deceiving.

'But let's leave them for now, and hear about Umar himself.

'As if at the throw of a die, his majesty called a halt to the feasting and celebrating and decided to undertake a journey, sending his wives and womenfolk ahead of him by cart from Namangan to Axsikent; he himself set off afterwards, accompanied by six trusted servants and forty guards. On their way there was a mighty act of God: sand and dust rose up and instantly turned the sky black; the wind was as strong as a hurricane. Their mouths and noses became filled with rough soil, their eyes bloodshot from the dust. The world around them was pitch dark, neither they nor their horses could see the road. They proceeded in single file, each clutching the harness of the horse in front, blindly following the Emir. When the sandstorm dropped they found themselves on the open steppe, back where they had started.

'The day was over, with only the cold wind blowing and the ravenous wolves howling: all their senses told them that night was falling, but their journey was nowhere near its end. One soldier called out to another, "Devils have surrounded us," and everyone was gripped by fear. First of all, four of the guards let the reins drop, and slipped away to find shelter to wait out the night. Another few followed suit, and after that a few more. By midnight the Emir had nobody left by his side, except for his six trusted servants. There was no light nor habitation in sight. As Shah Babur once said:

> "Our parting made the night woeful.
> There was no way I could find you again in that place.
> Woe is me, thanks to the tears in my eyes,
> The road was too muddy and the evening too dark."

When Abdulla's story reached this point, a prison warder, with the same cockerel's voice, sarcastically announced in Russian 'Bed time'. Jur'at stopped listening to and looking at Abdulla, and reluctantly ordered the men in the cell, 'Bed time! Lie down on your right sides!' Abdulla and Muborak found their places, tripping over other men's legs in the process. Too caught up in his tale, Abdulla hadn't been able to empty his bladder or wash as his faith required. He had to lie down on his quilt as he was.

That evening, Abdulla was still awake as midnight approached; in the darkness he drafted a letter to Rahbar, before finally obeying the cell elder's orders and turning over like all the others in his row, to lie on his right side. 'I have lain down on my side,' he prayed silently, 'let me rise up in my faith.'

CHAPTER 3

CRICKET

'The English have a game they call *kir-ket*: it's like our game of tip-cat,' said Muborak when he began chatting the next morning. Muborak spoke the drawling Bukhara dialect, replacing all his 'i's with 'e's, and whenever he spoke, his statements sounded more like questions. 'I myself saw it whenever I went out, at night or early morning,' he explained.

Abdulla, who had been holding back his bladder all through the night, could finally relieve himself and savour the pleasure of washing his face and hands. Now he waited for his sympathiser – the soldier from Qumloq – to appear. Had he said what his name was? Of course: as they say, eat the grapes, don't ask about the vineyard. Abdulla suppressed a laugh. He'd caught Jur'at the cell elder's way of talking. If you stick close to the cooking pot, your clothes turn black.

'I saw that game of cricket when we were in London...' Muborak pronounced it *kir-ket*, Uzbek for 'enter-go'.

'You're telling me you've visited London?' Abdulla was amazed.

'If you call a three-year stay a visit! That's why I'm in here, charged with spying.' But Muborak wasn't going to say more on this topic, and he went on to talk about kir-ket. Abdulla made a mental note that he would have to question Muborak about his life in London: he thought that 'kir-ket' must in fact be the well-known English game of cricket.

'The English stand on thick green grass in special white clothes and hit a small ball with a stick. Just like our tip-cat… If you hit it or, worse, it hits something behind you, someone else takes your place. That's why it's called enter-go.'

Muborak was about to launch into the details of the game when the cell door opened and two soldiers appeared. What a relief: one of them was Sunnat from Qumloq. 'Breakfast!' yelled the other, a Russian.

How many days had Abdulla been here? Would it be a whole week by this evening? Abdulla recalled the dawn he had seen seven days ago at home. A different life, a different era! After prayers at dawn that morning he had sat writing in his room; when he glanced through the window it was fully light. In fact everything was pure white and black: the summerhouse roof, the walls, the branches of the trees. There was just a hint of yellow or red in the sky. It was like the purple colour you see in New Year postcards, a colour deeper than red. In winter, the country-girls' cheeks took on that colour, as Abdulla remembered from his youth.

Another week had passed since then, another lifetime.

He went to get his millet porridge, which was dispensed from a ladle by the Russian soldier. As Sunnat poured the tea, he gave Abdulla a momentary look, and Abdulla responded with a gesture. Sunnat seemed to grasp his meaning. You can't go wrong with the right sign, Abdulla thought, happily returning to his place. Not letting the others distract him with their talk, he gulped down the unappetising gruel as though it were some delicious dish. To go up alone would be conspicuous; he waited a little.

'Who wants seconds?' the Russian yelled.

Abdulla's heart pounded. He got to his feet, holding his flattened piece of paper against the bottom of his bowl and went up to Sunnat. 'Here,' he said as he handed Sunnat the bowl and the scrap of paper, simultaneously holding his tea mug out to the Russian.

'What's this, you fucker?' the latter growled. 'Why are you shoving that mug in my face? If you want tea, he's the one to ask. Blockhead.' As if to show him contempt, or perhaps simply because he could, the young Russian soldier spat in Abdulla's face. It took every ounce of Abdulla's control for him to think of his letter, only his letter, and to turn calmly to Sunnat.

'You couldn't pour me some more tea, brother, could you?'

Even when he sat back down again, Abdulla's heart raced like an unbridled horse. Shame, anger that had no outlet, and fear coursed through his veins, because in prison an insult is not merely an insult, but a reminder of your position.

Abdulla didn't even hear the soldiers banging and clanging as they left, let alone Muborak's memories of England. He tried to console himself with thoughts of his letter, but even that seemed like a vain hope now; he was a desperate man clutching at straws. The world seemed to him to be utterly dark.

A few hours later Jur'at came up to him.

'I heard everything. You feel hard done by, but don't let it get to you, I'll teach that arrogant Russian a lesson myself. You'd best come with me, we'll have a little chat. A neighbour of ours has had a parcel delivered, so we can smoke to our heart's content.' Jur'at carefully led Abdulla by the hand to the far side of the cell, gesturing to Muborak, 'Ethnic minority, you can come with us.'

The cigarette calmed Abdulla: he drew on the tobacco as if he was smoking hashish, his lungs filling with the hot smoke, which seemed to penetrate even the tensed muscles of his mind.

'Lies don't work, so tell it straight,' Jur'at grumbled.

Now feeling more relaxed, Abdulla didn't need much urging. He continued his story from the day before.

'Well, my dear friends,' he began. 'In that dark night, with just six servants, Emir Umar was blundering about. He'd abandoned all hope, resigned himself to fate and to the devil's work. Then he appealed to Allah to make short work of the devil, by accompanying him in reciting "*La hawla,* There is no power and no strength except with Allah.".

'Thanks to God's providence, they finally heard something that was not the piteous howling of wolves or the wind, but the distinct bark of a dog coming towards them. This sound was so sweet to their ears that they eagerly spurred their horses towards it, and saw, squinting in the darkness, not the devil's lights but the lamps of Axsikent. They entered the city in time for dawn prayers, at the hour just before daybreak. As the Emir and his entourage rode up to the harem's tent, it was the turn of the beggars in the street to shrink back in fear and recite *La hawla,* believing that they were seeing the devil. The elderly harem servants, barely recognising them in their dishevelled headgear, met them with sobbing and weeping; the younger concubines giggled as they hurried to bring tea for the Emir. When the seven men looked at each other in the light of the camp fire and flares, they couldn't recognise one face from another. There were three Ethiopian pages in the palace, but Umar and his attendants were now blacker still.

'They were helpless with laughter, a kind of manic relief at having escaped with their lives.

'After they found water and washed their hands and faces, they looked more human and were able to relax. Over the course of the day, the guards who had lagged behind or got lost trickled into the city in dribs and drabs. They too were the subject of great merriment.

'"That damned lion made us lose our way," Umar concluded, eyeing the two teeth hanging round his neck.

'Again there was feasting, hunting and shooting, again games of knucklebones, and when they'd had enough of all this, they got up and set off for Kokand.

'As everyone knows, the Syr-Darya is not far from Axsikent. That spring the river had flooded so severely that the opposite shore was out of sight. Fortunately there were now boats and ferrymen approaching the banks. Waiting for the ferrymen, the Emir ordered his officials and servants to board a ship and cross to the other side. There was one frail vessel still left on the bank, but it had no one to steer it across. Emir Umar was stubborn, and would not wait for the other boat to return from the opposite shore: he ordered the twenty women in his harem onto the frailer boat and then boarded it himself with his son Madali and his nephew Hakim, as well as the man who had organised the crossing, Mirzo Rahim, Keeper of the Seals.

'Mirzo got down on his knees to plead: "I swear by Allah, Your Regal Majesty, this river thirsts for human blood. We are helpless as prisoners if we entrust our families to someone who has never in his life steered a boat. Trying to cross in this boat without a steersman is a waste of effort. It would be best if we wait for the other boats to come back!"

'But the Emir was not one to go back on his word. If need be, he would himself be captain. Four men harnessed their four horses to the boat, and sent it into the river. The horses had never in their lives seen water: they panicked

and started pulling the boat in all directions, putting everyone in mortal danger. The people in the boat yelled out,
the women cried for help. In this dreadful time of doom,
the horse that Hakim was holding on to broke free of its
reins and swam for the shore, and the boat started to spin
in the middle of the river.

'Then Mirzo Rahim moved to the middle of the boat,
fastened his belt as tight as he could, rolled up his sleeves,
slapped his own face and started tearing at his beard.
Everyone stared at him, stunned. He cried out: "Everyone
who is in the same boat shares the same soul! Now, listen to me!" The boat was being swamped by waves and
tossed about, now one way, now the other. Hakim, who
had lost his horse, was preparing to jump into the river.
He had stripped off his clothes, but stopped at Mirzo's
order: "Your highness, take hold of the horse and turn it to
your right!" He then ordered Madali and one particularly
strong-willed woman to rush forward and help him, "You
turn your horse round to the left!" Mirzo himself, with his
experience, mercilessly whipped the middle horse. In a
very short time all three were subdued by his courage and
began swimming in the same direction.

'The boat very quickly got back on course. Soon everyone who was travelling in it was safely delivered to the far
shore. Emir Umar took his sable-trimmed coat off his own
shoulders and presented it to Mirzo Rahim. Mirzo Rahim
expressed his gratitude by placing a little bag containing
around four hundred grams of tobacco before the Emir.
They smoked a hookah that day, desperately needing to
calm their nerves.

'After that they returned to Kokand, when, thinking
he had attained his desired goal, Umar was suddenly taken
ill; despite a thousand efforts by famous doctors, the Emir
was at death's door. Among the doctors attending to the

Emir was the Bukhara poet Hoziq, who later spoke of Umar's last moments. The Emir told Hoziq of the grief and pain he suffered, while Hoziq tried to raise his spirits:

"'What use is treatment, your reverence? My time is over...'"

"'My Emir, you will recover; despair is the devil's work.'"

'Then Umar rubbed his neck, smiled, and recited the following couplet:

Early morning among the flowers I heard it,
This magnanimous edict: all creatures are finite...

And with these words he drew his last breath. The washers removed from around his neck a strange amulet made from two lion's canine teeth. When they examined his body further, they saw teeth marks in several places.

'Some people said, "It was a lion's tooth that poisoned Umar." Others whispered that it was some sort of spell cast by the descendants of the Prophet, in revenge for the deceased Emir's impious marriages.

'The day that Emir Umar was committed to the earth, his son Madali was made to stand on a piece of red felt, and then enthroned as Khan of Kokand. The twelve-year-old Emir chose not to wear the lion's teeth he had inherited from his father: he wrapped them up in muslin, and kept them far from his body.'

———

Abdulla did his utmost to make this narrative like a fairy story, adapted for ordinary men's minds; the trouble with this was that he didn't know at what point he should end it. So he paused for breath and looked around: he saw that it wasn't just the cell elder Jur'at and his squat underling Muborak, but all the other prisoners around them who were listening to his story with bated breath. Seeing this, Abdulla adjusted his expression, and wiped the sweat off his forehead with his sleeve.

'Now it's somebody else's turn,' he said.

'Once you've started, see it through,' Jur'at countered. 'Right: this is what we'll do: if someone feeds us a cock-and-bull story and we don't notice, he gets the prize. Understand? Then give us the biggest cock and the biggest bull you've got, and see if you can pull the wool over our eyes! If a goat is born in a barn, then grass for him grows in the ditch, as the saying goes. Are we all agreed?'

Strangely enough, these words had an impact. First to put himself forward was Laziz; when he prefaced his story with a general introduction, it was obvious he had once worked as a Party lector: 'In the period you have been talking about, at the turn of the eighteenth and nineteenth centuries, the literature of the Uzbek nation consisted of two opposing currents: a feudal-clerical literature, and a progressive-democratic one.

'The most striking and obvious example of feudal-clerical literature is the man you have just mentioned, Emir Umar, who may have held supreme power as the Khan of Kokand, but whose writings are from an ideological point of view reactionary and, from an artistic point of view, formalist and dated. Their erotic themes are rubbish, they are panegyric odes, decadent in form, ideologically impoverished and artistically shallow.

'The most outstanding representative of progressive-democratic tendencies in literature is Emir Umar's wife Nodira Begum. In the work of this radical poet, if we take into account the era, her times and circumstances, celebrating in verse the truth about life was the basis of her genius. Her poetry reflected the sufferings and sorrows of the epoch, the local people's fears and worries: she used her pen creatively, longing for the freedom to work, to create and to live.'

Laziz talked without stumbling or digression, the non-sensical platitudes poured uninterruptedly from his mouth like water from a kettle.

'Let us cite two examples of Emir Umar's reactionary life, which offer concrete demonstration of its religious and dogmatic nature. In the bourgeois historian Fitrat's work *History of Fergana* it is written that Emir Umar subjected all his actions to the guidance of the feudal-clerical theologians' decrees. One day, passing by the hammam, he saw dirty water flowing out into a pool. He asked the theologians: "What does sharia law say about this water?" They replied, "This water is permitted, and it is flowing water, but nature does not recognise it." Then Emir Umar, relying on his religious mysticism, said "Nature has to be rejected in favour of the prescriptions of sharia law." To prove it, he scooped up a mouthful of this water and drank it up.

'The second example will show us Emir Umar's courtly aristocratic nature. Religion is the opium of the people, and when a place for religion, a madrasa, was being built, a foundation stone had to be laid. Then Umar turned to the crowd, showering religious propaganda on the people: "The foundation stone must be laid by a person who has unfailingly observed sharia law for their whole adult lives!" But to his astonishment, nobody from the class of hypocritical clerics and sheikhs had the heart to put themselves forward. Then the feudal ruler, who had devoted all his life to the pursuit of glory and to orgies, offered to do it himself: "I am the only person never to have broken the rules of sharia law in my lifetime!" This symbol of sycophancy and ideological impoverishment, this reactionary-feudal laid the foundation stone for the new building!'

Naturally, Abdulla was familiar with these events, although, true, the story was being told in a different language and style. Two things, however, astonished him: the first was that a Party activist, concerned only with the present and the future, should know about those times, and the second that, although knocked off his high horse, he was still firmly in the saddle. Here you are in prison, your Party has betrayed you, but you still won't give up your Red propaganda! You can call one an exploiter and a pessimist, and another a progressive democrat. But Laziz had moved on to speak of Nodira's love for the people and her humanism.

'From an ideological point of view, Nodira's poetry contradicts Umar's reactionary outlook and feudal literary and aesthetic principles. The basic reason for this, in our view, is to be found in a different way of viewing life's events and phenomena. Umar's rule was based on oppression and tyranny. He shed the blood of thousands of ordinary people, destroyed their lives utterly. In his poetry Umar averted his eyes from all this, he kept silent about it.

'Nodira was different. When the Emir goes off hunting game (Look at that: words like that from a Party man! Good for you! Abdulla thought to himself) or to a military campaign on his armoured horse, Nodira generally stays in Kokand and sees that the Emir's decrees are carried out. She had a good understanding of what was going on. She witnessed executioners drag innocent persons to their death; she had a rational, sensible view of the world, she tried to understand the essence of every event and phenomenon. She thought, she wondered, she queried, she sought answers, she suffered torments and used her pen to write about them:

> "I die in grief, I burn with sorrow, I can find no way out,
> In misery, summer and winter are alike to me as night."

Her failure to find a way out is only natural. It was nearly a hundred years before the October revolution; Karl Marx, the founder of scientific communism, had only just been born. The feudal-clerical tyranny and oppression would continue to rule over the working people.'

Apparently, Laziz considered that he had, at this point, completed his task. Nobody else knew what to say. Only Jur'at broke the silence, 'Thank you for the political education, comrade citizen… sorry, citizen comrade.' He sighed. 'There I was in my village, drinking kumys; now I scratch my arse, wondering why I came to the city.'

—

There was a brief silence, and then another man spoke up.

'Mulla Shibirg'oniy, from Afghanistan,' Jur'at introduced him. 'But at this point, a word to the wise: "Give tongue to a fool, and a spade to two hands." Go ahead, Mulla.'

'Of course, I am going to give you a story from our chronicler's history of the times of Emir Nasrullo. When Nasrullo was Emir of Bukhara, Dost Muhammad was on the throne in Kandahar, but the dethroned Prince Shah Shujah Durrani had struck a deal with Ranjit Singh of the Punjab: the famed Koh-i-noor diamond, in return for the aid of English troops, to help him win back the throne in Kabul.

'A Russian spy who had access to Dost Muhammad told him that, as a precautionary measure, the English were sending 50,000 soldiers with 30,000 camels from India. Dost Muhammad's entire army consisted of 2,500 soldiers and 45 cannons.

'Essentially, this massive invasion by the English meant the beginning for Kandahar and the end for Kabul. Dost Muhammad had no choice but to set off for Turkestan, and throw in his lot with Bukhara.

'Dost Muhammad, his followers and family were compelled to travel for some distance until, after many difficult days, they arrived in the glorious city of Bukhara. As soon as Emir Nasrullo heard about Dost Muhammad's arrival, he sent an appropriate number of his noblemen with a summons giving Dost Muhammad a safe conduct to come with his forces to the Emir's castle. But when Dost Muhammad arrived at the palace arrayed in his finery and bowed respectfully to Emir Nasrullo, the latter failed to stand up or make any move to greet him. In sight of everyone, Nasrullo remained seated, merely stretching out a hand. The incident was the talk of the town, making it likely that any meeting of the two Emirs would require interpreters and intermediaries.'

Abdulla looked around him. The heavy dose of Persian syntax in the Mulla's language had made some of his listeners yawn, and others start chatting among themselves. The Mulla himself was sensitive enough to take the hint; as the saying goes, 'the root is the basic part of the picture'. He tried to speak something like simple, intelligible Turkic.

'Put it this way,' he said. 'With praise to Allah, Emir Nasrullo said, "You're welcome!" and after a chat, ended the conversation with "Now you can go to your camp; let's meet later." Dost Muhammad quickly realised that whatever Nasrullo promised would be a lie. He spent days begging Nasrullo for his permission to proceed to Iran before this was finally granted, and he was given the best of Nasrullo's companions as a guide. When they got to the river Jayxun, the boatman there pointed out a decrepit boat. "You get in this one," he told Dost Muhammad, "the others can board separately." Fearing that he was to be drowned, Dost Muhammad took the Emir's travelling companion to one side, saying "Let's cross the river together." The boatman then warned the companion in Turkic: "If you try crossing in this boat, you're likely to drown!" Luckily, Dost Muhammad knew enough Turkic to understand this exchange: inevitably, he leapt from the boat onto the shore and headed back for the glorious city of Bukhara.

'It is with a heavy heart I must report that it was the month of January, the depth of winter, as luck would have it, and everything was covered in ice. Hearing that Dost Muhammad was back at the gates of Bukhara, Nasrullo ordered a trusted courtier to go and meet the group: "Dost Muhammad is not to enter Bukhara unless he dismisses his army; he can come in only with a small retinue". Dost Muhammad dismissed a thousand warriors; they wept at the wrong done to him, but dispersed at his command. To the sound of shrieking lamentation, Dost Muhammad returned to his camp. Just to live was now task enough, he had no way of achieving his goal.

'He and his princes found this life very hard. "We'll run off again," they decided, "and attempt to get to Qarshi." With seventy soldiers, his princes and nobles he set off for Shahrisabz. But the ruler of Qarshi put an end to his progress by giving battle, whereupon each Afghan found himself fighting thirty Uzbeks.

'Fleeing was the easiest option, but all eight princes were captured. Dost Muhammad and his sons were taken prisoner; the news of the turmoil would reach the ears of Emir Nasrullo.

'How shocked and dispirited Dost Muhammad was, when he saw his sons naked in the worst days of winter, starving and in shackles. As we can see, Emir Nasrullo inflicted repeated suffering on the unfortunate Dost Muhammad of Kabul, and yet took pleasure in these torments.'

At this point Jur'at raised the palm of his hand to interrupt Mulla Shibirg'oniy. 'If the patient is going to get better, the doctor comes of his own accord,' he concluded.

While Abdulla was still struggling to fit this proverb to the Mulla's tale, Jur'at offered a further explanation. 'The prison doctor will come at eleven. Vinokurov said that anyone with any illness, except for haemorrhoids, should speak up; otherwise, they can make themselves useful and put the cell in order. As for those with haemorrhoids, when you sit down, tuck in your arses.'

—

Abdulla had begun to notice something. Whether free or in prison, four men, even the cleverest, had only to be gathered together to start behaving like a group of delinquent youths. Their age – twenty, thirty, fifty – didn't matter: their attitude when they met was limited to 'Who's the strongest here?' and 'It'd be good if we could have a girl'. Everything they did was meant to show themselves to advantage, and none of their exchanges went beyond the first expression in Mahmud of Kashgar's dictionary: 'A man's strength is in his fucking'.

In enclosed groups this phenomenon was even more noticeable. Abdulla recalled his Russian-language school for Uzbeks, and then remembered the time he studied journalism in Moscow, his first spell in prison, his trip to a writers' congress in Tatarstan: everywhere the relationships were just as they now were in prison: this was the best place for observing and understanding them.

When the doctor came in to see them, it was the same: the philosophy of 'Who's the fighting cock here?' was particularly striking. Not one of the prisoners had the courage to say 'I have pain here,' or 'I've been injured'. The doctor was astonishing. He was swarthy, curly-haired and had an aquiline nose. He looked more like a Tajik than an Uzbek; in fact, you'd say he had Caucasian features, he smiled just like a Jew, there was a touch of Kipchak Turkic in the way he spoke. All in all, he was somebody who wanted to be liked by everyone.

When Abdulla's turn came, the doctor asked with a smile, 'Don't you have any pains anywhere, either?' and then began examining his head. He noticed a small sore on Abdulla's right cheek and asked, 'Have you ever had leishmaniasia?' Then he saw a hole, as if for an ear-ring, in Abdulla's left ear and whispered, 'What's that?' Abdulla whispered back, 'My mother's other children didn't survive, so she pierced my ear for luck.' The doctor's hands felt the injuries caused by Vinokurov's kicking. 'How did you get these?' he asked, but didn't press the matter when Abdulla kept silent. Then he examined the fur on Abdulla's tongue, gave him some medicine, applied ointment to his bruised rib-cage, and tightly bandaged a wound on his elbow that was beginning to close up.

'Now you'll be healthy as a brood mare, Qodiriy!' he said, clapping him on the shoulder.

Abdulla would have opened himself up to the doctor and poured out his worries, but the man and his fixed smile had already moved off, busy with other patients whose hidden wounds and osteomyelitis needed treating. Abdulla repressed his desire to talk, like a man with a chest cough.

In prison life, this sort of minor variation, these novelties not quite worthy of the label 'events', can nevertheless rouse the cell so that it hums like a wasps' nest for days on end. After encountering ordinary humanity, Abdulla began to contemplate compassion and love. He had been planning to write for the first time about the absence of love, about how love was abused and destroyed. In *Past Days* he had written about the love of Atabek and Kumush. *The Scorpion in the Altar* had praised Anvar's love for Ra'no, but in this new story, he realised, it was necessary to write about a different sort of love. A love that isn't particularly demonstrative, but involves fidelity and patience; a love, in other words, like his wife Rahbar's silent devotion.

What a predicament she had been subjected to, thanks to Abdulla! They had married, had two children, then when she was pregnant with a third he had gone to study in Moscow. And the first time he had been imprisoned she had been pregnant again, and with small infants to look after. Whatever Abdulla did she would follow, like thread pulled by a needle, and she kept the family together like a button in a buttonhole. Now, just as the children had grown up and peace and order returned to the house, Abdulla was in prison once more, leaving Rahbar to face all the troubles on her own. This was the sort of love that needed to be celebrated.

This was the spirit of what Laziz had been saying; or should he describe in this story the devotion which Nodira had tried but failed to express?

When I couldn't see your face, my tears raised a mighty storm –
Is it any surprise at all that the rivers rose in spate?

Those who are truly in love care nothing for the rage of the
   world.
Madness, take my misery, sweep this tumult to its fate!

When my love went away from me, my madness became a show,
But if I ever see him again, then there'll be a show to relate!

I'm entirely shamed in love, because I cannot reach my flower.
Help me: lead my disgrace towards a happier state.

Heavens, may your face freeze for the terrible hurt you've done –
You took mad Nodira's love away, and she is now desolate.

Again, Abdulla remembered the game he had played in trams and buses: the game of transporting the people around him to other times. Now, however, something 'clicked' in his brain, transporting the nineteenth-century poet-queen to Samarkand, Ko'birariq Street, Number 121, in the shape of Rahbar his wife, in whose voice he now heard those very words.

———

As soon as the doctor had left the prison, the midday meal was served. Whether this was due to a miracle worked by the doctor, or whether it was a form of inspection, this time the prisoners were given *moshkichiri*, a rice and mung-bean stew. It looked as if the cooking pot had soured it, but all the same it was the real thing, quite unlike the bitter stuff they were fed every other day. 'Now for a little after-dinner entertainment,' Jur'at exclaimed, 'let's take our mind off things again.' As Mulla Shibirg'oniy was busy reciting his noonday prayers, Muborak Kukhanov took the floor.

'In 1930 I went to England and stayed in the capital city, London. There's a district there called Golders Green, where our people, the people of Moses, live. I stayed with the Abramov family who owned sugar mills in Samarkand. When people heard I was from Bukhara, many Bukhara natives came to see me. A great number of rabbis came to pay me their respects. One person who came was not from Bukhara: he was a French Jew, and he told me that his grandfather, a Rabbi named Joseph Wolff, had travelled to Bukhara once, and wrote a book about it: *Narrative of a Mission to Bokhara*. The grandson gave me a copy; I've read it from beginning to end.

'In Emir Nasrullo's time, the Russian general Perovsky was planning to invade Khiva and Bukhara: he chose an

Englishman, Colonel Stoddart, to go ahead and survey the
lie of the land. The English ambassador to Tehran gave
Stoddart a thousand ducats and sent him to Bukhara. In
June 1838, two days before Ramadan, Stoddart reached
Bukhara and was put up at the house of the vizier Rais.

'Colonel Stoddart had brought with him a letter
addressed to Hakim the Chief Minister, but this man
had by now been executed, so he gave the letter to Rais
instead. Rais reacted with fury. "Do you know who I am?"
he menaced. "I'm the man who got rid of all the Emir's
enemies." Not to be intimidated, Stoddart responded iron-
ically, "I'm pleased to hear that the Emir has no enemies!"

'On the first day of Ramadan, the vizier told the
Englishman, "The Emir wants to see you; go on foot, past
the fortress to the Registon public square." Stoddart said,
"I don't go on foot to see my Queen, so why should I go
on foot to see your Emir?" He set of for the Registon on
horseback. The Emir had just emerged from the mosque
when he was met with the sight of a European on horseback and in uniform saluting him.

'The Emir didn't say a word, but sent a trusted aid to
enquire: "Why is that European on horseback blocking my
way?" "This is the English way of doing things," Stoddart
replied. "Very well," said the Emir, "proceed to the petitions chamber." Stoddart obeyed, but when the aide told
him, "Bow to the ground when you come to petition the
Emir," Stoddart angrily replied, "I bow only to God."

Then two guards came up and grabbed the Englishman
by the armpits: he shook them off. When he saw this, the
chamberlain thought he would have Stoddart searched.
Stoddart slapped his face and stepped up by himself to the
Emir's presence.

A courtier was standing by the door, reciting a prayer
in honour of the Emir. When he saw this prayer, Stoddart

too turned his palms upwards in prayer and recited a prayer in Farsi. When the prayer ended, the Emir too turned his palms upwards to recite the first surat of the Qu'ran.

"'You have a message for me?" asked the Emir.

'Stoddart handed over the English ambassador's letter.

"'Have you anything else to say?" the Emir added.

'Stoddart had a lot more to say.

'Then the audience was over and the Colonel returned to Rais's house.

'On the second day of Ramadan, the chamberlain came up and said, "Rais wants to see you!" Stoddart began putting on his uniform, but the chamberlain said, "No, go as you are." When Stoddart came into the courtyard and saw twelve men waiting there, his suspicions were aroused. The men went for his chest, twisted his arms behind him and tied them with a noose. To his dismay, Rais appeared: "You're a filthy spy. You betrayed Kabul!" The vizier pressed a dagger to Stoddart's breast, and Stoddart uttered a prayer in Farsi.

"'Take him away," Rais ordered. Stoddart was dragged out into the street, in the rain, for all to see; he was so humiliated, he wished he was dead. But they dragged him down the street and threw him into a dungeon.'

At this point Muborak broke off, leaving the prisoners gasping. Abdulla didn't know what to think. Who knows whether it was the novelty of the story that had captured them, or Muborak's simple but cunning storytelling? There was nothing fancy about it, he couldn't stick to the point, but it was still somehow bewitching. One or two prisoners, like small children listening to a folk tale, implored 'More! More!'

Abdulla himself had found something in some Russian

journals about two English spies sent to Emir Nasrullo's court: they had apparently been captured and beheaded. But this was the first time he had heard such a detailed description of their adventures in Bukhara, which Muborak claimed to have read in English books. But was it credible? There were stories gushing out of Muborak like a fountain! But if they were true, they would be invaluable for Abdulla, for the story he was devising. After all, there were no books for him to consult here.

As ever, Jur'at summed up for the group: 'A heron tried to act like a falcon and ended up stuck in the mud!'

———

After Muborak the Bukharan, nobody told a story. Their minds apparently dulled by the rice and mung beans, the prisoners took advantage of the holiday regime by dozing off as they studied the criminal code. With no talk to distract him, Abdulla let his mind wander where it would. Again, he recalled his wife and children, and that led to thoughts of Nodira and Oyxon. Quite possibly, Abdulla had paid more attention to Nodira than he had to Oyxon's love for the young Qosim. The more he thought about it, Nodira was not such an unhappy woman. She was Emir Umar's first wife, after all. How happy their life must have been, at first! They were one flesh, one soul, one spirit, as firmly bound to each other as two lines of a couplet:

> Though she is famed for being unique among beauties,
> There is one who dares to beg for her, like my mad self.

Umar loved Nodira as Nodira loved herself: what more can a woman ask of a man? Who destroyed their happiness?

> Oh angel, my poor hovel has fallen under a black enchantment,
> If nothing else, it was time's shadow on the wall.

You shouldn't put down on paper everything that comes to your mind. Who could have known that the 'shadow on the wall' would darken even the radiance of Nodira's bright life, and not for a brief time but forever? One day or another, what you wrote would come back to haunt you. If only Nodira could have guessed how her words would prove to be prophetic.

Where, Abdulla wondered, had he written about the dark days he was now experiencing? Did Oyxon's position as second wife have anything in common with his own imprisonment today? Was this what he had been secretly longing for, when he'd wished for a winter of uninterrupted work? Abdulla lay on his side as he mulled this over. His eyes weren't aware of anything now.

Abdulla had a dream in which his own mother Josiyat turned out to be in charge of Umar's harem. 'Where have you been?' she grumbled, 'We've not seen hide nor hair of you since you went off to that damned Kazan!'

Abdulla sought to placate her. 'Wherever I've been, I'm here now: but what are you doing here?'

'Oyxon's become like a daughter to me, she needs me to protect her. Your Madali doesn't impress me, not at all; he's a shitty sleeve, but look at him talking as if he were a man!'

'I've told him often enough,' Abdulla said defensively, 'that I'll tell his father. That seemed to frighten him.'

'Of course it didn't. Why should he be frightened of a dead man? Just now he came up to the door, that arrogant boy of yours, and said "At last, we can safely drink tea served by you."'

Still dreaming, Abdulla made an effort to remember that Umar really had died and that his teenaged son, dressed in white garments, had been put on the throne by the mullas and scholars.

'Well, it's time I was off.' Abdulla wasn't sure where he ought to go; all he knew was that it was incumbent on him to leave Oyxon; he averted his eyes from his mother's apprehensive face.

'No more slipping off to that ghastly Kazan, son!' Josiyat begged.

Oddly enough, after he left the palace Abdulla seemed to be heading for his house on Ko'bariq Street. It took him exactly two hundred and seventy seven steps to get to the front door. When he looked inside, there was nobody in. He dreamt that he called for Rahbar and the children, but there was no response. They must have gone to a wedding feast, he reassured himself, then went through into the garden, halting when he got to the summer house. It was beginning to get dark, and he was worried. This was no time for the children to be out! Then he spotted soldiers behind the wall, amusing themselves by lighting fires: they seemed to have surrounded the house and the yard. Who could they be? Abdulla began to panic. Perhaps it was just as well that his children weren't at home. But suppose that was because they'd been taken away?

But of course, they were Madali's guards. These guards seem to have taken Abdulla into custody, and to be keeping him under house arrest. Apparently, his recriminations against Madali's behaviour toward Oyxon had infuriated the young Khan. But now Abdulla was under lock and key, Madali was free to do whatever he liked.

———

When he awoke, Abdulla tried to order the scenes from his dream one by one: his mother, Oyxon's door, Madali, the way he counted his steps, his deserted yard, the guards surrounding his house… Some of these cheered him, others chilled his heart. Then he began looking for a way to interpret them. Dreaming of his mother Josiyat might mean her ghost had been badly upset. She no longer figured largely in his prayers or in his memory, nor had he performed any graveside rituals for her. He was her debtor in this world and the next. Two days after she died, before her body was committed to the grave, he'd gone eagerly off to Kazan like a dog wagging his tail. 'Have you got something boiling over there, you writers? To hell with writers!' her ghost called after him. 'When you were a baby, I pierced only one of your ears; I should have pierced both and put rings in them, then you'd stay where I can see you, like a pet calf, nice and obedient.'

But what did Oyxon have in common with his mother? Might she possibly be a stand-in for Rahbar? Except that, with her auburn hair, Rahbar was more like Nodira. And Nodira was the senior wife, above Kumush, Zaynab and Ra'no – the other women of the harem, his heroines. One day, when he was sitting weeping on the summer terrace, his son Habibullo had come over with Josiyat and Rahbar, saying 'Look, daddy is crying!'

'Hey, son, calm down, have your eyes been somewhere wet?' Josiyat asked.

'I've killed her! I've just killed her! I've killed Kumush with my own hands...' Abdulla was unable to hold back his tears.

'The boy is possessed!' his mother declared, reciting the prayer '*La illah*' before taking her daughter-in-law and grandson away.

But that night, it was Rahbar's turn to weep. 'You don't love me, you love Kumush and Zaynab!'

'Listen, Rahbar, they're not real, they're just figments of my imagination. Come on, stop it now.'

'Whoever heard of a man crying over someone he's invented?'

And now he had Oyxon as well. By this time, Sunnat from Qumloq must have gone to Abdulla's house and handed over his letter. Then Rahbar would find the manuscript, run her eyes over it and upset herself again! This was certainly no time to bring more worries down on her. 'Hey, don't bother yourself about it, daughter-in-law, my son has always been rather stupid!' his mother would have said, God rest her soul. Perhaps Abdulla should have thought more carefully about the contents of the letter. Mightn't Rahbar be thinking, even when he's sitting in prison, all he worries about is a manuscript!

To Abdulla, his soul seemed polluted, turbid, soiled. All his thoughts were of Oyxon. Had he turned into her young cousin Qosim, had he fallen in love with her? Or had he cast Qosim aside so he could have her to himself? Or a third possibility: was Oyxon herself a stand-in for Abdulla, imprisoned in her gilded cage, walking a tight-rope with every step she took?

When Umar was summoned from this world to the world of eternity, Oyxon's immediate thought was to rejoice; she was free! Was it possible that Qosim might overlook the fact that she had been married, since she had not borne Umar any heirs? After a great deal of thought, Oyxon decided to consult her father's close aide and the late Emir Umar's former bodyguard, her fellow-countryman Gulxaniy.

Using the wake as a pretext, she invited him to her quarters and was as frank with him as she would be to an older brother. 'As the saying goes, what a deaf man hears won't strike the eye,' Gulxaniy warned her, but undertook to negotiate with Qosim on her behalf. Even though she was outwardly in mourning, Oyxon's heart now knew a series of bright and cheerful days. Her black garments seemed to make her face paler, for now, truly, in beauty, the heart's house finds its radiance.'

She allowed her thoughts to linger on things of the past; a ladder propped against the vine stakes, the squeaking cart passing down the street, the warm, free breeze. She would go to Shahrixon on the pretext of seeing her siblings; she would leave with Qosim and start life afresh.

But then despair would set in again: Qosim would still be a young colt, while Oyxon was a widow, a barren flower. What reaction would they face if they sought to become man and wife? After all, Qosim's parents would have their own wishes and desires: they would want their son to set his heart on an blossoming virgin: could she spoil their happiness?

Just let the persuasive Gulxaniy come back after talking to the young Sayid.

All of a sudden, Abdulla realised what the cause of all these emotions was: hadn't he himself sent Sunnat to his house as a messenger, and weren't his emotions correlated to an expectation of good news? Once again Abdulla was plunged in his own thoughts, but this time Jur'at's harsh voice made the whole cell tremble: 'Get up, all of you! Why are you lying there like women in labour?'

———

'We have a Russian professor in our midst,' Jur'at announced, 'an archaeologist, one of those people who goes about digging things up. But he speaks decent Uzbek; let's hear something from him. Surely you can't be robbed twice of the same property? He can talk about Russian history, or ours, whichever he likes.' Jur'at clapped the rather frail old man on the shoulder as he offered him the floor.

'It's easier for me if I speak in Russian, but I'll have a go at Uzbek,' the old professor began. 'As the elder just said, I'm an archaeologist, which means I interpret the ancient world, but I do know a few things about more recent times, particularly the history of the "Great Game". Russia defeated Iran in 1828 and Turkey in 1829. And then Britain had the idea that if Russia came any closer to India there would be a rebellion in India, and that Russia must be preparing to invade Afghanistan.

'In the years 1829-30 the English spy Arthur Conolly travelled from Moscow to Afghanistan, and then went as far as the border of India to see which route the Russians might take. The routes according to him went through Khiva and Balkh as far as Kabul, and then via Khaibar to India. Shah Babur is known to have used this route. Afghanistan was then undergoing civil war. Dost Muhammad was in Kabul, Komron-Shah in Herat, and I can't remember who was in Kunduz, Balkh or Kandahar. And Ranjit Singh was the ruler of Kashmir.'

Listening to these words, Abdulla was utterly absorbed. Not only by the content of what the professor was saying, but by the way he expressed it. His language, with its loan translations from Russian, was like falling rain and rarefied air. In any case, even if it seemed at first to be too dense, it was, compared with Laziz's confused language, rather pleasant to listen to. Abdulla went on listening, as the professor's tongue pricked up men's ears.

'In 1832, the English tried to lay hands on Afghanistan. First they found Shuja Durrani, who was then in the Punjab. Shuja was allied to the English and the Sikhs when he besieged Kandahar. But Dost Muhammad came to his younger brother's assistance, and together they forced Shuja back to the Punjab.

'In 1836 the Afghans got into direct contact with the

Russians. Jan Witkiewicz, who had come to Bukhara to gather information, had a meeting there with Dost Muhammad and his spokesman Hussein Ali, whom he accompanied all the way back to Orenburg.'

Abdulla had studied Jan Witkiewicz's fate very thoroughly. He had even included some of it in his story, but as the tale of yet another errant man's unhappy fate, rather than as an aspect of the Great Game the professor was talking about. The professor's speech, however, took a rather broader view.

'In 1837 Hussein Ali received a letter from Tsar Nicolas I addressed to Shah Dost Muhammad; he set off with Witkiewicz for Afghanistan, but fell ill and died on the journey. Witkiewicz decided to deliver the letter himself, and arrived in Kabul on Christmas day. The British spy Alexander Burnes invited him to supper, and the two spies took a liking to one another over whisky and a quiet conversation. It became clear that what had collided in Afghanistan were not merely two men but two countries.'

Abdulla didn't listen much to what the professor said afterwards about the war between England and Afghanistan, and Russia's subsequent decision to invade Turkestan. He was preoccupied with the last scene: the two spies having a Christmas supper in Kabul. Abdulla would have written that scene up wonderfully. Not just their conversation, but the silences and what was left unspoken; everything that was understood, consciously or unconsciously, about the 'superiority' of the English over the Afghans and of the Russians over the Uzbeks. About the intellectual arrogance and cunning practices that both sides put such stock in in.

Abdulla had begun to bring this scene to life when the doors clanged open and the prison's miserable supper was brought in.

—

The reason he had thought of the food as 'miserable' became clear to Abdulla when the Russian soldier-cook called out, 'Come and get your *miski*!' Yes, eating from metal bowls really did mean a miserable supper. Who knows if the professor's Russified Uzbek might have suggested the thought?

The Uzbek language certainly is odd. You can hide yourself as a pronoun at the end, but that's also where the emphasis lies: it is marked. But if we look at the language of Navoi or Babur, which was influenced by Farsi, we find pronoun and predicate changing places, all much earlier than the Russian influence. Abdulla's thoughts reverted to Professor Zasypkin's narrative, or, to be precise, if one committed sacrilege, to Zasypkin's narrative reverted the thoughts of Abdulla.

Without a doubt, the meal they'd just had was very different from the Christmas Eve supper that Burnes and Witkiewicz enjoyed, but when you considered that all the prisoners were sitting in pairs, enjoying a barely audible chat, you couldn't help feeling that they were spies conversing.

Abdulla now focussed on the prisoner sitting next to him. The auburn-haired lad was nibbling away at his food like a marmot, and in between bites he was sniffling just like a marmot, or in a way, whistling. Abdulla nodded to him, saying 'Enjoy your meal!' as he pointed to the lad's bowl. The lad smiled between two noisy mouthfuls and said in Tatar, 'We're eating!'

Abdulla realised he was a Tatar and responded in Tatar, 'What else do we do!' and clapped him on the shoulder.

When the Tatar heard his own language spoken, as if exhilarated, he quivered.

'Do you speak Tatar, then?' he asked, unable to conceal

his joy.

'Not very well,' Abdulla admitted. 'I have read Ghabdulla Tuqay and Qayum Nosiri.'

Although those names sounded Tatar, they clearly meant nothing to the youth, but they moved him deeply and, once he heard his own language, he began opening his heart to Abdulla.

For some reason Abdulla presumed that this lad, too, would know a lot about the nineteenth-century, but no, the youth was neither a historian, nor a spy, nor a trader, nor a mulla: he turned out to be just an ordinary criminal. When he was released from prison in Samara, his mother had died, and his father was starving because of the failed harvest. 'Right, let's go to Tashkent,' said the father, and took his son to Tashkent. There, his father married an Uzbek widow and worked on a building site as a painter, a night-watchman and, when the occasion presented itself, as a bricklayer. He kept his son Rafail on as an assistant, to make sure he didn't go off the rails. Rafail's new stepmother Xosiyat worked as an office cleaner, when she wasn't making bread to sell at the market, and that was how the family survived.

It so happened that the stepmother got a job as a night cleaner in the local NKVD quarters, but somehow a few papers went missing. Inevitably, an interrogator used this as a pretext to make a pass at Xosiyat. When Xosiyat got home, she told her husband everything that had happened. The husband picked up a builder's mallet and went to see the NKVD man who employed his wife as a cleaner. In his efforts to restore justice, he entered the building, but never emerged again.

That day Rafail had gone to the Khiva open-air cinema and, when he came home he saw his stepmother sitting there abandoned and alone, tears falling from her eyes. She had been raped, but didn't dare go to the NKVD; and her husband, who had gone, had still not come home.

Then Rafail put the biggest screwdriver he could find under his shirt and went to the district NKVD, where his father had gone. At first they wouldn't let him in. But he was devious: 'I've come to expose some bad things my father has done,' he said, and he was taken to the office of the very interrogator who'd caused the trouble. When he looked, he saw his father, covered in blood, lying down, barely alive, in a corner.

He grabbed the screwdriver and thrust it into the interrogator's throat and then his chest. 'That's for my father! That's for my mother!' he said, as he ripped the scoundrel to shreds.

'Now I'm in prison,' this heroic young man said, baring his marmot teeth.

Abdulla was too stunned for words.

———

After the evening meal was over, the people once again 'assembled on the square'. Now everyone seemed to be burning to tell stories, to take this ritual to their hearts; some preferring to listen, others to disclose their innermost secrets. Whatever the case, the cell elder was not going to interfere with anyone: it freed the prison bosses from the danger of any trouble. No specially devised ritual would have done so well to keep the prisoners occupied.

'People, let's hear more about the English! Where are you, Muborak, ethnic minority?'

Muborak stood in front of the circle of men, put his hands on his hips in the Bukharan fashion, took a deep breath and plunged right in.

'Well, lucky brethren,' he began, as if imitating Abdulla. 'As you'll remember, we left Colonel Stoddart in the castle dungeon. That dungeon was worse than our prison, pitch dark, no lamp. Stoddart lay there without moving for two hours, and then a side door opened and a man holding a flare came in. Stoddart wondered if it was the Emir. He bowed low and said, "God forgive me, I'm innocent. I'm only an envoy. If my visit displeases his highness the Emir, let him give the order and I'll go!" The man, who was in fact the Chief of Police, promised to pass on Stoddart's words.'

As Abdulla listened to Muborak's story, he detected a change in his accent. Could he be acting a part? Who was he, really? But a moment later he couldn't help being sucked back in to the convoluted story.

'As soon as the Police Chief left, Stoddart was taken from the dungeon and thrown into a bug-infested pit with thieves and murderers. The Colonel got the other prisoners on his side by giving them some of his tobacco; smoking was the only way to drive the insects off their faces.

'The next day the executioner came down into the pit and delivered an ultimatum: either convert to Islam, or be killed. Fearing for his life, Stoddart gave in and pronounced the *shahada*. He endured two more months in that pit, before he was pulled out, tied up with a lasso and brought before the Chief of Police. "Your property has been forfeited and your weapon confiscated," the Chief told him. "The vizier has told his highness the Emir that your letter is from the Tsar of Russia: that it's false, a forgery, and you're an English spy."

"'I'm an envoy!" Stoddart insisted.

'The Police Chief interrogated him thoroughly and searched him. By now Stoddart was living comfortably in the Police Chief's house.'

The storytelling broke off here, almost as if the guards had been waiting in the wings; the cell door banged open, and a warder yelled: 'Prisoner Ma'sumov, for interrogation!'

Everyone fell silent. Little Sodiq, who had greeted Abdulla on his first day, put his jacket over his shoulders and felt his way to the door.

'The holiday's over!' a prisoner said. Someone else muttered under their breath, 'It's started.' The company that had only just formed was scattered, like ice crunched under a boot.

———

Five minutes or so later, someone else was taken off for interrogation, then another. After a while Sodiq returned, his arms and legs trembling; eventually, a moustachioed Russian was taken to replace him. 'So the game of cricket has started,' Abdulla thought darkly, 'one man in, another man out.' Was he going to be summoned? It was something he had to be ready for. They would try to stitch him up, but with what evidence?

Though the wretched Stoddart had been imprisoned in a strange land, while Abdulla had the dubious privilege of being locked up in his own country, what other difference lay between them? Like Stoddart, he had been thrown into a dungeon without any questioning, without any attempt to determine whether he was guilty or innocent; he supposed he ought to be thankful that the march of progress had replaced bug-infested pits with stinking concrete cells. The more things change, the more they stay the same: an expression never more true than when applied to human nature.

When Madali ascended the throne, he was at most fifteen years old; if Hakim's eloquent account is to be believed, perhaps even younger. But he wasted no time in weeding the field, eliminating one after the other of the viziers and beys whom his father had appointed. These men, all old enough to be Madali's father, were despatched to the next world as easily as though they were snot-nosed children. He had the burly Keeper of the Seals seized, his house looted and the man himself deported to Russia. Madali even beheaded his brother Abdulloh with his own hand. Those who managed to escape the cull would have their steps dogged by informers, for the teenaged Emir feared intrigue from every corner, and trusted nobody but his mother Nodira.

This was the time when Oyxon was waiting impatiently for Gulxaniy to return with the news from Eski-Novqat. Long before then she had finished this poem:

> Night and day, seeing shadows or someone watching behind –
> Haunting my loneliness, all of the day and all of the night.
>
> My terrors and anxieties are faint and shallow as breath.
> Yet at each step my grave's abyss looms ever nearer in sight.
>
> Like sharp splinters, or shards of rock in the mountains,
> Emptiness pierces my shoulders with a fear of light.
>
> At every lamp, my sombre soul hides in my shadow.
> As the lamp passes over, my soul hides in my body in fright.
>
> A mouth but no head is speaking the words, 'Turn around'
> But if I look behind, then there's only myself in sight.
>
> How strange that my fear of vanishing is frightening itself –
> A piece of bread is heaven, yes, but the oven's hell's spite.
>
> Oh you who pass, transparent in body, without a shadow.
> See me: my blood burns like the rising sun's light!

When Gulxaniy had finished his business in Eski-Novqat and was on his way back to Kokand, he was met by two of Madali's soldiers who claimed to have been ordered to accompany him. Although his heart missed a beat, he didn't let it show, and rode with them for two days' journey. In Marg'ilon they were met by the city governors, who gave Gulxaniy cause to rejoice: 'His highness Madali has given you Yangiqo'rg'on to rule!' The governor immediately threw a banquet in Marg'ilon fortress, where he sought to win Gulxaniy's trust with amusing stories and friendly jokes: 'I'm a governor, you're a governor, so there's no need for secrets between us,' he insisted.

Gulxaniy kept a cool head on his shoulders, parrying with his own jokes: 'A pock-marked butcher found a mirror when he was out walking. When he saw his ugly reflection, he lost his temper and smashed the glass, saying "Would you find anything good lying on the road?"'

The governor laughed long and loud, his flushed face reddening further; still he pressed Gulxaniy, 'Go on, tell us where you've been, what you've seen. Tell us all about it.'

Gulxaniy continued: 'A fox was walking down the road. It was pitch-dark. Snow and rain were coming down constantly, so the streets had turned to mud. The fox came across a young camel, sprawling in the mud and covered with dirt: the slime was glued to every hair on its back. The camel had escaped from the caravan leader; it was running away to the sun-baked meadows. Now it had encountered the fox. The fox greeted the camel and asked how it was doing: "Oh, your highness, you must be tired, where have you come from?" The camel replied, "I've come from the baths."

'"The fox replied, 'Good for you, you speak the truth, but you're nice and clean only from your head to your legs. To judge by your legs, you used the bath water only on your head and legs. Or had the bath attendant died and you couldn't find anyone to help you?'"

The oafish governor burst out laughing again, swaying from side to side and slumping onto the cushions.

After their instruments had been tuned, musicians assembled, and everything was done that was usually required for a party; music accompanied the conversation. Gulxaniy was not affected by the tiring journey or by the sweet wine, but the music relaxed him and, without getting up from his cushion, he fell into a deep sleep. As he did, his hand unconsciously strayed to the pocket where the sharp-eyed governor now detected a slight bulge.

The governor deftly snatched two letters from the pocket, and a dozen soldiers who had been lurking out of sight bound Gulxaniy's hands and feet and stuffed him into a woollen sack, which they flung that same night into the turbulent river.

CHAPTER 4

CHESS

The NKVD's millstones creaked into action. In the course of that night, many of the prisoners who lay close to Abdulla, packed like sardines, were summoned for interrogation; some would come back in an hour or so, downcast and sometimes physically beaten, while others didn't return until after daybreak. Naturally, nobody in the cell could sleep. Only recently the prisoners had been waiting for their turn to tell a story; now they were waiting to be summoned for interrogation, secretly rehearsing what they would say and how they would act.

If Abdulla had learnt anything from a life lived among Uzbeks, it was how to converse with them: he knew the importance of frank discussion and give-and-take chats. His novel *Past Days* had been written in the form of a series of conversations, one after another: no movement, no violent action, no wild confusion.

The great Mir Alisher Navoi had good reason to name the *Gatherings of the Elegant* as one of his greatest works. Abdulla recalled the *Babur-nama* by Shah Babur: 'One day, during a session of chess, Alisher Navoi was stretching out his leg. He touched Binoi's behind. Navoi made a joke of it, "It's a strange problem, isn't it: if you stretch out your leg in Herat, you touch a poet's backside." Binoi replied,

"And if you tuck your leg under yourself, you also touch a poet's backside!"

From picturing these two great men playing chess, and easing the tension from time to time with a joke or a saying, Abdulla's thoughts moved to his local tea-house in Samarkand. There, he had witnessed interminable conversations, or cheap talk as Josiyat would put it, carried on between friends playing chess.

One really skilled player was the poet Elbek. Whether it was because of something curmudgeonly in his nature, or whether he was just very cautious, or just combined meanness with the peculiarities of being a poet, he 'rubbed everyone's nose in the dirt', whether they were Uzbek poets or prose-writers.

In the years when they were all studying in Moscow, they once went together to Maryina Grove, which was full of Russians enthusiastically playing chess. This was the time when Alyokhin and Botvinnik were at the height of their fame, and every Russian with a chess set fancied himself a great player.

Being strangers away from home, the Uzbeks hung on to every penny, but Elbek was like a young cockerel eager to do battle. 'Forget it,' his horrified friends told him. 'We don't have much money as it is, don't go and lose it to the Alyokhins!' But Elbek gave them all the slip. In twelve moves he had one of the Russians check-mated, his Uzbek friends clamouring, 'Play for money! For money!'. Thanks to Elbek's mercenary nature, the Uzbeks' kitty trebled in size in the time they spent in that park. How could the unsuspecting Russians have known that they were dealing with the heirs of Navoi and Binoi?

Madali, who had taken the title of Khan before he had even put on a Khan's gown, was majestically reclining on his side, playing chess with his cousin Hakim, who sat with his legs tucked beneath him. Hakim's pieces were clearly doing well, his castles and bishops were excellently positioned, he could end the game in no more than ten moves; he had his queen waiting in the wings ready to unsheathe her sword and do battle at a moment's notice. Madali was fuming, seemingly about to explode with rage and frustration, when Hakim's skill abruptly failed him: one clumsy move, and his knight was swiftly taken by Madali's cornered bishop. Madali didn't hide his smile. Affectedly casual, he told Hakim:

'My soldiers have uncovered a plot.'

'Oh yes? What sort of plot?' Hakim frowned at the board, too absorbed by the game to look up.

'Your Oyxon wrote a letter to a young relative of hers, and we've seized his reply from the messenger.'

Not 'my mother', nor 'my stepmother'; 'your Oyxon'. Hakim could hardly fail to detect the ominous note in this. He knew Madali had not forgotten how he, Hakim, used to respond to Madali's improprieties towards Oyxon by threatening to tell his father Umar. Hakim had made a wrong move on purpose. Then, whatever you did, it was impossible to undo the damage caused by that move. The consequence of one blunder was an impasse with no way out.

'This was actually found in her possession?' Hakim asked, his voice showing how perturbed he was; as he spoke, he moved a useless pawn towards his opponent's knight.

'No, there was an intermediary, that's who we caught.' Madali took Hakim' pawn with his queen 'He has been sentenced to death.'

'Who was he?' asked Hakim, suddenly exhausted.

When he saw how unsettled his opponent was, Madali's eyes blazed.

'It was the man they called Gulxaniy,' he said, practically spitting out the name.

Hakim looked at Madali in horror.

'I've won!' Madali crowed, finishing the game in a way that would have been brusque in any dialect. 'You're all traitors!' he added. 'I'm going to crush the lot of you, one by one! Everyone who has committed fornication will be stoned as sharia law prescribes.' Then he began to laugh in a very odd way, far too knowing for his years, a laugh like the grinding of millstones.

———

While waiting for his turn to be interrogated, Abdulla only managed to get to sleep just before dawn. He had no dreams, pleasant or otherwise. If Jur'at hadn't called out 'Get up!' in the morning, he might have slept through noonday prayers as well as morning prayers. But he awoke with a clear head, as if he'd slept through the night rather than merely snatched a scant few hours. Sodiq was lying next to him, too distressed to get up; on Abdulla's other side, Muborak's place was empty. 'They took him away,' Sodiq said when he saw Abdulla's puzzled expression. Abdulla took his turn to go to the corner and relieve himself and then to wash his face and hands, something vaguely like an Islamic ablution ('God have mercy on me!'); then he sat down on his quilt. He wondered whether Sunnat might come today. If he did, he wouldn't have had time to visit Abdulla's home. He'd hardly go mid-week, on a working day. In any case, shouldn't he be cautious? Suppose the house was being watched by a policeman or somebody? God forbid they should find Sunnat going there. If he came today, then Abdulla would find an opportunity to speak to him, to warn him to be careful, to get a message through a neighbour – Yusuf, he could be trusted – rather than going straight to Rahbar herself. All right, let's wait until they bring breakfast.

As days and then weeks passed and Gulxaniy still failed to return, Oyxon began to worry. Worry was not the word: she began to panic, she was bewildered, utterly distressed. She was besieged by countless thoughts, but whom could she tell of her inner suspicions and alarms; if only she had someone to confide in.

Umar's sister Oftob had been like a mother to Oyxon, but after the death of the Emir and perhaps because of Nodira's reluctance, or because of the angry insistence of Nodira's darling offspring, the new Emir, she had been removed from court under various pretexts. Now, according to the gossip of the older harem ladies, she'd been packed off to perform *Haj*.

Hakim, her stepson, who once used to drop in from time to time and bring news, was now in a depressed state and walked about looking like thunder.

Poor Oyxon found herself all alone in the palace harem. She could not go to Shahrixon to see her siblings, since she was in mourning and unable to leave the palace.

One sleepless night, her mind clouded by dark thoughts, she sensed somebody's silhouette at the window. Alarmed, she immediately called for her maidservant: 'Gulsum, take a look by the door, someone seems to have passed by.'

Gulsum, who was busy with her own affairs, didn't hesitate: she went out to listen. She came back instantly and whispered to her mistress: 'Our new Emir, dead drunk.'

Oyxon needn't have sent her servant-girl out: the young Emir staggered in after her.

'Greetings… Mother, dear…'

Drink seemed to have knotted Madali's tongue, leaving

him stuttering his words. He could barely stay on his feet. Drunk or not, he was as sly as ever; his words as he entered Oyxon's chambers were those of an affectionate son visiting a beloved mother, but his manner went much further: he pressed his head against Oyxon's breast in a way that was far from innocent.

Overcoming her fright, Oyxon used both her hands to push Madali's head back, then forced herself to plant a chaste kiss on his forehead, above those greedy eyes. He plumped himself down next to her.

'My dear mother, sweet mother… how I've missed you…'

Oyxon was under no illusion; the teenaged Emir was only pretending to be drunk, behaving as though he felt for Oyxon the same affection he owed to his mother Nodira. Initially unsure how best to respond, Oyxon quickly made up her mind.

'Gulsum, tea! As quick as you can, and make it nice and strong!' As soon as the servant left to put the kettle on the hearth, Madali dropped his slurring act.

'You're too harsh! The only tea I want to drink comes straight from your sweet hands…'

'Gulsum!' Oyxon shouted in alarm. 'Attend to our Khan, give him water to wash his hands, and wait by him in case he needs anything else!'

Madali reverted to his previous infantile manner. 'My wonderful mother, my darling love… I'd give my life for my lovely mother… May you be as bounteous as the water, maidservant.'

Drying his hands and face with a towel, Madali gave Gulsum a furtive pinch before grunting at her: 'Off you go, Gulsum, bring us your tea.' The servant picked up the water ewer and went out to the yard.

Madali recited:

'Alas, because my beloved won't be my beloved,
Her grief slays me and she does not care.

My father wrote those words for you… I like these verses more… How about you, my love?' he said.

This sort of incident had occurred before, but now Oyxon was dealing not with a delinquent prince, but a fully enthroned Emir. Previously, she had been merely embarrassed; now, she felt disturbed to the bottom of her heart. She hurriedly summoned Gulsum again, but the cold weather was making the water slow to boil, and the girl was delayed. The young Emir seized his chance, speaking even more eagerly:

'Why should I hide from you that I have fallen in love?
There is no law to make the innocent deny it.'

By now Gulsum had returned with the tea, and Madali resumed his drunken act.

'Today it's going to snow, somebody or other put two letters in my pocket… letters in my dear mother's hand, in Oyxon's hand…' he said, as he pulled out two crumpled letters from his breast pocket, each folded over twice, and began to read out one of them. Oyxon recognised it at once, the letter she had written to Qosim, written on condition that it had to be given back: she felt faint.

Madali drank his fill of the tea he had been served, gave Gulsum another swift pinch, then added:

'There's no need, my love, to complain about a letter,
What mirror doesn't have a touch of rust?'

No slurring, no tottering: he got up from where he was sitting and left through the door, his steps swift and firm.

—

About half an hour later, Muborak returned to the cell, his spirit broken; he was followed by two Russian soldiers pushing a trolley with a jerry-can of gruel and a cask of tea. Abdulla looked through the open door behind them, thinking he might spot Sunnat's silhouette, but there was no sign. Perhaps it's his shift tomorrow, he told himself, determined to make the best of things.

Again, the unappetising, tasteless soup; again, another day. Muborak had sat down next to him; his arms and legs trembling, he seemed too weak to even think about food. Indifferent to his surroundings, he went on moving his lips in a whisper. Abdulla decided to listen.

'… comrade interrogator… in 1933 I was in London. I visited the grave of Karl Marx – "Proletariats of the world, unite!" The place was called Highgate… Then I went to the house of a relative called Philip Sosoniy. It was a big park called Cockfosters. Everyone has been there, from Charlie Chaplin to the Queen. The banquets you could have there, comrade interrogator!'

Muborak kept on talking, so quietly that it was almost inaudible.

Once Abdulla had finished his millet porridge, he got up to hand his bowl to the soldier-cooks. When he returned to his place, Muborak was telling Sodiq something, while Sodiq chewed his bread. Eavesdropping on a prison conversation is not approved of, but Abdulla couldn't help overhearing, however much he tried to block his ears to Muborak's words.

'I have a photographic memory: if I see something, I remember it forever.' Muborak tapped his forehead. 'Philip Sosoniy showed me the document which got Colonel Stoddart thrown into a pit on 31 December.'

When Abdulla heard the date, he shuddered and, without feigning anything, turned to face Muborak, who continued: 'Kamron, the Shah of Herat, wrote a letter on 20 August 1838: "O Emir, dear friend, I write in honour of our friendship. Great Britain is a very good country, it respects Muslims greatly. But it has become known that you have done something no Muslim ruler has done: you have arrested an envoy of Great Britain, Colonel Stoddart. Woe is you! Release him at all costs, and I shall intercede on your behalf."

'My friend Philip let me see Colonel Stoddart's letters, a great pack of them. One said, "On 8 July I left the dungeon and was free."' (At this point, Abdulla heaved a sigh of relief.) '"Believe me, I was taken to the executioner where they put a spade in my hand and told me to dig my own grave. As I said, his highness the Emir pardoned me. I was summoned before him and told, 'I'm giving you some soldiers of mine, you will be in charge of them!' I was then staying in the house of the Chief of Police."

'Another letter says, "The Emir has left for Samarkand. He ought to be advised not to hurry back. The English have taken over Kabul and rumour-mongers have raised the alarm. They're saying that the English will conquer Bukhara too, because I was thrown in a dungeon. The Emir is on his own, he doesn't trust any of his experts, and won't listen to any advice. The vizier seems to be doing a lot of good for me."

'Stoddart's last letter concludes, "The Chief of Police is ill, so I asked him to let me stay with his brother. I'm writing in the light of the moon from his brother's veranda, and Muborak, my loyal friend, is sitting next to me." That's what it says.'

At these last words Abdulla began to have serious doubts as to the plausibility of this story.

—

During the day, too, a couple of men were summoned for interrogation, but this was not the grim bustle of the night-time: leaving the cell during the hours of day was quite different. Abdulla recalled Cho'lpon's lines:

> The last light's gone… And from afar
> A terrible wailing hits the ear,
> Splitting the silence of the night
> What?
> What is it?
> What's that sound?
> Oh, I cannot help but hear.
> Is it the chant of some evil sprite,
> Or monsters bellowing underground,
> Or devils dancing on the hills,
> Or feasting in the steppe wolves' lair?
> Maybe the night's crying out its ills,
> Or daytime's howling its despair?

Abdulla loved Cho'lpon's poetry more than anyone else's. If in his younger days he had devoted himself to poetry rather than prose, this was the sort of thing he would be writing now. Not that he would have equalled Cho'lpon, but in Cho'lpon's poems Abdulla found the most precise expression of his own most intimate feelings. Cho'lpon had put his finger on, and seemed to dictate, the very words that he himself would have used.

'An unacquainted acquaintance' was Abdulla's phrase for it. In actual fact, when he wrote a prose piece, it too was a representation of this same 'known unknown' world. The known, the everyday, the petty and trivial, once plunged in the light of the unknown – and what was unknown, frightening and alien takes on a real existence and reverts to its real self.

In Cho'lpon's poem the 'last light' going out, 'the silence of the night', the 'monsters bellowing underground' are all of the same order. If Abdulla had learnt anything from any of his contemporaries, then it was without a doubt from Cho'lpon. The compositional harmonisation in *Night and Day* was itself a cosmic revelation. And Cho'lpon's innovations were not confined to poetry: he had introduced to the Uzbek novel a way of harmonising events and characters, balancing one love affair with another, or a fictional act of loyalty with a historical betrayal.

As well as being a fine stylist, Cho'lpon was a very modern writer. He never hesitated to employ so-called literary devices, whereas Abdulla was warier, always questioning whether readers would understand the significance of this or that. Abdulla had used some aspects of this style in his novella *Obid the Pickaxe*, but hadn't been completely happy with the work.

God grant that he get out of here safe and sound; then he would finish his tale of Oyxon and follow it up with a new, more hard-nosed novel, set in modern times. But would he dare write about the things he'd witnessed in this place? Jur'at the cell elder, Muborak the Jew, Mulla Shibirg'oniy, Rafail the Tatar, Vinokurov the Russian interrogator, Sunnat the Uzbek soldier... above all, he'd be writing about himself, his thoughts and his moral sufferings, his dreams and frustrations, the plans he'd conceived, leaving absolutely nothing out.

—

Abdulla was well aware of the enormous importance of tiny details for his story. So-called trivia was precisely what made a novel plausible and entertaining or, as he considered it, 'well-irrigated'. That was why he tirelessly and persistently collected details, trying hard to get at the very roots of every future hero. After that, his characters would begin to live their lives according to their nature. Jan Witkiewicz was one of these heroes. Abdulla hadn't yet begun to write about him, but he had sensed the presence of something that could be used in his story in this well-travelled man of the world. Why don't I get the professor to talk about him? he wondered, and approached the man who was selflessly enlightening the others sitting around him.

'May I join your circle?' he asked in Russian.

The professor didn't stop talking; he simply nodded as he went on with his narrative. 'We were excavating at Dalvarzin at the time, and some very old men explained to me that the etymology of the place meant, 'Dal's Wrestling'. Ali had seized Termez and was advancing to the north. There was a moat around Dalvarzin, full of water. When he reached the water, Ali couldn't see how to take the fortress. Ali was a tightrope walker: he threw a rope across the moat, apparently to reconnoitre; the daughter of the ruler of Dalvarzin fell in love with him. The girl wrote a letter to Ali, declaring her love. Ali replied, "If you love me, tell me where the water in the moat comes from." The girl advised him, "Throw a straw into the Tupalang river and dam the flow where the straw enters the moat." Ali did as she advised. When he captured the fortress, everyone in it had been reduced to a bestial existence. Only one dog was still moving. "This is my father Dal," said the girl. Ali asked, "What did your father feed you on?" "Bone marrow," the girl replied. "If you betrayed your father who fed you on bone marrow, could I expect any loyalty from you?" Ali hacked the girl to pieces. And that was how the place came to be called Dalvarzin.

Abdulla sat listening intently to this story. A pity there was no place for it in his own novel: it was lovely, though a bit of a muddle. When the professor came to the end of his story, he turned to Abdulla, as if to say, 'Fine: I'm at your service.'

Abdulla introduced himself: 'Abdulla Qodiriy.'

'Zasypkin,' the man responded.

'Yesterday you were talking about Jan Witkiewicz: I'm planning to write a book about those times…'

'Planning?' the professor responded archly. 'Isn't that rather risky in a place like this?'

'All the same, I'd like to know a bit about Witkiewicz.'

'What about him? Witkiewicz arrived in Bukhara in around 1836,' said Zasypkin, switching to Uzbek. 'Precisely a hundred years ago.'

'Speak Russian, please: as a child, I attended a Russian-language school. The language holds some wonderful memories for me.'

The professor reverted to his mother tongue. 'On 31 December 1835, 'Jan Witkiewicz entered Bukhara with a caravan. At the customs house the caravan was met by the Chief Minister himself. This vizier summoned Witkiewicz and asked: "Are you a Russian?"

'"I am," Witkiewicz said.

'"Why have you come here?"

'"By chance. I was travelling to retrieve prisoners from the Kazakhs. Snow covered the tracks, so I thought I might as well use the time to see Bukhara."

'"Do you have goods?"

'"No."

'"How about money?"

'"I have 200 gold roubles. Here, see for yourself!" Witkiewicz showed his purse to the Chief Minister. The vizier's eyes nearly popped out of his head, but he was too embarrassed to take this money openly, so he looked for a pretext.

'"In Bukhara, there is a law for everything, and that law says that you have to pay customs duty."

'"For us, too, the law is above everything. With pleasure!' Witkiewicz assented.

"'Do you know Alexander?" the Chief Minister suddenly asked.

"'The Macedonian?"

"'Not him: Alexander Burnes."

"'Ah, you mean the traveller? He praised you, Chief Minister, to me…"

The Chief Minister laughed briefly.

"'That Alexander gave me a book as a present…"

"'What was the book called?"

"'It had gold lettering…"

"'And its title?"

"'The binding was studded with precious stones…"

'By now Witkiewicz had allowed his pistol and rifle to be made visible. The Chief Minister seemed somewhat taken aback, and began calculating how much customs duty he should take from the Russian.

"'We take a fortieth part from Muslims; non-Muslims pay double. Armenians and Indians pay twenty per cent. That's what Alexander paid. As for Russians… ten per cent."

"'I'll check with the Khan,' the Chief Minister concluded. 'If we've taken more than the legal amount, we'll give it back."

And that was how Witkiewicz entered Bukhara.'

———

Jur'at clapped his hands to call for attention. 'Cleaning day, lads. If the camel shakes its back, the load goes to the donkey, as they say. Starting on the left, everybody takes turns to carry their bedding to the opposite corner, and without getting dust everywhere, do you hear? Sand gets into the well without food, you don't need me to tell you. Sodiq, you're the youngest, soak the broom so you don't

just spread all the dust about – got it? Then I'll begin!'
Jur'at rolled up his bedding and carried it off to the corner
by the door where the privy was; there, he unrolled and
shook each item out one by one. Meanwhile Sodiq dampened his broom and started sweeping Jur'at's place clean.

Someone in the corner grumbled: 'Two people mustn't
sweep at the same time, it's a bad omen, there'll be a corpse
leaving the house...'

Although Abdulla heard this remark, Jur'at was apparently too taken up with his work to grasp what was said,
and the job went on as it had started.

When everything was cleaned up, the refuse was piled
up in a corner and the brooms were stacked vertically over
the pile. The same voice as before grumbled barely audibly
from the corner: 'If you stand a broom on end, it's a bad
omen...' But this time nobody paid any attention.

'If your heart is sure, you needn't complain to the
world,' said Jur'at, puffing up his chest. Abdulla knew the
verse which contained the words 'the heart is pure', but
Jur'at's rather perverse character had now altered the line,
and Abdulla rather liked the way it now applied to himself.

'Come on Muborak, tell us about the English: we're
fed up with this life, skulking about: "White and gold the
caravans..."'

The eager little figure of Muborak rushed forwards to
the place of honour and, without a word of introduction,
he went straight to his story: 'I told you about the spies,
comrade interrogator.' (Only Abdulla seemed to notice this
slip.) 'The Emir had imprisoned Stoddart once before, and
again, he ordered him to be put away. After this second
arrest, the Emir personally handed Stoddart over to the
custody of his butler, who put the Englishman in a servant's room, without food. Naturally, Stoddart fell ill and
had to have a doctor come and look at him.

'After that the Emir passed Stoddart on to the care of a naib, one of the most notorious thieves in Bukhara. He'd been told many times, "Don't steal more than is decent!" But his greed knew no bounds. He made Stoddart write many letters to spies in Kabul and Khiva, saying that the naib had helped him, and ought to be rewarded. I've read these letters.

'One letter said that his health was not at all good. The fact that the English had captured Kabul and Herat gave him hope, but the possibility of the English attacking Bukhara was frightening.'

When Muborak's account reached this point, the door was opened with the customary force, and a soldier yelled: 'Rafail Ixsianov, out, with your belongings!' Everyone fell silent.

—

Poor Sodiq was floundering at dinner time. His trembling hands spilled half of his cabbage soup on someone else's bedding; hearing them curse him, he took refuge in his own corner and huddled there, immobile. Abdulla himself took Sodiq's half-full bowl and passed it back to the soldier-cook.

'You should have eaten it,' Abdulla said, trying to draw him out. 'The cabbage wasn't sour this time, it was actually quite fresh.'

But Sodiq simply sat there, as if struck dumb. His mood soon infected Abdulla. Rafail hadn't been taken away to be set free, had he? Why would they release him? Ever since these arrests began, Abdulla had never heard of anyone being released from detention. Why had Rafail been ordered to take his belongings with him? If he was going to be sent to Siberia, there had to be some sort of court trial, although people were saying that courts and trials had been replaced by the so-called *troyka* – groups of three brought together to deliver whatever sentence the authorities wanted. Was that what the wretched lad was now facing? Is that how they might deliver Abdulla's sentence, without calling him before an interrogator? By now he'd spent nearly ten days here, with no interrogator, no summons, and no judge.

What Stoddart had undergone was happening to Abdulla in his own country.

The events described by Muborak had to be checked with Professor Zasypkin. Especially whether the Russians really had been about to take Stoddart away with them. Would Zasypkin know about this? Hadn't all this happened after the business with Witkiewicz? In what way should Abdulla include them in his novel? Did they need to be there at all, or would the book then be too wide-ranging, causing it to crumble under its own weight?

He had to keep Oyxon in mind. After all, she was the heroine! He mustn't get so carried away with Witkiewicz and Stoddart that he forgot about the Emir's widow.

Nodira and Oyxon's relationship was what needed exploring. He had written enough about their life as Emir Umar's wives, but when, after Umar's death, Oyxon was wondering if she might leave the harem, why hadn't Nodira offered her any support? After all, everyone knows that power at that time rested with Nodira, not her teen-aged son, even if the latter had been newly enthroned. Still wet behind the ears, Madali preferred to amuse himself with his racing pigeons and leave the tricky matter of government to his mother: why was he allowed to make passes at his stepmother? Surely Nodira only had to say 'Boo!', and this thieving little tom-cat would have come to his senses? This was something that bothered Abdulla. It wasn't easy to penetrate a woman's mind. He might have sought his wife's advice, if she hadn't been jealous of his heroines… well, might it be precisely such jealousy that made Nodira happy for Madali to keep salivating over her junior wife? Or might she have actively encouraged the affair?

> Heaven and time set up a hundred intrigues thanks to jealousy,
> My glazed eyes stare amazed at the beloved.

After all, if jealousy could rouse heaven and time to intrigue, how much more easily could it move a human heart?

Shortly before the news of Gulxaniy's ill fate reached Oyxon's ears, she discovered that her father had been dismissed from the sinecure which Emir Umar had given him. Other officials were now in charge of weights and markets. After this snub, G'ozi-xo'ja took to his bed. But that was only the start of his troubles.

One day, after afternoon prayers, one of the older harem women came to Oyxon's quarters and announced, 'His highness the Emir is permitting your highness to go and see her father. The royal carriage and horses are harnessed, be ready quickly!' Oyxon didn't bother with perfume or make-up: she picked up her veil and made haste to get into the carriage that stood just outside the door. She threw her veil onto the wooden seat and ordered the driver, 'To my father's house!' The horses snorted and the carriage, with its decorative cloth roof, moved off. When they were approaching the gates of the harem palace, a strange noise was heard coming from the square. 'I hope the road isn't blocked, just when I'm in a hurry!' Oyxon shuddered with irritation.

Then the harem gates opened and the carriage moved out onto the square. In fact, the square was packed with a great number of people yelling and shouting: their attention was focussed on something. Had the Emir put on a public feast? Or was there a tightrope performance? But then there would be trumpets blasting away and drums beating. Leaving the palace fortifications, the carriage jolted over the brick-paved road down towards the square. Oyxon quietly lifted the silken curtain on her left. An enraged mob and a pile of stones met her gaze, and her heart missed a beat. Still, she could have passed on without looking, she had enough stones of misery hitting her own head: did her heart have room for a stranger's grief? But Oyxon held out for only an instant, before moving to lift the curtain on her right. In the middle of the square, a young man was kneeling, his white shift stained with bright red blood; his head was bare and his hands and feet were bound. The low-lying sun blinded Oyxon, and she wondered if what seemed like blood was just a reflection of the red evening light. Again, her heart sank.

The carriage had reached the square by now and had begun to pick up speed, drawing nearer and nearer to the middle of the square, where the young man knelt, his body upright. The red light spilled into the carriage, flooding Oyxon's eyes. Where had she seen a sun like this before? It was then that the crowd started screaming, and the stoning began; one missile clattered against the carriage's shaft. The driver lashed the horses, and they galloped off. Oyxon was paralysed with fear, she could not move her hand to lower the curtain. She saw the youth, in the middle of the square, bound and now crumpled. The red light throbbed between her temples. It was her cousin Qosim. 'God help me!' Oyxon cried, crumpling to the bottom of the carriage in a state that looked like death.

Her sisters came from Shahrixon and spent two months

looking after her. Nodira gave her a room in her own
chambers. Only her body returned to the world; her
soul did not. If only she could pour oil over herself and
set herself on fire. Or she could say she was going on an
excursion to see the spring tulips, then throw herself into
the Qora-daryo river. But either the human heart is as
tough as rock, or quite the opposite: after six months she
began to think about her paralysed father, her little brothers. It was then that something happened to counter this
treacherous world, this world of the flesh: Oyxon let her
eyes weep tears.

Even after she had recovered, Oyxon did not return
to her quarters: sensing the fears that besieged this junior
wife, Nodira set aside a room in her own house for her and
let her have more maidservants as well as Gulsum. Oyxon
could now bar her door and lock herself away. And there
was much to hide away from.

Perhaps because they were both the offspring of sayids, or because they shared the hostility of the late Emir's
senior wife, Oyxon had become close to Zubayda, the late
Emir's youngest wife. The girls spent hours in each other's quarters, gently mocking Nodira's sumptuous poetry
evenings and devising their own satirical lampoons. True,
Oyxon never breathed a word to Zubayda about Qosim:
this secret she kept buried deep in her heart. But Zubayda
was in every other respect Oyxon's confidante.

One evening, Oyxon arrived outside Zubayda's chambers to find Madali behaving as outrageously as he had
with her. Either because Zubayda was afraid of him, or
because she felt so downtrodden, she failed to object to his
lust. Oyxon didn't have the courage to burst in, but nor
could she retreat: her legs were paralysed. Thus she witnessed Madali the Fornicator committing rape.

Afterwards, Oyxon attempted to get Zubayda to say

what was on her mind. For some time the girl refused to speak out or complain: she remained mute. But one evening the sayid's daughter broke down, weeping on her fellow-wife's shoulder until all the bile in her heart was released. Just as they were cursing this scoundrel to hell, Madali burst in on them, reeling from drink. 'Have you been giving away my secrets?' he slurred, and then, before Oyxon's very eyes, hacked Zubayda, with her finely plaited hair, to death.

News of this grisly deed was only spoken in hushed whispers within the palace, but many of Madali's other acts reached the ears of the common people, who condemned him in the strongest terms.

Emir Umar had had a butler called Bahodir, whose wife had been Madali's wet-nurse. The butler's children were thus the young Emir's milk-brothers and -sisters, and Madali used to call Bahodir his father. This milk-father's wife was a woman of peerless beauty and charm. Spurning every form of honour and decency, Madali laid his lecherous hands on the foster-mother from whose breasts he had drunk.

As soon as Bahodir discovered this affair, he renounced his property, his wife and his children, washed his hands of the whole thing and set off for Bukhara. Once Bahodir was out of the picture, Madali moved his foster-mother into the chambers of the late Zubayda.

As if these foul acts were not enough, he recruited two whores, Xushhol and Bibinor, and gave them complete power over the Fergana region. They could go into any respectable house they liked and commandeer the most chaste veiled virgins for the harem. In a short time these debauched creatures became so rich from bribes that even the most respected and influential Beys of the Emirate of Kokand could not compete with their turnover, their splendours and their weaving looms.

Oyxon saw all of this, and she hid from it, like a hare that comes across a nest of vipers: she could do nothing but hope to wait it out, helpless and powerless.

One day Nodira decided to hold an enormous poetry contest in memory of Emir Umar: it was open to poets from far and wide, even those from foreign countries. When the day came, everyone in the palace rushed to the beautifully decorated hall to see Nodira, the queen of poets. Oyxon also appeared, dressed rather modestly out of consideration for the senior wife. What luxury, what splendour!

Nodira had introduced an innovation, one which seemed almost sacrilegious to some: the guests at the feast sat on their haunches around low tables with carved legs. Poets and scholars moved as they wished from table to table, trying the roast quail, baked pies flavoured delicately with herbs, tiny dumplings from indented wooden bowls. Cupbearers and serving maids carried jugs of fruit juice, and wines were served in crystal chalices specially imported from Iran. A great number of singers and musicians were gathered there; their tender music stirred the most deeply hidden feelings. Finally, a visiting Maulana declared the contest open by reciting in Farsi:

> A hundred different dishes have been made
> And countless tasty treats already laid –
> The mind is overwhelmed at such a spread
> And all the ceremonial greetings have been said.
> Appetite is boiling in the pot of pleasure.
> And nature is loath to give any measure.
> Rich foods and sweets crammed down by the hour,
> Then nature's inclined to turn somewhat sour...

Oyxon herself was similarly inclined; she was so revolted by all this nauseating falsehood that she slipped out of the hall and returned to her chambers. The party was in full swing, and the music and singing were audible even in her quarters. Oyxon found a bowl of sour milk and drank her fill of it.

All the maidservants were busy in the hall, leaving Oyxon alone in Nodira's apartments; she sat there, absorbed in her own thoughts, when a silhouette suddenly appeared at the window. The cry rose to Oyxon's lips instinctively: 'Gulsum!' Her voice was suffused with fear.

The door screeched open, and the silhouette spoke:

'There inside the window is my noble beloved,
At night she drinks wine, by day she is my desire.

'I made up that couplet especially for you. It came out well, don't you think?' Madali closed in on his stepmother.

A scream for help died on Oyxon's lips; she lay there like a corpse. Before returning to the poetry contest, her rapist recited over her, 'Your father is a G'ozi, a warrior for Islam; you too are fighting for your faith.'

———

In an attempt to overcome his anxieties, Abdulla sat down next to Professor Zasypkin and came straight to the point.

'There's something I want to ask you: did the Russians really attempt to save Colonel Stoddart?'

'As far as I know,' the professor said, 'an envoy was sent from Bukhara to Saint Petersburg in 1840, where he was received by Tsar Nicolas I and given a document addressed to the Emir of Bukhara. This document expressed approval of relations between Russia and the Emirate of Bukhara, and Russia's Tsar announced that he was sending an ambassador to Bukhara along with a specialist in mining work, which the Emir had requested.

'As a supplement to this document, the Russian vice

chancellor also wrote a number of letters to the vizier of the Emirate of Bukhara, in which the points of Tsar Nicolas I's document were repeated, with a request to treat their ambassador favourably, and to provide him with the means to return home at any time he wished.

'It was in this letter that we find Colonel Stoddart mentioned. The vice chancellor put it this way: "As is well known, his highness the Emir was intending to send the Englishman Stoddart together with the ambassador who has arrived here, but, fearing an attack from Khiva's forces, abandoned this intention. In accordance with the mutual treaty between Russia and Great Britain, this intention is very precious to us."

'"Since these former anxieties have vanished, we hope that his highness the Emir will now put his intentions into action. To deliver the said Englishman to us, the most convenient route is via caravan to Orenburg. There, a bold military governor will know what measures must be taken."

'I don't know exactly which words were used, but that was the general sense.'

Abdulla was convinced of the accuracy of Muborak's tale, whereas the professor, when he stopped at this point, had given more of a lecture than a narrative. Now he bent down close to Abdulla's ear and reverted to his odd bookish Uzbek: 'Why don't you ask the Kosoniy about the questions that interest you? He's an extraordinary historian.' Zasypkin pointed out the man who had complained about sweeping with two brooms and stacking them vertically.

'Of course, of course. I don't know him, though…'

'Come, I'll introduce you.'

The professor went up to a rather sullen-looking old man with bushy eyebrows and a wan face under a black and white skull-cap.

'Mr Kosoniy, allow me to introduce comrade Qodiriy,

the writer.'

Occupied by his own thoughts, the learned man looked slowly at Abdulla. 'Qodiriy the writer? I've heard of you,' Kosoniy said in a bored tone. 'I don't read modern writers, though; I read in the old Arabic script.'

The professor again put a word in: 'Comrade Qodiriy is writing about events of the nineteenth-century: about Madali and Nasrullo. I thought that the two of you could have a talk.' The professor went discreetly back to his place.

'So you're writing about the Khanate of Kokand and the Emirate of Bukhara? There's Abdulla Amiriy-Lashkar's *History of An Underage Prince*; also relevant is *An Account of the Blessed City of Kokand*, also *The Ghazi's Anthology*, Hakim-to'ra's *Historical Selection* – wonderful sources. Niyoz Muhammad of Kokand wrote the *History of Shah Ruh*, a book which was lithographed in Kazan.'

Kosoniy listed so many books, so many sources, that Abdulla's head began to spin. The older man seemed to sense this, fell silent for a moment, and gave Abdulla a penetrating look. 'To put it bluntly,' he concluded, 'there are a lot of books, and life is short.'

'You must have heard what Muborak was saying?' Abdulla enquired.

'No: what did he say?' asked Kosoniy with interest.

'Nothing much, just one thing,' said Abdulla, 'that the English came to Emir Nasrullo's palace.'

'Nasrullo wasn't the only one: your blue-eyed Englishmen also paid a visit to Madali in Kokand and Mirzo Rahim in Khiva. And it wasn't just the English, the Russians were at it, too; they were constantly rushing back and forth.'

'Did the Russians mean to rescue the English envoy Stoddart?' asked Abdulla, narrowing the focus of his enquiry.

'He may have called himself an envoy, but he was noth-

ing but a spy. Emir Nasrullo quickly saw through his slanders
and loose talk. He threw him in a pit a couple of times,
put him in a dungeon. The Russians sent their envoy to
rescue the unwanted colonel. In the circumstances, Emir
Nasrullo showed the Englishman a lot of favours, he gave
back the possessions he had looted from him. At that time,
Nasrullo had already decided to attack Kokand, but that's
a different story. The Emir's vizier meant to take Stoddart
into his own custody, but your Englishman begged the
Russians to intercede and ended up safe in their embassy.'

After this brief narrative Kosoniy gave Abdulla a fixed
look. 'It's time for afternoon prayers, I think. Are you a
believer, or one of the moderns?'

'Praise be to Allah,' Abdulla responded. Kosoniy slyly
winked at him and said, 'We're lacking a congregation, but
the two of us together will have to do: God will forgive us.'
He pointed to the space next to him, and Abdulla kneeled.

One peculiar thing about Uzbeks is that even if you are
a leading writer there will be plenty of people who don't
recognise you, and, of those who do, plenty who don't
give a damn about you. On those rare occasions when you
do come across someone who recognises you, it's you who
has to do the bowing and scraping. That was the position Abdulla found himself in. He was over forty now, but
compared to Kosoniy he was a young man, an apprentice,
a student: to put it in a nutshell, he felt half-baked. Once
prayers were over, he sat there nonplussed.

Kosoniy ended his prayer with the brief invocation and
then looked at Abdulla.

'Allah, hear our prayers!' he said.

'May He receive them!' Abdulla responded in kind.

'May I ask sir, what sins have brought you here?'

'Who knows?' Abdulla shrugged. 'I haven't been told yet. It must have to do with my writing. And you?'

'I opened a schoolroom to give lessons in the Arabic script,' said Kosoniy. 'Children don't get taught the old script in school these days. Our language and our history are being erased...'

'Language and culture is one thing, but there are a few things in our history that might indeed be better forgotten.' The words were out of Abdulla's mouth before he realised that this could be construed as the opening salvo in a familiar argument.

'You sound like one of those *jadid* – the new Uzbeks, as they call themselves. We had one in here before, Fitrat, his name was; we argued with him about the dispute between Europeanisers and traditionalists until our throats were dry. He'd even written a book on the subject, *A European's Dispute with the Bukharans*. A reputable scholar, but a bit too acerbic, a bit too highly-strung. Come on, let's drop it; you're obviously a proper Muslim, there's no need for us to disagree.'

'As you wish,' Abdulla sighed. Indeed, meetings at the Union of Writers had taught him the hard way that the saying 'Truth is found through argument' led to nothing but headaches and concealed hostility.

'It's best if we confine our conversation to historical topics,' Kosoniy suggested.

'Very well,' said Abdulla. 'You were saying that the English sent spies to Bukhara: what about Khiva and Kokand?'

'Oh yes, they sent their spies there too. The English first arrived in 1840 and presented himself to the vizier Mirzo Rahim as an ambassador. In their meetings, he tried to show Britain as well-disposed to Muslims, unlike treacherous Russia. "Russia has been at war with Turkey and Iran," he said, "and now the Tsar may well have evil intentions against you."

'After listening to what this rogue had to say, Mirzo Rahim wrote a letter to Emir Nasrullo, demanding he set Colonel Stoddart free. But this wasn't because he was at all intimidated by the false ambassador's empty threats to move the British armed forces from Afghanistan to Bukhara. He was more worried by the Russians; it was in the hope of establishing relations with them that he offered to help Stoddart. He sent an envoy to Bukhara. But the reply he got from Emir Nasrullo said, in essence: "The kindness and humanity which Stoddart would be shown in Khiva, he is here receiving tenfold."

'That was when the English took the decision to send their own Arthur Conolly via Kokand to Bukhara...'

—

Oyxon had been raped, her spirits trampled down. Now, at her wits' end, crying with pain, she heard from her father in Eski-Novqat that the anniversary of the martyred Qosim was being commemorated. Then, as winter gave way to spring, she realised that she was pregnant. She tried to weep, but had no tears; she wanted to kill herself, but she had long ago turned into a living corpse; she thought of fleeing, but her legs were too heavy, as good as shackled. She became addicted to beer and wine. 'My head is all dark,' she said as she drank. 'I'm living in a poem.' At other times, to get the delirium out of her brain, she would sit for hours with her maid Gulsum moving the pieces in a game of chess.

Nodira was disturbed to see her junior wife, a lady more nobly born than herself, surrender to fate in such a manner. She did her utmost to restore Oyxon to a fulfilling life: she held splendid poetry evenings, put on brilliant banquets, but none of this was of any use.

As soon as Madali heard that Oyxon was pregnant, he made the decision to marry her. He summoned his loyal council of clergy, and proposed a fatwa that would permit the marriage. But even among those lax and corrupt mullas, there was a one who had the courage to say: 'Your highness, sharia law holds a special provision for this affair. If you were to enter into marriage with your stepmother, then in the view of all four versions of Islam you would become an infidel. It would be better to carry on your former habit, fornicating with this lady in secret: it is permissible to get carried away. If your secret is revealed, you may be accused of fornication, but that is preferable to an accusation of apostasy.'

However, another mulla came out with a contrary opinion. 'Many clerical councils look down equally on fornication and apostasy. Be it great or small, a sin proven by fact is unforgivable and equal to apostasy.'

Madali could see that the clergy were making it impossible for him to get his own way. 'I summoned you to find a way around these stupid prohibitions. All you've done is shower me with pious rubbish, wasting my time. Idiots! Dried-up turbans!'

That same day, he went to a gambling house, one his father had frequented before him, where his friend the Chamberlain, a gambler and hashish-smoker, saw that the Emir was in a bad state.

'Ah, why make a mountain out of a molehill?' the Chamberlain said after Madali had told him of his trouble. 'Fine asses they are, your clergy! After all, when we were in our mother's womb, didn't we have a prick? And when we were being born, that prick touched our mother's vagina. Why is it permitted then, but forbidden later?'

This irreligious talk was like balm to Madali's ears.

'Thank God! Nobody's ever before said anything so apt to me,' he said, taking the gold-embroidered gown off his shoulders and giving it to the Chamberlain.

A few days later Madali summoned the newly appointed Sheikh ul-Islam, clerical judges, muftis and other clerical lawyers, and again proposed the question of his marriage. This council was new to sacred beneficence and loyal to Madali. 'In our opinion, this proposal is acceptable: based on the sharia, we issue a new fatwa in the name of the venerable mufti of the clergy, in the name of the venerable Kokandi, in the name of the venerable Qu'ranic teacher.' They issued it reinforced with seals and enormous flourishes of signatures.

True, according to popular rumour, one furious sheikh rode up on horseback to the Emir's palace, all the way in to the throne room without dismounting, where he told Madali to his face: 'You're a dog, you fornicator!'

The palace courtiers expected Madali to call for the executioner, but the young Emir restrained himself and only said, quite softly: 'If I am a dog, sir, then kindly leave this dog's land!'

After all this had happened, Madali acquired the nickname, whispered in the wind, of Madali the Motherfucker.

CHAPTER 5

PIGEON RACING

Madali the Fornicator had made the art of pigeon racing his hobby. It is generally known that since time immemorial this hobby has been popular with the rulers of Fergana. Shah Babur in his *Babur-nama*, writing about the death of his father, the great Umar Sheikh Mirza, says this:

> At this period, the uncanny event I mentioned occurred over Axsi fortress, which overlooks a deep ravine; there were buildings around the fortress. On a Monday, the fourth day of the month of Ramadan, Umar Sheikh Mirza was pursuing his hobby when he, with his pigeons and dovecote, fell into the ravine and in mid-air was turned into a gyrfalcon. He was then thirty-nine.

Madali the Fornicator collected pigeons in any province where fine specimens were to be found – Kashgar, Bukhara or Shahrisabz – and kept busy flying them. He was so devoted to this hobby that he left state affairs to his Chief Counsellor, while he had a decrepit-looking dovecote reconstructed with porcelain and silver nails, each compartment lined with ceramic tiles.

He was especially fond of two fluffy-legged pigeons, one white, the other black. The other pigeons were given ordinary grain, but these two he looked after himself, spoiling them with shelled pistachios and ground almonds with millet. This diet made their plumage shine, and the sight of them somersaulting in the air was irresistible.

Madali called the black pigeon after himself, and the white one 'Oyxon'; he delighted in watching them coo at each other, and would order his servants to bring him his side drum with the fish-skin head, gold rings and a hoop made from vines and ivory, on which he played an accompaniment.

The Emir devoted a great deal of time to training these two doves. He tied a silk thread to their legs, first teaching them to fly only over the roof. When they could be made to return to their perch by blowing a whistle and jerking the thread, he gradually lengthened the thread. The doves soared and tumbled like kites, but like kites, they were never truly free: after a while, Madali would always blow the whistle and reel the thread back in. That was it. The doves would fly back to their pistachios, their sunflower seeds and crushed almonds.

The doves must have been quite devoted to their master; he could send them off from as far away as Shahrixon or Axsi, and still they came back to the palace in Kokand. How strange, then, the Emir thought, that he could not manage to win Oyxon's affection! She had borne Madali two sons, but no motherly feelings towards them had been aroused in her breast. When she got drunk, she would scornfully berate Nodira, 'Look after your bastard grandsons!' Once or twice, when Madali had beaten her and dragged her around by the hair, it took all Nodira's strength to pull them apart.

Perhaps that was why Madali found consolation only in his doves, so beautiful, so biddable. Only when he sent them flying into the heavens could he forget the woman he told himself he loved and who he cursed for not loving him.

The last and coldest week of winter passed: it was early March. Abdulla had begun to lose count of the days he had spent in prison: he knew that it was now March only because he'd heard so from the others. What he'd lived through in those days, who his companions and neighbours had been, what he had talked about and to whom, how many dreams and thoughts he had mulled over, all that God alone knew; but one day after his evening prayers, he heard his name called out. After waiting for two months, anyone might be expected to conclude that nobody had any need of him; now, after being summoned when he least expected it, Abdulla was in a state of panic. Why had they summoned him? Had his hour struck? Might they possibly be setting him free? Nice surprise, hey, Qodiriy? His heart was racing. Unable to feel his legs, he stumbled towards the door. 'Hands behind your back! Follow me!' But surely, if he'd been going to be released, the young soldier wouldn't have used the familiar form of the verb?

The door slammed shut behind him. It was the first time in two months that Abdulla had left his cell. The soldier made him walk ahead. The corridor was much less dimly lit than the cell, and Abdulla was dazzled. The corridor was unbelievably long: on his first day he hadn't realised this, probably because of the beating he'd had at the hands of Vinokurov. He couldn't help clenching his fists. The soldier may have noticed, for he poked Abdulla's arm with his rifle: 'A step to the left, a step to the right, and I shoot.' Along the corridor there were more prison guards with weapons at the ready. Not a single Uzbek face among them. When Abdulla was almost at the end of the corridor, the soldier deftly pushed a side-door open. 'In!'

If he hadn't seen the table and two chairs there, Abdulla might have assumed the room was a slaughterhouse, but those familiar objects meant the nightmare eased, his heart slowed and he felt calmer.

'Stand in the corner!' a guard ordered. Abdulla meekly obeyed. Suddenly he recalled his Russian-language school, where he had first encountered that same expression. The memory aroused a smile which he had trouble suppressing.

At certain moments, time seems to show you its silhouette. Like a nimble snake, time moves from the caged lamp on the sloping concrete ceiling, down the pistachio-green walls to the cement floor, where it slithers away, swift as if scalded, out past Abdulla through the open door.

'Isn't time a bloodthirsty dragon?' Abdulla thought, before the sound of steel-tipped boots broke the silence. Crunching the cement floor as they came, the steps became more and more unmistakable, until Abdulla heard behind his neck a familiar voice: 'Abdulla Qodiriy? Prisoner Qodiriy, sit down!' it yelled. Abdulla quietly turned towards the voice, and saw, next to the warder holding his weapon at the ready, the interrogator Trigulov. Nodding at him as if to an old acquaintance, Abdulla sat down. Trigulov went round to the head of the table and sat on the opposite chair. He stretched and yawned.

'Good: are we going to confess?' he asked.

'To what?' Abdulla asked in genuine amazement.

'You can drop the naive act for a start!' The interrogator brandished the thick folder in front of him. 'The proof's all here. Talk about your counter-revolutionary anti-Soviet nationalist activity!'

'What counter-revolutionary activity, what anti-Soviet activity?' said Abdulla, uncomprehending.

'I'm the one that asks the questions here, not you! You're here to give the answers, you nationalist swine!'

'Show some respect!' Abdulla ventured, thinking to appeal to the interrogator's sense of reason. 'There are laws for everything…'

'I'm the law here! Don't you understand? You haven't seen what I can do to you yet, you counter-revolutionary filth! I crush people like you and throw out the bits! Hey, fuck your long tongue up to your blue veins!'

It was plain to see that here in this place, sense and reason, justice and faith would get Abdulla nowhere. However much this humiliation pained him, he had to observe the Russian saying, whip lashes are nothing to a sledgehammer. Abdulla shut his mouth and locked himself away in his own thoughts.

Madali the Fornicator dragged Oyxon about by her hair, slapped her face twice. 'Say you're sorry! Say you're sorry!' he said, forcing her to kneel to his mother Nodira. Oyxon froze: 'You bast..., you bast...' she whispered. When Madali heard this, he became hysterical and started kicking her. 'Shut your mouth! Shut up!' he roared, while Oyxon rolled about where she lay, her raven-black hair dishevelled. 'Infidel... Fornicator...'

'Come on, you're a sensible man. A prominent writer, no less! You want to get back to your children, your family. If you cooperate, I'll see to it personally that everything gets straightened out. You were arrested in 1926, too, and released safe and sound. This time we'll do the same. But only if you cooperate. Come on, let's begin with 1926. What were you arrested for then?'

Only Satan has no hope, Abdulla told himself, and began giving brief, succinct answers to the interrogator's questions.

—

Abdulla was left in peace for a few days. Knowing that he had been summoned for interrogation, the cellmates that he had become friends with came up one by one to see how he was. Abdulla didn't divulge anything to them. They tried their best to distract him, but Abdulla, in his nervous state, kept silent: he was waiting for his name to be called out again, and pondering what answers to give to the questions. What had they put into that folder? Who had been writing anonymous letters about him? What was he being accused of? He remembered reading articles in *Red Uzbekistan* and *Pravda of the East* about Cho'lpon, Fitrat and others, before they had been arrested. 'Enemies of the Uzbek people!', 'Death to the Traitors!': the titles had stuck in his mind.

Ever since 1936, his once devoted acolytes had been writing about him in ink of the deepest red: 'Abdulla Qodiriy's creative path'. Accusing him of not understanding the people, of being ignorant of the latest 'literary devices', they said his images were 'atypical', petty-bourgeois, and not proletarian. That was bad enough, but they also accused Abdulla of plagiarising his novel from the Arab writer Jurji Zaydan.

These thoughts numbed Abdulla's mind. Then Kosoniy, who had been sick and had just come out of the prison hospital, came groaning towards him: 'Friend, you look as if you're in the dumps...' Abdulla suddenly felt ashamed. Instead of sitting there looking sorry for himself, he should have gone over to the old man and asked how he was. Just because of a scoundrel of an interrogator, he had forgotten how to show human sympathy. In all sincerity, he asked the learned man for forgiveness.

'We can take a spoonful of bile out of your blood,' the old man joked. 'Come on, let's have a frank talk, otherwise you'll be sulking, and I'll be getting anxious. Last time you were wondering about the English spies. I've made a note of what I wanted to say about Conolly. The Chorasmian historians were knowledgeable people: they didn't leave out the tiniest crumb of information.

'When the English saw that Stoddart was sometimes free and sometimes imprisoned in Bukhara, they decided to send one of their cleverest and most skilful spies, Captain Arthur Conolly, to rescue him. But this time they had Shah Shujah's ambassador accompany him and, secondly, they planned to get the Ottoman sultan, Russia and the khans of Khiva and Kokand to exert pressure.

'Mirzo Rahim of Khiva received Conolly, but in the middle of the conversation he put a provocative question to him: "Tell me, who is more powerful, the English or the Russians?"

'"Both states are extremely powerful. England is older and wealthier, but Russia is now a great power and is constantly getting mightier."

'"What are their relations like?"

'"We are trading partners. Friendly relations are in the interests of both states."

'"Tell me then, what is Russia's attitude to us?'

'"According to the latest information, you have taken some Russians prisoner. Russia is angry about this. This year they haven't had enough camels to mount an attack, but they'll be looking to seize the first opportunity.'

'"If we returned most of their prisoners, would the Russians still have a quarrel with us?'

'"As far as I know, the prisoners were just one of their many demands. Perhaps you could fill me in as to the details?" But Mirzo Rahim refused to be drawn.

'"God alone knows what the Russians want."

—

'God alone, indeed,' Kosoniy repeated with pensive irony. Then he shook himself and looked at Abdulla. 'Let's hear something from you now, writer.'

Abdulla thought for a moment, then began his story: 'Let me tell you of an event I've read about in a number of books. At that time, the nobles of Kashgar wrote a letter to Madali of Kokand, complaining of the Chinese government's oppression and asking him to send Jahangir, descendant of the seventeenth-century Uyghur ruler-saint Afaq Khoja, to unite the Muslims against the Chinese. Madali summoned his counsellors, who cautioned that the peace treaty between Kokand and China meant this plea should remain unanswered. Then the Kashgar nobility contacted Jahangir secretly, and arranged for him to be smuggled out of Kokand with a number of his devoted followers.

'In a very short time, several thousand Muslims had rallied to his banner, bringing with them rifles and artillery, and Jahangir led them to Kashgar. When the Chinese government got wind of this, they went on the attack. A battle took place atop the mud walls of a saint's tomb, and Jahangir's army was defeated. Many men were killed, the survivors fled for their lives. Jahangir himself and forty of his close companions hid in the tombs of a nearby cemetery, where the ghost of Afaq Khoja appeared to Jahangir and reassured him of his ultimate victory.

'The fact of the matter was that before the battle Jahangir had sent a summons to the Jumbag' tribe; the latter answered willingly, though it was after dark when they arrived at the battle. Rallying the remains of Jahangir's force, they successfully routed the Chinese army. But they were worried by Jahangir's absence, and sent out search parties.

'Then one of the searchers spotted a tomb that he had

passed. But Jahangir and his forty companions seemed to have decided that this might be a cunning ruse by the infidels, and stayed put.

'When it was dark, a servant disguised as a beggar was sent out to assess the situation. When the servant saw that it was really Muslims who were celebrating their victory, he couldn't help bursting into tears of joy. The victorious Jumbag' people saw him, and said: "Why these tears, aren't you happy, Muslim?" It took him some time before he was able to speak to them coherently. Then Jahangir went from a tomb to the throne. Thus the hated Chinese rule in Kashgar came to an end, and a victorious Muslim government was installed.'

—

The next day, 10 March 1938, the interrogator summoned Abdulla again. This time he wasn't taken to a prison room, but upstairs to one of the NKVD offices. Although the curtains were drawn over the window, the sunlight still indicated that the outside world existed. You could hear the cooing of doves, people yelling, vehicles roaring, the sounds of life coming from the NKVD courtyard.

It was spring. When Abdulla was a young man, this was the season when he devoted himself to writing. The days began to get warmer, the flesh of tender greenery emerged from the soft earth, the apricot trees flowered the colour of roast maize, buds unfurled: all this inspired him. Later, as time passed, he changed, and began to write and plan in the long winter nights. Spring was the time to start gardening, tending the vegetable plot, and looking after the bees. Now, the vines were already bursting into leaf, filling with life-giving sap. Surely his eldest son Habibullo would have recovered by now: would he have staked the vines? For a moment Abdulla pictured his vineyard, the ladder placed against the stakes, the pure blue sky, and something else that touched him to the quick, but then he shuddered, and focussed on his immediate surroundings.

Trigulov was sitting with another NKVD man, another accomplice who had taken part in searching Abdulla's house. Without looking up from his papers, Trigulov pointed to a chair. Abdulla went towards it and sat down.

Trigulov dismissed the soldier who had brought Abdulla there; the soldier saluted and left. There was a silence. Abdulla used the time to look at the furnishings of the office, hoping to learn something about the character of its incumbent. After a moment or so there was a knock at the door, and a different soldier brought in Usmonov, the head of the Agitation and Propaganda Department of the Uzbek Central Committee. Once upon a time he had been a short, squat, flabby man; now he seemed to have become even shorter, thin and shrunken, and his eyes darted about like mercury. Poor wretch, was Abdulla's immediate thought; he was like a cushion from which the stuffing had been removed.

Trigulov gestured Usmonov towards the chair opposite him, then told the soldier to wait outside before addressing the two prisoners:

'Do you know each other?'

They nodded.

'Who is this man?' Trigulov said, pointing at Abdulla.

'The writer Abdulla Qodirov... sorry, Qodiriy...' Usmonov gabbled. The thought flashed through Abdulla's mind: they've broken him.

'And who is this?' Trigulov put the opposite question to Abdulla.

'Comrade Usmonov, head of the Agitation and Propaganda Department of the Uzbek Central Committee...'

'Former head!' Trigulov interrupted sourly. 'And now an opportunist Trotskyist. Isn't that so, Citizen Usmonov?'

'Quite so, comrade interrogator,' Usmonov replied with quiet desperation.

'Right, Citizen Usmonov, do you know Abdulla Qodiriy well?'

'Comrade interrogator, I know Abdulla Qodiriy as a convinced, hardened, counter-revolutionary nationalist. He has hypocritically concealed his bourgeois-nationalist nature and has deceived Soviet power…'

Usmonov said all this without drawing breath, without looking at Abdulla; he recited it quickly, like a boy scout reporting to his team leader.

'Tell me, Qodiriy, has Citizen Usmonov told the truth?'

'In part,' Abdulla said. 'I may, at one time, have been a nationalist, but I have never been a hypocrite and I have never deceived the Soviet government.'

'Usmonov, does Qodiriy's statement satisfy you?'

'No, it absolutely does not. Qodiriy is lying.'

'Very well: Qodiriy, do you admit your guilt?'

At that moment Usmonov clutched his chest and sobbed. His face and hands were wet with sweat. Trigulov called for the soldier standing outside, and shoved a document he had just written towards Usmonov, as fast as if he'd burnt his hand. 'Take him away,' he told the soldier, 'and see that the awkward sod doesn't drop dead on the way.'

Next, Trigulov showed Abdulla the record of the exchange which had just taken place, officially designated a 'confrontation'. 'Sign here where it says "Recorded accurately, and read by me".'

'Why should I put my signature to this pack of lies?'

'Listen, my boy, you're pushing your luck. Didn't every word written here come out of your own mouth? It did.

So sign it! You'd better not mess me around; if I get angry, I'll bring your wife here and pull her panties off.'

Abdulla bit his lip until it bled, and signed the papers.

Trigulov pressed a button on what looked like a radio. 'Next!'

Shortly after that, there was a knock at the door and Beregin came in. This was a man who had recently been working in the Central Committee, but who had previously been Abdulla's publisher. A charismatic man, for whom Abdulla had once had great respect.

'Do you know each other?' Trigulov began. Beregin, who hadn't yet sat down, and Abdulla, who had risen to greet him, simultaneously confirmed that they did.

'Who is this man?' the interrogator asked Abdulla.

'Qurbon Beregin, former director of the Central Committee Culture and Education Department.'

'Correct, accused Qodiriy. Who is this man?'

'Sitting opposite me is the writer Qodiriy...' Beregin fell silent. Abdulla looked at his dimmed and shrunken eyes. He knew him as a courageous man, not the type to sell out. But Beregin would not look at Abdulla, and went on to say in a voice without intonation: 'I know him to be a prominent participant in the bourgeois-nationalist stream of Uzbek literature. He has written major novels in an anti-Soviet nationalist spirit and has likewise helped our organisation to prepare professionals who were nationalists. He himself has never renounced his nationalism.'

When Abdulla heard these words, the image of a drowning man clutching at straws came to mind, and he recalled Cho'lpon's poem 'A Hand Stretched Out'.

Could he be pulled out by my hand?

Was he going to cast me on the land
To save me from the savage sea?
Could a man as deeply lost as me,

With his weary eyes, take my hand?

But Trigulov cut him off mid-thought: 'Accused Qodiriy, do you confirm this part of Beregin's statement?'

Abdulla felt a surge of pride in that poem, in that language, in that wretched people, in his own honest life; he lifted his head and said, 'Yes, I confirm it.'

And so I began to turn the pages
Of the tragic story of the ages.
Nervous, irritable and worse,
As I slowly find the mood for verse.

The clarity and firmness of this response made both the interrogator as well as Beregin take notice. A stray spark seemed to flash in the latter's dimmed eyes.

Trigulov hastily penned this response down on paper and leapt ahead in pursuit of his goal: 'Comrade Beregin, tell me, was the accused Qodiriy a member of your anti-Soviet nationalist organisation?'

The interrogator's sharp tone made Beregin relapse to his previous abased state, and his voice was flat when he replied, 'Yes, he was a member of our anti-Soviet nationalist organisation, headed by Akmal Ikromov and Fayzulla Kho'jayev.'

'I repudiate that part of Beregin's statement. I have never in my life been a member of any organisation.'

'Beregin, Qodiriy denies it. Are there any proofs of his membership of an anti-Soviet bourgeois-nationalist organisation? Perhaps in written form... can you cite them?'

'In 1932 Fayzulla Kho'jayev proposed that I should republish works by Abdulla Qodiriy written in an anti-Soviet nationalist spirit. In particular, he mentioned the novel *Past Days*. He drew up a contract with Abdulla Qodiriy and took it upon himself to send these works abroad. Kho'jayev would not have taken this much trouble over an outsider who was not a member of our organisation. I have kept written proof of this.'

'What do you say to that, accused Qodiriy?'

'I have never been a member of any organisation, including these anti-Soviet bourgeois-nationalist organisations. I'm a loner, an independent writer.'

'Take that man of yours away!' Trigulov snapped, pointing to the crestfallen Beregin.

> I began to tell these plaintive tales
> Of hands stretched out from the shore,
> Of untrodden paths through lonely vales,
> Where I seek my desire or more.

—

By the time Abdulla got back to his cell, everyone had lain down to sleep. Had those two short confrontations really gone on for such a long time? In his mind Abdulla went over and over the questions and answers, unable to get away from one particular thought: these men had been crushed, ground down to powder. But what did Trigulov's threat, 'I'll have your wife brought here!' tell him, what did it indicate? Could he have found evidence of Sunnat delivering a letter once a month? Should Abdulla write to Rahbar and tell her to move to the country? God forbid: those people were capable of anything. Prisoners would tremble with fear as they told stories of Room 42: might that have been the room where Vinokurov had bruised Abdulla on his first day?

If they brought his wife in and violated her, could Abdulla stand it? What could he do to stop it? He might attack one man, but there were a thousand of them. He had said at the time that he would kill Vinokurov, and meant it; but he hadn't done it, and his desire for vengeance had melted like the winter's snow.

'God forbid! God forbid!' Abdulla prayed as he lay down. Rahbar had to move to the country, otherwise they would crush Abdulla with their pestles and mortars. But could he stand up to them on his own, could he summon the strength?

—

They said things to frighten him: 'We'll make you watch us behead the servants who came with you!' Then it was, 'Become a Muslim!', forcing Stoddart to recite the *shahada*. Even this did not seem to be enough: they made him undergo circumcision under the supervision of the chief Islamic judge. The poor colonel, a man getting on for fifty, his 'reed' broken, wrapped in a blanket, stayed in the house of the chief of police; he pressed a piece of burnt cotton to the wound until it healed. After that he was put in the care of the Chief Minister, who housed him in his handsome guest chambers in the fortress.

The Chief Minister took an instant dislike to Stoddart. 'He's not a real Muslim!' he told the Emir. 'He pisses standing up!' This time the colonel was imprisoned in the 'Cold House', a damp and airless room more like a deep pit, where the prisoners were given only water.

Fortunately for Stoddart, one of the jailers turned out to be a pleasant man: he helped the colonel smuggle letters out of the country by passing them on to one of his servants, who crossed the border to Afghanistan hiding in a camel's pack-box.

The only difference between their situations, Abdulla thought, was that Stoddart at least had his country's support.

His thoughts turned to the wretched Beregin again. Abdulla hadn't known Usmonov quite so well, so his provocative language hadn't stung him so badly, but Beregin was someone he'd respected. True, Fayzulla Xo'jayev had singled out Abdulla and Cho'lpon for his approval, calling them 'the pride of our literature and language' and had given them money every time he saw them. In 1932 he had in fact said, 'It would be good to publish *Past Days* in Kashgar, in the Arabic script.' But how could anyone talk of an organisation? Did an Uzbek mixing with Uzbeks now count as being a member of an organisation?

—

Who else was Abdulla going to be confronted with? The specific charge was membership of an anti-Soviet nationalist organisation. Had Abdulla been recruited, like a bride who was married off without being aware of it? Writers are a crazy lot, you probably couldn't confront them with each other; if you have to confront one, then it would have to be with politicians and officials like the men he had faced the day before. Which others might they try? He had to make use of Sunnat, and get Rahbar to leave for the country as quickly as possible.

The door opened and Abdulla's name was called out again. Gathering his wits, putting his hands behind his back, he was about to leave when he saw it wasn't for interrogation or confrontation but for a shave and a haircut.

Abdulla remembered the barber, and gave him a friendly greeting as he sat down on the stool. Why decide to give me a haircut in the middle of confrontations? he wondered. 'What more is there to discuss? Has the case been decided? Am I being prepared for execution? If they're going to shoot me, would they sit me down first to tidy me up? Am I being made presentable before they take me to one of the higher-ups? Who?

In prison every tiny thing takes on boundless importance: who, when, where, for what reason? Question after question worms its way into your brain. Turning it into a something like a silkworm hatchery, your thoughts are the mulberry leaves the larvae feed on, punctured as if by an awl. The Jewish barber wouldn't talk in the presence of the guard, but his thoughts seemed to seek expression in his constant sighs, his sniffling and the smacking of his lips. He must have a lot on his mind, too, Abdulla decided.

A shave and a haircut were, perhaps, the only service in prison provided by someone else. The barber's warm hand brushing his nose and ear reminded Abdulla of his mother Josiyat washing his hair when he was a child: he couldn't keep the tears from filling his eyes. The barber took a white napkin and discreetly wiped this moisture away while powdering Abdulla's face.

'Thank you,' Abdulla said as he got up from the stool.

'You're wel…' the barber began, but was instantly cut off by the soldier.

'No chatting!' the Russian barked; he quickly led Abdulla away, not back towards the cell but in the opposite direction. Where is this guard taking me?' Has my time come, then? In such a senseless way?

The soldier pushed open a door on his left. 'Comrade Captain, I've brought him,' he said as he saluted. When he entered the room Abdulla clenched his fists reflexively: Vinokurov. His heart began to pound. His face first turned pale, and then flushed bright red. He's going to hit me, he's going to hit me, he told himself, mentally preparing to hit back.

'Sit down,' Vinokurov barked, pointing to a chair by the desk; 'You're free to go,' he told the soldier. The soldier retreated out into the corridor, letting the door slam shut behind him. Abdulla's last link with the outside world was broken.

He would grab him by the throat! He would go for

his windpipe. As Abdulla sat down, the blood rushed to his eyes.

Suddenly Vinokurov stretched out a calloused open palm to him: 'Forgive me, Abdulla!' he said.

Abdulla was stunned: he felt lost. Was this a dream, or reality? Had this devil some trick up his sleeve?

'Forgive me, Abdulla,' the guard repeated in a cracked, muted voice. 'I hit you too hard... I'll understand if you can't forgive me. But we're human too, you know. I'd been drinking too much that day. I'd had it up to here,' he said, pointing to the throat which Abdulla wanted to sink his teeth into. 'I don't get a New Year's break, not even a single day off. Nothing but arrests and arrests and knocking people about.

'Last Sunday I tied up my vines and secretly went to church: 6 March was Shrove Sunday. One of my writer friends was there. Apparently, you and he studied together in Moscow. He said your work is wonderful, he praised you to the skies. He even told me you'd attended a Russian-language school... How did you end up packed off here as a nationalist?

'You should write about us, Abdulla, about the fear we feel in our throats: today it's you here in jail, and tomorrow it's me they'll put inside...' Vinokurov struck the breast pocket of his tunic with his clenched fist.

Could he be drunk? Abdulla wondered, but the only smell he could detect was that of tobacco.

'You still don't trust me, Abdulla, I can tell by your eyes. All right, don't. But to make up for the wrong I've done you, I can offer you my help. True, you understand, I can't let you out of here. I'm only a pawn in this game. But tell me if there's anything you want to say to your friends.'

A whole swarm of butterflies emerging from their cocoons – no, a whole flight of doves flew out of Abdulla's mind. He was utterly bewildered: he couldn't understand whether this world was one of truth or of lies.

'All right,' said Abdulla. 'But in Russian fairy tales you get to make not just one, but three wishes. So here are my three little wishes. First, tell Beregin I don't bear him any grudge; second, let Yunusov know I have his gold watch; third, the most important, tell Cho'lpon that his wife came to ask me to write a letter to the authorities, but there were no authorities left to write to. I did write to Aleksei Tolstoy, but I received no answer.'

'Then might you forgive me?' Vinokurov asked, taking his calloused hand off the table, while still holding it palm up in offering.

—

After such a full day, sleep was the last thing on Abdulla's mind. Was Vinokurov merely pretending to be an ally? If it was a trick, what could be the point of it? The jailer had offered to help Stoddart and his people out of self-interest, but Abdulla didn't have any hidden gold, nor did he have the Queen of England to back him. If Vinokurov was looking after his own interests, there was no sign of it. Seemingly, he was just a man asking to be forgiven.

Did Abdulla have to accept his apology? Time may have healed his physical injuries, but what about his moral suffering? If it was true that Abdulla now held the upper hand, should he have used it to his advantage somehow? If Vinokurov could arrange a confrontation with Beregin, or Cho'lpon, then it might be possible to put some trust in him.

'I met a writer in church,' he'd said. 'He praised you to the skies.' Which writer? A Russian, obviously. Could it be Borodin? But Borodin was a Tatar. Nikitin? He's a militant communist, wild horses couldn't drag him into a church.

Sheverdin, then? That could be it... Sheverdin was from Samarkand, but had studied in Moscow. Abdulla had seen him once or twice there at the houses of other poets. In 1931 he wrote a fairly good review of *Past Days*, and had contributed a foreword to the Russian edition of *Obid the Pickaxe*. But he was a Party loyalist; still, who knows, after hearing unbelievers like Vinokurov talk about Shrove Sunday, a writer might well go to bow and cross himself.

The order rang out: 'Turn over onto your left side!' Sniffling and groaning, the prisoners obeyed. Abdulla spared a thought for Jur'at, who had disappeared without trace after he had been taken out for interrogation a fortnight previously. He'd like to ask Vinokurov what had happened to the big man. After Jur'at, the notorious thief Gena of Tashkent had been moved into this cell with five of his underlings, and the thieves had soon asserted a hierarchy over the 'politicals'. 'Now we'll show you what life is like in a prison camp,' they said, and that was the end of the Chaghatai Symposiums. Jur'at would have had something to say in such circumstances: 'The sparrow bust its gut when it tried to walk like a stork.' Now anything sent from outside, tobacco or the like, was swiftly confiscated by Gena and his men. The most nourishing food was reserved for them. When sugar was handed out, they took it as a tax. The politicals were mostly elderly intellectuals, so the thieves had only to say 'Chuh' and they would give in. When Abdulla was off being interrogated, they'd even taken Professor Zasypkin's gold-rimmed glasses.

Should Abdulla try to get involved in this business? Could he ask Vinokurov to do something about it? Don't be naive, Abdulla! You're as easy to catch as a cat having its fur stroked! Mightn't Vinokurov himself have arranged for these thieves to be shoved in with the 'politicals'?

Could he ask Vinokurov to arrange a visit from

Rahbar? Would such a thing even be within his power? He had himself said 'I'm just a pawn in this place.' No, Abdulla was raving. Never mind bringing his wife here, she had to be sent off to the country, well out of sight. As far away from Samarkand as possible.

———

On the evening of 13 March Abdulla was taken again to Trigulov's office. The setting sun soaked in through the drawn curtains, penetrating the secret space of the room. Seeing sunlight for the first time in two and a half months, Abdulla had to screw up his eyes, and his flesh shivered. But an inexplicable feeling of joy arose in his heart.

This time, as well as Trigulov and a sergeant, a third person was in the room. Abdulla allowed himself a frivolous thought: They're going to marry me off again! The third man turned his face towards Abdulla. He vaguely remembered this person, his smooth round face, his broad shiny forehead, his barely discernible staring eyes, the imperceptible smile always ghosting his lips. Where had he seen him before?

Sitting down, Abdulla remembered: he was a teacher of literature at a pedagogical institute. In 1935, when this institute had been set up in Tashkent's Mirobod quarter, a group of writers had come there for a meeting organised by this teacher, whose name was…

'Do you know this person?' asked Trigulov, nodding towards Abdulla.

'Yes, it's the famous writer Abdulla Qodiriy.'

Abdulla was embarrassed. If he was asked now, what name would he give?

'Do you know Nazrulla Inoyatov?' asked Trigulov, almost as if he had read Abdulla's thoughts.

'Yes,' Abdulla hastily replied, and trying to overcome his

embarrassment, said with more respect than was needed: 'He's a teacher of literature at the pedagogical institute.'

The slight smile did not leave Inoyatov's smooth face, and this too gave Abdulla an involuntary spark of joy.

'Inoyatov,' said the interrogator, 'do you confirm what you earlier admitted, that you were part of an anti-Soviet bourgeois-nationalist organisation?'

Nazrulla's face didn't change. 'Yes, I confirm everything in full!' The smile still lit up his face.

'What have you got to say about the accused Qodiriy?'

'I know Abdulla Qodiriy as a dyed-in-the-wool nationalist. Our organisation valued him highly as the most prominent representative of the Uzbek bourgeois-nationalist movement. Because his works served the aims of our organisation. I have no doubt that, even now, Abdulla Qodiriy is of those same opinions.'

So much for you! thought Abdulla. They've really worked you over!

'Accused Qodiriy, do you admit this?'

'I admit the nationalist part. Up to 1932 my writing was nationalist. I don't deny opposing the Soviets – then. But in my novel written in 1932 I had moved to support the Soviets...'

'Inoyatov, were you a member of the nationalist counter-revolutionary organisation "National Independence"?'

Inoyatov didn't frown even for a moment. 'Yes,' he said softly, 'I was a member.'

'Was Abdulla Qodiriy also a member of "National Independence"?'

'According to one of its leaders of the organisation, yes.'

'Very good. Qodiriy, do you admit to being a member of this counter-revolutionary organisation?'

'No, I don't. I've never been a member of any organisation. I have never even heard about this so-called "National Independence", never mind been a member of it; as I've explained, the nature of my writing means I couldn't have had any connection to it.'

'You can see, Inoyatov, that Qodiriy denies what you yourself have demonstrated and shown. How do you explain this?'

'Abdulla Qodiriy is lying. The leaders openly and publicly talked about his being a member.' Inoyatov's face maintained its friendly smile, while Abdulla's was frozen in disbelief: the promise of springtime had disappeared without a trace. Abdulla was prepared to accept the charges of nationalism, of counter-revolution and a thousand other political crimes, but the charges which this man had sprung on him – an accusation based on lies – was something he was not going to put up with under any circumstances.

———

The first time he was arrested, Abdulla had ended his last speech to the court with the following words:

> I request the judges of this just court: even if I have been slandered in every possible way, personally, and by falsification, because of a misunderstanding, I shan't be acquitted, but will be found guilty. At the very least, perhaps because of the prosecutor's negative attitude, you may also intend to sentence me to the highest measure of punishment. Since there isn't a trace of malice in his heart, a simple, naive, young man with a clear conscience much prefers death to such humiliation. As certain persons will have hoped, I have already died a moral death. Now physical death no longer frightens me. This is what I await and this is what I request from the justice of the court.

Now he was utterly bewildered, as he ran these words through his memory. Preoccupied by his thoughts, he didn't even notice that Inoyatov had been taken away, and that his place had been taken by the teacher Yunusov.

'Qodiriy, do you know this man? Who is he?' Trigulov had to repeat his demand.

Abdulla shuddered. He leapt to his feet and tried to offer his hand to Yunusov. Trigulov took fright.

'Get back down!' he yelled, his voice breaking. Abdulla hastily complied.

'I repeat, Qodiriy! Do you know this man?'

'Yes, I know him. How are you, sir? This person is the teacher Yunusov.'

'How about you, Yunusov, do you know this man?'

'Yes, I do. This is the writer Abdulla Qodiriy.' The teacher's face was wan and had lost all colour. He had been one of the very first to be arrested. I expect he's been inside for a year now, thought Abdulla. What vicious things have they done to transform a man who used to be so full of life? It must have been in the 1930s when the two of them made a trip to Samarkand and Bukhara. Abdulla was looking for material for a story about a concubine, and Yunusov, then a respected teacher, was collecting folk stories. Abdulla remembered his constant loud laughter as they trekked round the towns and villages with Elbek and Cho'lpon. Now this same man was swollen like a pumpkin, like a man stung by wasps.

'Yunusov, under the leadership of the enemies of the people Akmal Ikromov and Fayzulla Xo'jayev, you...'

The same old record on the same old gramophone: how many hundreds of times has he repeated such interrogations? After so many times, you might well begin to believe it. Saying 'halva' once doesn't bring a sweet taste to your mouth, but after a hundred times, your teeth will start sticking together.

'Qodiriy, Qodiriy! Do you confirm what Yunusov has said?'

'Yes, I do. Some of it. Yes, I have written from a nationalist point of view, but I've never been a member of any organisation. My novella *Obid the Pickaxe*, which I wrote in 1932, is very pro-Soviet…'

'You're lying! You finished writing *Obid the Pickaxe* in 1935 when it was published. But you promote nationalistic ideas in it. Do you admit your guilt?'

'I consider the novel *Obid the Pickaxe*, which I finished in 1935, excuse me, to be neither nationalistic nor anti-Soviet.'

'Yunusov, tell me, what nationalist anti-Soviet organisation was Qodiriy a member of?'

'Both Abdulla Qodiriy and I were members of the To'ron society in 1919. He took part in that organisation's meetings.'

'Qodiriy, do you admit this?'

'I do not.'

No, Abdulla thought, staring at Yunusov's exhausted expressionless face, Vinokurov didn't pass on my words to him, and even if he did, my friend has already said goodbye to this world. Without bothering to check what it said, Abdulla signed the piece of paper that the interrogator put in front of him.

The confrontations meant Abdulla had missed the midday and evening meals of soup and scraps, and nobody had thought to put a bit of bread aside for him. If only there were something to chew on, he thought, as he resigned himself to fasting until breakfast the next morning. Abdulla went back to the confrontations as he sucked his teeth. Then he recalled what he had been thinking about and went over to Kosoniy.

'I hope my question doesn't seem rude, but have you ever in your life sold anyone?' he asked.

'In what sense? Do you mean as a slave-trader?

'No, no: in the sense of telling lies about them.'

'Then, my dear boy, you really must cast the noose a little wider,' Kosoniy began. 'In al-Ghazali's book *The Revival of Religious Sciences*, the third chapter 'Way to Perdition', the section 'The Tongue's Calamities', there are twenty misfortunes that can befall because of one's tongue. Among them are empty talk, spite, debauchery, reciting poetry, scolding, cursing, telling lies, gossiping, slander and similar misfortunes. We need to talk only about the couple that interest you. When you say "selling people", primarily you would have spiteful talk in mind. Spiteful talk, in al-Ghazali's opinion, comes from being inclined to arguing and protesting. As Allah's Prophet, peace be upon him, said in one of his hadiths, "Anyone ignorant enough to indulge in spiteful talk incurs the wrath of Allah until he renounces it or dies." There is another misfortune of interest to you: the inability to keep a secret. In our prophet's hadiths it is said, "A man who says something in an assembly while looking around him is entrusting his words to his listeners." According to tradition, Muawiya told a secret to Walid son of Utbah. Walid went up to his father and said, "The Emir of the Faithful has told me a secret, let me reveal it to you." His father said, "Don't tell me under any circumstances! Secrets must be kept secret. Don't be a slave to sin!" There's another misfortune relevant to our conversation: that of telling lies. "Preserve yourself from lies, they are the same as debauchery, and both of them are hell," said our magnanimous Prophet. Yet another: "Lies are one of the doors to quarrelling."

'Luqman the Wise told his sons, "Son, preserve yourself from lies, because they taste better than sparrow meat. Not many people are free from them." But in sharia law, there are situations where lies are permissible. Our magnanimous Prophet apparently said, "If a man has put things right between any two persons, or has spoken well to exalt what is good, he is not a liar." Ato ibn Yasar relates, "A person asked our Prophet: 'Messenger of Allah, may I tell my wife a lie?' The Prophet decreed, 'There's nothing good about lying.' The man asked, 'May I promise to give my wife a few things, one way or another?' The generous Prophet decreed, 'There's no harm in that.'"

'These things lead to what we call a happy relationship, my dear boy. But this not all there is to it. As for the misfortune of gossip, we must include this in the question you asked. In our merciful Qu'ran's Sura al-Hujurat, Allah the all-Highest commanded: "Do not say bad things behind one another's backs. Would any of you like to eat the flesh of his brother when dead?" Our magnanimous Messenger has said, "On the night I was ascending to heaven, I saw a group of people who were scratching their faces with their fingernails. I asked the angel Gabriel, 'Who are these people?' and Gabriel said, 'These people were gossiping and revealing each other's secrets'." Al-Ghazali cites eight reasons for gossip: vindictive denial, trying to please someone, taking advantage of something, blaming another person for one's own disgrace, showing off, envy, playing a joke, or mocking someone, belittling someone…'

'For the sake of good relations, so that I don't cause you any upset, I shan't speak to you of other misfortunes of the tongue, listed by al-Ghazali, which include invention, literature, poetry; let me just cite a legend from Kashifi's *Education of the Just*. "The tyrant Hajjoj was threatening everyone. When it was the turn of a mulla, the latter responded: 'O Emir, don't kill me, because I have been truly faithful to you!' 'What have you actually done for me?' Hajjoj demanded to know, and the mulla said, 'Your enemy so-and-so was gossiping about you and spoke about your debauchery. I forbad him to do so and protected you from being abused in the future.' When asked for a witness, the mulla pointed to another person present at this session. This person confirmed his story. 'Yes, he was telling the truth, he saved that man from the sin of gossiping!' Hajjoj then questioned this second man. 'Then why didn't you join him in opposing my enemy?' The reply came, 'Because I, too, am your enemy. It was out of the question for me to take your side!' After that Hajjoj ordered both men to be released – one for his loyalty, the other for his honesty. And thus the saying came about: 'A lie can sometimes serve a man, but the truth will serve him better.'"

—

That night, hunched over with hunger, listening to his empty stomach rumbling, Abdulla wondered: had Kosoniy actually answered his question? Then his thoughts went further back to the teacher Yunusov. Anyone writing in their native language was by extension a nationalist. If a man didn't love his people, if he didn't value his own language, why would he become a writer? But this didn't mean believing that one's own people and one's own language were the only ones in the world! Every trader praises his own wares in the market. Only, what was meant by an 'organisation'? True, many years ago Fitrat had formed a group called the Chaghatai Symposium, but if those utterly frivolous sessions of literary chat and gossip could be called an organisation, then all of Uzbekistan was up to its neck in them; every tea-house a rebel headquarters, every town quarter where people wore national headgear a military detachment.

Abdulla remembered the hospitable household of a friend who lived in the same quarter, and who, when he came across Abdulla's son Habibullo in the street, used to tell him, 'Go and tell your dad: "The drums are banging, to say that for those who have money things are fine; for those who haven't, too bad to tell." He'll understand.' As soon as Habibullo passed this on to his father, the latter would stop work, because he knew that the message meant this friend was coming back from work at the theatre with a group of friends: poets, singers, lute players and comedians. Abdulla had an image of himself going to the house, seeing the pond in the middle of the yard, a weeping willow by the pond and a burnt-clay bench surrounded by peonies. Then someone would pick up a tambourine and, after Abdulla had shaken all the assembled guests' hands, the singer, tightening the cummerbund around his waist, seemed to project his voice not into the air, but inside himself:

> Let the morning breeze hear my plea,
> Let the morning breeze hear my plea.
> Her eyes bright as Venus, her hair wild and free
> The grace of a cypress, brows black as can be!
> Let my prayers be heard by this shimmering beauty.

Everyone found his words heartbreaking. Who but an Uzbek could understand it?

Two days ago, Abdulla had started to weigh up Nodira's sufferings and torments. From the day she had ended up in the palace as first wife, she'd been seen by the whole world to be in a relationship with a nonentity. Her husband Emir Umar had impregnated her three times, in quick succession; taken two other wives; and made her a widow at thirty. All she had experienced with her husband was some ten marriage feasts and fifteen banquets. His departure had smashed her responsive heart, like a porcelain bowl, in two. If only she could see his offspring turn out like the husband whom she could no longer see. But they couldn't stand the sight of one another; they were at daggers drawn.

She sent them on errands in different directions: she was a loving mother.

The eldest, Madali of the blazing eyes, persecuted all those close to him and repelled all good men. 'Don't interfere! I know best!' – he refused the advice of all but intriguers and prostitutes. Scholarship died out, poetry faded. As if that wasn't enough, he had to have whatever he saw. When a viper-like passion burned his soul, nothing could restrain him from forbidden vices: he drank wine, he smoked hashish, he gambled, he raced pigeons, he fornicated with his former wet-nurse and married a woman who had been his father's wife.

His mother was shattered. To whom could she complain? Who was there in this world who might listen to her? Nodira could confide the pain and the misery that had befallen her only to Kokand paper.

> Oh heaven, you killed my very soul, you did.
> You made me weak by leaving me, you did.
>
> My cries are deadly arrows, each one –
> You turned my body to a bow, you did.
>
> Heaven has not been loyal to you, my soul –
> Though you tried and questioned it, you did.
>
> You stained with tears each inch of my cheeks.
> You whitened my face with grief, you did,
>
> You turned a tryst into a parting, oh heaven.
> You made spring die into autumn, you did.
>
> You have suffered so in secret, Nodira.
> Your lonely heart from strangers, you hid.

—

The next day, when Abdulla was expecting a confrontation or an interrogation, and trying to follow the thread of logic in Nodira's poem, a thought occurred to him that made him shudder inwardly. After two and a half months in prison, with nothing but time on his hands, there was one topic he hadn't even considered to himself, let alone discussed. Uzbeks have a custom of never calling a scorpion a scorpion: instead, they call it 'the thing with no name'. Was that why they could talk freely about Emirs Nasrullo, Umar and Madali, Shah Dost Muhammad and even Queen Victoria, but wouldn't dare mention *his* name? In the first draft of *Obid the Pickaxe* he did mention *his* name in two or three unimportant passages. The interrogators did not hesitate to bring up the names of those 'notorious enemies of the people' Ikromov and Xo'jaev, but they never once let their mouths utter *his* name. Yet *he* was the heart and soul, the beginning and the end, of all the things taking place around him. It was *he* who had sent Abdulla here, *he* was the reason why the interrogators were questioning Qodiriy, it was because of *him* that friends turned into enemies, and conspiracies were dreamed up by the interrogators. What was *his* mysterious secret? When Abdulla had gone on a trip to research Nasrullo's history, the Tajik writer Sadriddin Ayniy had passed on the following anecdote. At one of the ceremonies in the Kremlin, *he* had got up, lifted his glass and proposed a toast: 'To the great Tajik nation, its extraordinary art and literature, to Omar Khayyam, Rudaki and Firdousi...' Ayniy was so gratified at this rehabilitation that he shouted out in broken Russian, 'Bravo. Old literary critics caput!' Everyone was dumbstruck. But *he* seemed not to have noticed anything: he lifted his glass and said again: 'Because of Omar Khayyam's, Rudaki's, Firdousi's and Jami's literature...' And Ayniy, filled with pleasure and enthusiasm, again shouted out, 'Bravo. Old literary critics caput!' The rest of the gathering was as silent as the grave. The learned Ayniy boldly strode towards *him*. Utterly bewildered, *he* began to back away, pretending to be suddenly occupied with something he had dropped, and vanished under the table.

Two burly bodyguards seized Ayniy and twisted his arms behind his back. *He* pretended to have found what *he* was looking for and returned to *his* seat. Later *he* sat down next to the Tajik Party secretary and asked, 'Who was that old man? What was he shouting?' The secretary explained, 'He was a former elder. Up until today, the poets of old were said to be feudal reactionaries. He was so pleased and inspired by what you said, that he applauded "Bravo!"' Then *he* stood up, went up to Ayniy, and gestured at the guards to let him go. 'What is your name?' *he* asked. Ayniy bowed. 'I am the impoverished Sadriddin Ayniy.' Then *he* gave Ayniy *his* hand and said, 'Let's get acquainted: Jughashvili.'

—

'That man of yours was a coward. A cowardly heart and a pock-marked face. The coward raises his fist first, as they say.'

Ayniy considered other writers to be mere scribblers, beneath contempt, but he was fond of Abdulla: he wouldn't even offer tea to the others, but when Abdulla visited his house in Bukhara he laid on generous banquets. In a sense, he considered Abdulla his teacher, as the latter had helped him polish his Uzbek. Given the man's sarcasm, it was just as well that he'd migrated to the rocks and mountains outside Stalinabad. If he had stayed here, wouldn't he now be confronted with others, who would certainly remind him of his indiscretions: 'What rubbish you used to come out with!'

Abdulla got no sleep that night. By morning, his whole body was shaking, small blisters breaking out on his hands: finally, he realised what was going on. It was the return of an old illness, which he'd had when he used to keep bees. His flesh itched, then it turned red; after that, it was covered in a khaki-coloured rash which finally hardened into watery blisters.

'It's because you've been eating too much honey,' the local Uzbek doctor had told him at the time. But what honey could he have been eating now?

Ever since Muborak had become chief storyteller to Gena of Tashkent, scuttling nervously at the thieves' beck and call, Abdulla had barely been able to share a word with him. Yet wasn't that Muborak standing over him now, hands on hips in his unmistakable Bukharan style?

'Is something wrong, brother? You're awfully quiet – perhaps a story would cheer you up? I've got one about Emir Nasrullo; one of our people wrote it. "The Emir was handsome, quite impressive, with black eyebrows, though he was of middling height. His cheek sometimes twitched, he had a low voice and a forced smile. He dressed like anyone else. He took away the mullas' authority and put himself in charge. When he came to the throne he killed all his brothers, except one who ran away.

'He issued a fatwa: "The Emir is the shepherd, the people are the sheep. The shepherd does whatever he likes, including taking a man's wife if he wants her, for the shepherd is shepherd to the ewes, too." The Emir had four wives, and four hundred concubines.

'It's said that the Emir was born to a Persian concubine of his father Emir Haydar. The Turkmen have a saying, a horse and a donkey give birth to a mule; an Uzbek and a

Persian give birth to an Emir.

'The Emir had concubines of all nationalities, but he never touched women descended from Moses.

'The Emir's power was unlimited. No letter came into or out of the Emirate, not even one between husband and wife, without the Emir being aware of its contents. He even recruited poor street urchins to tell him what was being said in the markets. What husbands said to their wives, what masters told their servants: everyone started to spy on each other.

But the Emir was also spied on...'

Either Muborak was called back to Gena, or he finally noticed the severity of Abdulla's situation; at this point, Abdulla himself was not able to tell. By nightfall he felt he was on fire, by morning he was becoming delirious. He could respond neither to Gena's orders nor to Sodiq and Muborak's care. Someone banged on the door to summon the doctor; it took more than one injection for Abdulla to regain consciousness. When he opened his eyes, he saw the prison doctor taking his pulse.

'You writers are a rather fragile lot,' the doctor commented. 'Diabetes, tuberculosis; though I'd say you were a bit tougher, Qodiriy, judging by your pulse. It will all go smoothly for you now; here's some Brilliant Green ointment for you to put on your sores. But keep them away from water.' He turned and whispered something in Sodiq's ear.

Writers with diabetes? Cho'lpon was diabetic: what was happening to him in this place? Abdulla struggled to remember what he'd been thinking about before he fell ill. Was it about poetry as the bedrock of Uzbek literature, and how he'd planned to demonstrate this by including a lot of

poetry into his new novel? His mind jumped ahead: 'Who tricked all *those people*? Cho'lpon, of course: a poet. Using *those people's* language for their slogans and panegyrics, he laughed out loud at them. Abdulla began to remember:

> Interpreter for millions – a new kind of poet
> Dedicated to today
> Every year, he makes a new melody
> Everywhere, every farm, every factory
> Every worker is singing this melody.
>
> At the start of every worker's shift,
> He sings all the words out quietly
> And a pioneer – who never met a poet –
> Is praising the lyrics eruditely.

And in another poem, 'Remembering the Sun of the Caucasus', he says something that hints at a certain Caucasian:

> The lord of this land is an entirely new man.
> Will his pride let him ask help heaven's help? No!
> He'll order the heavens to work – that's his plan
> If you're angry, yes, light your fire – go!
> But he'll make the flames dance to his tune
> You'll follow his ways, all too soon.

So here it was, the bountiful harvest of everybody, put away into the state's innumerable prisons. Oh Cho'lpon, shouldn't you have left your last line as:

> He'll make you his prisoner, soon.

Again, Abdulla remembered with regret his intention to write a novel about Cho'lpon. Even after Cho'lpon had returned from Moscow, the Red writers gave him no peace. Abdulla could still picture the unfortunate poet at the Uzbek Writers' Union meeting of spring the previous year, left to the mercy of the dogs.

'Comrades, forgive me, but for reasons beyond my control I am always made to speak when I have a headache. It may be because of this that I can't express my thoughts as I wish. Firstly, I must answer three questions posed in comrade Beregin's speech. Then I'll say what I have to say. Comrade Beregin was right to point out my mistakes, I freely admit these mistakes to everyone here.

'I must settle my accounts with respect to G'ulom Zafariy. This man once came to look for me in the Union's garden. I shall explain why this person came to see me. I have diabetes. I have been to Moscow and other places for medical consultations, seeking treatment for my illness, but not finding any good medicine anywhere, I turned to folk healers who recommended black mulberries as a medicine. Although I consider myself an intellectual, I trusted this advice and asked Zafariy to bring black mulberries with him. He came after I'd gone to bed, when it was night, and so he went to see So'fi-zoda.

'The next day I was invited to So'fi-zoda's, and that's where we talked. It was then that Comrade Shams informed me that this business was wrong. His rebuke was justified. That was when I stopped meeting the two men. After these words, Comrade Shams summoned me for a reprimand. I then told Comrade Shams that I needed people's criticism and help in order to correct my own mistakes. This is the second time that I've been advised about correcting myself.

'If anyone thinks that we can correct our old mistakes in just two or three days, then you are wrong. You can correct us by summoning us, helping us to understand and then bringing us into the fold of society. We carry on with our path to life. But if there are obstacles on that path, you are answerable.'

Sitting among *those people* Abdulla saw that Cho'lpon

was mocking them, and he himself laughed without show-ing it. This poet, monumental in his originality, was greater than the rest of the Writers' Union put together, yet *they* behaved as if they were the wise fathers and Cho'lpon a wicked child. In one of his satirical articles of the 1920s, Abdulla had wished that Cho'lpon were more devilish; now the poet appeared to have taken this advice to heart.

'How have you been educating me over these past twenty-one years? I'm still not a member of the Union of Writers, who knows why: I applied to join a long time ago. Because of this, my works have to be closely analysed. A month after my arrival here, my poem 'The Lute' was published. If I am a nationalist, if I am so reprehensible, then why have you made this work available without a foreword? A foreword is clearly necessary to give me a rap on the knuckles, and establish the proper context so young people won't be led astray. And then there was my novel. It sold out, but try to find anyone who owns a copy! That novel, too, came out without a foreword. That was six months ago, and still no one has picked up their pen to write about it. I did read one article in *Young Leninist*, but that was nothing but praise, which is obviously no good to me. In Moscow, we were meant to read this work at the Union of Writers so I could get some constructive criti-cism. Eleven people came to the first session, seven to the second, and by the third we were down to four. None of the Union officials bothered to show up. And as a soci-ety we should be educating a former nationalist! Mistakes aside, I simply can't continue working under these condi-tions.'

Some of the simpletons claimed that Cho'lpon had sided with the Soviets. True, when Abdulla first read a poem from the much-denigrated *A Capella*, his hair had stood on end. After everything that had happened,

Cho'lpon had dedicated it to the Party's xvIth Congress. But then, after a dozen lines of Party waffling:

> For the sixteenth time, we're gathered here
> We have grasped the very roots of life!
> We are the power that moves life!
>
> The living will not turn around
> The dawn will not turn red
> Death will bless us on the ground
> Darkness will salute from the poor instead
> To the lords of the lie.

'You're skating on thin ice, friend!' was Abdulla's immediate thought, but to himself he said, 'Good for you, poet!'

And these were only what had been published. There were also unpublished poems, one of which Abdulla memorised:

> Here you see a map of Moscow:
> Grab it by the handful now!
> Hey, look there's Moscow's daughters' hips.
> The capital's fake and luscious lips.
> Can't swallow, 'til you give a piece.
> Her plan is grasping and increase.
> Bit by bit, she pockets more.
> What will she give back? She'll make you sore.
>
> Moscow's not the place for you, man
> Oh, the thirst of 'Cotton-stan'!
> Sixty years you've been her friend
> But 'take, not give' is Moscow's end.
>
> A'lamov wrote Ikromov a letter
> But it was lost under a car, they say.
> That's why your life will never get better.
> But what's wrong with A'lamov's way?
>
> Make a space for the new Uzbeks' game:
> They're all overjoyed, to 'Make Their Own Way'.
> As for you, there's 'Reproof!' and 'Shame'

If you're breathing... just die today.

Who told you to be born Uzbek in the end?
Why, 'Misfortune' is the Uzbek's dearest friend.

———

On 20 March, Abdulla – barely alive – was taken again
to Trigulov's office. This time he was confronted with an
irrigation expert who worked in Kazakhstan. After the
revolution, Abdulla used to encounter this man now and
then at gatherings of friends in Tashkent. But it was the
same old record, the same old song: 'I have known Abdulla
Qodiriy since 1919 as a dyed-in-the-wool nationalist. He
and I were both members, first of the 'National Union',
then of the 'National Independence' organisations'.

What has happened to poor 'To'ron'? Abdulla wondered sarcastically.

'I've never been a member of any organisation! I've
never been a member of any organisation!' All Abdulla
could remember was repeating this several times: then his
head began to spin and he lost all his strength. When he
opened his eyes, he was back in the cell and Sodiq was
pressing a wet towel to his head. He became delirious; he
was tormented by nightmares where he was either in a
palace or in a cell, surrounded by both acquaintances and
strangers. He heard musicians playing sad tunes. He saw his
mother Josiyat as a young woman, dancing with his father
in the middle of the room. 'When your father married me,
I was sixteen, and he already had a beard that went down
to his belly button!' she complained, just as she did in real
life. Abdulla grew angry. Why were his parents making
fools of themselves in front of other people? He meant to
have a stern word with them. But, bewitched by the musicians' playing, he couldn't help joining in the dance. He
started twisting and spinning, and with an enchanting girl

in his arms. He looked around, meaning to ask his Rahbar who she was. He spotted his wife sitting in a corner, but then she and the beautiful girl both vanished. Still, Abdulla went on dancing. He was stumbling and, when he looked down, he saw a silk tassel tied to his ankle. Someone was tugging at him, tugging, and whistling as they tugged…

Drenched in sweat, Abdulla woke up. Sodiq was by his head, Muborak by his feet; Kosoniy was sitting a little further away, intoning a healing prayer.

'You've had an attack of malaria,' Sodiq told him.

From that day on Abdulla's thoughts became acutely lucid. The next morning, when he was summoned to Trigulov's office, he was so weak he could barely move his legs, but his mind was as ready for battle as a charger.

'I don't wish in the least to conceal my nationalist views,' he said. 'My views on the nation were formed even before the October revolution. I was brought up in this spirit by the Islamic reform movement of Jadidism. I didn't assimilate the idea of Soviet power. I considered myself to be a national writer. My novel *Past Days*, begun in 1919 and published in 1925, was a national novel, opposed to the Soviets. In it, I described our history before the Soviets came. True, "Down with the Soviet government" is not openly said in this novel, but it is implied.' Abdulla briefly paused for breath, wiped his dry lips and continued, 'From 1926-8 I wrote another historical novel, *The Scorpion under the Altar*. In it, I distanced myself a little from the national idea; that is why the work is half-baked from a political point of view. But it does contain a certain amount of nationalism, as well as relics of the past.

'Between 1932-5 I wrote my most recent work, the novella *Obid the Pickaxe*. Its contents are close to Soviet themes: in other words, it's about a collective farm being set up. But I did express my doubts about collective farms.

If that is an offence, then I admit my guilt.'

Abdulla's throat had dried up. 'Oh, the thirst of "Cotton-stan"!' But as long as he had the strength to hold out, he was not going to ask for a glass of water from the interrogator, who had himself worked up a sweat writing down what had been said.

'Which anti-Soviet organisation, exactly, has benefited from your activities?' Trigulov asked, looking up from his papers.

'As a nationalist, I was working for the Uzbek nation, which wanted to overthrow Soviet power. My novels and press articles were against Soviet power, and in this respect my work can be used as an argument against Ikromov and Xo'jayev. It was on their orders that my writings were published and circulated on a massive scale.'

'When, by whom, and into which anti-Soviet bourgeois-nationalist organisation were you recruited?'

'I have been involved with nationalists for a very long, but I have never been a member of any organisation.'

'You're lying, Qodiriy! We have ample proof linking you to both National Unity and National Independence. How can you deny this?'

'I repeat, I have never been a member of any organisation, and nobody has ever recruited me.' Abdulla's mouth was so dry that his tongue stuck to his palate, making his speech sound heavy and slow.

'You're lying! You were present in this room when Nazrulla Inoyatov said you were a member of National Independence! The others have also confirmed this.'

'And I have denied this in their presence and in yours! Yes, I am a nationalist, and yes, I have been active in spreading nationalist ideas in literature and in the press. But I tell you again and again that I have never known or been a member of any organisation, neither National Unity nor

National Independence.

True, just once in my life, I did try to join an organi-sation – To'ron, in 1917. For reasons I do not know, they wouldn't have me. But I have had nothing to do with any of Ikromov's or Xo'jayev's organisations.' (I wouldn't be a party member, Abdulla thought of adding, nor work in the commissariats. But he held his tongue.)

Flinging down his pen, Trigulov made a show of his irritation to the sergeant standing next to him. 'At the last confrontations it was proved in full that you were a member of anti-Soviet bourgeois–nationalist organisations headed by Ikromov and Xo'jayev. Are you ever going to tell the truth?'

'They said I was a nationalist at those confrontations. I acknowledge and confirm the truth of that. But I have not been a member of any organisation. I said so at those con-frontations, and I say it again now: those statements made about me are baseless and unjust. I have had nothing to do with Akmal Ikromov and Fayzulla Xo'jayev.'

Abdulla felt his sight dimming and his head throbbing. If he had to repeat these names one more time, he felt sure his brain would burst. Was this all a delirious illusion? Was he still suffering from the effects of malaria?

—

At midnight, the questioning continued.

'We have shown you a letter written by Fayzulla Xo'jayev in his own hand, which shows that you, together with organisation member Beregin, re-published your nationalist anti-Soviet books and that they were exported abroad. Do you acknowledge this?'

'Yes, I do. In summer 1932, my work *Past Days* was set in Arabic script in order to be sent to Kashgar. This job was entrusted to Beregin. I didn't object to this, because

I had been informed before that there were people in Kashgar who had read *Past Days*. This book of mine was widely circulated there. At the time, an important trader had come to Tashkent from Kashgar, intending to talk to me about *Past Days*. I never met this trader personally, but I heard about him from a friend at Uzbek State Publishing.

'You are concealing your links with foreign intelligence services!' (Good God, thought Abdulla, as if this wasn't enough, he's making a spy out of me now!) 'Tell me the name of this "trader"! The whole truth: what instructions did you take from him to undertake your treasonable activity?'

Abdulla was dumbfounded. When he was a child, the Russian language and literature teacher at his school invented a game to develop the children's vocabulary. The first child had to devise a sentence and say half of it; the next had to catch the sense and continue, but stop before he finished the phrase. Each successive child continued, with the sense becoming gradually vaguer. By the time they reached the end of the class, it would be twisted beyond all recognition. Abdulla was reminded of this game now. Could that man, in his official epaulets, seriously believe the rubbish he was coming out with?

Or this might be a variation of the game that Jur'at had started: mixing lies and truth until they could no longer be told apart?

'Qodiriy, I asked you a question. You think you can gain time by keeping quiet?'

'I absolutely deny having any connection to treacherous activity of any sort. I've never had connections to any intelligence services, I've never ever carried out anyone's instructions. I don't know the name or title of the trader from Kashgar.'

'So you say. But you do know Zahriddin A'lam – and

we know him to be an agent of the English intelligence services. Tell us then, what was the basis of your connection?'

'As far as I know, Zahriddin is a major religious figure. The reason for my being connected with him is that I also believe in God. But our views were somewhat different. Because my religious views are peculiar to me. But I've never had any working connections with this man. I certainly never knew him to be a spy.'

'All right, in what way were your religious views expressed?'

'If Zahriddin can be counted one of the conservatives, compared to him, I am a jadid. What I value in Islam is Allah, all the rest is nonsense invented by the clerics.'

'You're being deceitful again. We know that you are a Baha'i.'

'I used to know some prominent Baha'i leaders, it's true. And in 1936 they tried to lure me into that movement. But I categorically refused to convert.' (Is there anything they don't know? Abdulla almost admired their thoroughness. Wherever three people met, the third man was one of theirs; if four people got together, the fourth would be one of theirs; if five were in the same place, the fifth would be their man…)

'In 1936 you took an active part in a meeting of religious leaders, where the politics of the Soviet government were discussed in a counter-revolutionary spirit. Do you confirm that?'

'Yes, I do. In summer 1936, at the house of a cleric who was a friend of Zahriddin, we quite openly discussed taxes and the state loans. Personally, I didn't take part in the discussion, but I fully supported what was said. If that is a crime, then I am guilty of it.'

An endless refrain again began to sound in Abdulla's

ears: *La hawla…* There is no power and no strength except with Allah…' he whispered to himself. Was this just a musical refrain, or his interminable illness plaguing him anew? He hastily tried to distract himself.

Uzbeks have a curious belief: if a woman is overly fond of a neighbour or relative, then her next child will resemble this person. The neighbour of Abdulla's family garden was an Auntie Tursun: from time to time she would drop in to see Abdulla's mother: 'Josiyat, my dear, what a fine son you've given birth to: I read everything Abdulla writes, I can't put it down! He writes as if inspired! And how does he think up all those words? To think his father was illiterate! A nightingale born of a shrike, that's what he is.'

Josiyat very much disliked this praise from 'that birdbrain Tursun', and when the latter left, the old woman would call her grandson Habibullo over and fumigate him by burning Persian rue. 'Trying to put the evil eye on my son, damn her eyes!' Nevertheless, though she was over forty, Tursun had a child by her sixty-year-old husband, and the child was the spitting image of Abdulla: he even had a pierced ear!

The older Oyxon's eldest son grew, the redder his black hair and eyebrows became, and the bluer his eyes. His movements became energetic; those who observed him compared him to a crackling bonfire. Oyxon felt flooded with love for her son, and nicknamed him her Gulxan, which means 'bonfire'. She couldn't bear to be apart from him. Her younger son by Madali was also growing quickly, becoming more and more obviously unlike his father.

Oyxon's affection for her sons grew as she spent all her time with them, telling riddles, doing calligraphy, or reading *A Thousand and One Nights*. Suspicions began to gnaw ever more sharply at Madali's heart. He would watch them furtively, then look in the mirror in his room and compare his nose and eyebrows with his sons'. After that, on the pretext of swordsmanship practice, he took both princes to his dovecote. One of them yawned, the other pinched his nose: 'Ugh, they stink!' Another day, he gave each son a drum: one started rolling it around like a wheel, the other set it like a cap on his red hair to make his younger brother laugh.

Madali was having bad dreams: in his dreams, he beat Oyxon even more brutally than in waking life, pounding her face like dough. But even that didn't calm his mind. The worm of doubt became a leech, then a snake; the snake turned into a dragon. One day he got drunk and burst into Oyxon's chamber while she was putting the children to bed; the furious Emir dealt his wife a brutal slap in the face, then waited for her to shriek. But Oyxon covered her mouth with her hand and did not utter a sound: she didn't want to wake the children.

'Tell me, you slut,' the Emir rasped, 'who fathered those children of yours?'

Oyxon's eyes froze with horror and astonishment.

'I'll cut the heads off your bastards!' he said, drawing his sword.

Oyxon shook her head and bent her white neck, as if to offer it as a replacement.

This outraged Madali even more: 'Who have you been cheating on me with, bitch?' he said, grabbing her hair.

Oyxon did not utter a sound.

'You were sleeping with Gulxaniy, you filthy whore,' said Madali, spitting it out at last.

He put the blade right against Oyxon's neck, and again she silently shook her head.

Madali struck his wife in the face with the pommel of

his sword. Blood dripped onto the bed.

'I've killed them both, Gulxaniy and Qosim; now I'll cut the throats of the lot of you!' hissed the Emir. It was then that Gulsum came in and raised the alarm. Oyxon fell upon her two children, who had woken up: a furious tumult ensued. The Emir flung down his sword and stormed out of the room.

CHAPTER 6

GUESS WHO HIT YOU

Bokhara, Dustar Khaunchy's House in the Ark,
Tuesday, 26 January, 1841

My dear Todd,

The fear of uselessly sacrificing my own life and that of the messenger and all concerned in forwarding letters has kept me strictly silent. I now venture to speak out, upon the strength of the very high favour in which I am with the Ameer; but he is very uncertain; and should a secret letter from you or Cabool now be found out, the heads of the merchant on whom it might be found, and mine, would not be worth ten minutes' purchase.

I beg of you, therefore, and Mr Macnaghten, not to send any such letters. On the 25th of October, by the Ameer's order, I wrote a letter to Government, requesting a treaty. That letter will, I trust, be the beginning of useful negotiations, and end, as everything here, to the firm establishment of British interests at Bokhara [...]

My release from all restraints took place on the 8th of October, but I was still surrounded by spies. On the 17th of January my dwelling was changed to this most agreeable one, where I was with the former Vizier five months; he is now Governor of Charjooy. My employment for the last two months and hereafter is to translate from my books, the greater part of which they have found and given me back, what I think useful for this country; and, besides this, the Ameer called for an account of European armies. On 15th of January the Ameer [...] sent a clever man to help me [...] Whatever I require in money or kind for my

work, I am to receive from the treasury, as I now do in fact.
In four days I made a looking-glass, and delighted the King
much by sending it to him. They never knew before how to
plate glass, and the Ameer has long been anxious to know the
secret of how this is done. It may seem trifling and ridiculous to
dwell on a looking-glass, but my object being his favour, I am
glad by all means to have secured it. My books have thus been
of the greatest service. I will thank you to send me as many as
possible, and some medicines and tests for minerals, or rather
for stones containing metals. Make them all up with any letters
you may have for me, and lots of newspapers, in two parcels:
one containing books alone, and the other containing the letters
and papers, and writing-paper, ink, pens and pen-knives. Let the
bearer come openly, and leaving No. 2 with his baggage, let him
take No. 1, with a letter from you to the Shekawol, requesting
him to represent to the Ameer that as you learnt from Cabool
that the Ameer required translations for his service from me, you
have sent some books to aid me, […] I wish also the following
books procured for me, and sent: Reid's *Chemistry*, Copeland's
Medical Dictionary, some books on Diseases and Prescribing […]
on Bees and Hives […]. some copperas, soda-powers, pencils,
colours and brandy (French) will be welcome. The barouche I
speak of as likely to win the Ameer's heart (to be sent after he
has apologised) […] need not have silver or gold about it, as the
Ameer votes himself a Soofee […] It should have harness for
two or four horses, separate: Indian-rubber linen folding-head
instead of thick leather, silk inside instead of Morocco lining and
cushions, and high wheels […] Very strange it may seem that after
so long a silence I should write in this manner, but I consider that
the interests of Government, especially in keeping the Russians
out of this (who hitherto have no hold whatsoever here) will
best be answered by my stopping here doing my best to keep the
Ameer to us […] for there is only one man to be considered here:
as Boney said, 'Je suis l'Empire!' […]

Thank God, I am relieved, and now quite at my ease, and, please
God, I will serve on here till all is as right as Government and my
friends could wish.

My dear Todd, yours most sincerely,

Charles Stoddart

'It's from Joseph Wolff's book,' Muborak whispered, when Abdulla had read these three torn-out sheets. 'Moshe the barber is one of us. If we ask, he can bring more...'

Abdulla was amazed. Did he need this sort of document? True, he was learning much he'd never known about the history of Uzbek khanates, but were such articles of any use for a novel he planned to call *The Harem Girl*? What could they have to do with Oyxon? On the other hand, how could he write about the nineteenth century and leave out the Great Game? Didn't he see himself as a national writer? If you're a national writer, and don't know the grindstones through which your nation's history has passed, and the consequences for its fate today, are you worth even tuppence? All right, he would familiarise himself with the documents that Muborak had obtained – God knows from where – and then see, as they say, if he was 'a king or a donkey'.

First, though, Abdulla recalled another letter, one that made tears of distress well up in his eyes. A letter from his mother Josiyat, dictated to one of her grandchildren and sent during Abdulla's studies in Moscow. 'Abdulla, son, come back as quickly as you can from those Russian lands! The world is unreliable, sufficient unto the day is the evil thereof – to put it bluntly, you might not see me again!' Abdulla sensed that his mother was being underhanded; he replied with a letter that was even more sly: 'Mama, you write that you're on the verge of death, and that I have to come at once. Don't be afraid. It's not your turn yet; before you die there are your older sisters, Aunties Ubayda, Buvma and Rokiya. There is a long queue to get through.' One day, at a wake, Abdulla's Aunt Rokiya asked her younger sister: 'Josiyat, you're not ill, are you? You haven't caught something, have you?'

'I can't seem to catch my breath these days, it'll be the

death of me, sister.'

Then the eldest sister, who had a sarcastic streak, said, 'I'm the one who this talk about breathlessness should worry, because it will be my turn first to die, then Buvma's, then yours, Rokiya, and Josiyat only after her. That's what her son Abdulla prescribes.'

—

Muborak was having a hard time of it.

'You're lucky to have that skin disease,' he whispered to Abdulla as one of Gena's henchman barked at him to come over. 'Nobody will touch you. I wish you'd infect me with your sores.' Before Abdulla could think of any meaningful response, Muborak hurried over to the thieves. He was their human punch bag: every day they played tricks on him, such as: 'showing the stars', which involved pulling the sleeve of an old sweater tight over his head then pouring water over him, or they would blindfold him and make him pretend to be their driver, ordering him, 'Turn right!', 'Old woman on the road!', 'Stop!', 'Cat crossing!' 'Look out: policeman!' When the Jew was exhausted, they kept the blindfold on for a game of 'guess who hit you'. The thieves beat Muborak mercilessly, and even if he managed to identify the author of the blows, they would continue to torment him, leaving off only when they were bored or Gena's fancy turned to a story.

Abdulla's thoughts of intervening, vague as they had been, had vanished: his illness and the endless interrogations had left him thoroughly exhausted, too exhausted to do anything but feel guilty relief that Muborak's observations were correct, and the thieves were leaving him alone.

This time, at least, he was thankful that Muborak had been called upon in his role as court jester rather than punch bag. His stories seemed to put Gena in a lenient mood, and the other prisoners always used these interludes for some conversation among themselves. This time, it was Kosoniy who moved over to Abdulla.

'Sir, it seems you've finished your business upstairs; for the last day or two you've been worried, haven't you?' the elderly man enquired.

'Who knows? I've said everything that was on my mind, now they'll need time to digest it,' Abdulla responded, lifting his shoulder as he stretched out where he lay. Then something occurred to him, and he looked as if he meant to investigate further. 'Mr Kosoniy, did Nasrullo, Emir of Bukhara, really write a letter to Victoria, the Queen of Britain?' he asked.

'Not only Nasrullo; Timur, or Tamberlaine as he was known to the English, also sent a letter to a British monarch. Emir Nasrullo Baxodur-xon, who interests you, sent his people with a memorandum for Queen Victoria a week before New Year, when the English spy Stoddart was in Bukhara.

'Once I learnt this letter by heart, together with His Excellency Navoi's *Collected Letters*, as a model example:

> Let it be known to her who has the highest title and noblest position, the sun in the constellation of happiness, the pearl in the sea of nobility, who irrigates her splendid realm in the garden of the world with the river of justice, who nurtures the flowers of stability and prosperity in this realm, who is as great as Jamshid, as just as Faridun, the queen of the kingdom of Christ, the ruler at the court of Jesus, the guardian of the highest dwellings of the Roman peoples of Europe, that at this moment, by the grace of the most High and Just Allah, the man writing to her is seated unshakeably on the throne of state which he rules, as her obedient servant, in the hope that the rays of truth will illumine our common goals.

'Come, my dear sir, you're yawning, I shan't burden your head with this florid style, let me just give you the essence of what was said.'

'Not at all,' Abdulla protested, 'I wasn't yawning. But that style...'

'To put it briefly, the Emir was writing about how he was entirely fair and impartial in his treatment, including of Russians or other foreign traders; if they didn't bring trouble on their own heads, he would receive them with justice and hospitality. For example, take Stoddart, who writes that when he first came there he had no knowledge of the local customs and couldn't help but cause offence, whereas now, once he had understood and explained the errors of his ways, he was forgiven and restored to his proper rank.'

—

At night, when everyone had lain down to sleep, the iron door was opened.

'Qodiriy, out!' the order rang out. Abdulla flung his gown over his shoulders and moved towards to the exit. Behind him he heard Sodiq mumble a prayer, 'God preserve you!' Whether Sodiq was saying this prayer for Abdulla, or whether he meant the preservation for himself, the sound of a man's ordinary voice seemed to fortify Abdulla.

The soldier acting as duty warder led him down the corridor, but in the opposite direction from usual, away from the stairs. So this was not going to be an interrogation. For shooting, though, they would have taken him out into the yard. Surely they didn't use the prison building as their slaughterhouse? No, because in that case he would have heard the sound of gunshots. You couldn't cover that up, the whole cell would talk of it. Just as the notorious room number 42 was common knowledge.

No, there was to be no firing squad today. Instead, the

soldier brought Abdulla to the room where he had first been questioned. Trigulov sat at the head of a long table, Abdulla's thick case file in front of him.

'Sit!' Trigulov said, then gestured to dismiss the warder. The soldier left and stood outside the door. Trigulov lit a cigarette, and pushed the cigarette case towards Abdulla.

'You smoke, don't you? Take one.'

When he was with the others in the cell, Abdulla did enjoy the occasional smoke. For some reason he didn't push Trigulov's hand away, but took one cigarette. Trigulov offered him his own lighted cigarette instead of a match. Abdulla lit his cigarette and drew deeply. The mild, warm smoke filled him with a feeling that he had forgotten. The tobacco's effect went quickly to his head.

'I've been reading you, and you're not bad,' Trigulov conceded. 'You really captured Berdi the Tatar! And the way Xayri keeps quiet while letting herself be kissed and embraced... "If the heifer doesn't make eyes at him, the bullock won't break its halter," isn't that how you put it? Very good! Shodmonboy's going to marry his daughter off to someone else, isn't he? He's making Berdi work for him for fifteen years, and all for nothing, isn't he? Berdi will take an axe and hack him to pieces, won't he? Just like in Dostoyevsky.' Trigulov was making every effort to show off his knowledge of literature and especially of *Obid the Pickaxe*.

'You know what? I've written a few things myself, now and then, though I don't have time for that these days,' the interrogator said, opening up.

Abdulla remained seated, enjoying his cigarette. Where was all this heading, he wondered.

'Things aren't looking good for you!' Trigulov continued. 'I've questioned a number of your colleagues, and what they've said...' At this point he seemed to lose the thread of his thoughts, and he broke off halfway through: 'If you're a writer, then you ought to see people for what they are. I'm going to read, and you're going to tell me who it is: are we agreed?' He didn't wait for an answer.

'Abdulla Qodiriy is considered a true nationalist. He was previously a wealthy trader, an exploiter of the working classes, whom he forced to work for him in his business. At that time he maintained close relations with Muslim clerics of a counter-revolutionary bent, such as Zahiriddin A'lam. These associates have been made to answer for their criminal activities.

'In 1936 a group of Uzbek writers travelled to Kazan. There, while staying at the Soviet hotel, Qodiriy is quoted as having said: "By deliberately cutting food supplies to Tatarstan and the Volga German Autonomous Republic, the Soviets have caused a famine. Humanitarian assistance is being prepared in Germany for Tatarstan and the German Autonomous Republic." He also said, "The Soviet Union is weaker than Germany: if there's a war, the Soviets will lose."

'"Spies from among counter-revolutionary nationalists who have infiltrated our literature have split Uzbek literature..." No, that's not it. Here we are: "Of the bourgeois nationalist apologists, who have been praised to the skies and take pride in this praise, the first and foremost is Abdulla Qodiriy. Until the final day of victory over the bourgeois nationalists, Abdulla Qodiriy faithfully served the bourgeoisie..."' Trigulov glanced at Abdulla. Not seeing a response, he passed on to another document.

'"Abdulla Qodiriy has always cited his work *Obid the Pickaxe* as proof that he has become a supporter of the Soviets. In truth, he has only been wearing a mask in order to struggle against the Soviets."'

Still Abdulla kept his thoughts to himself. Trigulov

moved to the next document, his face brightening as he cleared his throat and read out: "'The novel is written in the pompous, hyperbolic, florid style of the old literature, dead and artificial. Otabek shows bravery only in matters of love; when the people are suffering, when he should be showing his social side, he hides under his quilt.'"

Trigulov shut the thick folder with a flourish 'They're all in here!' he pronounced. 'Qurbonov, Oxundi, Kahhor, Nazirin and Husainov.' This time, the interrogator seemed not to expect any reply, and the two men puffed at their cigarettes at silence. Trigulov exhaled two circles of smoke, 'What shall we do now?' Holding the smoke in his mouth a moment longer, Abdulla raised his eyebrows as if to ask, in what sense?

'You and I ought to write a fine detective novel, with a secret policeman as the hero! Come on, sign this, with yesterday's date.' He passed Abdulla a piece of paper marked 15 March. 'I have been informed of the end of the investigation. I have been shown the investigation's materials. I have no complaints about the investigation.'

Abdulla picked up the fountain pen and wrote, 'I have never been a member of any anti-Soviet organisation.' Then he signed at the bottom.

—

After breakfast, when the more simple-minded prisoners sat down to play their card games, Muborak took the opportunity to pass Abdulla a sheet of folded paper: 'For you to roll yourself a cigarette, brother.'

Bukhara, March 29, 1841

My dear Conolly,

 1. I have the honour of transmitting a copy, in Persian, of a letter written by desire of the Ameer from me to you, the original

Persian having been submitted to and approved by him this day. [...] Of course Orgunj and Kokan would never, any more than the British, submit to have their Government communications dependent on the pleasure of the Ameer of Bokhara, however much the British may desire, as it is their interest, that the Oosbeg rulers should be at peace with one another and their neighbours. [...] The high tone of the expressions of the letter will not mislead you [...] I may add that you will only consult the Government interest, or your orders, whatever answer you may give to this communication will neither give offence to the Ameer, nor be prejudicial to me in his eyes.

2. It occurs to me that going yourself to Kokan might excite unnecessary jealousy in the mind of the Khan Orgunj, as well as lose the thread of your communications with him, without, on the other hand, your having an opportunity of doing anything effectual at Kokan, as your stay would be short.

3. The Kokan chief is raising soldiers after the European system. He gives them very little, and they are drilled in parties of ten and twenty at separate places by Cabool people and some Persians, who ran away from the body of soldiers kept up here by the Ameer.

4. [...] I enclose a copy of the letter of the Ameer sent to the British state. You, therefore, also, must act so that whatever treaty or communications you make with other countries of Oosbegistan, be not made without the Ameer's knowledge and assent, because he is the chief Sovereign of the Oosbegistan's dominions. [...] you should constantly send me all your news.

5. [...] my sincere thanks to the Khan Huzrut for sending his Elchee to request my release. [...]

6. Should you require money, I can supply you, or, if you prefer it, send me bills in my name. [...]

I have &c.,

Charles Stoddart.

'Roll a cigarette, quick,' whispered Muborak. 'They're

coming.'

Debating the relative merits of their countries' literary traditions was a popular pastime among the more intellectually inclined of the prisoners, not least because it gave them the chance to show off their knowledge. The other pleasure it provided was that of argument, as when Abdulla, sitting with Muborak, Kosoniy and Mulla Shibirgoniy, praised the lyrics of Bedil.

'But Bedil is one of ours,' the mulla exclaimed. 'He wrote in Dari, he's the master of Persian poetry!'

'True,' Abdulla countered, 'but his family were Chaghatai, and that makes him an honorary Uzbek.'

'But is he well known among the Uzbeks?' the mulla asked doubtfully. 'His style is a little Indian, after all; even the Iranians don't rate him as we Afghans do. For instance, his couplets on the theme of "The Mirror"; there are plenty, but would you be able to recite them?' Without waiting for Abdulla or Muborak to respond, the mulla began, reciting first in Farsi and then in Uzbek:

> Anyone looking with wonderment has no business with eyelashes,
> The mirror's chamber is closed, it has no door or wall.

'In other words, the eye is the mirror of the soul. When it is struck by wonder, the soul's closed cage becomes an open room.'

Kosoniy seemed to want to challenge this interpretation, but, remembering the rules of the game, waved his hand and recalled another of Bedil's couplets:

> Enchantment cannot deal with our sorrows,
> Breath on the mirror's chamber will not be air.

'If you breathe onto a mirror, the mirror's surface clouds over, just as our griefs and sorrows are not abolished, but only briefly masked, when we allow ourselves to be enchanted by the beauty of poetry – or the pleasures of fiction.' Kosoniy directed this last at Abdulla. 'Your Cho'lpon used to be good at this game. Are you his match?'

Abdulla took up the challenge:

> Should the battlefield of lust draw dust on the path of desire,
> If you breathe in or out at the mirror facing me, the breath
>   stretches out and goes.

'Do I have it right, gentlemen?' Kosoniy and the mulla nodded. 'What the poet is trying to say is this: if you are possessed by lust, and have gone in for the dust of desire, look at the mirror: it will start to breathe as you breathe in and out. This is a rough summary, of course, you can extract a dozen meanings from this couplet.' But this time Muborak intervened:

'We Jews put it simply:

> Ashamed of its love, the heart retreats, look,
> This mirror does such work, look.

> 'The mirror doesn't know what it serves: love, shame, or the poet.'

———

It was now that Captain Arthur Conolly came to Kokand from Khiva. 'You see,' Madali crowed, 'none other than the Queen of England has shown me respect: she's sent her ambassador.' He gave a feast in Conolly's honour, showed him his pigeons and his drums, introduced him to his mother Nodira and to the ladies of the court. 'This English dervish has come from Delhi. Look, he's brought me a picture of the Taj Mahal, and this enormous mirror!' The womenfolk were particularly pleased by the full-sized mirror, and the pleasure they gained from it was embodied in a poetry contest 'The Mirror'. Conolly spoke Farsi fluently, and knew Mughal poetry like the back of his hand.

He too took part in the contest, reciting a couplet which he tried to put into Ottoman Turkish:

> The heart's page, without the writing of your wounds, is lonely
> and empty,
> Our mirror reflects authority, or the perspiration of pearls.

While he stumbled over the Turkish, Oyxon stole a glance at this gigantic, blue-eyed European, who reminded her of her old friend Gulxaniy: the same majestic stature, the same good looks, the same gift of the gab. At first, this resemblance was a source of sadness for Oyxon, and then she worried that Madali would be jealous of the attention she was showing the foreigner; luckily, she was saved by the fact of Uzbeks seeming to regard Europeans as aliens – a European, after all! – and thus not worth considering as men. In this sense, Madali showed himself indifferent to Conolly's presence, treating him as if he were a *mahram*; gradually, Oyxon gathered the confidence to let her gaze linger ever longer on this cheerful, talkative foreigner; with the warming fire of memories of Gulxaniy, she found pleasure and enjoyment in looking at him.

Conolly knew a couplet about a mirror, but only in the English translation. First he recited it in his lisping English, then attempted to put it into Ottoman Turkish:

> I shall see the morning overthrown with age, fire will come from
> my tongue,
> Ah, if it is taken away, my choice will make the mirror fresh.

Then they all tried to work out the original couplet. Oyxon sent Gulsum to the library and had the poetess's *The Hidden One's Anthology* brought from there. After turning the pages, Oyxon exclaimed 'I've found it!' She recited the couplet:

> The morning I greet with tears and sighs,

No breath can burnish my mirror of desire.

The contest was not over. Conolly produced a copy of the *Babur-nama* featuring several colour-plates, which he passed around for everyone to see: 'This is the Red Fort, which Aurangzeb captured when he killed his brother Dara Shikoh; that's where he locked up his own father Shah Jahan, and where he put his daughter Zeb-un-Nisa under house arrest. In this same prison Dara Shikoh had kept his son (and Aurangzeb's nephew) Suleiman Shikoh,' said Conolly, telling of the last bloody days of the Mughal emperors, keeping his audience captivated until past midnight. 'To keep his throne and crown, Aurangzeb killed his brothers and imprisoned both his father and his daughter. At the end of his life, he wrote a testament bitterly repenting all these acts.' Conolly presented a copy of this testament to Nodira, whose passion for all things Indian he had cleverly picked up on. Other souvenirs from his time in Delhi were handed around. Leaving Oyxon until last, while everyone else was cooing over their own gifts, he gave her a portrait of the Queen of England getting into a barouche; very discreetly, without anyone noticing, he winked at her.

—

'Did you say Conolly?' Muborak chimed in. 'We've got him, too. We've got them all. We brought them from England. Let me tell you, brother, this story is very interesting. Just give our brother Moshe a bit of time, he's got a lot on his hands...

'When we arrived in London, all I had to do was say we'd come from Bukhara and my God, the invitations came flooding in, everyone's door was open to us. We were guests of the grandsons of the English rabbi, Joseph Wolff. Rabbi Wolff went to Bukhara half a century earlier, looking for Stoddart and Conolly. And when he came back, he wrote a book as thick as a brick. We've all read it.'

Abdulla was both perturbed and intrigued by these stories of the English: in what sense could they connect with his novel? The more he heard of Muborak's eager storytelling, the more Abdulla realised that they were mixed up in everything, impossible to leave out.

'Chief Minister Hakim realised that his influence on Emir Nasrullo was waning. He presented himself to the Emir, he bowed to the ground thrice, then kneeled, reciting a solemn oath. The Emir asked: 'What is your complaint?' Hakim said, 'Your Majesty, I have served you and your predecessors until my hair has turned white, and in doing so have acquired neither wealth nor power. I have thought only of your majesty's glory. I have compared you to Timur Lang, to Alexander the Great. Well, then, what have I done wrong that you no longer require my advice?'

The Emir answered this question with another: 'If you want something, why not say so?' The Chief Minister said: 'Why does Your Majesty turn to ruins the magnificent creations he has built? Why, after capturing the English foreigner, was he brought to Bukhara? England is a powerful kingdom, India is its province. The English have given refuge to two Afghan rulers. The infidel Ranjit Singh is threatening to invade Afghanistan, and if he succeeds he will not hesitate to attack Bukhara. Furthermore, Russia and Khiva have trained their eyes on us. The Shi'a kizilbash troops are ready to unite against us. May Allah preserve us from them all! There is only one way to save ourselves from these impending disasters: strike an alliance with the English.'

Nasrullo waved his hand, as if to say, is that your advice? I've understood! You're free to go! Hunched, the white-haired Chief Minister left the Emir's presence.

Believing him to be in the pocket of the English, the Emir killed this old-fashioned man, who had once put him on the throne!

—

The Islamic New Year had now passed. After this, the days would become hot, the apricot and cherry trees must have been setting fruit already. Very soon, the strawberries would be ripe. The Chorsu market must be full of greens: Chinese rocket, wild garlic, coriander and spring onions. The children would go to the Jar Canal to gather sorrel and mint. Was there any prospect of Abdulla tasting Rahbar's delicious herb samsas?

> The dear spring is on its way. The dear spring will soon be seen.
> The time is shortly coming when we see her dress of green.
>
> Spring's silken skirt is stroking
> Across the head of the damp black earth
> Renewing its power and provoking
> The black treasury to its gold give birth.
>
> May our land be filled with growing!
> May our souls smell spring's sweet coming!
> May our hearts with its spirit be bursting!

Abdulla had fallen asleep with bittersweet thoughts clouding his mind: he was awoken by the sound of his name, and led out into the corridor. This time, he was taken to see Vinokurov, who dismissed the escort before addressing Abdulla.

'I've done everything you asked, Qodiriy. I'm guessing Yunusov has already had a confrontation with you: he was weeping. Beregin hasn't said a thing. Cho'lpon asked me to give you this piece of paper here. Take it and read it, don't be afraid! Then you can use it to roll a cigarette, unless you've given up smoking.'

Abdulla unfolded the proffered paper, and recognised Cho'lpon's old calligraphic hand.

'My dear Abdulla,

No person, no wave, no typhoon, no fire!
In my eye is the light of a grievous surrender.
Oh, my fiery past, conceal your face,
You have satanic, unjust powers.'

Beneath these lines was a decorative signature, done in the Arabic script: 'Cho'lpon.'

Abdulla glanced up at Vinokurov, 'May I write a few lines to him now?'

'As long as there's nothing anti-Soviet in them, brother.'

'Nothing at all, just a few lines of verse. A poem to keep his spirits up.'

'Just don't write in the Arabic script,' the turnkey ordered. 'I'll need to read it myself before I pass it on.'

Abdulla took the sheet of paper he was offered, and wrote:

When the lies and falsehoods start,
That, awaking from sleep, we send into existence.
A time will come when swords never stay in their scabbards
And at that time we'll fly off as far as the blue sky.

Then he returned the paper to Vinokurov.

'Nobody in the cell is giving you a hard time, are they?' Vinokurov asked.

'Not me, no; but Gena and his crew are throwing Muborak about like a stuffed toy.'

'Well, you tell me if they start on you!' Vinokurov slipped the piece of paper into his breast pocket and shook the tobacco out of two cigarettes into Abdulla's cupped hand. 'If they see you in the cell with cigarettes, you'll be in trouble,' he explained, 'they'll think you got them in return for snitching.' He waited for Abdulla to hide the tobacco in his pocket, then shouted to the soldier by the door. 'Take the prisoner back to his cell.'

———

Two days later, Muborak gave Abdulla the document he had promised, in exchange for enough tobacco for a roll-up.

> If I reach Khiva, it is my wish to pass on afterwards to Kokand. Our relations with Khiva are fairly firm. Until Russia's quarrel with this state is ended, we will not change our relations with the Khan of Khiva: we will only look after our own interests.
>
> But if the Russians besiege Khiva, we will find other ways of getting to Kokand, and, winning over Fergana in the Emir's favour; we will promote our idea of a union of peaceful Uzbek khanates in an independent Turkestan.
>
> Arthur Conolly.

Into this document Abdulla rolled up the tobacco Vinokurov had given him two days previously and then lit up. After his first puff, he passed the cigarette to Muborak. He wondered how Muborak managed to get any document he wanted into this place so easily. It had taken him enormous trouble to get just three very brief notes to his home, smuggled through Sunnat, and he was too afraid to attempt communication in any other way. The last thing he wanted was to get his family into any danger. But Muborak had a family that was preserving these documents: he'd said so himself. 'My people at home have made plenty of copies, so don't worry about using them to make cigarettes!'

Whatever was going on, Abdulla still didn't fully trust Vinokurov, although in one thing, at least, the Russian wasn't deceiving him: he had passed on Cho'lpon's letter.

Muborak seemed to have noticed that the tobacco was different; frowning, he turned to Abdulla when a sudden shout from Gena made him jerk. With trembling hands, he passed his cigarette to Abdulla before hurrying over to join the thieves. At first, Abdulla allowed himself to be lost in his own thoughts, smoking and contemplating the Englishman Conolly. But the noise from the far side of the cell was gradually building to an uproar, making it impossible to think. When Abdulla looked over, he saw that the thieves had embarked upon a new form of cruelty. They had blindfolded Muborak as if for a game of hide and seek; one thief then climbed onto another's back, opened his fly and stuck his penis straight into Muborak's face, accompanied by screams and laughter.

Abdulla leapt to his feet without thinking what he was doing, marched over and struck the thief in the face with as much strength as he could muster. There was a brief, stunned silence, during which Abdulla had just time enough to feel his heart sink when he heard a small voice pipe up behind him: Sodiq. 'Beat them up!' And that was all it took. A moment later, all the 'politicals' – those who had the physical strength to do so – joined forces in attacking the criminals, while the weaker ones wailed and called for help. When the soldiers rushed in, stamping their feet, they had to tear the prisoners off each other. Gena and his crew were hauled out of the cell, and Kosoniy was appointed elder.

—

Madali was as changeable as the weather in winter. After hours spent happily flying his pigeons and banging away at his drums, the Emir would abuse the first person to cross his path. Drunk on beer, he would stagger to the harem and torment his wives, not sparing even the two prostitutes he'd set up as his procuresses.

One day he got it into his head to invade Jizzax, and set off with a mass of soldiers from Fergana. He delayed the journey by resting at some places where he pitched camp. One night, he got roaring drunk, left behind a hundred thousand soldiers and went off on his way with only a hundred men. When his generals, alarmed, saw that their Emir meant to go to war with just these hundred men, they tried all they could to dissuade him. Refusing to dismount, Madali shouted back at them, 'I am a warrior for God. We'll smash Jizzax and its troops in battle. I'll lead the attack myself!' The generals replied, 'Your Majesty, you are the ruler of a great kingdom, but Jizzax castle has three thousand well-trained soldiers occupying it. Come, leave them to us; we'll encircle Jizzax with our full force, while you stand back to enjoy the sight.' The Emir appeared to have been won over, then suddenly rode away towards O'ratepa. Any who dared to go after him were cursed by the generals, but that didn't stop his courtiers and companions from following in their leader's suit. The Fergana army, abandoned by its ruler, remained pitched midway between Kokand and Jizzax. Only a week later did that army limp back to Kokand, straggling and destitute.

And this was the kind of stubborn, fickle character which Conolly now found himself having to contend with. The previous day Madali had shown Conolly his fluttering pigeons and boasted of his extraordinary drums. Today, he accused the Englishman of being a spy working for Nasrullo. 'You've come to reconnoitre, then tell him the easiest route from Bukhara to Kokand!' Madali was on the verge of throwing Conolly into a dungeon. But the Englishman used all the cunning he had:

'If there is any force opposing English interests in Turkestan, then it is without a doubt Emir Nasrullo. He

is not only sowing trouble between the Uzbek emirates and creating the conditions for a Russian conquest
of Turkestan, but he has spat in Britain's face by holding
our officer Stoddart for the past two years. Tell me, Your
Majesty, how can I possibly be working for such a man?'

Madali may have been drunk, or have been smoking
hashish. He mumbled: 'If you're not a spy, why were you
planning to go to Bukhara after you left here?'

'To rescue my brother officer.'

'You ignorant fool,' Madali scoffed, 'Nasrullo will
throw you in the pit alongside him. When you're rotting in
his pit, squeezing out your pus and sores, you may remember what I've said.'

'Your Majesty, if you wish to ease my situation, then
allow me to obtain a letter of recommendation and an
inscribed amulet for my journey.'

'Do as you like, then!' Madali exclaimed, exasperated,
and set off for his porcelain dovecote.

—

The ornamental royal carriage followed the Kokand streets
in the direction of the Shaykhon district. Inside, Oyxon
had drawn back the silk curtain, and the sight of Conolly,
who was sitting next to the driver, made her heart miss a
beat. She suddenly recalled another carriage, another journey. It must have been the scent of spring in the air – it
was the time when the daisies, the amaranths, the early
roses and the aromatic basil were wafting their fragrance
through the town – that made her head swim.

She remembered her childhood days in O'ratepa,
when she gathered mint and sorrel by the canal banks, its
crystal-clear water, and her grateful mother stuffing samsas
with the herbs. If she closed her eyes, she could still see,
quivering in her imagination, the pure blue sky which had

finally emerged from winter, to be flung over the tall pop-lars like a gauze cloth.

The carriage rolled on, cutting through air that had cooled after sunset, but the evening held no fears for Oyxon, nor did the chill distress her. In the calm, she recalled a couplet she had written some time ago:

In this world of mine, like a deaf-mute looking round, I suffer for love,
In this sky of mine, like the day plunging, I blush a hundred times.

For some reason, these thoughts, her racing heart, her shallow breathing, were centred on the figure of the ath-letic foreigner sitting on the other side of the curtain.

Good, Oyxon thought, he reminds me of Gulxaniy, but why, when he requested a letter and an amulet from one of the *Haji*, did I offer to take him to my revered father? Granted, it was the Emir who gave the order, but might my father not chase us away from the door, saying, "To hell with his majesty the Emir!" Is this my way of repaying him for the portrait he gave me? He gives me the Queen getting into her barouche; I give him myself, rid-ing with him in one of our carriages?' As if searching for a sensible answer to her questions, she raised the curtain a fraction and saw red hair curling over Conolly's neck from under his headgear. Gulxaniy, then Qosim, and after that her father passed through her mind.

After leaving the palace, there seemed to be nobody about. Conolly seemed to sense that Oyxon's attention was fixed on him; to lessen the awkwardness, he began to sing. The song was in a language of which Oyxon knew not a single word, and the tune itself was strange, not at all like our grave, drawn-out melodies – even the sad notes had a playfulness about them. Conolly's voice grew gradually louder; it had something of the stormy sea hitting the rocks about it, of broad green meadows and forests, and above all a yearning, a heartfelt longing for these things. Oyxon's mind fitted the music to a couplet by Nodira:

> With cries of woe, the hoop of time has broken free of the
> beloved,
> My great grief, oh heart, is that you ignore my sorrowful state.

Does Conolly have a wife or a beloved waiting for him in his country? she wondered. She didn't think anyone had thought to ask him that. Startled by where her thoughts were taking her, she shook herself and laughed aloud. Really, was she looking for another rival wife in a foreign country when she had a harem full of them here? As the laughter rose to her lips and filtered out from behind the curtain, the song being sung on its other side died down.

———

Why not? Abdulla asked himself. Though this would have its critics – he remembered how much abuse was hurled at *Past Days*: 'How could Otabek marry Kumush without his parents' consent? No Uzbek would do a thing like that!'

One evening, Abdulla was summoned to the door. Now that farce they called an interrogation was over, was Vinokurov's conscience bothering him again? But it was Trigulov who had called for him.

On the interrogator's desk was the same old fat dossier; but this time Trigulov left it closed.

'Well, Qodiriy, will you smoke?'

Abdulla took a cigarette from the offered case. Trigulov said: 'Take a few more, only it's best to squeeze the tobacco out into your pocket: if they catch you with cigarettes in the cell, you'll be in trouble.'

What trouble? Could they all be trained to say exactly

the same things? Vinokurov had used those very words. Abdulla extracted another two cigarettes from the case and tipped the tobacco out into his pocket, then lit up one for himself. He nodded at Trigulov as if to say, at your service.

'The novel I've been planning will be set in a prison,' Trigulov began. 'The main hero is a prisoner. But not just any old prisoner, no; he is an extremely unusual man. He doesn't get on with anyone around him, because he's a theatre director, a playwright. He's used to everyone dancing to his tune.'

Abdulla drew deeply on his cigarette. Not a writer, but a playwright: he could be grateful for that, at least. Trigulov went on: 'The prisoner is given a death sentence. True, there hasn't yet been a trial, but the interrogator has whispered it in his ear. Because of this, the prisoner washes his hands of this world. When he gets back to his cell, he invents games based on everyday senseless things that have happened in his life, since he hasn't the strength to face what is coming. Petty, trivial things: extra summons to see the interrogator, a routine confrontation, another prisoner joining him. Nothing changes. The extraordinary man is left to his own devices. Outside prison he has a wife and children. He thinks of them, for want of anything else to do, and amuses himself in idle chat with the other prisoners: that's all he does.

'One day the prisoner is in solitary confinement when he hears a noise. As if someone is digging the ground up with a pickaxe. The next night, the same sounds are repeated. At first the sounds seem to be some way off, like a ticking clock, but every night they get louder and closer. Someone's digging a tunnel, the prisoner concludes. One night a corner of the extraordinary prisoner's cage collapses, a hole opens up, and out pop the prison chief and the interrogator. When they see the prisoner's dumbfounded face, these two tricksters laugh themselves silly.'

As if interested to see the effect of his words, Trigulov fell silent for a while. Abdulla hid behind his smoke and tried to guess what lay behind all this.

'Don't think, Qodiriy, that this has any connection to real life. It's only something I've made up.' But Abdulla was well aware of the effect that the 'made-up' could have on real life. You could surrender to inspiration and write about the most unbelievable things, and five or ten years down the line, this same 'made-up' thing would turn up in your life.

'"All right, don't be disheartened," those two officials tell the remarkable person as they lead him to the pit. There are trenches leading from this pit like a spider's web to every cell in the prison. Realising that these two men were preoccupied with their conversation at this point, the theatre director slips unnoticed into the underground passage and, after many twists and turns, finally emerges at the surface. He sees the lights of the city glimmering in the distance. After all that humiliation, his heart is excited by freedom, and he heads for the city. But before he takes five steps he comes up against a paper wall and tears it down: he has come back to the prison chief's office. Naturally, the prison chief and his interrogator are waiting for him. Again, uproarious laughter breaks out.

'The novel is made up of scenes like this. So our remarkable theatre director, who used to believe himself in charge of the play, is in fact just a character trapped inside it. What do you say to that, writer?'

'I'll have to think about it,' said Abdulla.

—

When he looked at the men around him, messily fussing and bustling about, the superiority of himself and all his countrymen was brought thudding home: how in heaven's name had he become so inextricably entangled in their pointless occupations, their senseless intrigues? More to the point, how was he going to get out of such a quagmire? From 22 February 1841, on the orders of Emir Nasrullo, Colonel Stoddart stayed in the house of the Naib Abdusamad: a native of Tabriz whose notoriety stretched from Baghdad to India by way of Kabul – all of which places he had been forced to flee when his various schemes were uncovered. His chief talent lay in ingratiating himself with intemperate rulers, and as the success of this was usually in proportion to the latter's depravity, he had fallen on his feet with Nasrullo in Bukhara. He had been quick to smell the potential for extortion in having an envoy of Queen Victoria under his 'care', and was likewise keen to scotch any attempts by which Stoddart might win Nasrullo's favour and thus his freedom. After inspecting the Emir's troops and proposing that he replace compulsory service with a volunteer army, Abdusamad presented the idea to Nasrullo as if it were his own. When mineral ores were found near Samarkand, Stoddart tested them and drew up a plan for extraction: but it was Abdusamad who showed these papers to the Emir, receiving the praise and the gold-embroidered gowns for himself.

These tricks might not have been so serious, if he were only to stop at them; but, like a tax collector mounted behind his victim, he was determined to squeeze everything he could out of Stoddart. 'Aren't I the one who rescued you from the pit? The Islamic judge and the Chief of Police are both in my pay. If I want, I can have you thrown as food to the worms and insects. So write to your chiefs that, in exchange for the help I've given you, they are to open an account for me in India with two thousand pounds in it. Until I receive confirmation of that, you haven't a hope of getting out of here.'

On the next occasion this devil had a new request: 'Write to your chiefs.' Abdusamad presented himself to the Emir on 7 March and told his Majesty, 'Sire, according to my information, Stoddart never gave you on any occasion a letter from the British government confirming his authority; is this true?' The Emir has confirmed this. So Abdusamad said, 'I have information regarding such a letter.'

'What does it contain?'

'In it, the British government announced its gratitude to you, warns you about plans by the Russians and Persians to attack the Uzbek khanates. Their advice is to return your Russian prisoners to their homeland, so as not to give the Russians any pretext for war. I can quote: "It is in the interests of both Bukhara and Britain to keep the Russians away from the Uzbek khanates. My appeal to you, your Majesty, is a recognition of your high reputation among the Uzbek khans. The British have sent Stoddart here to ensure unity among the Uzbek khans."'

'Word for word,' Abdusamad warned Stoddart; 'and none of your tricks. If I find out you've been deceiving me, I'll see you rot. Now write to your government that they are to draw up an agreement of friendship with Bukhara, with the Nayab Abdusamad named as intermediary, and including a provision for the appropriate fee.'

Though Stoddart understood that he was becoming this man's puppet, he could do nothing to stop it, for Abdusamad had imprisoned all his servants, and set spies to keep watch on him day and night. His situation, then, was desperate, and worsening by the day.

—

Abdulla kept returning to what Trigulov had said. Was the

talk about a prisoner who'd been sentenced to death – the interrogator who whispered it into his ear – a hint about his own fate? What stopped Trigulov saying so outright? Was he afraid of breaking the law? Abdulla permitted himself a wry smile. Was it possible, then, that the interrogator really was a frustrated would-be writer? Then write about your father, about your mother, about your Tatar homeland, even about Tashkent which gave you refuge... but perhaps, after spending so long in this line of work, all he knew was this prison and the prisoners in it.

The cell doors clanged open and Sunnat entered with a Russian soldier. When Sunnat's eyes met Abdulla's, the latter felt his chest tighten. He hadn't seen the Uzbek soldier for so long that he'd stopped expecting him. If only he'd known he would be coming back, he could have had written another note, ready to be passed to the outside world. Though he longed to rush forward, Abdulla held himself back, waiting until the queue of people thinned before going up to get his food. He let the Russian soldier give him his bowl and then deliberately dropped it onto Sunnat's trolley. Sunnat and Abdulla bent down together to retrieve it, exchanging hurried whispers.

'They've moved to Ko'kterak.'

'Did you see them?'

'The neighbours told me.'

That was all there was time for. Sunnat ladled porridge into Abdulla's bowl, the Russian soldier gave him a piece of sour-smelling black bread and a mug of stew-like tea. His heart relieved, Abdulla went back to his place.

—

A prison runs on its own timetable. Not just in the sense of what time its occupants must get up, or have meals, or see the barber. If your name is called out in the daytime or the evening, then it's either for questioning, for a confrontation, or, in the worst case, to Room 42 for a thorough beating. If you leave at midnight, your neighbours who lie down next to you know not to panic, that you'll be back among them by morning, rubbing your sleepless eyes. But if it's that hour in the night just before dawn prayers, when you can't distinguish a black thread from a white one, the man whose name is called awakes with a shudder, or writhes on the ground, or clutches at someone's side – before he is subjected to force, and dragged off, trying to conceal himself, clinging to a hiding place he will not return to, or weeping openly, begging for mercy, as he begins to embrace his fellow-prisoners. Only the strongest recite the *shahada*, say farewell to those around them, and then stride off towards the exit and are transfigured, into the dark. All those who are left behind either recite their prayers or weep quietly. Or sit together, unable to settle down and go back to sleep until morning comes. Everyone knows the fate of those who are taken out at that early hour.

Over two nights at the end of March, names were called out: the mulla first, then Kosoniy at dawn the next day. Perhaps because the surviving prisoners didn't know what the mulla was accused of, or because Abdulla was one of the few who had conversed much with him, his disappearance did not affect them too badly. But when Kosoniy had his name called out, everyone awoke. The elderly man walked around to look at everybody, taking the time to say to each, 'We commit all of you to God!' As he went out, striding purposefully towards the light coming from the door, Abdulla felt a sense of something left undone, like a dark pit in his heart.

Sitting in his place, and without making a sound, Abdulla began to weep. He wept as much as he could in that dark hour. He wept as he recalled his mother, who hadn't lived to Kosoniy's age; he grieved for the wife and children he had failed to make happy; for his friends lying here in neighbouring prison cells; his tears were bathing the defunct and forgotten, his wretched people and their errant history, of whom beautiful, betrayed Oyxon seemed such a potent symbol, her memory in danger of being lost along with her poetry, another chapter of Uzbek literature brutally excised.

> The moth in its flame was burning, the candle was slowly weeping.
> The air was split by lightning, I was scorched with the pain of parting.
> And for my heart's sharp suffering, the world was bleakly weeping.
> Every thorn on the mountain of grief, pricked my toe and made it bleed.
> My beloved showed no mercy, lovers were sadly weeping.
> And was there anyone at all who knew of my pain indeed?
>
> Oh yes we laughed with our mouths, but our hearts inside were weeping.

———

Now that Jur'at and Kosoniy were no more, Abdulla felt that all the prisoners around him were somehow ephemeral, and thus it was imperative to get all the information he could from them. Those he singled out were Professor Zasypkin, now appointed elder; Muborak; and the Party functionary Laziz, whose incessant chatter used to irritate him. With these people Abdulla now sat talking for hours on end, for it seemed as though he was preserving their transience for all eternity, all the wisdom and intuition they had to offer.

Spring was now nearly over, and his soul longed for other things: to witness the bees toiling without end, buzzing around the blossoming trees in the orchards; to walk out into the open fields and be swamped by tulips and red poppies; to take deep, deep breaths. But every cell of his nose was saturated with the smells of this dark, airless, stinking cattle shed, and the only possibility left was to indulge in idle conversation.

When Conolly left Kokand for Bukhara, Oyxon was heartbroken. She was not consoled by noisy excursions to the countryside with the harem ladies to celebrate spring; she was not comforted by the gardens' regal flowering. It was during this period that she found solace in an unexpected corner: from Uvaysiy, a woman old enough to be her grandmother. Until then Oyxon had not let her come close, for she considered Uvaysiy to be Nodira's disciple. But when she looked at her with clear eyes, she saw not a scheming rival but a woman who, like herself, lived a lonely and precarious life. Uvaysiy's husband had been killed in one of Umar's senseless wars, her son had been exiled to Kashgar, her daughter had died in childbirth. Uvaysiy had neither a home of her own nor any independent wealth; she scraped a living from giving private Qu'ran recitals and from teaching at houses which she visited with her three-year-old granddaughter in tow. Later this was no longer sufficient, she had no choice but to move to the palace, with all the miseries that entailed.

Walking with Oyxon in the gardens, Uvaysiy recited one of her latest verses:

> When you shoot arrows at your rivals, don't kill me who is
> already dead,
> The people have set my life on fire, don't burn me who is
> already burnt

'You're the same age as my daughter, your highness; when I see how you grieve, I myself grieve. People of passion must expect to have suffering souls. But if you do not open your heart to someone, that heart will eat itself alive.'

Oyxon responded by quoting the older woman's own words back to her:

> If I ask for a token of love for my lover, she'll kill me: if I don't ask, I will die.
> If I open a love shop for sufferers in love, she'll kill me; if I don't ask, I will die.
>
> Don't torment me with jealousy, death, if my beloved talks to a stranger.
> If I bark like a dog in her mansion, she'll kill me; if I don't bark, I will die.
>
> I have no choice but to be patient, whether I wish it, day or night.
> If I wander through the streets like a vagrant, she'll kill me; if I don't, I will die.
>
> I am withering from separation, but she told me: stay away,
> If I visit sweet as a flower, she'll kill me; if I don't, I will die.

Uvaysiy herself chimed in, summing up:

> She's ashamed of me, she debases me; and this vain world banishes my spirit.
> If poor Uvaysiy remains a beggar, she will kill me; if I don't, I will die.

From then on, the two women understood one another perfectly.

In prison everyone harbours doubts and suspicions about everybody else. Anyone might be an interrogator's informer, willing to sell someone else down the river, just to save their own skin. Prison life makes men keep their mouths tight shut. I won't let my heart be burnt because of my tongue, is what prisoners say about themselves when they avoid saying too much. But in prison, being prison, there are times when a man feels bad and can't stand being in this situation: like shouting 'The Emperor has no clothes' down a well, he can spill all his unspoken secrets. So it was, when Professor Zasypkin and the Party activist Laziz were arguing about what the Russians had contributed to Central Asia.

'All right,' Zasypkin bleated, 'suppose the Russians hadn't come to Turkestan. Wouldn't Central Asia then be the same sort of place as Afghanistan? But now we have universal education and a health service, factories and plants, collective and state farms...'

Another prisoner overheard them and broke in: 'Look at Iran or Turkey. They haven't been under the Russians or the British. All the same they are developing! Take India which has been an English colony: poverty and ignorance.'

'I'd say the same,' said Zasypkin. 'The English brought backwardness and ignorance, but the Russians came and gave culture and civilisation a head start.'

'But do you call what the Russians brought civilisation and culture?' Laziz put in, shaking the two tufts of hair over his ears. 'I'd like to say that as well as progressive tendencies they brought negative phenomena into life here, including diseases like alcoholism, female depravity, immodesty in the life of local people...'

'You should read your literature more carefully!' Zasypkin moved to the attack. 'Read the memoirs my colleague Professor Fitrat wrote before the revolution. Or read Sadriddin Ayniy's *The Old School*. Then you'll get an insight into what was going on in people's lives before the Russians came here.'

'The Russians can't take the credit for that,' the third prisoner contended. 'In the Middle Ages, when Russia and Europe were still in the dark, the Islamic world already had universities; medicine and other branches of science were advancing, there were new discoveries every day, and everything was progressing.'

'Karl Marx talks about development having a spiral form,' said Lazi, anxious to give this discussion a theoretical basis. 'The law of antithesis…'

Abdulla was listening to this argument from the sidelines. Laziz-zoda's Party said, 'Truth emerges from argument.' But in most cases, on the contrary, truth died during the dispute. Truth was many-sided, it was richer than the false information that you got from a book or a newspaper, which you swallowed undigested. More often than not, truth wasn't fastened to a single word, like a fish hanging securely from a rod. In fact, a flash of truth might perversely emerge in a tone or an unfinished phrase. But the moment you seize on it, that flash vanishes like sunlight glancing from the mirror to the wall.

—

Riding across mile after mile of the waterless Jizzax steppes on his way from Kokand to Bukhara, Conolly was absorbed by his thoughts. After arriving in Kokand, what was his goal, and what would he have to show for it when he returned? At first sight, everything seemed to be as it should. He had managed to instil into Madali what the English wanted, by praising the Emir's pigeons and drums. He had explained in detail that the Emir of Bukhara was the main obstacle in getting the Uzbek khans to stand up against the Russians. 'The Emir of Bukhara has singled you out as an infidel! That's what the Khan of Khiva told me.' Then Madali lost his temper, proving the success of

Conolly's efforts. But something else was bothering him.

The Khan of Khiva had told him how, on learning of this Madali's marriage to Oyxon, he had written a letter to Emir Nasrullo: 'My elder brother Madali, considering his father's widow to be a permissible bride, has married her. The holy city of Bukhara is the capital of the clergy. What decision would they take on this matter? You are the greatest ruler of Transoxiana. What do you say to this revolting action?'

As soon as Emir Nasrullo received this letter, he summoned the senior clerics and Islamic judges to his presence and issued the *fatwa*:

'As the head of Islam, any person who is Emir of the Islamic community has a duty to observe and fulfil sharia law. Should any such person turn his face away from Islam in the slightest, they can no longer be counted an Emir. *Nauzanbillahi* – I seek Allah's refuge – Madali, being an Emir of Fergana and Turkestan, has married his late father's legal wife and entered a form of matrimony with her, *nauzanbillahi* – I seek Allah's refuge – *nauzanbillahi*. In accordance with the verses of the Holy Qu'ran, the sayings of the Prophet, peace be upon him, the four sects of Islam, the decision of the theologians and the *ulema*, he is an infidel. Islamic Emirs and all Muslims have the right to execute this outlaw.'

According to the Khan of Khiva, Emir Nasrullo was ready to attack Kokand. 'The woman is said to be a peerless beauty,' Mirzo Rahim had remarked, 'which might explain Nasrullo's sudden burst of religious fervour.' A woman so lovely she sets one Emir against the other; Conolly naturally thought of the Greeks' Helen.

Just as naturally, he meant in Kokand to see with his own eyes the now legendary Oyxon. This was the curiosity not merely of a man, but of a sophisticated, seasoned traveller. And saw her he did. Conolly had spent half his life with men like himself, explorers and conquerors – and not merely of geographical territory. Four officers only had to get together for their banter to turn bawdy, and a debate to start up on the merits of women of different nationalities. One man would praise the flirtatious French, another the passionate Italians; another would boast of his Spanish conquests, while others would praise the exotic Indians.

But only now did Conolly understand the words of Hafiz:

> If you fall in love, no matter whether Turk or Tajik; Hafiz, create
>   sayings for your love,
> Write in the language you know.

and Shakespeare:

> But love, hate on, for now I know thy mind,
> Those than can see thou lov'st, and I am blind.

———

On 1 April, a cruel joke was played on the prisoners. That morning, a soldier had come into the cell, called the names of seven men and told them to get their things together; they'd been pardoned, and were free to go. They bundled their belongings together and lined up behind the door, not even taking the time to throw thicker clothes on over their nightgowns, so fearful were they of missing this chance. When the night warders yelled out, 'April's Fool', the entire cell felt as though they'd been punched in the collective gut.

On that topsy-turvy day, everything was flipped on its head: at dinnertime, they were left not with the usual foul bread and gruel, but with a steaming cauldron of plov. Granted, it had been overcooked, but the rice was fresh, it had carrots, and it was seasoned: in short, it was the real thing. Abdulla hadn't realised how much he'd missed the taste of it. And this was spring, a time for picnics: when you'd throw your overalls over your shoulder and go to Pushkin Park with your friends, where every one of the Green Ditch teahouses claimed their plov was the best. But who would be there now? Who would have the heart to go out and eat plov in times as dark as these?

In the evening Abdulla was summoned to see Trigulov again.

'The guards had an April fool's joke, I hear,' the Russian laughed. 'At least you weren't put on the list of those to be freed, were you?'

If Trigulov had begun their talk in any other way, Abdulla might have kept his usual silence and not risen to the bait. But the moment he heard those words and saw that smile, the conversation got off on the wrong foot. The veins on his temples swelled: 'I'm a free man anyway,' he snapped.

'Yes, if you're talking about inner freedom. You're the cat that couldn't get its tail out of the trap and said, "Ugh, it stinks anyway". You'd do better to listen to me. Have you thought about what I said the last time we met?'

Abdulla maintained a stubborn silence.

'I've decided I shan't make my hero a theatre director. I'm making him a writer instead. A spinner of fictions, locked up in prison.'

Abdulla barely suppressed a shudder. It was true that Muborak was next to him in the cell, and heard him raving in his sleep, but where did this man get his information from?

'Everyone gets on well with him. The prison officers, the prisoners in his cell, the interrogators, they all treat him politely. A prisoner's ordinary daily life. He senses some current at work under all this, but can't get to the bottom of it. What is actually going on? What sort of process, what sort of game? The prison chief arranges a meeting for him with his beloved…' (Is he alluding to Vinokurov? Abdulla wondered.) 'And more scenes like this… The writer's only link with the outside world is through writing.' (Does he actually know? Or is he just guessing, and waiting to see what might hit the mark?) But nobody pays him any mind. Ordinary life goes on, but the underlying process – if you like, you can write it in capitals, PROCESS, nobody can makes any sense of the PROCESS – gradually it sucks him in, like a storm, like a maelstrom, like a sinkhole.'

As Trigulov spoke, his lips dried and sweat broke out on his forehead.

'What do you think? I've thought it out pretty well, haven't I?' he said, eyeing Abdulla; but his expression changed when he saw the prisoner staring him straight in the face.

'Do you think you're a puppetmaster and we are just puppets?' Abdulla's voice was shaking with anger. 'You're counting your chickens before they hatch. When the cow drinks water, the calf licks ice – that applies to drivelling errand boys like you. You'd do better to lick the arse of the cow that gives you milk.' Holding nothing back, Abdulla spat into his pale face all the humiliation that had accumulated inside him. Trigulov slammed his fist onto the desk and yelled in Russian:

'Take him away to cell 42! I'll see him rot!' he said. Two soldiers grabbed Abdulla from behind, twisting his arms behind his back, and dragged him out of the room.

The soldiers flung Abdulla into the familiar cell 42, and set about giving him a beating. Then Vinokurov himself came in: 'Leave him, I'll sort him out myself,' he said, ordering the soldiers to leave.

Abdulla was badly beaten, but not completely crushed; he gathered all his strength: 'Now my hour has come, for what happened on New Year's Eve,' he said, readying himself to go for Vinokurov's throat the moment he got near enough. Two or three minutes passed as dusk thickened. When the soldiers' footsteps had faded into silence, Vinokurov spoke from the far corner of the room: 'Abdulla, it's me…' His voice sounded friendly, but Abdulla had no faith in this comradely approach. These devils tried to lull your vigilance, as if you were a lamb, with their April fool's joke, and then they flung themselves on you like wolves.

'Abdulla, it's me. Calm down…' Vinokurov was repeating.

No, Abdulla thought. They're all the same! They're not to be trusted.

'Here, wipe your face,' said Vinokurov, passing him his own freshly laundered handkerchief, folded four times. Abdulla paused. When I go to take it, he'll kick me, he told himself; slowly, he stretched his hand out for the white object. Vinokurov did not move. Abdulla brought the handkerchief to his face without unfolding it. The perfume of attar of roses struck his nostrils: it was what he had used every day when shaving. For some reason, it brought tears to Abdulla's eyes. After all this, he thought, feeling himself go to pieces, he'll beat me to death. But one instant passed, then another, and still, Vinokurov did not make a move.

In the semi-darkness Abdulla could not hold back the tears provoked by the attar of roses. Tears for his lost faith that some small scrap of goodness might be left in the world.

———

Or was it because of the April fool's joke that Vinokurov

had refrained from kicking him and staving in his ribs? All these things could not be a dream, for Abdulla still had in his pocket the handkerchief folded four times. The men around caught a whiff of the scent and asked in amazement, 'What's that smell?' As the hour for dawn prayers approached, another prisoner was taken away. Jokes aside, in the most professional demeanour, the wretched victim made a gift of his glasses which were held together with thread to Professor Zasypkin, thrusting the glasses at him like a souvenir, before groping his way towards the door.

Several days passed uneventfully. Then one day, towards evening, Abdulla's name was called in the usual way, and he was taken down the long corridor; this time, though, he was ushered in to an office far more magnificent than Trigulov's. Under a portrait of Stalin, holding a pipe that looked like an Uzbek boy's pissing pipe, sat a major with bushy eyebrows and an Armenian aquiline nose; Trigulov sat next to him. Abdulla could see his file, an even bulkier folder than before, lying on the table.

The major gestured him to sit.

'Accused Qodiriy, the investigation of your case has been completed. Do you have any complaints?'

Abdulla froze for a moment. If the mulla has no tricks, the congregation's in trouble, he reflected. What kind of trick was this sly Armenian playing? When the world was on fire, was this the time to dry your trousers?

'Silence implies consent,' said the major, translating a Russian cliche into Uzbek. 'If there are no complaints, then sign here.'

Abdulla signed the paper without even looking: he was in a strangely querulous state of mind.

The major took the signed document back and gave him another sheet of paper.

'Here's your indictment. If you want to, read it here, or

if you prefer, take it with you.'

Abdulla stared at the document:

> Indictment. In the case of the accused Abdulla Qodiriy, who has
> committed crimes, as specified in articles 58, 64a and 57 of the
> Uzbek ssr criminal code.

> As has become clear in the course of the investigation of the
> criminal activities of the bourgeois-nationalist anti-Soviet
> organisation operating in Uzbekistan in agreement with
> right-Trotskyists, the accused Abdulla Qodiriy has been an active
> member of this organisation. For this reason Abdulla Qodiriy was
> arrested on 1 January 1938 and has been held accountable as an
> accused person.

Abdulla read the printed words, but he could not process their meaning into his brain. Hadn't that scheming Tatar said, 'Everything is as usual, but underneath it is an abstract essence of a PROCESS'?

True, there's something here about the October revolution and his participation in the satirical magazine *The Fist*; the novel *Past Days* is mentioned, too, as are *The Scorpion under the Altar* and *Obid the Pickaxe*, also noted on this sheet of paper. It's all familiar, but distorted somehow, made to sound like some official decree. There's a paragraph about *Past Days*:

> This novel, approved by the leaders of the anti-Soviet
> bourgeois-nationalist organisation of Ikromov and Xo'jayev, was
> widely distributed among the population of the national republics.
> Furthermore, the novel was sent to eastern countries on the
> instructions of Xo'jayev.

But the book never came out in Kashgar – the intermediary never even went there!

> Before being detained, he gathered anti-revolutionary elements
> around him and took part with them in anti-revolutionary
> activities. He made contact with foreign countries.

Accordingly, the indictment, composed of charges against Abdulla Qodiriy, is presented for the consideration of the Military Collegium of the Supreme Court of the USSR.

Assistant Chief of IVth section of IIIrd administration of the NKVD of Uzbekistan, Lieutenant N. Trigulov.

"Agreed," Chief of IVth section, Major Apresyan.

Well, now I know his name, thought Abdulla, and raised his gaze to look at Apresyan.

'You're free to go,' the Major said, and then smiled gently. 'No, not in the full sense of the word.' Switching to Russian, he ordered the guard in Russian, 'Take him to the cell for the indicted.'

After that, you could expect only death.

CHAPTER 7

CRISS-CROSS

When Abdulla woke up the next morning, there were only two other prisoners next to him in the cell. At first sight they did not look like Uzbeks. The smaller and more sinewy one was Russian-looking, but he had a goatee. The other was snoring: giant, reddish, rather like the Tajiks of Badakhshan who dye their beards with henna. They must have been given a 'deregistration voucher' from the Soviet Supreme Court, Abdulla thought to himself, which is what they call a ticket to eternal freedom. Waiting for death, as Abdulla was.

On that note, he began to study his cell for 'the indicted', for those 'of no further importance'. It was very different from the one he'd known just yesterday. The walls were wet, made of peeling mud, and were plastered not with cement but with hay: more like an earthen pit than a concrete bunker. Is it supposed to get us accustomed to the grave? Abdulla wondered. Breathing was easier – the air here was rather cleaner – but the smell of damp was stronger, too.

The smaller, slightly jaundiced prisoner turned over in his sleep, chattering about something in a strange language. Could he be a Latvian?

Half an hour or so later, the fat man woke up and,

surprised to see a new prisoner in the cell, rubbed his eyes and drawled, 'Salaam aleikum!' 'Aleikum,' Abdulla replied. The fat man woke his companion and told him something in their unintelligible language. The latter didn't bother to wash his face before greeting Abdulla.

As a new arrival, the onus was on Abdulla to introduce himself first. His new neighbours each shook his hand, but neither gave their name.

'You don't speak Farsi, by any chance?' the smaller, older, man asked.

'I speak a little, but I understand it better,' Abdulla explained.

'I expect you speak Turkish better?' the giant asked in Ottoman Turkish, and when he saw Abdulla nodding, said: 'We're English.'

'Oh my God, what a disaster! What are the English doing here? Are you explorers? Or naive Communists from the Communist International: "came to flirt, ended up hooked and married"? How long have you been here?' They shrugged, so Abdulla repeated the question in Farsi.

'Here? In this place?' the older man pointed to the hay in the cell. When Abdulla's gesture confirmed that he was understood, he replied, 'Four months.' The bigger man added in Turkish, 'Four months here.'

'In December?' Abdulla asked in simple language.

Both nodded.

'How long have you been here? I mean, in Uzbekistan?' Abdulla asked in several languages.

The giant pointed to the other and said: 'He three years, me six months.'

Had they not managed to learn a little Uzbek in three years? Had they not even been outside Bukhara? Not that any of the arrogant Russian nightingales who'd been eating the bread and drinking the water here since the

Revolution had ever got round to speaking even a word of Uzbek. At least one could be grateful that these two spoke good Farsi.

'Why are you here?' the sinewy one asked.

'Nationalism,' Abdulla replied. The Englishman raised his thin eyebrows: he hadn't understood.

'I am a lover of my nation,' Abdulla put it in Farsi. The sinewy Englishman raised his eyebrows again.

'I'm a nationalist,' Abdulla said, in Turkish this time.

The burly man tried to explain something to the older one and seemed to get it across, but the smaller man's pale eyebrows were still raised.

'How about you?'

'We're said to be spies,' the red-head replied, first in Farsi, then in Turkish.

'Well, how about that! In my indictment it says 'organised connections with foreign countries', so now they can put 'shared a meal with English spies' without any need for written evidence. Or is this just another one of Trigulov's tricks? A clever twist for the novel he thinks he's writing? No, he hasn't got the authority for something like this, much less the imagination: it has to be someone a bit higher up the ladder; probably that Armenian major.'

Noticing a wave of anxiety cross Abdulla's face, the older Englishman carefully told the giant something in his own language. Are they planning to kill me? Abdulla wondered, casting a worried glance at the red-bearded man. He wasn't strong enough to tackle him, let alone strangle him. That red-skinned monster could deal with Abdulla one-handed. What's more, if he was a spy, he must have known ways of killing people with just one finger. On the other hand, Abdulla reassured himself, if he's such a professional, why did he let himself get put in here? 'Who's your interrogator?' he asked.

At that, the Englishmen again raised their eyebrows, and Abdulla racked his brains for the Farsi for 'interrogator'.

'Who carries out your inspection? Who's your inspector?' he asked in Farsi.

The older man seemed to have understood: 'Ameer Nasrullo,' he said.

Just then, while Abdulla was pondering, their fragmented conversation was interrupted by a hatch in the ceiling opening: as if into a well, a container was lowered by rope from the hatch: a brass tub holding three loaves, and a brass jug of tea. Abdulla was amazed. Who's up there? he wondered, looking up, but the hatch had slammed shut, while the red-haired giant reached out for the tub.

—

Abdulla was taken aback by the sight of these infidels reaching for the bread without having washed their faces. He looked at the corner where there were usually two buckets: one empty, to use as a latrine, and one with water; this time, though, he could see only the one empty bucket. So those warders weren't even giving them water to wash with!

The thick-set Englishman offered Abdulla some of his bread, and tea which, oddly, was served in an earthenware bowl. The bread was a real flat loaf, and the tea was made with proper green leaves, not the brick tea Abdulla was now used to. 'They're mean with the water, but not with the food': the NKVD's attitude to foreigners was puzzling.

After a breakfast, the foreigners washed their faces and rinsed their mouths with what was left of the tea. They signalled to Abdulla to do the same, before moving back over to their bedding. Abdulla washed himself in the remaining hot tea; when he put his hand in his pocket, he found the handkerchief, slightly blood-stained, but still smelling of attar of roses. Pulling it out to dry his face and hands, he glanced around again. Was this Vinokurov's idea of humane treatment?

The smell of perfume was unmistakeable as it spread round the pit. The Englishmen seemed to detect it, and gave Abdulla a meaningful look when he went back to his place.

It took time for a conversation to take shape, and when it did, it was fragmentary: it got no further than: 'What do you do for a living?', 'How old are you?', 'Do you have a wife and family?'. The Englishmen questioned Abdulla more than he did them, but he still managed to learn that the older one had a wife and children, and the younger one was single but had an elder brother working in Afghanistan.

They went on stumbling and stammering, but an hour passed without the conversation making any sense. Then the two foreigners had a long exchange of opinions in English, before they asked Abdulla's pardon and sat down to play their everyday game, which involved sweeping aside the hay and straw on the floor, drawing a grid like a chessboard in the earth, and then filling in the grid with words.

Abdulla didn't understand the words but he had no trouble grasping the game itself. For example, the old man would get three points for writing the three-letter word 'dot'; then the red-headed man would add two letters to make a longer word and thus get five points. The words could be extended horizontally or vertically. It took them an hour to fill all sixty-four squares. Abdulla judged by the big man's laughter and the old man's dour expression who had won and who had lost.

When the old man lost, he frowned and picked up his

Bible. The younger man, flushed with success, began a conversation with Abdulla in Ottoman Turkish, which the old man could not understand.

'Have you been to Kokand?' he asked Abdulla, using the familiar form of the verb.

The familiarity made Abdulla squirm, but he remembered that Turks addressed everyone like that, indiscriminately.

'Yes, I've been there. I've even written a book about it,' he replied. 'That's what I do: I'm a writer. My novels *Past Days* and *A Scorpion under the Altar* are both set partly in Kokand...' But this, of course, was too much for the Englishman, who clearly had no idea what Abdulla was talking about.

'I have something,' he said. 'From Kokand, but I cannot read it.'

Opening what looked like an amulet from around his neck, he extracted a fragment of what looked like Kokand paper: he proffered it to Abdulla somewhat boastfully. Abdulla took the piece of paper – though he almost dropped it in astonishment when he saw that it was indeed genuine ancient Kokand paper – he unfolded it and read the couplet, written in Arabic script:

> Now Russian, now Circassian, now Muslim, now Christian,
> Between one world and the other I can't find room for the
>   *shahada* prayer.

'It's from a ghazal by our great poet Mashrab. Do you understand it? Mashrab says, "Today I'm a Russian, tomorrow a Circassian" – you know, from the Caucasus. Do you know the Caucasus? Baku, Mount Elbrus, that's where the Caucasians live. "The day after tomorrow I'm a Muslim, and the day after that, an unbeliever".'

'Why would you be a Russian today?' the Englishman

asked. 'You're an Uzbek, aren't you?'

'Yes, I'm an Uzbek. Mashrab was speaking meta-phorically; he meant, "I can be whoever I want: Russian, Circassian, Muslim, unbeliever…"'

'Does he say that if you become a Russian, an unbeliever, you'll be killed?' the Englishman asked, muddling the sense of the verse even more.

'Look,' Abdulla tried another tack, 'forget all that. Were you able to be a Muslim here?'

The Englishman looked suddenly uneasy, glanced at his elderly compatriot and mumbled something in English.

Abdulla was baffled by this reaction: what could he have said that had touched a sore point? Then the younger man looked at him and said in a solemn voice: 'My faith is between me and God: it would be easier for me to die than to desert it. Even though my friend here may have pronounced the *shahada*. After all, as it says in the Qu'ran, "*La ikrakha fi ed-din*, there is no compulsion in faith." I was invited here as a guest, so I deserve to be treated like one, respectfully and honourably.'

He reached out for the Kokand paper; Abdulla put it back in the amulet and hung it around the man's neck.

—

The Englishmen also had their meals lowered on a rope, like a bucket being lowered into a well, and theirs came in a wooden tub, not an old jerry-can. Abdulla had judged correctly: special food was reserved for the Europeans. Theirs was some sort of fatty stew, with three hot flat loaves to mop it up and a pot full of fragrant green tea.

The older man, now somewhat cheered, used the end of his spoon to make a mark on the wall. 'So we don't lose count of the days,' he said.

They eagerly devoured the fatty stew, served on a real

plate: they wiped it clean with pieces of bread, which they then ate. The older man then said: 'My friend suggests we play Criss-Cross in Farsi.'

Abdulla consented, they cleared the straw from the ground again and drew a grid.

'In Latin or Arabic letters?' asked Abdulla.

'Latin,' said the younger Englishman. 'You start.' He had written in the centre of the grid: 'Oyxon'.

'Are you fond of the theatre?' asked Abdulla. If they'd been to Kokand there was a good chance they'd seen a performance of *Maysara's Antics*.'

The Englishman shrugged: he hadn't understood. Abdulla sang him sotto voce an aria:

> Now the contract has been signed
> Oyxon is forever mine.
> Maysara, cook a dish of plov,
> Today I consummate my love.

The younger Englishman then said in Turkish: 'Write down the verse for me. Did you compose it yourself?'

'No, they're by my late friend Hamza Niyazi,' said Abdulla; he took the Bible the Englishman proffered and, whispering 'God forgive me', used the Englishman's sharp pencil to write on the last page, which was blank, the verses composed by his friend, a poet who had been an unbeliever and a ladies' man.

The game went on.

———

Supper came earlier here: they hadn't yet digested the stew served for dinner when a tub of milk-stewed rice came down from the ceiling. Was everyone treated so generously while they waited for Moscow to confirm their death sentence?

One thing in particular struck Abdulla about the two Englishmen. While they were frank and devoted to one another, they were at the same time mercilessly sarcastic. The old man was somewhat reserved and formal, whereas the younger was more rough and ready, yet with a severe, austere air, and this must have been the reason for the nature of their interaction.

The older man's official status was reflected in his uniform, which looked like a railwayman's, whereas the red-headed Englishman wore a mishmash of European trousers and a ragged sheepskin coat that wouldn't have looked out of place in the streets of any Uzbek town. The way they ate their rice and milk – Abdulla's fascination overcame his sense of decorum, and he couldn't help but steal a look – was further proof of their strange habits. The old man rolled the rice in his mouth from side to side, chomping at it, while the younger man gulped it down almost without chewing. After finishing their supper in silence, they put their bowls back in the tub and began drinking tea. Brewing green tea so late was not a good idea; Abdulla sighed at the thought of the night ahead.

Each man surrendered to his own thoughts; their mood now turned from the day's events and hovered on the verge of a sort of despair.

Once they had drunk their tea, the Englishmen reverted to their own language, discussing things between themselves. Abdulla felt a little awkward, not sure whether he ought to move away and leave them to their own devices, or whether that might be construed as rude. Then the younger one addressed Abdulla in Turkish: 'If we have a talk with the city's Chief of Police and get you released from here, would you take a letter from us?' At first Abdulla thought he had misunderstood; he looked to the old man, who repeated the same thing word for word in Farsi.

Abdulla was at a loss. There were several reasons for doubt. This situation was so far outside his experience… and to be turned into a courier? Abdulla had his pride: this was not, after all, some English prison, this was Uzbekistan, Abdulla's motherland, where he enjoyed a certain standing. Even in prison, such hierarchies were still respected – no, *especially* in prison, where God knows there was little else to cling to.

All right then, let's dismiss all that as the obtuse arrogance of Englishmen; what did they mean by 'having a talk with the city's Chief of Police'? Were they seriously suggesting that they had some power over such a man? If so, what on earth were they doing here? They were prisoners themselves, what was this nonsense about them being able to get Abdulla released? He had already fallen for one April fool; he wasn't about to be taken in again. As Trigulov said, underneath all this there is a gigantic PROCESS, not a natural drift. But the Englishmen continued, in all seriousness, trying to inveigle him.

'Don't be afraid,' said the younger one, 'there's nothing subversive in the letter, it's only a request to some people in London, to whom we owe money and made promises, to carry out our last wishes.'

Abdulla grew wary again. There was every possibility that this was all some trick of the NKVD's; a piece of theatre. Petty tricks were played by petty men like Trigulov; someone like Apresyan might try his hand at a bigger deception. Suppose Abdulla took the bait and accepted the letter, wouldn't they then have enough to frame him on charges of spying and fraternising with foreign nationals?

'Here, you can see for yourself,' said the younger man, taking a thin sheet of folded paper from the older man and offering it to Abdulla. Abdulla unfolded the letter and glanced at its contents.

'But I can't understand it,' he said. 'I don't know any English.'

'I'll translate it for you,' the big man offered. 'It's addressed to my elder brother.'

My dear John,

We've been here in prison 87 days without changing our clothes, eaten alive by insects. Since my confinement I have been unable to spend any money, and I calculate that all my savings together with my life Insurance will do more than make me free of debt. Send Elliot Macnaghten my love with the money which is due to him. I think that this will satisfy. William, Helen (Frank Macnaghten) are all assured of it, but I have never sufficiently thanked them for their kind pecuniary assistance, which I would now repay. To Eliza, Matilda and Emily send my best love. You, my dear John, need no declaration of my affection for you. There is an old man in London, known to Mrs Orr and to my friend Mr Allen the bookseller in Leadenhall Street, to whom I intended to give half a crown weekly for the rest of his life. I sent home a year's allowance for him and Mrs Orr promised his pittance should not fail. In the event of my death, pray let this allowance be continued to him by some of the family. He is a worthy old man. Send my love to Mrs Orr. A great many valued friends to whom I should like to express it come to mind, but I cannot now peculiarise them all.

At this point it was too much for the red-headed Englishman: the effort of translating, the difficulty of remembering. He made no sound, and his countenance was unaltered, but when it was clear that he was not going to continue, Abdulla took the letter from his hand, folded it again and put it in his pocket. The older Englishman went up to the younger and clapped him on the shoulder as if to comfort him. The red-bearded man stood up, picked up the teapot and wetted the hem of his shirt with the tea dregs. Then he went to the older man, gently removed the latter's uniform and began anointing with his shirt hem the sores and ulcers and carbuncles which covered his flesh. Then both of them kneeled facing the wall and began to pray aloud.

Abdulla went to the other corner of the pit, sat down, spread his gown over the straw and began reciting the prayers he had missed. In the darkened cell one prayer was in English: 'Our Father, which art in heaven, Hallowed be thy Name. Thy Kingdom come. Thy will be done on earth, As it is in heaven. Give us this day our daily bread. And forgive us our trespasses, As we forgive those that trespass against us. And lead us not into temptation, But deliver us from evil. For thine is the kingdom, The power, and the glory, For ever and ever.'; the other was Muslim: 'In the name of Allah the merciful, Praise to Allah, the Lord of the inhabitants of the world, the merciful, the forgiving, the lord of the Day of Judgement. We bow down to thee and we call on thee for help: lead us along the straight road, the road of those whom thou hast blest, not of those who have incurred thy wrath, nor the path of the lost…'

The prayers that evening mingled and merged, and ended alike with the same word: 'Amen'.

CHAPTER 8

DEBATES

When Abdulla awoke in the morning, Muborak was next to him as before, but all the other men around him were strangers. A different cell again. Every morning, in order to begin life anew, a man has once more to recall where he was and what happened the previous day, like an embroiderer having to pick up her stitches.

Where had the Englishmen vanished to? Had he dreamt them? He would have sworn that you couldn't have dreamt up such things with such clarity. Abdulla put his hand into his pocket. Yes, there it was, the letter that the red-headed Englishman had given him. He then checked his other pocket. The handkerchief, folded four times, the barely perceptible scent of attar of roses.

Ashamed to have missed his early morning prayers, Abdulla got to his feet and looked around. Two buckets in the corner, as usual, and the walls were made of concrete. He looked at the ceiling. No hatch, just an ordinary light bulb behind an iron grille. By its weak light, he could make out the faces of some ten to fifteen prisoners lying on their backs, and his heart leapt when he saw who they were: there was Anqaboy, there was Fitrat, there was... someone Abdulla did not know. His heart pounded when he thought Cho'lpon might be there. No, he couldn't see him. Unless he was in the far corner...

Despite the early hour, when everyone was asleep, this cell seemed to be airier and less crowded than the previous one. Although it was half the size of the other one, there must be fewer people in it, Abdulla thought, as he hastily washed his face and hands. When he got back to his place and had a look at the far corner, alas, there was nobody he knew there, neither Cho'lpon nor anyone else. He recited the morning prayer he had missed, put his hand back in his pocket to take out the letter, quietly unfolded it in the semi-darkness, and, trying to convince himself that it was real, looked at the unintelligible words. Although it was written in English letters, when he looked at the very beginning he could read the Latin script, and when he saw 'Bukhara, The Ark, April 1842', his heart missed a beat. His eye immediately skipped to the end of the letter. Yes, as he had anticipated, the signature was 'A. Conolly'. Abdulla's head began to spin. Every day in his prayers to Allah he had asked, 'Preserve me from madness!' His prayer seemed not to have been granted. Now he beseeched, save me from disgrace and scandal! To lose your wits here in prison, surrounded by enemies, would be insupportable; worse, it would be downright dangerous No, he had to regain control of his mind. Yesterday had not happened. Muborak must have put this letter in his pocket. If he hadn't, then Abdulla must have been distracted when Muborak showed it to him and said, 'Brother, read this before you smoke it,' and Abdulla must have absent-mindedly shoved the piece of paper in his pocket. All right, as soon as Muborak woke up, he'd ask him about it.

Or was this some complicated game on the part of the NKVD? What would they have to gain from such an elaborate trick? If they were sentencing Abdulla to death, they had no need of such things.

When Abdulla had first arrived in Moscow to study, he was given a place in a hostel on Novolesnaya Street. At the hostel he met two of his neighbours: one was the Ukrainian Sergei Berezhnoy, the other was a Kazakh, Serik Saktaganov. Both had started their studies a year earlier, and therefore took Abdulla under their wings. They shared a room, studied, ate and relaxed together, and very soon the trio was inseparable. The two senior men knew Moscow like the back of their hands; they took Abdulla to the Vakhtangov theatre, to poetry evenings at the Polytechnic Institute to see Mayakovsky, famously as tall as a lighthouse, or to see the world-famous dancer Isadora Duncan when she came to town.

But they were not just interested in the arts: when summer came, once they were free of classes and examinations, they went to Sokolniki park, cycled at Vorobinye Hills, or watched the races at the Begovoi hippodrome.

One day they went to a pine forest outside the city to swim in the Moscow river. Berezhnoy had grown up by the River Dnieper and was a natural swimmer, but Serik, a man of the steppes, was not to be outdone, boasting of how he used to take girls out to Lake Balkhash. Only Abdulla, who had plunged just a couple of times into the muddy waters of the Anxor, turned out to be incompetent.

The others dived in, saying 'Let's swim to the other side!' Abdulla's heart sank, but youthful pride wouldn't let him hang back and, reluctantly, he joined in. Although it was mid-summer, the Moscow river's cold waters and Abdulla's chilled body began to feel it by the time he'd swum a quarter of the way across. His heart was pounding, but pride in his courage wouldn't let him give up, and he went on splashing away at the surface of the water. His friends had overtaken him and weren't looking behind them. Gasping for breath, at the end of his tether, Abdulla managed to get halfway, with one silent thought striking his brain: if I turn back now, the distance is the same as if I go ahead.' His arms and legs had lost all feeling, but he began desperately using them to fight the evil spell of the current and the freezing-cold water. The boundless current then swallowed him: it wasn't Abdulla's helpless arms and legs that felt it, but his throat, from which the life was draining. Just like a piece of straw, so a living being needs to swallow only two gulps of water: the Moscow river water reached Abdulla's throat and he lost consciousness. Could death really be so quiet and anonymous?

When he surfaced, not knowing which world he was in, Sergei was standing over him, and Serik was sitting there smiling, 'Well, diver, were you looking for pearls at the bottom? You could have called for us!'

That summer, their studies over, the two of them left: Sergei for Murmansk, Serik for Magadan, and they vanished without a trace from Abdulla's life. After their departure, before he met Cho'lpon, Abdulla was left on his own.

One by one, the prisoners began to wake up. Fitrat was one of the first to rise. As soon as he saw Abdulla, he leapt to his feet and rushed forwards; the two men embraced, too choked to speak. That dawn, this noble person washed his face and hands with his transparent tears.

Then he sat down facing Abdulla, regarding him without saying a word, only shaking his head. His heavy sighs woke Muborak.

'Hey, teacher, are you here too?' he said on seeing Fitrat; then he spotted Abdulla: 'Thank God, we're all together again.' A simple man, he hadn't realised that this cell was for prisoners under sentence of death. 'When I was in London, I saw a museum where they make men out of beeswax. Just like real live people. There was Stalin with his moustache, there was Churchill smoking a pipe, and our Joseph Wolff, too. Now we look as if we were made of beeswax, too.'

Muborak rubbed his eyes and fell silent for a while; then asked: 'Why aren't you talking?'

What would the two of them have to say? Everything about their situation was perfectly clear, so what need was there for words? As Cho'lpon put it:

> I have no sleep like you in my eyes, oh cloud,
> I want a lifelong silence like death!

———

As the other men woke up they started to gather around the new arrival. Everyone in this cell seemed to have their own way of preparing for their execution: there was no appointed elder, so they got up and lay down as they liked. The men around Abdulla began questioning him, asking about life outside, assuming he'd only just been arrested. After informing them that he had been in prison for three months, Abdulla talked about life in Tashkent before then. As they talked, the iron door scraped open, and they were brought the usual thin millet gruel and pale brick tea. When everyone was busy with their food, Abdulla turned to Muborak.

'We Uzbeks have a game with a calf's carcass called bozkashi; the Indians have invented chess. You were saying once that the English have their own game, cricket: what's the Jewish national game?'

'Debating,' Muborak replied without having to think about it. 'Where you have ten Jews, you'll have eleven points of view. And storytelling, of course! How about it? I could tell you more about the English spies Stoddart and

Conolly; it's a curious story, oh yes, very curious.'

'When Conolly arrived in Bukhara from Kokand, Emir Nasrullo insisted that he was a spy like Stoddart, that the two of them had turned Khiva and Kokand against Bukhara. He had them both locked up in a pit in his palace, the Ark – a terrible place, much worse than what we have here! Soon there were rumours that the two men had been beheaded. But nobody had seen their corpses, so nobody could be certain. One year later, Joseph Wolff arrived in Bukhara. An extraordinary man, a brilliant mind: he'd studied Near Eastern languages and spoke fluent Farsi. He was a Jewish Christian – one of the converts – and he travelled all over: Egypt and India, Ethiopia and Yemen, Afghanistan and Bukhara, wherever our people lived, preaching to them as a missionary. A real man of the world! So when a committee formed in London to try and help Stoddart and Conolly, he volunteered his services. Joseph Wolff was warned not to go – Nasrullo was known as 'the Butcher of Bukhara' – but he was a brave man, and obtained letters of recommendation from the Ottoman Sultan and the Shah of Iran. In the end, though, he was lucky to escape with his life – some say Nasrullo would have had him executed if the Persian government hadn't intervened; others, that the Emir was so amused by his outlandish dress (he presented himself in full clerical garb, which really must have looked quite funny) he decided on a whim to let him go free.'

—

While Muborak was describing Joseph Wolff's reception by Nasrullo, rattling away in a breathless rush as though he was under some strange compulsion, his food had grown cold and one of the prisoners had taken the bowls away, so that he was left with only a few mouthfuls of tea with which to sustain himself.

Only half-listening to Muborak's flow of talk, Abdulla was trying to make sense of what was happening to him. Whether it was all a dream, a piece of theatre, or the visions of a deranged mind; how had he not made the connection at the time? Didn't the older one say 'Ameer' and 'Nasrulla'? But even that hadn't rung the smallest bell in Abdulla's brain. And he called himself a writer? You're nothing but a naïve idiot, a simpleton, a ninny, just as your mother always said! Abdulla cursed himself, then stuck his hands in his pockets: one had a handkerchief folded in four, the other a letter folded double. Yes, both of them were safely where they should be.

In the novel that Abdulla had planned, all the knotty sections were now loosened up; there were just one or two things that remained ambiguous. To shed light on these, the Englishmen would have been handy; at the time they were in prison, Emir Nasrullo was readying his troops to march on Kokand.

By then Madali had been living as his stepmother's husband for several years. Why then did the Emir decide to act only after Captain Conolly had arrived in Bukhara?

After breakfast, when the soldier-warders had left, Fitrat came and sat with Abdulla: he looked anguished, and was reluctant to talk – until Abdulla asked the question he seemed to have been expecting.

'Have you seen Cho'lpon?'

'We were taken to a confrontation,' Fitrat said. 'They tried to set us up against each other. What times are these, Abdulla, dear fellow? Is this the revolution we fought for?'

Fitrat heaved a deep sigh. 'Cho'lpon is ill. He's got diabetes. And heart trouble, too. They've destroyed him. Everything we wrote in our books is coming to pass.' In the most melancholy voice imaginable, he recited a poem of his that had once been popular:

> Do you have amongst you, disguised as humans,
> Tricksters and deceivers, two-faced demons,
> Leeches that suck the blood of their kin
> Tigers that feast on their comrades' skin
>
> Do you have tyrants who burn their own land
> As fuel for the fire of their cooking pot stand?
> Do you have traitors who make their living
> Selling their nation, their people and everything?

Abdulla responded with another of Fitrat's poems:

> Why do they live, when they are unmoveable,
> Why have they been given wings, when they cannot fly?

For some minutes the two men lapsed into silence. Then Fitrat felt the need to speak:

'I've been classified as an English spy. Have you ever even set eyes on an Englishman?'

———

Nasrullo took a liking to Conolly; the red-headed giant reminded the Emir of the local Badakhshan Tajiks, a sharp contrast to the jaundiced, asthmatic old Stoddart. His knowledge seemed just as good, yet he was much more easy-going, more like a Muslim, with none of Stoddart's arrogance or stiffness.

So far the conversation had been about the Emir not sending Stoddart away. On the one hand, Stoddart had proved very useful, he had brought order to Bukhara's soldiers and armaments. He had made a third-rate army into a passable one, and from passable it had become first-class. He had exposed the weak points not just of the English, but of the Russians, Persians, Afghans and Indians. And the benefits he had brought to mineral extraction, the gold deposits he had discovered near Samarkand! Now that the gold had been panned, the treasury was stacked with ingots.

But more important still, Emir Nasrullo was keeping that dry stick Stoddart hostage. The Russians were pleading for him, and because of the Russians' vulnerability, he could now be friends with them. Meanwhile the Persians and the Ottoman Sultan were also showing favour to the Emir.

Now, with Stoddart's help, he would rein in the arrogant English. 'If you want me to release you,' he said, 'then insist on an agreement between your Queen and Bukhara.' The English were rushing about all over the place, firing off letter after letter.

But once Captain Conolly had been lured to Bukhara, Nasrullo's plans altered slightly. The Emir now had a choice: Conolly's a good man, the Emir thought to himself. But he must be good in the future, too. He can replace at one go that arrogant pale-face, and that Iranian crook Abdusamad. For now, though, the Emir would keep these thoughts to himself.

Emir Nasrullo questioned Conolly several times, sometimes with Stoddart, sometimes alone. He gave Conolly hard but furtive looks, studying and testing him. Now he was pleased with his very satisfactory plan.

Conolly had come with a well-meaning study of the weak points of the Kokand khanate.

In face-to-face conversations with Conolly the discerning and sharp-witted Emir had detected one other thing. That sturdy colt of an Englishman talked a lot about

Madali the Fornicator marrying his stepmother Oyxon. And every time the red-head talked about her, his blue eyes blazed under his bushy eyebrows. She had hooked that dervish's heart, and since it was hooked, then Emir Nasrullo knew very well how to keep this giant fish hooked to his rod.

For the time being, as insurance, he would put both the Englishmen in prison – not his own, but Abdusamad's. His chief artilleryman was a volatile, slippery character, but also useful, at least for the time being; likewise, the English could be kept as potential bargaining chips, or even freed if they proved their good intentions. But if they stepped out of line, writing any letters they shouldn't, Abdusamad would also be implicated – and ultimately blamed for their demise, in case any foreign powers were to get involved. The Persian was said to be fabulously wealthy, and the royal coffers could always do with some additional lining. Two birds with one stone – or, as the Uzbeks say, the calf bleats until it gets to the straw barn. For now, Nasrullo would give them all plenty of rope. Then, once Madali had been dealt with, he could decide whether to take up the slack.

———

If anyone knew the history of Bukhara, it was Fitrat, a native of the city… He had even written a tragedy, *Abdulfayz-xon*, based on Bukhara's history. Abdulla had drawn on this book for a great deal of information about the Emir's court and its intrigues; he had first read in this tragedy about the endless plots and constant bloodshed in the fight for the throne. It also taught him about the time-serving and pompous religious servants and noble-born clerics. Fitrat had read writers like Shakespeare: 'There you have passion in the oriental style, tragedy in the oriental style,' he said, when attempting to write something grave, but there was something missing in it. There wasn't one single proper hero in it. There was an Abulfayz-xon, but he was overshadowed by a Hakimbiy-atalyk. While Hakimbiy seemed to be the hero, he in turn was destined to be overshadowed by his son Rahimbiy, and then there was the rather weak young princeling Abdumo'min's story. But as well as all this, the language and the staging was heavy going... Yet there were the games played to get the throne, the Forty Daughters' Dungeon...

Fitrat seemed to have guessed what Abdulla was thinking: 'My dear Abdulla, I heard that you are thinking of writing a novel about Bukhara's history: how will it end?'

Having written a work on Uzbek morphology and syntax, Fitrat always structured his phrases faultlessly.

'Yes, I've started writing it. Actually, it's more about the Kokand khanate, the period of Emirs Umar and Madali. But there are parts which deal with Emir Nasrullo, too. I've started it, but my work's been badly hit.' Abdulla smiled wanly and pointed to the windowless walls around them.

'They haven't taken the manuscript, have they? Is it somewhere safe?'

'Apart from one or two final chapters, I've saved everything.'

'Well done. In these uncertain times one can't be too careful.'

'Professor, there's one thing I was going to ask you. In your *Abulfayz-xon* you show both Hakim-biy and Doniyol-otaliq. Didn't they live at a different time from Emir Haydar and Emir Nasrullo?'

Professor Fitrat raised both hands, as if to say, 'I admit it'. Then he said: 'You've studied history thoroughly, my dear Abdulla! Good for you! You know very well what being a writer involves: you add some things, you patch up a few places. With *Abulfayz-xon,* what I had in mind was to write about the Great Game, not just about the Shah of Iran, but also about the Russians and the English squaring up over Turkestan. Unfortunately, the times are wrong for it. So this tragedy exists only in fragments.'

Abdulla was ashamed of his early opinions. Before this conversation, he had been thinking that there was no single hero, that it was a bit of a mess.

'Stick to the point, talk about your novel, what's the novel about?' asked Fitrat. 'According to Musayyana, you said "If I write this book, nobody will bother to read *Past Days* or *The Scorpion under the Altar*." Is that true?'

'Who knows?' Abdulla shrugged. 'I had big plans, but I forgot to say *inshallah*. What's the novel about, you ask? About an unhappy woman who was wife to three rulers.'

'Oyxon?' Fitrat shivered.

Abdulla nodded.

'It looks as if you're writing about yourself,' the professor concluded.

Suddenly Abdulla felt engulfed by a wave of resentment: 'How is that?' he asked, trying to be as formal as he could.

'So I've hit the nail on the head,' Fitrat smiled faintly, 'When you respond to a question with another question, that's a sign you're at a loss for an answer. That incomparably beautiful lady was betrayed on all sides. And isn't the same true of your incomparable literary talent? It's been betrayed; is there anyone left who wouldn't sell it down the river?' he said, like a surgeon inserting a probe in someone's eye, and with repeated stabs of the knife, bringing out what had been concealed deep inside Abdulla.

—

If there was anyone in the world who knew Oyxon's secret, it was Uvaysiy. All the love that she had felt for her late daughter Oftob-oyim was now devoted to Oyxon: she loved her like a daughter. But she had no idea what was going on in Oyxon's soul.

After Conolly left Kokand and set off for Bukhara, a deep and irreparable crack opened up in Oyxon's heart. She could not settle anywhere. 'What can you tell me about the foreigner who's become your follower? Whom have you recommended him to?' she asked her ailing father, trying to trace his movements. At other times, without letting the women of the harem know, she visited Uvaysiy, but she could get no relief from her distress.

She felt like submerging herself in wine and beer, but alcohol could only cloud what she was feeling, not abolish it.

Then, using a hundred different ploys, she had one of her father's followers disguised as a dervish and sent him to Bukhara with a note for Conolly, and, just as she had once waited for Gulxaniy to return from Eski-Novqat, all those years ago, she began to wait for this young wandering dervish to return.

For a woman getting on for forty, such passion was fraught with disaster. Vague desires were all very well for a young person falling in love for the first time, but for a woman of her age passion could no longer be thought of in the abstract; it was deeply entangled with the realities of life. Only now, in that relatively late stage of her life, was Oyxon truly able to relate to those verses by Nodira and Uvaysiy. After she had spent two months burning with a mix of love, fear and desperation, a young man came from Bukhara to G'ozi-xo'ja's house, dressed in the patchwork shirt and conical hat of a wandering dervish, where he informed Oyxon that the English Captain Arthur Conolly had been thrown into the Forty Daughters dungeon.

—

'There is still a lot we don't know regarding Nasrullo's campaign against Kokand,' said Fitrat. 'Historians usually refer to a letter he had from Sultan Muhammad, Madali's younger brother. Supposedly, this letter was what led the Emir to attack Kokand, overthrow the infidel Madali and restore the proper rule of Islam. But a question arises: Emir Umar passed away in June 1828. Not long after, his heir Madali married both his wet-nurse and then stepmother, the khan's widow Oyxon. Why didn't Emir Nasrullo start his campaign then, after these outrageous actions; why did he wait ten years? No, there must have been something else behind it.'

Abdulla wasn't sure whether to voice his own conjectures. If Professor Fitrat had asked, 'My dear Abdulla, what is your conclusion?' he would have poured out everything in full. But Fitrat went on talking as if he were back in the university giving one of his famous lectures.

'In Ibrat's *History of Fergana*, war between the two khans broke out due to a dispute over the Lashgar fortress. In Xudoyorxon-zoda's *Historical Collection*, this event is linked with something more remote. Madali's younger brother Mahmud was caught plotting against him, and fled to Shahrisabz. There he wrote a plea to Emir Nasrullo, complaining that Madali's depravity made him unfit to rule. Emir Nasrullo invited Mahmud to come to Bukhara and received him with great honour in Samarkand, and gave him Urmeton and Falg'ar to govern.'

Abdulla already knew these facts, but he was waiting to see what conclusion Fitrat would draw from them. The former professor continued:

'These were the times when the lying sheikhs of Fergana were plotting. One of them returned from the *Haj* claiming to have brought a hair of the prophet with him; he displayed this false relic first in Namagan and then, when his fame had spread, all over Fergana: he seduced a thousand simple-minded men into becoming his followers; another sheikh began dancing about on stilts. There was no shortage of imbeciles willing to take orders from them. A third trickster sheikh started a new heresy: he got his followers to make flags of coloured rags and painted sticks and walk the streets, shaking them in a religious trance.'

Now this was something Abdulla hadn't heard about. Fitrat interpreted superstition and sectarian beliefs from his own atheistic point of view, which was bound to distort them; still, these incidents might well warrant inclusion in Abdulla's novel. He could picture it now: mutes following the blind, cripples following the deaf.

'Fergana was rotten to the core; Madali called a council of the chief clerics. But, afraid of provoking disturbances if they attempted to combat heresy by force, they washed their hands of the present situation, saying: "It's preferable to take measures at another time and in another place."

'Madali then called a council of his army commanders. Some declared the need to prepare for war; others were more ambivalent, "Is it worth putting our trust in the words of spies and messengers? Bukhara is a long way from Kokand."

'Among these was a group of commanders who had conspired with Mahmud-xon and were still in secret correspondence with him. Mahmud-xon was soon informed of the outcome of the council, and he in turn passed the news on to Emir Nasrullo.'

'What does Hakim's *Selected History* have to say on the subject?' Abdulla asked, happy to play the part of a devoted student.

'Much the same, although for the war, and the fate of Oyxon and Madali fate in particular, it gives a somewhat broader account. But none of that casts any light on the cause of the war.'

Abdulla hesitated. 'No,' he said.' Perhaps not.'

Emir Nasrullo had gathered his troops and gone to attack Kokand, taking all his counsellors and high officials with him, leaving only a couple of minor viziers behind in the fortress: if there was ever the time for Conolly to make his escape, it was now. But what could one do in this situation? He could not abandon Stoddart; he was the reason he'd come here, after all. And now the old man seemed on his death-bed. When would the Emir return from Kokand? As far as Conolly could tell, Kokand's forces were disorganised, there was no discipline, their armaments were old. They weren't fit for a prolonged battle. But could the outcome of any war ever be certain? Fergana's people would meet the Bukharans in battle even if they had only pick-axes and sickles.

As he had done countless times already, Conolly chewed over his encounters with Nasrullo. When talking to Stoddart, the Emir's cheek would twitch with barely-suppressed annoyance, but with Conolly he was all smiles.

What mistake had Conolly made to lose the Emir's favour? This question was a constant torment to him; if only he could find the answer, he felt he might regain Nasrullo's sympathy and be taken back into his confidence.

One thing he had noticed was odd: every time he had mentioned the name of Madali's wife Oyxon in the Emir's presence, Nasrullo would shudder as if with distaste, then shift about as if bored, then straighten up as if coming to a decision. Each time, he would switch the conversation to another subject, to the unification of Turkestan, for example, stressing all the ways in which Turkestan could not simply be considered another Afghanistan.

Was Oyxon the real reason for Conolly's imprisonment? Could Nasrullo want this Helen for his harem? If so, why hadn't he got on his horse ten or twelve years ago, and competed for this trophy as though she were the prize in his beloved bozkashi? Or was it Conolly himself who had provided him with the perfect pretext?

—

For some reason, Abdulla was growing reluctant to share this period of history with anyone else. As Fitrat carried on with his exposition, Abdulla felt a pang of jealousy; he recalled Nodira. Hadn't he once dismissed her as a jealous wife? True, at one time she had been just that, then when power passed into her hands, she resorted to underhand cunning... but the result of that cunning was to free her from her former jealousy and to draw her into new griefs and troubles, of which Madali was always the greatest cause. No sooner had Emir Umar passed away, and his son, the fifteen-year-old simpleton, had taken the throne, Nodira became de facto ruler of the Kokand Khanate: she only had to raise an eyebrow for heads to roll. Her one petty act, more suited to a jealous wife than to a powerful, liberal ruler, had been to encourage her son in his pursuit of Oyxon, but that had backfired. Even though he beat Oyxon and tormented her, she had only to raise one of heavy curved eyebrows and the young Emir was putty in her hands.

True, thanks to Uvaysiy's diplomacy and to Oyxon herself, Nodira eventually established a kind of truce with the woman who had once been her rival wife, and was now her daughter-in-law: they had taken each other's measure. But then another misfortune befell Nodira. Her two sons could not stand each other! Two heads won't fit in one cooking-pot, as they say. So her favourite, Mahmud, went into exile, first to Qarshi and then to Shahrisabz, where he married a girl of dubious heritage and ended up in misery, without a title. A mother's heart is not a melon to be divided in two and handed out, 'This half for you, that half for you'.

> An evening separated from my beloved leaves me unable to suffer any more,
> Have mercy on me, there is no way I can suffer more.

—

'The Iranian Abdusamad played a large part in these scandals and quarrels,' said Fitrat. 'Nasrullo began his attack on Kokand by laying siege to the fortress of Yom. When the Emir had encircled the fortress, he summoned Abdusamad and granted him royal favour: "Today is yours. Today, apply all the knowledge you have acquired from the English! Prepare the cannon and guns: let the fortress have a hail of gunfire."

'Abdusamad the Artilleryman bowed and placed the guns on a hill; for three nights and three days the fortress was under a hail of gunfire. The men in the fortress held out heroically: they immediately extinguished the places that caught fire, they rushed about. But on the fourth day, the cannonballs hit their own stores of gunpowder. An unimaginable fire broke out, impossible to extinguish. The fire spread to other buildings: half of the fortress and its inhabitants were burned alive. The fire made the night as bright as day. The fortress gates were opened and the Bukharan army rushed in; its governor was caught and bound hand and foot; Nasrullo had him beheaded on the spot.'

'Professor, this Abdusamad was a real scoundrel!' Muborak chimed in. 'Joseph Wolff wrote a lot about him.

Just listen to this: after nine years in Bukhara he had amassed a vast fortune, about sixty thousand gold pieces: enough for him to build himself a palace outside the city walls. He got the money through extortion and embezzlement, but he was sly; somehow, he always managed to contrive it so that somebody else's head got the chop. He seemed to have a knack for ingratiating himself with rulers, impressing them with the knowledge and sophistication he'd gained from his travels – he was forever boasting to Nasrullo about how well he understood the way the Europeans' minds worked, having had so much contact with them at Dost Mohamed's court in Kabul. So of course, when Joseph Wolff turned up, Abdusamad greased a few palms to arrange a private audience.

"'The Bukharans doubt me, and say I'm on the side of the English; the English suspect me of seeking to undermine their intentions here. But I'm merely an intermediary – all I want is that the two countries should be at peace. I've done all in my power to get Stoddart and Conolly released. I even promised the Emir a thousand gold pieces from my own savings, but he insists that they're spies, and that the penalty for spying is death. Such a barbarous people! And Nasrullo is the worst of them. Did you know he murdered all his brothers, so there would be no challenger for the throne? If he didn't need my services, he'd have had me executed too, as a sympathiser. I've been sticking my neck out, you know. For two years he hasn't paid me my salary.

"'The English government is known for its generosity: for twenty thousand gold pieces, I am ready to strike a blow for your cause. The gunpowder stocks are under my control – I can invite Nasrullo to a circumcision feast, then blow him up.'

"'The English government would never have a hand

in such a bloody conspiracy," Joseph Wolff rebuffed him. "Kings are God's shadows on earth."

'Abdusamad changed the subject. "There are Russian slaves here, about twenty of them. I can sell them to you. All twenty for a thousand gold pieces. A bargain, wouldn't you say?'

At that time the campaign against slavery was at its peak; there was no question of the English refusing money for this purpose, so Joseph Wolff agreed to Abdusamad's suggestion, even though it disgusted him to do business with such an unscrupulous man, who seemed obsessed with extorting money. Joseph Wolff, you know, was a principled man!'

None of Abdulla's previous books had featured battle scenes, except for a couple of passing allusions in *Past Days*. It had never seemed quite right to describe events that he had not personally experienced. A man who'd never been to war writing about a battle was like a woman who'd never had children describing childbirth. But if he didn't talk about the war between Kokand and Bukhara, his novel would not be complete.

He had been travelling in the Fergana valley to research this new novel when he came across a very elderly man who claimed to have witnessed the war first-hand. He would have had to have been over one hundred years old; which was perfectly possible judging by the way his bones were almost poking through his papery skin.

'Do you remember Madali-xon being killed, sir?' Abdulla had asked.

'Yes, I remember. He was killed by Nasrullo-xon.'

'And where were you at the time?' The old man frowned and replied rather slowly: 'In Khojent.'

'You didn't see Nasrullo's troops, did you? What route did he take to get to Kokand?'

'Through Khojent, of course... It was spring. The Emir's troops came through in small groups. After two or three days, the news came that Madali-xon had been killed...'

'You didn't happen to see Emir Nasrullo, did you?'

The old man opened his dull eyes wide and waved his withered hand: 'How could I? I wasn't at Khojent when he was...'

All you could get from conversations like that was one or two anecdotes. Abdulla then reread the war scenes in Shah Babur's memoirs. He learned something from Shah Babur's elegant style. Compared with other writers, Babur's history was always specific, always written as if by one who had witnessed the events with his own eyes. His work might be one-sided, but it was always sincere, concrete and vivid.

After listening to what Muborak, Kosoniy, and Fitrat had told him, Abdulla had come to a conclusion: he would describe the war through the eyes of the duplicitous Abdusamad. This man of the world had spent a lifetime surviving wars and battles, like an unsinkable fishing-line float. War was a profitable vocation for him; one or another ruler would hire him to train up a battalion as you might hire a fighting cockerel.

It would mean introducing a whole new narrative strand – could his novel really take it? On the other hand, was there really any workable alternative?

If he looked at everything through Emir Nasrullo's eyes, the account would be one-sided. Bringing in Nodira and Oyxon, he could show the tragedy of war through its collateral damage; he wouldn't be able to show the battles themselves through their eyes, though. No, it had to be

Abdusamad.

Abdulla began sketching out the battle scenes. After what happened in Yom fortress, he would have to give an account of how Mahmud betrayed Nasrullo by switching to Madali's side. This affair happened in several stages. First of all, Mahmud took O'ratepa at the head of Nasrullo's vanguard, which Nasrullo then gave him for his own. At the same time, the Emir of Bukhara sent an envoy to instil fear in Madali: 'We won O'ratepa with ease. Give us the Khojent, Qurama and Tashkent provinces, too, and the Kipchak steppes in their entirety: if you don't, beware!'

Madali had lost his best commanders at O'ratepa: he was quivering with fear. 'All right, I'll give Khojent to Nasrullo, with property and taxes in tribute,' he said, send-ing an envoy with the keys to Khojent castle.

Nasrullo sent Madali back this message: 'If Madali comes out to greet us, I shall give him back his property. If he doesn't, he had better look after himself.'

Bewildered, conflicted, Madali did not know what to do. Then a wandering dervish, a former copper-worker, came in from the street to beg an audience with the Emir: 'Your Majesty, I know how to wipe out the Mangits for good. Nasrullo and the rest of his family will never trou-ble Kokand again. All you have to do is allow me to take over the government for one day.' Desperate, clutching at straws, Madali assented. The copper-worker went outside and got the entire population of Kokand to assemble on the main square. 'I have taken over power!' he shrieked. 'The hand that's been lying idle should be raised!' He directed the people first at Madali's courtiers, whose houses were looted, and who were then humiliated by being made to mount donkeys facing the tail. The two prostitutes-turned-procuresses Xush-hol and Oshula had their houses burned down. The mob burst into the harem and Oyxon barely managed to flee, seeking sanctuary in her father's house, where she wept so many tears her body seemed a salty wasteland.

All this has to be described in detail, Abdulla thought. Might this uprising need its own chapter? In a single day all of Kokand went up in flames, like a field of dry Persian rue catching fire. The most important nobles and religious leaders went out and pleaded with the people: their intervention succeeded in quashing the uprising.

The beleaguered Madali sent nobles and clerics to Emir Nasrullo with gifts and greetings. They returned after having obtained a truce. But Nasrullo gave Khojent and Tashkent to Mahmud and he himself went back to Bukhara.

And at that point Nodira made her appearance, shuttling between Kokand and Khojent, where Mahmud had based himself. No one knew her sons' personalities better than her; by making various appeals, she was eventually able to get them to agree on a treaty of division: Mahmud got Khojent, Tashkent and Qurama provinces, the Kipchak steppes and G'urmsaroy, while the remaining part of the Kokand khanate stayed with Madali. Thus, the entirety of the former Fergana Khanate fell under the control of these two brothers, Nodira's sons. When Nasrullo heard that Mahmud had betrayed him by cutting a deal with Madali he was enraged, and in the month of Savr 1257 moved his countless soldiers in the direction of Kokand.

———

Kokand was drowning in uprisings. The day before, a mob had burst into the palace, looting everything. As soon as she found out about the rioting in the city, Uvaysiy rushed

to the harem, found Gulsum and told her to dress Oyxon
in the oldest, most ragged clothes she could find. Then
all three women put baskets on their heads, as if they had
been delivering loaves of bread to the palace; with this
makeshift disguise, they managed to get through the mob
to the Sheikhan quarter, where they sheltered in the house
of Oyxon's father.

Nodira was in Khojent visiting her son Mahmud: that
lessened Uvaysiy's troubles a little.

> For clever people among fools it is better to be insane,
> It is likewise better to stop at a mountain inn when the mob is
>   mad.

Talk spread like wildfire through the streets and alleys of
Kokand: 'The Emir of Bukhara is coming to capture the
city!' Others said joyfully, 'Now Madali the Fornicator will
be overthrown, and Mahmud will rule instead.' A hundred
people had a thousand ideas; the town was seething with
rumours.

Sitting at the feet of her paralysed father, who was
on his deathbed, Oyxon remembered her childhood in
O'ratepa, when, gathered round a campfire, the children
listened to Gulxaniy telling fairy tales and funny fables.
Once again, she saw the modest cottage in Shahrixon with
its vineyard, and she remembered Qosim, a lad like a willow branch in spring. In her father's aged, noble face, the
image of the young man was just discernible; she could
sense its reflection.

What is going to happen now? Oyxon wondered bitterly. If the enraged populace found her, they might say,
'All the trouble is because of her!', tie her to the back of a
horse and drag her at a gallop over the bare ground. Who
would feel any pity for her?

Or would she be saved by Madali, who had brought so

much misery upon her head?

If the Emir of Bukhara should capture Kokand, would Conolly be among his troops? Oyxon only had to indulge such a supposition for her heart to feel a piercing pain. This piece of flesh had died some time ago, it seemed to have turned into something hard and sinewy, but it still ached. Could the human heart really be so tough and enduring?

Even if Conolly came to Kokand, what could that change now? Oyxon chased away such aching thoughts and turned back to her pallid father. After G'ozi-xo'ja was dismissed from his post, his health had rapidly deteriorated. According to people at the market, customers were once again being given false weights, cheated and insulted.

Gulsum entered with two bowls of noodle soup, disturbing Oyxon from her thoughts.

'One is for your father, the other is for you,' she said, setting the bowls on the tablecloth. 'Take it while it's hot. I'll see to the master myself.'

'How about yourself, aren't you going to eat?' asked Oyxon anxiously.

'I'll eat later, with Uvaysiy.'

'Where is Uvaysiy?'

'On the veranda, writing.'

'Haven't you called her to come and eat?'

'She said she'd come when she's finished.'

'Father can sleep,' Oyxon decided, 'I'll feed him later myself.'

She and Gulsum had begun to drink their soup when Uvaysiy came in and whispered, 'Is the master asleep?'

Oyxon nodded.

'Madam, I've written a poem for you. Take it and read it.' Oyxon moved her bowl aside. Gulsum left the room to fetch Uvaysiy some food. Uvaysiy began reading in a deep voice:

To be loyal to those who've suffered, it is good.
To nurse those hurt by love, it is good.

But be merciless, hunter, to the injured heart:
Aim straight for the target, it is good.

If I meet you on the road, take my life;
Part my soul from my body, it is good.

You robbed me of your lovely eyes, oh my buyer
You made me cheap and my loss dear, it is good.

You knew beauty all too briefly, oh my heart;
Now fade quickly in the winehouse, it is good.

Stop this strife and noise, Uvaysiy, for your lover,
Only row when God is judge, it is good.

Just then, G'ozi-xo'ja trembled and woke up.

———

On the seventh or eighth day Sunnat again brought breakfast to the cell. Abdulla sensed that the Uzbek soldier had
something to tell him, so was in no hurry to queue up
when he went for his food. Bending over the jerry-can,
Sunnat whispered, 'There's a letter,' then shouted, 'Hold
your bowl properly!' as he handed Abdulla the letter which
he clutched close to the bowl. The bowl of rice and milk
was lukewarm, yet Abdulla felt as though his hand had
been burnt. This was the first time since his arrest that he
had a letter from the outside world. He felt like one of
those students who came to an exam with a crib sheet, that
drops off the desk in sight of the teacher: Abdulla worried his clumsy fingers might drop this note at the wrong
moment: he could feel everyone's eyes on him.

He told himself he was being ridiculous. His cellmates were busy eating their morning rice and milk, heads
bowed, spoons scraping against their bowls. Still, he had a

problem: you couldn't just roll a cigarette at mealtimes. If he'd been back in his old cell nobody would have paid the blindest bit of attention, but here...

Abdulla managed to slip the piece of paper into his pocket, but his heart would not stop racing. Who is this letter from? If it's from Rahbar, is everything all right? Has anything happened to the children? His thoughts expressed themselves in wild shapes, his mind gave rise to countless thoughts, he couldn't taste the bland rice and milk he was eating, and swallowed it without chewing. He downed the brick tea in two gulps. Some of the prisoners around him were still eating, some had finished. He looked at Muborak.

'Muborak, is there any of your tobacco left?'

Muborak first pulled a piece of paper out of his pocket and offered it to Abdulla; then he began searching his other pocket for tobacco.

Abdulla was in a fix. He had taken out his own letter, but he couldn't read it because Muborak was offering his own piece of paper! Abdulla could hardly insist on using his own paper; that would be sure to excite suspicion. He had no alternative but to accept Muborak's offering. He stiffened; would it be more from those Englishmen? And if so, what would that prove – that he was going mad, that he was being gulled, or neither? But the letter was written in Farsi:

> With greetings and prayers, we wish to make known that your kind letter has indeed reached our hands, and that its content is as clear as day. The news of your imprisonment in the dungeon of darkness is a cause of endless pain and torment to us. Thanks to the intrigues of enemies, we too are expelled from our palace to the house of our father. Searching for a way to relieve you in your difficult situation, we have decided to ask the greatest of Sayids for support, in the hope that his reverend opinion should hold sway with your captor.

Being apart from you grieves us, so that our days seem overcast;
the smoke of the evening dusk is made darker still by our sighs.
Have pity and come quickly, as soon as you can! With frank
hopes, Your Oyxon.

This document might seem a forgery, but the Farsi was
faultless: nobody today could forge such elegance. For that
reason, instead of asking, 'Where did you get it from?' or
'Who passed this on to you?', Abdulla merely said: 'Who's
it to?'

'To an English spy,' Muborak replied with a wink.

—

Abdusamad hated war with all his heart. There were quieter ways to make money: extracting bribes and taxes from
foreigners who came to Bukhara, collecting ransoms for
freeing prisoners, profiting from selling slaves… why put
his life at risk, when the gold piled up?

And instead of that, he had to put his life at stake, and
go and do battle. Fortunately, Abdusamad didn't have to
get on a horse and head the charge against the enemy.
Here it was hard to find anyone who knew about guns,
so Abdusamad was much in demand. So now when thousands of soldiers were moving from O'ratepa to Khojent,
Abdusamad could remain in the rearguard, in relative
safety, with the draft horses pulling heavy gun carriages.

What a life he had led! A tyrant in Tabriz had threatened to cut off his ear, so he ran away from his home to
serve someone else. From there he was forced to flee his
country for good, to India. He stuck to the English. He
learned a lot, but he realised he would never become a
man of importance with them, and set off for Afghanistan,
where he'd had to endure a spell in prison before earning
Dost Mohamed's trust. He was over forty now, getting on
for fifty; much of those years had been spent wandering

the world, with little time for life's pleasures. But he had landed on his feet in Bukhara.

The people here were so outstandingly backward, he had found a position and a rank befitting him! But what Abdusamad thought of as the Bukharans' barbarism was a double-edged sword. When the Emir's blood boiled and he called out 'Sentence!', whether you were a vizier or a governor, or minister of foreign affairs, the executioner would have your head off its body before you had time to protest, leaving your convulsing corpse attempting to say, 'I'm innocent, I'm innocent!' The Emir was beginning to fall into frenzies. Abdusamad had witnessed these summary executions too often. If he got back safe and sound from this war, then he had to start thinking about his future. In Bukhara he had amassed considerable wealth, squirrelling the money away in an English bank. Now the time had come to settle in some quiet corner of India, where the people were as simple as sheep and nobody would bother him. Maybe just one or two local English governors, with whom he could find a common language…

Abdusamad approached the Khojent oasis as if it were a reflection of these dreams. What great man had not besieged this city: Alexander the Great, Genghis Khan, Timur Lang, Shah Babur. And now it was his turn.

But Abdusamad's thoughts of a leisurely siege were interrupted when a messenger rode up from the vanguard: 'The enemy's not in the fortress, he's waiting in open country. Get ready for battle!'

So that's it, thought Abdusamad. He had neither the endurance, the energy, nor the desire to go into open battle. The odds of being badly injured were far too high for him. He had to think quickly, and send his own messenge to the Emir: 'His majesty should hold back the troops, and prepare the right and left flanks for battle; meanwhile the artillery should advance to the front and fire cannon at the enemy army. When they begin to panic, then let our army attack.'

The Emir quickly responded, 'Excellent!' Abdusamad moved his gunners to a hill on the western side of the battlefield, stopped the horses and aimed the line of cannon at the enemy. 'Fire!' The Kokand soldiers were overcome by confusion and panic. Ash and dust on one side, smoke on a second side, fire on the third, shrieks of despair on the fourth. At this point, the right and left flanks of the Bukharan army flung themselves onto the Kokand soldiers with cries of 'Kill! Kill!' Hand-to-hand battle began. At first, arrows snatched from the quiver and fixed to the bowstrings flew whistling through the air, then came the clash of Yemeni swords, ringing as they hit each other, hammering against shields and crunching human bones: the noise drowned out everything. Abdusamad held back his gunners, then prayed to God that the Kokanders, though much reduced in number, would not break out of their encirclement; it would only take a few to split off from the main battle and make their way over to the artillery for Abdusamad and his gunners to be hacked to pieces; they might even turn the abandoned guns against the Bukharan side.

No, Abdusamad had been right to keep the Bukharans close to one another, and to move against the left wing, where apocalyptic panic was moving eastwards to the Syr-Darya. Arrows and swords made sparks fly from helmets, screams were heard as spears pierced men, there was shrieking and whinnying when a horse was speared, headless corpses hacked in half were trampled under the hooves of maddened horses. The battlefield became a slaughterhouse, the green grass was turned red, the ditches were filled with a mixture of clay and blood. A soldier came up to Emir Nasrullo, who was watching the battle's progress from a hill, and flung down a decapitated head. 'Gadoy-bey, Keeper of the Seals,' voices announced. Less than a minute later, another head was thrown at the Emir's feet, like a carcass in a game of bozkashi: 'Bahordir-xo'ja, Receiver of Petitions'. In a short time, the Khojent Chief Minister's head was lying at the Emir's feet, and it was obvious that the scales of victory were weighed in favour of the Bukharans.

Now Abdusamad bowed to Emir Nasrullo like a horse that had won a race, and the Emir, in high spirits, applauded him as one. Soon the Khojent commanders who had been wounded in action were brought from the battlefield. Fixing them with a look of furious hatred, the Emir called out 'Sentence!' The executioner beheaded them on the spot, and the battle was settled.

—

Abdulla was in a state of panic. Unable to read the letter he was clutching, his eyes turned in one direction, then another, his mind was in disarray, directed elsewhere; he struggled again to focus it. He recalled the annihilation of Passion in the eighteenth-century Uzbek poet Nishotiy's *Beauty and the Heart*. The old poets knew everything. Every generation says, 'We have come anew to the world, we shall create the world anew!' But the world is the same old wooden tub built over the freezing cold. Just a little worse, you might say, the old men, like the prophet Jonah, had also been in the whale's belly. But every new generation begins life like the previous ones, banging its head against a rock until its neck is firmly out of joint. Philosophers were all very well, but how was Abdulla going to read the letter? If he had wait until evening, his heart would burst. He thought up a dozen ploys, but greater than any human ploy was Allah's, as it appeared; before dinner, Abdulla's name was called and he was taken out of the cell.

At first, Abdulla was taken aback: was it really him they were summoning? After all, the interrogations were over. If he was being taken out to be shot, they'd wake him just before dawn. And there were a lot of people in the queue ahead of him.

Only when his name was repeated did he stand up and move to the door. The soldier-guard, instead of taking him upstairs, hurried him along him to the prison interrogation room. The door to the room opened, and Vinokurov was standing there. He sent the soldier off and whispered to Abdulla: 'It's Trigulov who's summoned you. He'll be down in a minute. I thought I'd see you first, brother. Today it's our Easter: "Christ has risen!"' He then bent towards Abdulla, embraced him and kissed his cheek.

Abdulla had known this ritual since he was a child. Every Easter five or six Uzbek and Kazakh children from his Russian school would go to the New City Russian quarters, knocking at all the doors and saying in broken Russian, 'Christ has risen!', just as people used to go from house to house at Ramadan. It was the custom for smiling grannies and granddads to open their doors and, when they saw the children dressed in their school uniform, respond tearfully, 'He has truly risen!', offering the children colourful painted eggs, never boiled, and sweet, slightly burnt Easter cake.

Remembering the custom, Abdulla responded reflexively, 'He has truly risen!' Vinokurov's eyes shone. Taking painted eggs from his inside his tunic, he put them into Abdulla's pockets.

'You can eat them in the cell, brother,' he said, and hurried from the room. Abdulla looked around in amazement, then put an ear to the door. He could hear only

Vinokurov's departing footsteps. He thrust a hand into his pocket, and pulled the letter out from under the eggs… no, the wrong one! Ah, this one… The fumbling gave him a burning feeling, and sweat broke out on his forehead. Yes, this one… now to unfold it… how clumsy his fingers had become… he should have played cards with the thieves. He opened it; graph paper, the kind from a school workbook, and his son Habibullo's angular writing; so he had recovered!

> Greetings, father dear! Are you all right? We're fine, so don't worry. Mother is in the country. I'm taking care of the garden. Your son, Habibullo.

Steel-tipped boots could be heard approaching down the corridor. Abdulla hastily crumpled the letter and thrust it into his pocket just as the door swung open.

'Ah, Qodiriy, still alive?' Trigulov went to his side of the desk and sat down, gesturing to Abdulla to sit at his own place. Abdulla sat on a stool that was fixed to the floor. He had allowed himself to get worked up; sweat had broken out on his forehead at the sight of the interrogator. He quickly took himself in hand. Trigulov sat there looking at Abdulla through narrowed eyes, then lit a cigarette and blew the tobacco smoke at him.

Enjoying yourself, are you, you scoundrel? Abdulla said to himself.

'I thought you were supposed to be a national writer? Funny how the entire nation is against you.' Trigulov tossed a pile of newspapers at him.

'Death to the traitors!', 'Uzbekistan's workers demand that the enemies of the people be shot!', 'No mercy to the rogues,' shrieked the headlines. In one or two places he saw the names 'Cho'lpon' and 'Qodiriy'. Abdulla's heart sank. As if this wasn't enough, Trigulov passed him yet another piece of paper, the size of a human hand:

> The Uzbek ssr Chief Administration for Literature and Publishing, Uzbek Literary Administration.

No. 287. 15 April 1938.

to Comrade N. Trigulov, 4th section of Uzbek ssr NKVD State Security Administration.

We inform you that all books and pamphlets by the unmasked enemy of the people Abdulla Qodiriy have been, on the basis of the 1937 inventory, removed from circulation.

Head of the Uzbek Literary Board, Askulov.

'Your writing, your life, will vanish without a trace. Didn't I tell you to listen to what I said? You refused. So you have only yourself to blame.' He puffed stale smoke in Abdulla's face, apparently relishing every moment.

'Our novel is getting along fine without you,' he said suddenly. Yes, he really did say 'our novel'. 'Everyone's sold you down the river: your pupils, your friends, your colleagues, your readers. I'm the only one who hasn't changed my attitude. I myself will write what you've refused to.'

Abdulla looked at Trigulov with astonishment, and the interrogator tried to make himself clear:

'About your life,' he explained. 'Come on, let me read you a bit, so you see the line it will take.' He put a few sheets of paper into a copy of the magazine *The Earth's Surface* and started reading directly from them, or so it seemed:

'The following words were written in this letter: "As you said, I've rejected both worlds, and I've renounced my religion. Now an avalanche of problems is falling on my head. I haven't got a single confidant or close friend left. Come, let's leave this town and this region for good!"

'After reading the letter, the wife, without waiting for the man who had brought it, wrote a reply: "My depraved husband! Have you really not read *A Wise Man's Spring*? Have you never cast an eye on Barxudor Turkman's *Assembly of the Beautiful*? At least you've studied *The Parrot* and *Four Dervishes*, and I've seen you handling a copy of *The Doors of the Main Mosque*. In all those books, at times when men had authority, what good did they get from women; what kindness can you expect when you are empty-handed? That's what they think. Knowing all this, how can you call upon me to join you?"'

As Trigulov's voice grew steadier and his reading became more professional, the blood rushed to Abdulla's eyes, and breathing became progressively more difficult. The moment Trigulov came to the words, 'When he received this letter from his wife, who was hiding in the country...' Abdulla hurled himself across the desk.

'I'll kill you, you son of a whore!' But the papers slid under him and Abdulla's outstretched fingers missed Trigulov's throat, grasping instead a fistful of empty air.

Trigulov howled for the guards. Two soldiers burst into the cell, flung themselves on Abdulla and twisted his arms behind his back, then started slamming his head against the desk as papers flew everywhere.

Abdulla tried to resist, until Trigulov's steel-tipped boot struck him in the head.

When Abdulla, barely alive, was flung back in his cell, Muborak and Professor Fitrat used wet rags to wipe the blood from his face and head. They burned all the papers they could find, including the letters they found in Abdulla's pocket, and rubbed the ash into his wounds. At midnight, when everyone had lain down on their sides, Abdulla dragged himself to the latrine bucket in the corner, took the crumbs of the smashed eggs out of his pocket and emptied them into the bucket.

—

In addition to the pain, which made it difficult to lie comfortably, the extract that Trigulov had read made it impossible for Abdulla to get a wink of sleep that night. Whether a novel or a story, Abdulla never wrote straight through from beginning to end. He would make an outline of the work's essence, and often he would work out every detail of the denouement. Sometimes he would start a first draft before the final scenes were clear in his mind. After that he would make the story follow his outline. True, it was not impossible for the story to take unexpected turns as it developed, but its unity and form were more or less preserved, thanks to the structuring effect of the plan. The extract that Trigulov had read was one of the last episodes he had written, among the papers he had hidden in the summerhouse.

In it, Abdulla had described how, after losing the battle for Kokand and hiding in a village in Andijan, Madali sent a letter to Oyxon. Trigulov had recited what Abdulla had written almost word-for-word: it was impossible that it could be a coincidence. The moment the interrogator pronounced the words, 'wife who was hiding in the country', Abdulla realised that this 'authorial addition' was a deliberate provocation, and the son of a whore had traced Rahbar to where she was hiding.

Couldn't he have left his wife in peace? Was there anything these devils were not capable of? If Sunnat turned up in the morning, he'd have to speak to him. Could he get another letter sent to Rahbar? Could he tell her, 'Get away as far as you can, to Kazakhstan, or Bashkiria!' Those places would be quieter for Uzbeks. Remembering the note from his son Habibullo, hot tears started to Abdulla's eyes. What had he said? 'I'm looking after the garden. Don't worry.' Now that his eldest son had recovered, was he able to attend his medical courses? Abdulla was proud of Habibullo; he had acquired his father's quick wit and insight into people. When Abdulla was writing *Obid the Pickaxe*, he would get up from the low table to stretch his legs and call to Habibullo, who was doing his homework in the next room: 'Now, sir, let's hear something from you.' His son would then recount interesting anecdotes, moments Abdulla himself had ignored. One day in the hottest time of summer, when Habibullo was watering the roses in the garden, their neighbour the mulla dropped by: watching the young lad at work, he asked, 'Son, how far do you think the scent of those flowers can reach?'

Habibullo didn't understand what the mulla was getting at: he kept quiet. The mulla said: 'At most, the smell of these roses will reach the end of the lane. But the flowers of paradise spread their scent as far as a man can walk in three years...'

'He's just like your character Kalvak-Maxsum,' Habibullo then said; a perceptive remark.

His garden. Fitrat had taken the handkerchief out of Abdulla's pocket and tied it over Abdulla's forehead, covering the wound made by Trigulov's steel-tipped boot. When he worked in the garden, Abdulla used to tie a handkerchief round his head to protect it from the sun. How were the vines doing this spring? Had Habibullo spread and fanned the new shoots to the wooden hoops and stakes? One or two cross-ties for the new shoots were broken, the stakes had nothing on them. Would his son be able to cope with this? Had he found the tools?

Now the vines would be bursting into leaf, the perfect time to make dolmas. The cherries, apricots and peaches would have set fruit, and the old women would be warning

the children not to eat them when they were green, otherwise they would get goitre. Not that Josiyat or Rahbar
could control the children. But Habibullo was a sharp lad:
he wouldn't let anyone break the branches with green fruit
still on them.

But what could they do with the orchard this year?
Would they have the money to buy tomato seedlings?
Radish seeds were cheaper, and there was some left over
from last year in the shed. He hadn't written about that.
Well, as long as Habibullo wasn't expelled from college.
But what would they have to eat over the summer? Would
they spend their time in the country? If their neighbour
Yusuf hadn't been arrested, couldn't they borrow some
seed potatoes from him? He needed to write to Habibullo
about that. Should he take the risk of asking Vinokurov
personally? He already had his head wound bandaged with
Vinokurov's handkerchief: thanks for that, but no more,
Abdulla told himself. He had been writing books since his
youth, he thought he knew people; now he realised that
he had been mistaken.

———

After re-harnessing the horses to the guns, Abdusamad
and his gunners were the last to enter Khojent. When
Emir Nasrullo took the keys to the city from its elders, he
ordered, 'There is to be no looting in the city'. Because of
this, the people of the city gave their blessings, praising him
for ridding them of Madali's infidel tyranny. The banks of
the Syr-Darya were crowded: those who had feared the
city would be looted now returned to their quarters, while
those who had hidden in their houses ventured outside,
some to make plov, some slaughtering sheep, some bringing basketfuls of bread, some bringing beer and wine out
of their cellars, all in gratitude to the newly arrived victors.

The night passed in games and laughter around bonfires, to the sound of drums and shamus. At first light, Khojent's Sheikh led morning prayers in the mosque, and Nasrullo moved his vanguard off toward Kokand. In no time at all, the soldiers remaining in Khojent had looted so much that the inhabitants weren't left with even a piece of cloth to cover their loins. Abdusamad set his gunners loose in the jewellers' quarter, where they filled an entire cannon barrel with gold: necklaces and bracelets, medallions and earrings, turban jewels and nose pieces. Then they stuffed a rag down the mouth of the barrel to cork it, and Abdusamad positioned himself close behind it as he finally left the city.

———

The next morning, neither of the soldiers who brought breakfast was Sunnat. Abdulla had thought it was his turn, but that was wishful thinking; there was no set timetable, no use pinning your hopes on probabilities. The bruises and swellings from yesterday's kicking now began to throb painfully. Everything looked black to Abdulla, and Sunnat's failure to appear left him in despair. He didn't get up for breakfast; in fact, he couldn't get up. Rather clumsily, Muborak fed him oatmeal gruel with a spoon, despite Abdulla insisting that he eat his first.

'Eat well, brother, and you'll get your strength back,' Muborak said.

'For now, you shouldn't try to talk; I'll tell you a story while you have your tea.' Abdulla tried to listen, but his aching body and grim thoughts broke his concentration, so the story was like a watercolour soaked in water: its forms were unrecognisable, changed to such a degree that they began to resemble some fabulous account, the kind that wouldn't have been out of place in *A Thousand and*

One Nights.

In Bukhara, something unexpected happened to Abdusamad: he fell in love. The story's heroine was Rohila, daughter of the widowed Jewish silk trader Ilyos. Rohila was as beautiful as the moon, the mere sight of her smile was enough to leave a man bewitched, mind and soul. Her arched eyebrows seemed to shoot arrows, killing any man in front of her, her face was a pink as a tulip, her mouth was as tiny as a ring for a little finger, her navel could hold a cupful of oil, her buttocks were like two heavy bags of sand, just the shadow of her eyelashes falling over her breast was enough to enthral even a blind man to her beauty and begin to tell black from white.

At first Abdusamad decided to intimidate Ilyos, and threatened to have him locked up. But Ilyos, who supplied the Emir's harem with the best silk, and was in favour with Nasrullo, threatened to beat Abdusamad at his own game. As for money, Ilyos had more than he could count; as for rank, whether by underhand means or not, he had so much that any higher would only make him dizzy: would an Israelite lag behind a Shi'a? Abdusamad was ablaze with frustrated desire; never had he imagined such a disgraceful defeat. Nothing would make an impression. In his dreams, he pounded Ilyos' fortress with an endless barrage of cannon fire, but this was nothing to the onslaught which the idea and image of Rohila was having on his own fevered mind.

Finally, Abdusamad decided that he would win Rohila's hand by means of a trick. Weren't the two Englishmen staying in his country house? Ilyos would dearly love to establish a trade with their country. Abdusamad spread the rumour that the two men were back in favour with the Emir, and that he would soon release them, allowing them to return to England. Abdusamad announced that he was giving a feast in their honour, and invited Ilyos, suggesting that the two men might like some silks to take back with them.

Ilyos and all his family turned up at Abdusamad's country manor in their string belts. And what a magnificent banquet Abdusamad laid on! But Ilyos, like a growling guard dog, refused to move an inch from his daughter's side. Abdusamad had his butler mix cannabis seed with the spices in the guests' plov. At midnight, when the Israelites were moaning in their sleep, he achieved his aim; the beautiful Jewess was in his arms.

> How good it is if the two of us can have a tryst in your garden,
> If my hand can be on your neck, my mouth on your ear.

—

Like a man who had eaten cannabis, Abdulla was unable to distinguish dream from reality. Whether it was Muborak telling this story, or whether he had concocted something pleasant from odd phrases Muborak had uttered, what difference did it make? In prison every man longed for a woman, that was why the story had taken such a turn. Even if he called Fitrat to hear this story, the latter would only recite his famous lines:

> My darling one, may God preserve you
> From the evil eye, may he ever save you.
> You're so lovely may nothing depress you.
> My crimson flower, my shining star,
> Linger a while, let me see you.
> Are you the cure for my soul in grief?
> The throne of my heart? My belief?
> My goddess, is that what you are?
>
> My goddess, is that what you are?
> By what name should my heart address you?

Anqaboy never so much as glanced at Abdulla. And yet they had been close friends, they used to go together to Abdulla's house in the country. Why was he keeping his distance? Surely his nose wasn't still out of joint from that article?

In the mid-1920s Abdulla had published a humorous article titled 'A Wish' in the newspaper *Turkestan*. In it he wrote 'For our poets and prose-writers today: fairness for Fitrat, inspiration for Elbek, madness for Cho'lpon, patience for G'ozi, idleness for Sanjar, new secrets to emerge in Samarkand for Hoji Muin, sobering up after intoxication with Halima for G'ulom Zafariy, "Bukhara's Executioners" for Sadriddin Ayni, an idea not excluded by the Party for Mirmuhsin.' Anqaboy took considerable offence: 'Why didn't you include me in that list?'

In actual fact, as Fitrat then told Abdulla, 'if resentment was flying past in the air, Anqaboy would jump up and grab it.' Ah well, everyone's nature was God-given.

An Uzbek's wits are holistic, accumulative. From childhood, it was drilled into our minds together with our mother tongue: if you start an idea, take it to the finish line! This is because the Uzbek language's structure is such that until you get to the end of a verbal phrase, in order not to miss the meaning of the verb, whether the sentence is a question, a supposition or an exclamation, or a sizeable exposition, you won't know what it means. This was the motive power running through Abdulla's novel. But Muborak, in his disordered way, had confused everything with his intervention. A verb – an action that was being kept for the end – had been uttered too early. Abdulla had allowed himself to be seduced by details of his account, and now the whole structure of his carefully planned novel was threatening to burst apart.

Abdulla had to get back to his Uzbek way of doing things.

Madali had lost Khojent, but he still ruled Kokand, though Nasrullo was moving his troops in that direction. Abdusamad might well be sick of war, but he would go on following his Emir's troops, safe in the rearguard with his cannon full of gold.

Not far from Kokand, Nasrullo pitched camp. Madali sent his son Madamin with two senior clergy to meet him, together with the treaty that had been signed the previous year. Nasrullo summoned his counsellors. At this conference, Abdusamad was the only one to have lost all appetite for war; cautiously, he addressed the Emir: 'Let me say a few words, if your majesty does not find them tedious.' The Emir responded, 'What words? Speak!' And Abdusamad said, 'Khojent has been taken, and that is good, but Fergana is a bigger state; think how many soldiers, how much state money would have to be expended on its conquest. Now Russia's intervention is a local danger, as the Englishman Conolly has already warned. If you show mercy, and get Madali to repent of his infidel ways, let him rule Khojent, making him subject to Bukhara: a single, united Emirate would be a shield against any enemy.' But this speech was not to Nasrullo's taste; in front of all his other counsellors, the Emir kicked the kneeling Abdusamad in the mouth. 'You want to run away without finishing the job, you tanned fox!' Privately, he thought: once your cannons have done their work and Kokand is ours, I will deal with you and your Englishmen together.

With Madali's envoys as hostages, including his son prince Madamin, Nasrullo advanced his troops to Kokand.

—

Abdulla's bruises and swellings were fading now; he had listened to another dozen or so of Muborak's endless stories, but there was no news from Sunnat. When he and Fitrat sat down to talk that morning, breakfast was brought by a Russian and an Armenian. Inquiring after Sunnat might arouse their suspicions; they might well report him to the prison chief. Sunnat was Abdulla's only link with the outside world; it would be better to treasure this link by keeping it secret.

When he'd eaten his portion of millet porridge, Abdulla turned to Fitrat. 'There's something I've always wanted to ask you, Professor: why, when you've written about several of our classic poets – Yassaviy, Mashrab, Turdi – have you never set pen to paper about Nodira and Uvaysiy?'

Fitrat thought for a while.

'You're right,' he said. 'I've never written anything about our women poets. For one thing, I've read them mainly in anthologies. I've never found a single lyric by Nodira that's any good. Uvaysiy is much stronger, but if one starts writing about her, then you can't leave out Nodira, and life's too short to write about all of them.'

'In my opinion, Professor, you're too dismissive of Nodira. She's quite equal to our other poets. And then look at her life, so full of tragedies.'

'Yes, good for you!' said Fitrat. 'Here you've hit the nail on the head. "Her life full of tragedies," you say. But none of these tragedies can be detected in the verse itself. It's all unhappy love, grief and separation; the classic themes, in other words, nothing concrete from her own life. With Uvaysiy, on the other hand, you see it all right there on the page: the heartbreak of losing a child, the struggles of making a living, of old age as a woman. Speaking to God, she says:

Perhaps this message will reach the Prince, and my cry will pass

through nine heavens,
Say a prayer, erring Uvaysiy, my shoe is missing, have you got it?

In another lyric, she said:

Today, left by the beloved, Uvaysiy, abandon noise and scandal,
It is better for you to make a row when God is the Judge.

Look at her daring: she talks to God as an equal!

Abdulla agreed with Fitrat on some points, but insisted that Nodira not be discounted. 'She was also a poet of considerable daring. Think of these lines:

Whoever as a slave decreed, oh King of the world,
The probability of Nodira refusing Your way?'

'All right,' said Fitrat, 'daring aside, this is what I want to say: you can't find a single poem of hers that is based on her own life's tragedies. Tragedies like, for example, her two sons, Madali and Mahmud, opposing one another, like Mahmud getting married in a foreign city and writing to his elder brother asking for money, only for Madali to say, "He's not worth the expense." If historians can write about this, why can't Nodira?'

'She kept it all hidden,' Abdulla said in her defence.

'Keeping one's troubles to oneself is praiseworthy for a mother. But we weren't talking about the real woman Mohlaroyim, were we, but about Nodira, as she called herself?'

Fitrat had been an eager debater ever since his youth; he was now riding his hobby horse, ready for a contest, making his snorting horse break into a gallop.

'Or take Emir Nasrullo's second campaign against Kokand, after he had conquered Khojent: Mahmud betrayed him by switching to his elder brother Madali's side. When Mahmud arrived in Kokand with his troops,

Madali, who hadn't cared tuppence for his younger brother, now clutched him to his chest. Nodira, too, embraced her son, kissed his face and forehead and wept her fill. The very next day, one son renounced the throne, and the other stepped up to take it. A Shakespearean tragedy! But will you find a hint of such tragedy in Nodira's collected works? It's all:

> Oh, cypress-slim beauty, rare are your thoughts,
> The soul is burnt by a promise of a tryst with you.

'But that is a splendid poem,' Abdulla laughed.

'You're a writer, you're no critic: your weapon is not your mind, but your feelings, your trade involves finding nobility even in a scoundrel,' Fitrat said, waving his hand half in jest.

———

There was one secret that Abdulla kept deep in his heart, away from Fitrat or anyone else, that he didn't trust even himself with. Yet it held the kernel of the impulse to write this novel.

It had happened when he visited the Fergana valley to gather material for *The Scorpion under the Altar:* in the town of Shahrixon he came across an old man who possessed an anthology of poems from the Khanate period. The poems it contained were of varying quality, but one line bewitched him: 'Hassan, bereft of Husain.' When he asked after its author, the hint came that it was Oyxon, the pride and glory of Shahrixon.

There and then, the first spark of a new secret was lit inside Abdulla, and Ra'no, the heroine of *The Scorpion under the Altar*, was deposed from her prime position in his heart. However hard he tried to find Oyxon's other poems, he had no success; no one he encountered had ever seen her writing in any anthology, and people could recite no full poems, only odd lines. Yet these odd lines of Oyxon's were every bit the equal of Nodira's and Uvaysiy's couplets.

The lure of a lost manuscript is one of humanity's eternal temptations. Our ancestor Adam's first poem; the *Mushaf* of Fatima, daughter of the Prophet; Ibn-Sina's *Eastern Logic*; Yassawi's secret aphorisms… and these were just the Islamic works. If you included the lost books of other cultures, the list would number thousands, from St Margaret's gospel to the history of Genghis Khan.

Abdulla, too, had fallen into the trap. For over ten years he roamed Bukhara and the Fergana valley in search of Oyxon's collected works. In the course of these searches he managed to reconstruct the odd couplet here and there, but he found no trace of the compendium he was after.

He was convinced that if he had found a collection of Oyxon's poetry, it would have been acknowledged as the most powerful ever written by an Uzbek woman, topping even that of Nodira. Abdulla's enthusiasm really knew no bounds: if he had found that collection, he thought fever-ishly, not only would it provoke a revolution in the history of oriental classic literature, but all the secrets of the wom-an's life would be revealed. Somehow, it had come to seem to him that only when he knew Oyxon's life from begin-ning to end would he be able to bring his own life to its conclusion, to resolve the thoughts that had been plaguing him.

The previous year he had cast the net wider, touching on his quest in a conversation with Cho'lpon, who hailed from Andijan in the Fergana valley. Soon after, he brought Abdulla a whole lyric by Oyxon. Abdulla pressed him to reveal where he'd got hold of such a find, but Cho'lpon refused to give up the secret: eat the grapes, don't ask about the vineyard. Abdulla knew that Cho'lpon's father and mother both wrote lyrics. Might he have got it from an anthology kept in their house? Was that how Cho'lpon became famous – plagiarising the work of long-forgotten poets? Then he laughed at himself. His friend was fond of jokes: might he not have written the poem himself? Abdulla could still remember every line:

> You have turned to look with tears, oh my beloved, what did I do to you?
> You have thrown a stone at a mare, my beauty, what did I do to you?

> What I knew as earth – the anvil, the grain – is strewn in my dreams.
> The sharp wits are with you, I am ignorant, my pomegranate, what did I do to you?

> Water and blood were my eyes' tears, my patience swelled in my blood,
> Close and trusted friends are strangers to me, my talisman, what did I do to you?

> The caravan passes, my beloved departs, the open road for you, sobbing for me,
> I have constant business in the market – my face, what did I do to you?

> The night you died at my feet, where's Iraq, China – where?
> Today you take your stick and we part, my smoke, what did I do to you?

> I stand, mother of a bastard, alone at the scene of the Last Judgement,
> I ask even in the midst of fire – my flame, what did I do to you?

> My question to you, oh blanket, why is my loneliness so uncanny,
> The scythe reaps, the barley falls, I'm asking, what did I do to you?

> You have put me into the fire, then you have taken me into ice

and snow,
Look what you have done to me, my game of chance, what did I
do to you?

I see everything this moment, in this matter my blindness is a lie,
Once love has gone, death is the gardener, my anguish, what did
I do to you?

Whether she is a tree, your Oyxon, or a spike, the apple has lost
its dust,
Give pardon, grace and absolution, oh my Absolute, what did I
do to you?

No, Cho'lpon hadn't written this. If Cho'lpon's pseudonym had replaced Oyxon's in the poem's refrain, it wouldn't
have fitted the rhythm. And its cry was clearly that of a
woman. There was real thirst for love, Mashrab's madness
and ambition in it, which was something that Cho'lpon's
poetry lacked. That was why, years before, Abdulla had
jokingly wished him madness. Just when he was pestering
Cho'lpon, 'If you could find one complete poem, then
you really ought to find the collected poems in the same
place!', his friend was sent to prison. This single lyric was
all that was left to indicate the existence of a collection.
Abdulla still wasn't sure which part of his novel to put it in.

A few days previously, and in as casual a way as he
could manage, Abdulla had asked Muborak whether he
happened to know anything about a collection by Oyxon;
Muborak had responded with his usual alacrity, 'When I
was in London, a relative of mine showed me Conolly's
diary, which mentioned a manuscript collection, brought
from Bukhara. He wanted me to read it; unfortunately, I
was due to leave the next day.'

Could Oyxon's collected poems be preserved in faraway
London? If so, was there any way to retrieve them? Abdulla

had to laugh at himself. This truly was a kind of madness! Did he think he himself could fly as free and far as these wild dreams of his? Here he was in prison in Tashkent, contemplating a trip to London; worrying about a long lost manuscript – which might not even exist – when his own novel, the culmination of his life's work, was unfinished; as for what he had written down, Allah alone knew where those manuscripts were now.

Basically, this temptation, the nature of the discussion was too exalted: in this black place the works of Oyxon or of Abdulla would, faithfully or erratically, interpret the radiance and reflection of tablets written in heaven, while anyone else's emulation or capitulation would be equal to rebellion, even outrage… In this sense, there was no question but that the dark place to which our father Adam and mother Eve were expelled was far worse than this trivial prison.

———

At dawn on Wednesday 23 Safar 1258, when the solar drum beat out the rhythm for the start of battle and the dawn shawms chased away the army of darkness, Emir Nasrullo had his army assembled for inspection and ordered Abdusamad, with a vanguard of furious red-turbaned artillery soldiers, to prepare the cannon. The governors of Samarkand and Urgut took up position on the right flank with their forces, while the Chief Counsellor and the ruler of O'ratepa moved towards the city under the Nasrullo's command.

The citizens of Kokand were now under Mahmud's rule; day and night, their new khan kept his soldiers and mercenaries busy digging a moat around the city, ringing it with stakes, earth and rocks: the whole thing was completed in under three days.

But when Abdusamad's Shi'a gunners starting shelling the city from the west, its fortifications very soon turned to ruins. When battle broke out, the common people showed a lot of courage. Where the Bukharans breached the walls, these breaches were quickly filled; the Kokanders counter-attacked on all sides; armed with sabres and rifles, they made sorties against the enemy.

It was then that in the centre of the city two sheikhs led their followers in a revolt, proclaiming to all: 'The spirits of Holy Bukhara have told us that the ancestors have rejected Madali and his family, and that from now on all Fergana shall forever be the fief of the Emir of Holy Bukhara!'

One group went to loot the markets and shops, another set off to rob the treasury. Another battle began inside the town against the rebels; several Kokanders were martyred in this conflict.

Thanks to this internal rebellion and the constant pounding from Abdusamad's artillery, the Bukharans broke through the defences and entered the city. By noon, Kokand was completely encircled and was left to await its fate.

Seeing that the outcome was hopeless, the two royal brothers lost all interest in crown and throne: united in their approval of the principle, that only a coward wouldn't flee, they both fled the city, in opposite directions.

Then looting and robbery broke out in Kokand. Streaming into the ruined palace, Abdusamad's red turbans got to work. If in Khojent they filled just one cannon barrel, here they managed two or three, with gold and silver, pearls and rubies.

Also on 23 Safar, but in 1938, Abdulla's name was called out and he was taken out into the corridor. When he is wholly absorbed in his own thoughts, it is hard for a man's mind to surface from their embrace. One can imagine the writer's situation, as he drifts in his fantasies. As he was leaving the cell, Abdulla was asking himself, 'Were our outer defences fortified? Were barriers built outside? There mustn't be a rebellion within the city. Who can be trusted to deal with it? The enemy is at the gates, the guns and cannon are ready to fire. Merciless, pitiless. They'll massacre your mother, your wife and children, they'll loot all your possessions…'

A door was opened, Abdulla was pushed into a room; only Vinokurov was there. For a moment Abdulla seemed to come back to reality, but then the vortex governing his thoughts began seething again.

Hadn't Abdusamad said, "The best way to deal with the Russian threat would be for Bukhara, Kokand and Khiva to unite. By creating one single empire out of three khanates, it can be a shield against any enemy who attacks us…" And didn't Nasrullo reward him with a boot in the mouth? Perhaps Vinokurov, too, would kick Abdulla in the face with his steel-tipped leather boot.

'Abdulla, it's me, what's wrong with you?' Vinokurov was quivering with amazement and alarm. 'Do you still not trust me? Here, Cho'lpon has sent this for you.' Vinokurov offered him a sheet of paper.

Abdulla took the paper: he was assailed with doubts. Whether this was all an illusion, or nervous exhaustion, Abdulla's thoughts couldn't escape from the abyss, however hard he resolved to return to reality. 'Who is this letter really from?' Vinokurov stared long and hard at Abdulla.

'You still don't trust me, do you? What do I have to do to earn your trust?' Vinokurov pulled his revolver out of its holster and waved it in Abdulla's face. 'He's bound to shoot me now,' thought Abdulla. 'So that's why my mind has been falling apart — somehow, I knew the end was coming' Suddenly, everything inside him went quiet, as quiet as falling snow. Then Vinokurov grew hysterical.

'There's only one bullet in the barrel, I'm going to spin it now. Now, let's see what happens: I'll hold the revolver to my head. See if I'm pretending!' Vinokurov pressed the trigger. The revolver clicked, and Abdulla's heart nearly burst.

'Do you trust me? Now do you trust me?' Abruptly enfeebled, Vinokurov let himself slump heavily onto a stool.

Silence ensued. Abdulla's trembling fingers unfolded the piece of paper:

> An empty cemetery in the pitch-black night:
> Imagine a lonely traveller strayed.
> Yes, you're afraid! You're afraid!
> But on the horizon a little light,
> Three or four stars always shimmer –
> You can just see by the light they made.
> Your frightened heart stops, but a glimmer
> Of hope towards your eyes is born.
> This is the light of freedom's dawn!

At the bottom was a postscript: 'Abdulla, remember this sinner in your prayers.'

CHAPTER 9

RUSSIAN ROULETTE

Summer in the prison began with ominous news. In the notorious Room No. 42, Vinokurov had shot himself. Some believed the news, some didn't, some seemed to know the details: he had been drinking and decided to play a game of Russian roulette. Others, determined to put the most favourable interpretation on it, said that he had been exposed for beating prisoners. Only Abdulla could truly say he was sorry; not just sorry, he found himself waking abruptly at night, remembering what had passed between them. True, he had never trusted the Russian; he had hated him from the start, and his heart had not thawed on further acquaintance. Vinokurov had frightened him with his night-time game of Russian roulette, but this hadn't given Abdulla any faith in him as a human being. No, as Rahbar always said, Abdulla didn't understand people, he merely invented them.

Death never comes singly. A week after Vinokurov's suicide, at first light, Muborak's name was called. The wretched Jew ran from one end of the cell to the other, as if hoping for a place to hide.

'Brother, tell them, I'm no crook,' he said, clutching Abdulla to his chest and sobbing quietly. But two soldiers seized him by the armpits and dragged him off.

When the sun is in Gemini and heading for Cancer, the season of death begins, thought Abdulla. This season of death had been already on his mind. However much Abdulla sought to delay it, his narrative rushed ever faster towards its tragic finale, like water racing into a river's vortex.

When the news that Kokand has been captured reached the palace, Madali gathered up everything left in the treasury and set off for O'zgan castle, the most heavily fortified place in Fergana. Mahmud, seeing that the situation was hopeless without support, fled Kokand with his closest companions. The abandoned city was victim to such looting that nothing was left of the houses except for the carved woodwork and the cobwebs in the reception rooms. The common people had not even been left anything to cover their naked bodies! The Bukharans raped their women and girls; all the wells were filled with blood, and the streets with puddles of tears. The girls, their heads and feet bare, were mounted behind the Bukharan riders; women slung onto their horses as if they were goat carcasses, and taken off wherever the soldiers wanted.

As for Madali, he was galloping over the steppes and the foothills with his bodyguards towards O'zgan, but his horses and pack animals were quickly exhausted, and they were forced to stop for the night in Marg'ilon.

In the morning, they set off again. Mahmud-xo'ja Marg'iloniy, a Bukharan who had been brought up in Fergana, decided on his own initiative to hand over Madali-xon and Sultan Mahmud-xon to Emir Nasrullo: this man sent squads of his men in different directions. Meanwhile, Madali, who had lost his horses and become separated from his courtiers, reached a village in Andijan province. He stopped here in the house of the village elder, dressed up two of his adjutants as merchants and sent them to Andijan market to buy horses and pack animals. He sent another close associate to Shahrixon with a supplicatory letter to Oyxon, who was hiding there with her younger sisters.

We know what happened when Madali's envoy reached Shahrixon, so let's listen to what happened to the two idiots who had gone, dressed as merchants, to Andijan's horse market. When they had bought the horses and pack animals and were riding back to Madali, they were inter-cepted by one of Mahmud-xo'ja's fast-moving horsemen. After some words had been exchanged, the quick-witted horseman realised who they were and who the horses and pack animals were meant for. The horseman got the envoys to tell him everything: where Madali was staying, and in whose house.

When the two hapless 'traders' got back to the elder's house and Madali realised what had happened, he hurried to get his horses ready for departure; but it was too late.

By now Mahmud-xo'ja and his fifteen horsemen had surrounded the elder's house. When Madali saw this, he and his warriors decided to fight back. If a fight broke out, Madali could not be killed, as Nasrullo had not passed a death sentence on him. So Mahmud-xo'ja cunningly dismounted, kissed the ground in front of Madali and, bowing low, said: 'Your highness, I was about to declare holy war against the Emir of Bukhara and raise the flag for the nation of Fergana, but a courier has ridden in from Kokand to say that the Emir wants to make peace between your two states, with the intention of returning to Bukhara after restoring you to your throne.' Mahmud-xo'ja swore so many oaths that Madali, trusting the word of a *Haji*, set off back to Kokand.

As he approached the outskirts of Shahrixon, Madali

once again sent a trusted companion with a letter for his wife Oyxon. In this letter he informed her that the Emir of Bukhara was restoring him to his throne: 'Oh faithless woman, who has broken her marriage vows, whatever tricks you may be up to, go back to my harem!' He entered Shahrixon on the pretext of needing to shoe his horse. When the messenger found the family where Oyxon was hiding and handed her the letter, this unforgiving beauty responded: 'Go and tell that womaniser Madali that a man who expects a pretty girl to be faithful must have a temperament expert in patience, if he is planting a flowerbed in burning heat. Has he not heard this poem by Hafiz?

> I said, learn to show love to those who have shown fidelity,
> She said that very little will come from the moon-faced beauties.'

When the messenger whispered this message to him, Madali fell off his horse and wept loudly. His tears mingled with the dust, he yelled out a quatrain by Shah Babur:

> Separated from you, this night is one of grief for the heart,
> I have not kept my tryst with you, this was the point.
> The fumes of my groans, together with the tears from my eyes
> Made the path muddy, the night was dark…

—

Vinokurov's suicide in cell No. 42 led Abdulla to recall the fate of Jan Witkiewicz.

Before bringing Witkiewicz into the novel, Abdulla had used his friend Aleksei Tolstoy to obtain a number of relevant documents from the Russian archives. Among them was Witkiewicz's report on his journey to Bukhara in 1836, on a reconnaissance mission on behalf of General Perovsky of Orenburg.

Abdulla had already sketched out the episode in which Witkiewicz arrived in Bukhara with his caravan. But he hadn't yet written about his encounter with the Chief Minister Hakim.

Witkiewicz's account of Hakim runs: 'A cross-eyed, cunning, mercenary old man, the owner of a large capital, richer than any other Bukharan, even the Emir. He is responsible for the kitchen and stables, the court and its administration; he is everything: the courts, the police, the water-supply and the officialdom – he is first vizier in all spheres, He also controls the customs, which are wholly answerable to him.'

Witkiewicz visited the Chief Minister eight times. He openly hinted that a bird in the hand was better than one in the bush: in other words, the English were far beyond the mountains, whereas the Russians were nearby; thus, it was with them that Bukhara ought to trade. He tried to get some Russian prisoners freed, hoping to take them back with him, but Hakim was too cunning to take the hint: 'The Russians are perfectly happy where they are; they've kept their religion, and they get drunk as lords on holidays.'

One particular aspect of Witkiewicz's tragedy occupied Abdulla's thoughts. Before shooting himself, the Pole must have thought, 'Here I am, trying to do good for those backward Asiatics, and I've been turned into an agent of the Tsar's government. And for what? That same government has focussed their politics on Turkey and Iran; nobody cares about Bukhara or Afghanistan. As a youth I swore to liberate my motherland from Russian colonisation; now here I am sticking the heads of other nations into that same noose...'

Abdulla discussed his ideas at length with Fitrat, recalling other nations which had somehow ended up enslaving the foreign peoples they claimed to want to make happy, from the Russians in Uzbekistan to the British Raj in

India.

'My dear Abdulla, one thing can't be denied: we've allowed ourselves to get sucked into a quagmire. I've written a lot about it, as you know. Not the Reds' rubbish about Soviet times: the times of the Emir of Bukhara. I've thought a lot about why the West forged ahead, while our Islamic East lost the advantage and let itself stagnate.'

'And what was your conclusion?' Abdulla was genuinely interested.

'There were a number of causes,' said the Professor. 'Firstly, during the period known as the Enlightenment, they agreed to a certain distinction: give God what belonged to God, and man what belonged to man. Though this is by no means alien to us. As far back as the 1300s, in Bukhara itself, the Sufi His Majesty Baho-uddin Naqshband's motto was "The heart for God, the hands for labour." And people say something similar now: "Yours is the effort, mine is the prosperity."'

'So why did it work for them and not for us?'

'They backed up their motto with a system of education. They founded universities, they developed humanitarian studies, they made inventions and discoveries. Until the *jadid* schools came along, we only had religious studies. I spent fifteen years in a madrasa, I know it inside out,' said Fitrat.

'Later, they began to acquire a sense of freedom, first in reasoning, and then in their personal life. Something called initiative awoke. It was the era of heroism, and of enterprise: some men discovering America; others went to the North Pole, some grazed sheep or produced milk. The main thing is that this gave rise to constant competition. A rational process became the basis of the economy.'

'Would that be right for us? We're an Islamic people in all respects. We value the family, we value our local neighbourhood, the city... the motherland, the nation...'

'This is precisely what I'm talking about,' Fitrat said impatiently. 'All right, what I'm saying seems to go against your views, but take a look at yourself, at your books! What made your Otabek unique? Forget about what he says, which is directly opposed to public opinion; pay attention to his actions. He married Kumush without telling his parents! What would you have said if something like that happened in your neighbourhood, in your society, among Uzbeks?'

Fitrat's sharp eyes glinted as his stare held Abdulla.

'My friend, the thing that made you Abdulla Qodiriy was precisely that inner freedom, a free sense of identity. But the West's defeat of the East has another basis, too.'

'What basis?'

'The strength of its laws. To stop other people's freedom encroaching on your own, equality before the law is necessary. Needless to say, I'm not talking about the law which has led you and me to be sitting here today.' Fitrat permitted himself an ironic smile. 'But not the sharia law of the days of Islamic judges, either. Did you know that in the time of Emir Nasrullo, whom you're so interested in, those same Islamic judges and mullas issued a fatwa in favour of pederasty?'

'But that's not so bad,' Abdulla joked, 'compared with the fatwas in Kokand that allowed Madali to marry his stepmother.'

'Equality before the law is the foundation for equality of opportunity. Combined with personal initiative, as I said, this is the step which would take us from yesterday's poverty to tomorrow's prosperity.'

Abdulla meant to say something about Obid the Pickaxe and Berdi the Tatar, but decided to keep his objections to himself. A man can be lectured to, but as a result the thought would die.

—

What kept Abdulla alive was his novel. Otherwise, his state of mind would be no better than that of the NKVD officer Vinokurov (whose first name Abdulla had never asked about) in Room No. 42. True, Abdulla had no weapon with which to shoot himself, but if a man is tired of life, he will find some means or other to end it. All he needed was willpower and the wish to die.

Just as Professor Zasypkin was in a hurry to finish his game of chess, so Abdulla wanted to finish his novel, even if he didn't finish writing it, but just thought it out to the end. Why? Because when you bring something to a conclusion, things you don't know will be revealed to you, and then you will no longer regard the work as something you did personally, a part of yourself: you will accept it as if it were a revelation from the blue. 'Was it really me who wrote that?' you will ask, staring at your handwriting in disbelief.

Mahmud-xo'ja Marg'iloniy, who had tricked Madali into setting off for Kokand, gradually dispersed his companions and associates; by the time they got to Marg'ilon, Madali was completely alone, deprived of both his horse and his golden gown. A man who used to keep thousands of thoroughbred racing horses in his own stables now lacked even a donkey; forced to ride in a cart, wearing an ordinary striped gown, he finally grasped the full extent of his woes. As they were approaching Kokand, he begged and pleaded, 'Don't take me into Kokand by daylight, *Haji*! Let me enter under cover of darkness!' But the

treacherous Mahmud-xo'ja turned a deaf ear to his pleas.
In broad daylight, he paraded yesterday's Khan of Fergana
through the streets, for all to see his destitution. Even those
who had once complained of Madali's tyranny wept out
loud when they saw state to which their Khan had been
reduced. Mahmud-xo'ja Marg'iloniy delivered Madali
to the blue pavilion that the latter had built, where Emir
Nasrullo awaited him. Once the two rulers had set eyes
on each other, Nasrullo waved his hand: 'To the prison!'
Imprisoned in his own palace, the Khan said not a word,
absorbed in his own dark thoughts. When the time for
night prayers approached, he lifted his head and addressed
one of the guards, who was sitting nearby: 'Not a thing
has passed my lips for three days. Could I trouble you for a
bite to eat?' 'Ask your father to satisfy your whims! This is
all you'll get from us.' The guard thrust a brass ewer of icy
water forward. The Khan fell silent.

As Madali raised the ewer to his lips, about to slake his
thirst, two executioners loomed up in the dark, grabbing
him by the armpits, so he could offer no resistance. They
dragged him off unwashed and unrelieved, to be questioned or tortured.

—

After night-time prayers, Abdulla's name was called out,
and once again he was taken outside. Has the sentence
come from Moscow? he wondered as he was led out.
Yet again he was taken to one of the prison's interrogation rooms. As usual, Trigulov was sitting there with his
revolver on his belt and his sergeant's stripes on his collar.
Apart from his remark 'This time, if you go for me, I'll
shoot you on the spot,' everything was the same: the thick
criminal file in front of him, and on the other side of the
desk the stool fixed to the concrete.

Abdulla abruptly realised that he harboured no resentment, hostility or desire for retribution towards the man
watching him. He sat down on the bench that Trigulov
indicated with a receptive look that said right, I'm ready.

Trigulov seemed to be in no hurry, taking a deep draw
on his cigarette as he perused the papers in front of him. It
didn't look as if a sentence had come. That devil couldn't
have held back from saying so straight out. Was he going
to boast about his writing exercises again?

'You must know what happened to Vinokurov?'
Trigulov asked.

Abdulla nodded.

'They say the two of you had a relationship: is that so?'

'He was a warder, I'm a prisoner, that was our relationship,' Abdulla said brusquely.

'The soldiers saw him give you a cigarette.'

Haven't you done the same? Abdulla wanted to say, but
instead he came out with a scornful: 'Didn't you see him
beat me till I bled, knock the living daylights out of me?'

'That was his job,' Trigulov sneered. And since we're
on the subject...' Here we go again, thought Abdulla, but
resolved to be patient.

'Has it never occurred to you that an interrogator and
a writer have quite a few things in common?'

Only we don't lock people up, but Abdulla began to
have his doubts as soon as this thought popped into his
head: unless prison is something invented, a work of art.
Trigulov seemed to have heard this: he continued.

'Don't both seek to uncover the secrets of a person's
soul? Why does your Berdi the Tatar take an axe and split
Shodmonboy's head in two? Why does Obid the Pickaxe
join the collective farm, when he is so dissatisfied? That's
something an interrogator has to investigate.'

It occurred to Abdulla that if the sergeant managed to

get inside the world of his books, he would lock up practically everyone he met there – both Berdi the Tatar and Shodmonboy.

'There are differences, of course, but a novel is an enquiry into a human being's spirit, his identity, in much the same way as a prison interrogation – isn't that so, my learned writer? This isn't one of those interrogations, of course, just a friendly chat, so you don't have to answer now. Let me just tell you a story, and you can draw your own conclusions. Ah yes, I meant to say, here's a cigarette, here are the matches, go on, make yourself at home.'

If there had been any fly on the wall, they might have thought that here were two friends having a heart-to-heart about some lofty matter. The fact that one was an executioner, and the other his victim, would not have been immediately apparent.

Abdulla smoked, and went on listening. Trigulov's voice was low as he began his story:

'In the Russian province of Penza, on the Sura river, lies a village called Delino. It's mainly settled by Tatars. But these are baptised Tatars; in other words, forcibly converted. The story of their conversion goes back to the middle of the nineteenth century, but it might have happened even earlier. In the 1830s a priest was sent to this village, and he called upon the Muslim Tatars to convert. He promised money to some, allotted plots of church-owned land to others, and he tried to frighten the rest with deportation to Siberia or imprisonment behind stockades. The village elder may have been frightened, or he may have been greedy; in any case, he was the first to convert. A few of his relatives followed suit, and these men then united to persecute the rest. First, they demolished the village mosque and built a church in its place, then they began levelling the Muslim cemetery. People endured this as long as they could, but one night they set fire to the priest and the village elder's houses, killing them and all their relatives.

'After that, mounted Cossacks came from Penza to attack the village. It was a massacre; the village was drowning in blood. Those who escaped fled to the forest, but it was winter, and many died of exposure. Those that were caught were sent to Siberia. The chief was a young man called To'raqul; sheltered by kind-hearted people, he eventually made it through the forests, where he joined a caravan than was on its way to Bukhara.

'Here he married a Jewish widow called Rohila who had converted to Islam; they had children. But Rohila the Jewess died. When the Russians invaded Turkestan, the roads to Russia were open, and To'raqul, near the end of his life, returned with great difficulty to his home village of Delino. He took his eldest son Ishoq with him. Nobody in the village recognised him, everyone had long since accepted Christianity, except for a handful of old men. He kept himself to himself and prayed at home. Time passed: his son, influenced by boys his own age, changed his name to Isaac and decided to marry one of the baptised girls. His father drove him out of the house. Around then, the son of the village elder who had been murdered in the insurrection, now a man of high rank, returned to Delino, recognised To'raqul and handed him over to the police. The old man was sent to Siberia.

'When Isaac heard about this, he took his wife and his only son Nurlin and fled to Bukhara.'

When the tale reached this point, Abdulla realised whom this story was about. 'Ah yes, I've got it. The man facing me is State Security Sergeant Nurlin Ishoqovich Trigulov.'

———

For the first time, Abdulla felt a surge of pity for the interrogator. It didn't matter whom you stuck a needle into, they all bled and suffered. For instance, Vinokurov, whom he considered more a devil than a human being, had shot himself. And just now Trigulov seemed to have told Abdulla that the stories and the suffering the latter spent his time inventing had nothing on real life. And yet, wasn't there something suspicious in his mentioning the Bukharan Jewess Rohila? Could it be that this was all a game? As Mayakovsky himself had said: 'We were born to make fairy tales reality.'

Why had Trigulov told him this story? Was it to assert his claim to be a writer? Or was it a reproach: 'You've been ignoring me?' Once again, the end of the thread seemed to be missing, and Abdulla's thoughts were hopelessly confused. He could no longer trace them back to their beginning: they had drifted in various directions, they overflowed like dough in a bowl. If you turned the tray upside down, you'd squash the dough, crumple the tablecloth, and dirty the seat covers. The best thing was to look after your own affairs, not to stray from your familiar pastures, not to stumble away from your tether.

Now that Mahmud had abandoned his mother Nodira and fled Kokand, renouncing his crown and throne, he reached Shahrixon with his suite. From Shahrixon they were heading for Andijan, where, by getting reinforcements in the fortress, they could rouse the Kyrgyz against the Bukharans. But the citizens of Shahrixon were enraged that their Emir's wife Oyxon had been expelled from Kokand back to her native city, and when they found out that Mahmud had arrived in their city they swore that they would hand him over to Emir Nasrullo. At night, when the Khan and his noblemen had gone to sleep, the people fell upon them when they least expected it, and bound them hand and foot. They ripped the Khan's clothes off and covered him with an old blanket. 'See, I put that boot on the throne, now you've untied it,' said the Khan, regretfully, his hands and feet oozing blood. But was anyone listening? Alas, no: they put him on a cart and sent the horses galloping off towards Kokand.

Once he arrived in Kokand, when the people of the city saw the newly dethroned Khan in such a lamentable state, they sighed sadly. They groaned at the world, the treachery of perfidious fortune. The captors quickly dashed to the palace to get their rewards. Emir Nasrullo merely caught a distant sight of Mahmud: he spat and gave the order, 'To prison!' Mahmud-xon was taken to the same place where the young princes, Oyxon's two sons by Madali, were already languishing in captivity.

Looking around in the pitch darkness, Abdulla felt them there: Madali and Mahmud, Nodira and Oyxon, all awaiting an answer. Their eyes all asked the same questions: what have you done to us? Why have you put us in this setting? Reproaches and warnings echoing off the walls.

I'm just like you! Abdulla wanted to say. There's no difference between us! but his tongue refused to form the words. He could have played the omniscient author, told them that this was just a foretaste, only he could not meet their flashing eyes. As for them, did they have any idea of what awaited him? Why then did they all stay silent?

—

When the men who had handed Madali over to Emir Nasrullo returned to Shahrixon, they showed everyone the gifts they had received and told the story of those who had been imprisoned in the palace. Oyxon became pensive when she heard what they had to say. Had she done the right thing in rejecting her husband? In refusing to protect Mahmud from the citizens of Shahrixon? In not helping Nodira, the senior wife, to flee here? Didn't Oyxon have a hand their imprisonment? Or, as Hafiz put it:

My heart is a treasury of secrets, yet the hand of destiny,
Slamming its door, gave the key to the tormentor of my heart.

Was this hand of destiny their way of avenging themselves? No, Oyxon was tormenting herself needlessly with these questions, she had been born unlucky: whatever she set out to do in this world, nothing but harm ever came from it. She had found joy in the hilly steppes of O'ratepa, and her father, destitute, was exiled to Shahrixon; she had loved the young Sayid Qosim, and had been forced to marry Emir Umar. But the 'predator' who violated Oyxon had not lived for long. He passed away at the age of thirty, as if Oyxon's silent curses had reached the ear of God. Just as she was rejoicing in her new-found freedom, her stepson Madali, a still more brutal predator, had cast aside religious teachings to marry her. As if that were not enough, he had Gulxaniy, who had done no wrong, drowned, and the innocent Qosim stoned to death. Now the executioner must be sharpening his sword over Madali's head. May none of this be blamed on Oyxon! She'd had two bastard sons by Madali. Only recently had she developed any affection for them, then that jealous jackal sent one as a hostage to Emir Nasrullo, and locked the other one up in the palace. Now both of the innocent princes were in prison in Kokand, waiting for death. If only Oyxon were not held accountable for all these deaths in the next world.

What could she do, sleepless at midnight? Her prayers

went unanswered because of her sins, and now God would not listen to her. Perhaps she should go and surrender herself to Nasrullo? She could say, you started a war against Madali, but I, not he, am to blame for his apostasy. Kill me, and let the others go! She could say this; yes, this was what ought to be done. That would bring about God's mercy, and if the Emir's wife's prayed to the Almighty for her children, perhaps he would allow her life after death!

Abdulla awoke at midnight, soaked in cold sweat. Why was he trembling? What had he been dreaming of? Where did the nightmares and delirium come from? However hard he tried, he couldn't remember the dream that had reduced him to this state. The shade of his mother Josiyat seemed to have appeared from afar. 'Child, you've seen the devil!' his mother had said one day, when Abdulla was sitting on the veranda, weeping bitterly after 'killing off' his heroine Kumush. But he hadn't killed anyone off today, he hadn't even intended to make an attempt on anyone's life. He looked about him. He was lying in a row of men, each waiting for his death. What unconscious thought had woken him? Should he yell out? Call for someone? Call for help? It was pointless; Vinokurov himself had known it. It was all in God's hands. If an earthquake struck that same day, prisoners and guards would meet their deaths together. 'One single Shout!' as the Qu'ran says. And this concrete prison might be the only hole left in town. A mouse-hole is worth a thousand shillings, after all.

But this wasn't why Abdulla was trembling. What then was the reason? Was it the deaths? Vinokurov; Jur'at, the lover of proverbs; Professor Zasypkin; Kosoniy's and Muborak... Wasn't Abdulla in some way to blame? But how? Had his own wretched fall from grace brought down these other men? Was that what Trigulov had been hinting at? The dying die not for themselves but for others; that was why it was easier for whoever died first. What should Abdulla do? Confess all his crimes, existent and non-existent, and ask to be shot as soon as possible. But who would be saved by his death?

In trodden mud the horse leaves behind,
In marks on grass you sometimes find,
In the darkness of words to which I'm blind –
There is nothing more than chance.

Substance and nothingness made and remade,
The shade of a tree and a sketch of the shade,
An image's reflection, a reflection displayed –
Are just coincidence's dance.

Strange relics from a Stone Age site,
Moths scattered by the light,
Signs in the stars in the black of night –
Are false spirits that lead us on.

Cast off, we seek your name in all –
In drops of rain or how crumbs fall
Or a wandering dervish's death call
Which are flawed when found, flawless when gone.

'My dear Abdulla, you're a writer. And the sort of writer, as Cho'lpon liked to say, that would not be born to an Uzbek mother in a hundred years. Why don't you write about all this?' Fitrat exclaimed the next day.

'About all what?' Abdulla replied.

'The situation here, of course,' Fitrat replied, waving his hand around him.

'It's not as if I've been sent here on creative leave,' Abdulla demurred.

'Well, that's fair enough. But if you had the opportunity to write about it, wouldn't you?'

'Who knows? Anyone who's gone through something similar himself will take it with him to the grave. Anyone who hasn't will simply say "There but for the grace of God!" I'd say that there's nothing here one can make literature out of.'

'You're giving an answer from a professional point of view; my question was from a human one.' In any conversation with Fitrat, even an ordinary exchange would run into difficulties. Meanings would multiply, merge and divide, and the result, like any equation, would end as a zero sum.

'Very well, from the human point of view: there is death here, but no love. It's hard to make literature out of nothing but death; that's why I wouldn't write about this place.'

Abdulla said all this impromptu, but when he thought about it, all his books had been structured on the same basis. Even his old story, 'Dance of Devils', linked the horror of his father's death with a beautiful angelic figure. You could not make literature out of meaningless death. Death had to interact with life. Life was not more expressive than love, because love was a life-giving force. Perhaps he ought to say these things outright to Fitrat, who valued logic and precision most of all. But then, there was no need to labour the point; a hint should be enough for an intelligent man.

'So you don't think there's any mystery to all this?' Fitrat asked.

'There may be, but the mystery of waiting for death has nothing to do that of of being torn away from life: I'd say, rather, it simplifies it.'

'You've convinced me,' said Fitrat. 'Think of da Vinci's *La Gioconda*. It's a portrait of a woman. She's not exactly a beauty, but she's certainly not ugly. Her hair is neither curly nor straight, you can't tell if her smile is amusement or reproach, whether she wants to embrace you or push you away. Her breasts are neither exposed nor concealed, the spectator can call her hands, folded on her chest, delicate if he wants, or if he prefers, he can call them rough. So wherever you look, you find – as our leading literary figures would say – a mix of earthly and divine love... If only one picture were to be left in the world, then this is the one to be set aside as the most perfect and the most full of life. This is the secret of painting and literature: the blend, the balance...'

Belatedly, Fitrat appeared to realise he wasn't in a lecture hall; he looked around and fell silent.

'It must be the same with literature.' Abdulla added pensively. 'Words not only reveal and proclaim, they also keep things hidden.'

'Quite right,' said Fitrat, animated again. 'The heroes' actions, the author's narration, it all has to keep to this dictum, isn't that so?'

'Yes,' Abdulla agreed, but that affirmation didn't lessen the grimness of the scene he had for so long been sketching out in his mind.

On Saturday, just before early morning prayers, four executioners entered the room where the Khans and their offspring were imprisoned, took Madali, Mahmud and Madali's son Madamin by their hands and wordlessly led them out. Outside was still as dark as inside, too dark to distinguish a white thread from a black one. So the Khans stumbled and tripped as they crossed the brick courtyard towards the garden, following their executioners, the commander of the army and the Chief Minister, who was holding a lantern and a lamp. They cringed as the night air numbed their flesh; they had gowns over their shoulders to ward off the cold breeze, but still it bit in to their bones. The pitch-black garden was utterly soundless; then the Chief Minister appeared, holding a lamp, frowned at the dark and stood there as if to meet them. The branches and twigs were motionless, somehow expectant. In the quivering light of the lantern the only moving things were the shadows of their legs, even the shadows of the trees were still invisible: a pitch-black wall rose up to the heavens. They guessed that they had reached the edge of a pond. Suddenly the stars seemed to have fallen at their feet. The heavens now opened like an overhead hatch. Then the Chief Minister put the lantern on the ground and rapped out a single word: 'Sentence!' Two executioners threw themselves on Madali, knocked him to the ground like a fettered sheep and executed him, parting his head instantly from his body. The spurting blood spilled onto the garden soil.

Although Mahmud didn't see his brother's death, he sensed what was happening by the convulsions of the body and began to recite the *shahada* of repentance. The young Sultan Madamin, standing behind him, uttered a scream. Then two other executioners fell upon him, making a martyr of a flower that had not had time to bloom. Mahmud prayed even more fervently. Heads and bodies were mingled with earth and blood on the ground, and when the executioners tried to grab Mahmud, they were confused as to who would hold him and who would axe him, but the head, parted from the body, hit the lantern with a thud, and the light went out, leaving everything totally dark.

Only the executioner's rasping breath broke the silence of the darkness before dawn. From afar, like the shriek of a soul, a solitary cockerel crowed.

—

Does your hair and your beard somehow stop growing in prison, or, like a pale potato thrown into a pit, grow, but turn white as they do so? Back in the hands of Moshe the barber, Abdulla could not help but wonder. As before, Moshe huffed and puffed as he sharpened his razor, as if he was about to cut Abdulla's head off his body; again this huffing and puffing seemed to express all his feelings, and from time to time he would turn to the soldier standing by the door and look at him askance, as if to say, what are you hanging about there for? You could tell by his face that he wanted to say something to Abdulla, but the soldier was an obstacle, forcing the barber to limit himself to even more stertorous puffing. Moshe's strange movements had an effect on the soldier, who abruptly announced that he was 'going for a piss,' and left Abdulla in Moshe's care. Abdulla pricked up his ears: well, now, out with it! But Moshe simply went on puffing as before. When Abdulla saw that Moshe looked unlikely to speak, he himself hurriedly asked, 'Excuse me, did you know the late Muborak?'

Moshe shuddered. He had never been seen or heard talking to the prisoners. First of all, he furrowed his eyebrows, as if to say, what did he say? Then he seemed at last to have understood, though he responded with a question instead of an answer. 'Why?'

Abdulla was too hasty to be logical: 'What do you mean, why?' he replied.

'Why "the late"?'

'Have I got it wrong?' said Abdulla, wasting time.

'Why do you call him "the late"?' Moshe asked politely. 'And what makes you think I don't know him? He's my nephew,' he said, and was about to say more, when the flip-flop of the soldier's boots was heard, and the barber reverted to his huffing and puffing. Abdulla became deeply thoughtful.

If Muborak was a close relative of Moshe, who knew Muborak himself as his nephew, could he possibly not have been informed of his demise? He worked here, after all! Would they have fought to keep his execution a secret from him? Certainly not; Moshe's response was so natural and astonished, as if he had seen his nephew only an hour before, and he seemed stunned that Abdulla should call him 'the late'. What did this imply? Could Muborak be alive?

Then what did it mean that they came to take him away, to be shot? If only he could have questioned Moshe just now. But all he got from him was that huffing and puffing and Moshe's furtive glances at the soldier.

As Moshe was finishing his work, Abdulla's thoughts were still confused. If only Vinokurov were still alive, perhaps he could have asked him. But this was pointless speculation; when he'd had the chance, Abdulla had lacked the courage.

Once he was back in his cell, Abdulla was unable to solve the puzzle Moshe had set him. Should he tell Fitrat about it? But, for some reason, Fitrat had never liked Muborak. At first, he had interpreted this as professorial jealousy, but later he saw that the rivalry ran deeper than intellectual one-upmanship and the fact they came from the same city. Abdulla didn't enquire into the source of this animosity. For that would have required some deep and painful thoughts.

But Fitrat was a perceptive man. He approached Abdulla, and deliberately began with a joke: 'Did you give a tip for your shave? You look younger now. It's a pity that, according to your theory, there are no women in here:

you've become an eligible young man again.'

Abdulla was confused: 'What theory was that?' But then he recalled their earlier talk, and his conclusion about the search for a path – about a novel not succeeding if it was about death without love. These patterns seemed to have trouble forming in Abdulla's brain, and Fitrat, sensing this, went on:

'I've thought about what you said yesterday, and you're right. Death on its own doesn't amount to a tragedy, it must involve love and life as well. I too have thought a great deal about Nasrullo's murders. If the Emir had killed only the Khans, that wouldn't have amounted to a historical event. But here we have Nodira's story. According to the *History of Fergana*, the executioners slaughtered Madali first, then, when they seized his son Madamin, the lad shrieked and wept, wanting to say goodbye to his mother. Nodira couldn't bear this, and said to Nasrullo, "You monster, his father committed a sin, but what did this innocent boy do to you? You merciless hangman, you have drowned Kokand in blood. I curse you before God, may you go blind, may you be deprived of everything! May you drown in your own blood, may you lose your royal status and be destroyed." Foul curses came to Nodira's lips, and all these words rebounded on her. Nasrullo then sentenced them all, including his pregnant daughter-in-law, to be beheaded.

These were scenes that Abdulla had saved when he was beginning his novel; he was jealous of the account as Fitrat had set it out. Stop it! he felt like blurting out, cutting the Professor off in full flow. This was for him, Abdulla, to tell, these tragic scenes needed to be expressed differently. But he told himself to be calm. How could he be jealous of a story, as though it belonged just to him? Even if he wrote it his way, this would only be one way of treating it. For that reason, seeing that Fitrat had become pensive, Abdulla responded, 'What's interesting is that a poet called Fitrat, a contemporary of Nodira's, wrote a poem about those deaths:

> Fitrat, tender-hearted by nature, wanting one night to tell
> The history of this royal death,
> Said in his tipsy state: 'Now is gone
> All joy in the land of Fergana.'

Fitrat responded with a grim laugh, 'Who will there be to write history for us?'

—

Abdulla did not tell Professor Fitrat the final part of the scene, which he was saving for the novel's climax.

Early one day, before morning prayers, Oyxon was speeding in a cart from Shahrixon: she entered the outskirts of Kokand when the call to prayer was sounding out. She was determined to see the Emir, to confess herself guilty of every sin committed, in the hope of saving the lives of Kokand's ruling family. But at heart she was worried. The sun was rising in an overcast sky – the cart was moving at a gallop – like a decapitated head soaked in blood, the sun was rolling along the horizon, and its rays were like swords with blood-stained blades, making Oyxon anxious. 'Faster! Faster!' she urged the driver on. Just as she realised she was entering Kokand, she felt herself to be in as ravaged and hopeless a state as the streets. From the clutches of one predator into the presence of another... Now the Shayxon district where her father had lived was below her; she left it behind. As they neared the Emir's harem, the sun, still on the horizon, vanished behind trees and buildings. She had to get there faster, faster!

At first they wouldn't let her enter the palace. She tugged the rings off her fingers and gave them to the guards. 'Only as far as the harem,' they said, as they opened the gate. Once inside the palace, there wasn't a corridor or a hatch that Oyxon didn't know. She sent Gulsum, who had accompanied her in the cart, to find out what was going on, while she meant to cross the garden that linked the palace chambers to the blue kiosk. Cherries were ripening there, beginning to take on the colour of blood: everything was a reminder of war and haste, the leaves and the fruits now had a covering of dust, in the flowerbeds along the garden edges. Some of the flowers had faded, some had withered.

'They've been neglected,' Oyxon thought sadly, as she headed through the trees towards the pond. This had once been the legendary bottomless pool of paradise: from it, through the trees, an invisible bright-red sun emerged. Oyxon's vision blurred. It seemed to her that on the opposite side of the pool some people were lying fast asleep. What lazy gardeners, instead of tending the garden, they're lying asleep without having even washed! When the cat's away, the mice can play, so that's it! The shout was ready on the tip of her tongue. Then, as she approached the edge of the pool, the slumped figures solidified into the headless bodies of men and women. She shrieked, and collapsed unconscious.

Imagining this episode, Abdulla found himself wanting to defend and protect Oyxon; at all costs, Gulsum had to be the one to find her unconscious, not the soldiers and the Chief Minister who would take her to Nasrullo. 'Why have I started interfering with their business?' he asked himself. 'My task is only to give a picture of actual events, as described in history.' But at heart he was against this approach, and searched for pretexts to avoid handing Oyxon over to that butcher. 'It's strange,' thought Abdulla. 'I began the novel by showing Nasrullo as a bozkashi player: wasn't that the aim? And now, when we get to the end, who gets the prize carcass but him? So why am I deluding myself? What has changed in the meantime? Is it history, my heroes, or myself? Why am I so firmly in Oyxon's camp?'

—

In his youth, Abdusamad had an ear cut off by the ruler of Tabriz; in India, the English had sought to imprison him for misappropriating government money, and he had been forced to make his escape to Kabul; there, Dost Muhammad had threatened to blind him for treachery, and he had only just got out in time, disguised in a woman's burka. The siege of Kokand had proved extremely profitable for him, but Nasrullo's volatility was worrying; Abdusamad's mouth still smarted from the Emir's boot. Was it perhaps time for another moonlight flit?

If so then now was the time, while the Emir was drunk with victory, celebrating his slaughter of the Kokand Mangit dynasty with beer and flirtatious Fergana boys. Should Abdusamad make his escape via Kashgar? But he was loathe to abandon Rohila now that he had her in his power. And what about the Englishmen, still locked up in his palace? Might they not still prove of some use? There was more to be got from them, Abdusamad was sure.

The older one was clearly ill; if they took him with them, he would only slow them down. And two was unnecessary. Abdusamad would find some way to prompt the Emir to sentence Stoddart; then Conolly would be easier to persuade.

Did Abdulla need to let Abdusamad meet Oyxon? With Conolly in his power, his communication closely monitored, there was no way that the Iranian could have failed to learn of the Englishman's connection with Madali's wife; as with every other piece of knowledge that came into his hands, he would have been thinking carefully about how to put it to the best use. But logic was one thing, and Abdulla's approach was another: he was fiercely protective of Oyxon. About a week earlier, when he imagined Conolly's journey over the Jizzax steppes, he had planned to 'rhyme' Conolly's thoughts with Oyxon's as the novel approached its finale. But now these plans had changed. He would not elaborate on the Jizzax steppes, nor on Oyxon's thoughts, nor on that devil Abdusamad's ever-grasping hands. At the very most, he would write: 'Seventeen days after the defeat of Kokand, Emir Nasrullo rounded up all those in Fergana who had great intelligence or beauty and elegance, and herded them off to Bukhara for resettlement. He put on the throne of Kokand an utterly inept man.'

Abdulla was now interested in just one thing: solving the puzzle left by Muborak, which was every bit as tricky as the one that prompted Hafiz to say: 'Whoever looks at this puzzle, their wisdom has never solved it, nor ever will.'

In one of the papers Muborak had left behind there was an extract from a letter written by Arthur Conolly in prison: 'The Uzbeks make agreements without being accustomed to keeping them. So it is doubtful if they will carry out the obligations they have undertaken.' Was there a hint in these sentences? If the Uzbeks were unreliable and untrustworthy, was the implication that, in relations with them, the best weapons were lies? If the Uzbeks couldn't be trusted, why did Conolly's ruler, Queen Victoria, nevertheless write a letter to Emir Nasrullo? Perhaps this was Muborak's secret: was the letter which never reached Emir Nasrullo buried somewhere?

Her Majesty the Queen to the Ameer of Bokhara:

Victoria, by grace of God Queen of the United Kingdom of Great Britain and Ireland, Defender of the Faith etc., etc. to His Highness the Ameer of Bokhara — Greeting. These are to inform you that we learnt with great pleasure from our trusty subject Lieutenant-Colonel Stoddart that you desired to enter into friendly relations with us; and our pleasure was increased when we received your letter, conveying to us your wishes in that respect. We accordingly desired the Governor-General whom we had set over the countries of India, in order to rule those countries in our name, and to communicate on our behalf with the Princes and Lords whose dominions are near to India, and distant from our capital, to consider of the means by which your wishes for friendly intercourse between our States could be most effectually gratified, and to give you such proofs of our good will towards you, as might convince you of the regard which we felt for your person and Government.

But rumours have reached us that evil-disposed persons have suggested to your mind doubts as to Stoddart's being really one of our servants, and as to the friendly object of his mission, and therefore we now acquaint you that Stoddart is indeed our servant, and that he was sent to Bokhara by our commands, to testify to you the interest which we felt in your welfare, and our desire to promote a good understanding between our servants in India and your Government. We expect that having this assurance from ourselves, and being convinced of our friendship, you will send back to us our servant Stoddart with all haste, and that you will authorise him to acquaint us with your wishes as to the manner in which friendly intercourse shall, in all time to come, be maintained between our dominions and the countries ruled by you. And as we understand that another of our servants, Conolly, is also at your capital, which he was invited by you to visit, we trust that, being now informed of our desire that he should return to our presence, you will dismiss him also from your Court, and direct that he, as well as Stoddart, shall be conducted in safety to the frontier of some friendly State. Our satisfaction will be complete when these, our servants, shall appear before us, and shall report to us that you are in the enjoyment of good health, and that the riches and prosperity of your house are on the increase. And with this we bid you heartily farewell.

Given at our Court of London, the 3rd day of December, in the year of our Lord 1842. Victoria R.

Why had Muborak not shown these letters to Abdulla? After all, if it hadn't been for his intervention, those super-fluous Englishmen would never have got into the novel in the first place! Was Abdulla aware of the novel's ending, but ignorant of the true outcome of Conolly's part in what he himself had called the Great Game? Were some devils twisting things to make Muborak seem an English spy? Wasn't spying one of the accusations against Fitrat, who was now waiting for death? Abdulla's head began to spin. Various scenes, ones that he had never heard of, began to emerge, like muddy liquid boiling over from a bubbling black cauldron. He suddenly recalled a story by the poet-ess Dilshod that he had read in her collected works: Emir Umar, when he finally conquered O'ratepa and broke down the city's resistance, took revenge for that rebellion by hanging 1,213 men and driving another 13,000, barefoot and bare-headed, to Fergana. Among these, driven into the desert, forbidden to build themselves a house for seven years, was Sayid Go'zi-xo'ja and his unfortunate family, in which Oyxon was still a child. For the duration of seven years they could only live in an open hovel. After those seven years the deportees' settlement of hovels turned into Shahrixon, the 'city of the Khan'. Dilshod herself, with three other beauties, was taken into the Emir's harem: one by one, they were washed, perfumed, dressed and presented to the Emir. The Emir had no idea that Dilshod was a poetess: he gave her a testing look. He showed her a pomegranate on a low table and asked her, 'What do you have to say about that?'

Her blood boiling, Dilshod answered: 'You've filled it with blood!'

The Emir was about to summon an executioner, but Nodira was lurking behind a screen, sensing a possible rival; she came out between them and hurried Dilshod away from the furious Emir's palace. Then Dilshod recited this couplet to her:

> Umar-xon is a tyrant's name; famed as a poet,
> This oppressor saw our beauty and became oppressed.

While Abdulla wondered what part of the novel this disruptive scene ought to be in, other scenes were uprooted, like weedy grass, from his brain. When Emir Nasrullo conquered Kokand, he ordered all the books that Nodira had spent years collecting to be burnt. The books were hurled out of the palace library and destroyed in an enormous bonfire. The librarian of the Bukhara palace, Junaydullo Hoziq, approached Emir Nasrullo, bowed down and pointed to one of the books, saying: 'Your Majesty, if you will pardon me, that book *The Secret Collection* is very rare, the only copy in the world. Let the order be given not to burn it.'

'Shit!' the Emir told Hoziq, his inflamed eyes popping, and gestured for the books to be burnt. Hoziq backed away without a word.

That night, at a victory feast to celebrate the conquest of Kokand, the Emir addressed his chief librarian. 'Recite a couplet in honour of our victory,' he ordered.

Then Hoziq recited in Farsi:

> You have dressed yourself in false witness,
> You won't be undressed until the day of resurrection.

Emir Nasrullo turned pale. He was on the point of ordering 'Sentence'. Hoziq sensed this and, to save his life,
produced another impromptu couplet:

> God does not touch the sinful joker,
> King, God's shadow, do not lay hands on him.

The Emir then had mercy on the poet and let him depart.
Hoziq, with the help of friends, immediately fled to
Shahrisabz. But the vindictive Emir, once he had returned
to Bukhara, secretly included a thief among four revered
clerics and sent them to Shahrisabz; in the depths of night
these merciless executioners broke through a roof, and
struck the learned man three blows with a sword, parted
the venerable head from his pure body, and took it in a
sack for Emir Nasrullo.

    The season of death, indeed.

—

The closer the novel came to its end in Abdulla's imagination, the more he began to dislike it. It couldn't be said to
be progressing in all its finery. Usually, a narrative begins
to move towards its end after the climax, the knots have
been unravelled, the complications have been simplified.
But life around the novel (if only you could call it life!) was
restoring the tangles and knots, and was doing all it could
to make more and more obscurity out of the clarity. At the
start of his imprisonment, everything was as crystal-clear as
a winter's day: who was a friend, and who an enemy. Hafiz
had something to say about this:

> Love seemed easy at first, but then the complications came.

Sunnat had vanished into thin air. Vinokurov had shot himself, Muborak had mysteriously disappeared. Trigulov had finally shown himself for what he was. Emir Nasrullo and Conolly, by coming back to life, seemed to have tainted Oyxon's final stages. The work Abdulla had sketched out last autumn was now shrivelled up, and his impatient brain was seeking to bring it somehow back to life…

Fitrat came up to Abdulla. He seemed to know all about Abdulla's thoughts.

'My dear Abdulla, there's a story I've been keeping for you' he said. 'It's about how I nearly became an English spy. I wasn't going to tell it to anyone, but now there's no sense in keeping anything secret. Tomorrow or the day after, in a week or a month, they'll get round to shooting all of us.'

Ever since his youth, Fitrat had learnt how to reveal the essence of what people said and what they kept hidden in their hearts. Effectively, Fitrat was the man who had introduced modern literature to Turkestan. His collection of poetry *Clamour* had raised an outcry such as no other book had done. When Abdulla was still a youth, he had secretly copied out poems from *Clamour* and learnt them by heart. And now Fitrat, out of the blue, was revealing his private thoughts about death, so that secrecy seemed to disappear: yes, indeed, tomorrow or the day after, or in a week, or in a month they would get round to shooting everyone, but each person took a different attitude to reality or inevitability. Anqaboy became unsociable, reproachful and absorbed in his own thoughts, as he finished thinking out his *Divine Tragedy*. But Fitrat – if only slightly – was more inclined to talk, as if there were hitherto unthought or unspoken ideas to be expressed, so as to unburden himself of them. And Abdulla, gritting his teeth, was prolonging his novel, as if that would stop him being despatched to the next world.

Fitrat suddenly looked at Abdulla's pensive face: Should I tell him, or shouldn't I? he wondered doubtfully, but then decided to speak, for his own sake, if not Abdulla's.

'It was late autumn in 1919. It was the time I was publishing the newspaper *Freedom* in Tashkent. Circumstances forced me to make a secret trip to Bukhara. So I decided to join a group of Afghan traders, pretending to be one of them. Among the people we trusted in Bukhara was a certain Mirbadalov, a Tatar. He had come from Russia as an interpreter with the Russian army. He married a Bukhara woman and stayed on.'

Busy at first with his own thoughts, Abdulla now began to listen with interest. But Fitrat – as if cutting a leather sole with a cobbler's knife – was carrying on:

'When we stopped at the caravanserai, I took the opportunity of secretly going to their house. I found out that they had some tricky guest at their house: an English spy, Frederick Bailey. That night at the Mirbadalovs' house, over a meal of plov, we got to know this Englishman. At the time, as you know, I had published my articles 'The English in Turkestan' and 'Eastern Politics' in *Hurriyet*, and was absolutely opposed to the English. Feigning ignorance, Bailey asked me about English policies in India and Afghanistan, and, in passing, corrected me on some points. I spoke out about everything that I thought at heart. In those days I was obsessed with the idea of 'Indian resistance', so looking at that arrogant gentleman, I concluded by saying that India, Afghanistan and Turkestan should determine their own fate.

'After that dispute, we decided to meet Mr Bailey again, face to face in the Nazarov passage. He was frank with me from the start. "I'm a British officer, I'm preparing to leave for home via Mashhad," he said. "You seem an intelligent man, and you clearly know Bukhara like the back of your hand. If you help me with a few things here, I might be able to do the same for you in Afghanistan."

"'Well, what would you need?" I asked.

""First of all, can you arrange for me to meet the Emir?" he asked.

'Of course, I was one of the Emir's most bitter enemies; if he'd learned I was in Bukhara, he'd have had me bound hand and foot and thrown off the highest minaret. But I wasn't about to blow my cover; instead, I affected to be humble: "I'm a petty trader, the Emir and I are poles apart."

"'Does the Emir understand French?" Bailey was disappointed, but after he asked if the Emir spoke French and I told him that yes, he'd learned it as a student in the Pages' Corps in Russia, he seemed to think that would solve his problem. Before we parted, we fell to talking of other things; I don't remember now quite how we got on to the subject, but he told me that he'd learned something quite extraordinary from some of the Bukharan Jews: apparently, Emir Nasrullo didn't have the English spies Stoddart and Conolly executed at all. The older one fell ill and died of natural causes; the younger then converted to Islam and became a confidant of the Emir, who had him married off to some Kokand beauty. According to the Jews, you can find his offspring in Bukhara: they call themselves Xonaliev.

This contradicted everything I knew from the historical sources, which state that in June 1842, when Emir Nasrullo returned from conquering Kokand, he sentenced Stoddart and Conolly to death and had them publicly beheaded. Though no one seems to have witnessed this; the sources all re-tell the story from secondary accounts…'

'Qodiriy, out!' a loathsome voice yelled in Russian.

—

This time he was taken not to the prison interrogation room, but upstairs to the NKVD office, where the Armenian Major Apresyan had read out his indictment to him. Apresyan showed Abdulla where to sit, and when he was seated, Apresyan went to a piece of equipment that looked like a radio, and pressed a button. A crackling noise and a familiar voice sounded out: 'But two days later we did meet, as we agreed, face to face in the Nazarov passage. He was frank with me from the start. "I'm a British officer, I'm preparing to leave for home via Mashhad," he said. "You seem to be an intelligent man. You know Bukhara like the back of your hand. If you help me wherever possible with one of two things…'

At this point Apresyan pressed the button again: the familiar voice coming through the crackling sound stopped, together with the familiar harmony. The room was plunged into silence. It was a hot, sultry summer. The merciless sun was blocked out by the heavy white curtains; through the open windows behind them came loud offerings of praise for the Soviet people and their leader Comrade Stalin, followed by exultant cries of 'Death! Death!' Abdulla had seen gramophones and radios, but he knew nothing about this sort of equipment which could record voices, and in a prison, too. What else did these devils have up their sleeves?'

Apresyan gave Abdulla a condescending look. The sense of it was plain: you're all puppets in our hands.

'Did you understand?' asked Apresyan. 'We have information about everything. Everything about Bailey's work in Tashkent, Fergana, Chirchiq and Bukhara has been documented.' He tapped a thick file on the table in front of him. 'We are aware of his meetings with *basmachi*, *jadids*, counter-revolutionaries and social revolutionaries.

'So, comrade Qodiriy, as for you,' he said, changing the subject, and seeming to go back to his expositions. 'You take pride in calling yourself a nationalist, and you have refused to collaborate with us,' he said, giving Trigulov a meaningful look. 'But imagine things as a writer, not as a citizen. We are going to use the words which that stinking old man Fitrat just said to you, but we shall say that what he said was passed on to us word-for-word by Abdulla Qodiriy, the pride of Uzbek national literature. In fact, apart from you, he didn't say them to anyone else. Isn't that so? Well, what did he say at the beginning?' Apresyan pressed the button.

'My dear Abdulla, there's a story I've been keeping for you,' he said. 'It's about how I nearly became an English spy. I wasn't going to tell it to anyone…' Another gesture, and the hissing and crackling and the familiar voice broke off.

'This is a provocation,' said Abdulla angrily. 'I'll inform Fitrat!'

'You continue to underestimate us. We're not going to give you another opportunity to meet your precious professor. *A Thousand and One Nights* goes on and on only in fairy tales. We can put a stop to all this here and now. And in Fitrat's broken mind, all that will remain is the thought that the pride of Uzbek national literature has turned out to be a lying traitor. We'll even let the old man go free for a year to spread the word for us. We can cast our rod quite far out, as they say.'

Abdulla knew that they were cunning, but this new plot crushed him. As his spirits sank, he felt for a while how incredibly tired he was. If Abdulla valued anything in this world, it was his honour. He owed his first term of imprisonment to that, when he demanded a death sentence to defend his honour. But now they had trussed him up like a puppet, hand and foot, and soiled his good name. What options were left to him?

'You fancied yourself as someone who determines the fates of others, an engineer of human souls,' Apresyan continued in perfect Uzbek. 'But our works have turned out to be stronger than yours.' He gave Trigulov another meaningful look.

'Usually we work to a "Storm and Stress" formula. But because of our respect for you, Qodiriy, we can give you time on your own to think over what we've said. What do you think, comrades?' Apresyan looked at Trigulov, who nodded his assent.

'Good, we have an agreement.'

CHAPTER 10

CHASING THE WIND

Abdulla was now put into a solitary cell. In the confusion of his thoughts, he didn't know what to give priority to. Should he think about Fitrat, or himself, or Apresyan and Trigulov? Which one to begin with? If he pulled one thread, the others would be tangled. So Abdulla had no choice but to say to hell with the lot of them.

But his thoughts returned increasingly to his own situation. What did Apresyan want from him? What were they playing at? They had already drawn up an indictment, which bore absolutely no relation to whatever Abdulla did or said. Or was the indictment too shaky on its own, did they need a confession to make it stick?

He had already admitted responsibility for being a writer who had written nostalgically for the nation. All right, he had as good as conceded he was a nationalist. In that sense, Shakespeare, Hafiz, Cervantes and Tagore were all nationalists. This amounted to proof that they were members of an organisation. But if there was no organisation, then how could Abdulla be considered a member? Surely a group of people having a chat in Moscow's Pushkin Park or Tashkent's Dormon Gardens wasn't sufficient to constitute an organisation, was it?

If it was, then a morning meal of plov would have to

be renamed a National Union, and plov in a teahouse, The National Bloc. 'On the occasion of our son's circumcision, we invite you to a "National Union".'

Their game was clear, Abdulla felt. They were less concerned with making the charges stick, and more with making everyone betray one another, Uzbek betraying Uzbek, Kazakh – Kazakh, Russian – Russian, until no group was left uncontaminated, building a Traitors' Nation, a Renegades' International, a humanity of double-dealers… If they broke Abdulla, what hope was there for the nation, or even humanity itself?

What purpose did Abdulla have in mind when he first sat down to write his novel? Wasn't he inventing a new sort of fairy tale, like *Takhir and Zukhra*, the Turkic *Romeo and Juliet*? Once upon a time there lived a just king, Umar, a lover of hunting and of poetry. On one hunt, a member of the royal family, a military commander called Mahmud-bek, was shot by a stray arrow: the King came up to him, and put the commander's bleeding head on his knees. As his strength failed, Mahmud-bek said, 'My lord, my wound is serious, and now I must depart this world. May I be so bold as to make a bequest to you: my beloved only daughter, who is old enough to marry. Take her into your palace and have her educated, so that our family connection is not broken…' Thus he breathed his last.

After burying his friend and minister with the highest honours, Umar honoured his bequest by taking his daughter Oyxon into his court and entrusting her education to his senior wife, Nodira.

A number of years, full of splendour, passed in Umar's life: feasts every other day, poetry contests, night-long banquets with wine. Wild parties at their zenith. One day, Umar slipped away from one such orgy to the harem. Stumbling slightly from the drink, he went to Nodira's chamber. There he found her, sitting with an angelic young girl of between ten and twelve, who was learning a poem by heart. As soon as they saw the King standing opposite, the two of them bowed to him in greeting. Umar couldn't take his drunken eyes off this slender maiden: he was bewitched by her peerless beauty. Nodira invited Umar to take a seat and gave the girl permission to leave. When the girl had gone, the King wiped his cracked lips and asked, 'What girl was that?'

'How can you have forgotten?' Nodira replied readily. 'She's the girl that your late relative Mahmud-bek bequeathed to you, his daughter. Your majesty has been so busy with palace affairs that it's not surprising if he has forgotten his harem.'

'Excellent,' said the King. 'In three or four years' time this girl will be a perfect beauty. Then I shall marry her.' And he recited this couplet:

> The face of a noble flower, eyes that slant like narcissi,
> No rare jasmine nor moon-lit tree is like her.

At this, Nodira was left in distress, biting her lips till they bled.

This *Takhir and Zukhra* fairy tale was one thing; the fruit of his shaken mind, the novel he now was writing, was another. What an ending he had arrived at: hadn't it all come to an impasse, the tragedy of a wretched woman betrayed by her father, her family and her beloved? Wasn't the concoction of endless misfortunes that made up Oyxon's life (Umar's and Nodira's betrayal, Madali's infidelities, Nasrullo's latest passion) a reflection of the nation? When and how had Oyxon's tragic life-story turned into Abdulla's own? Abdulla's father used to say, 'Devils will possess your mind, son, if you let yourself be swept away by whatever thought blows into your head. Don't ever forget the story I told you about the devils' dance.' His mother Josiyat kept nagging him, 'Child, if the devil gets your mind one day, you'll only have yourself to blame.'

He remembered how Gogol had burned his manuscripts. Had it helped? All it had done was to deprive him of his senses. If the NKVD hadn't burnt Abdulla's manuscripts yet, it was doing so now. But what could that do? Temptations were not to be found on paper, but inside one's heart and mind.

During his preliminary work on the novel, Abdulla had come across a legend among the chronicles. A certain king had married a girl much younger than himself. One day, the king returned from hunting, and a servant was waiting for him:

'Your majesty, have mercy on me, but her ladyship is behaving suspiciously,' he said. 'She has locked herself up in her room with a large trunk, big enough to hide a man. This was your grandmother's trunk. What her ladyship is doing with it, we do not know.'

'A lot of things were kept there...'

'If you look inside the trunk, it would not be surprising if you found something rather bigger than various things, sire...'

The king found his wife in her room, staring sadly at the trunk.

'What's in the trunk?' asked the king.

'Is your question due to the servant's suspicions, or because you don't trust me?' the king's wife countered.

'Talking about it is a waste of time, wouldn't it be easiest if you simply opened the trunk?' asked the king impatiently.

'No,' replied his wife.

'Is it locked?

'Yes…'

'Where is the key?'

'If you dismiss the servant, I shall give you the key,' said her ladyship, to cut the conversation short.

The king summoned the servant and dismissed him. Her ladyship gave the king the key and left the room with a regretful sigh.

The king, left on his own, thought long and hard. Then he called for four slaves, ordered them to pick up the trunk and take it to the garden, dig a deep pit and bury it there.

Neither the king nor his wife ever referred to the matter again.

At one point Abdulla had intended to incorporate this parable into one of his chapters. Now he didn't know if it was suitable. Perhaps its import was quite different. 'Wouldn't it be better if I buried the novel somewhere secret without ever finding out quite what's inside it, just like that trunk?' But, instead of the trunk, he himself was the one who had been buried.

As a boy in the Russian-language school, Abdulla had been taught by a man named Pugovkin. One day this teacher brought a gigantic mirror to the class for the children to draw their reflections. When Pugovkin stepped out of the classroom, a couple of boys, wondering what the other side of the mirror was like, clumsily swung the mirror round. When they took hold of the back, the glass crashed down and smashed to smithereens. Leaping up to try and hold it, Abdulla was the last to see his reflection in the mirror; that reflection shattered into pieces, one holding an ear, another his neck, and a third his mouth, and yet another an eye…

Abdulla was left amazed; the sum total of the shattered pieces seemed somehow to preserve the whole of his face. The merging of the oneness, he would call it now.

Perhaps the previous scene should be moved to Bukhara? Oyxon and her property brought to the fortress, when Nasrullo goes to Oyxon's chamber and bursts in on her sitting next to an enormous trunk. 'Give me the key, you bitch!' he tears the key from her hands, and opens the trunk. Inside, he sees with horror the enormous mirror and his vicious, ugly face in the mirror multiplied by three. In fury he draws his sword and hacks, hacks, hacks at this looking-glass... The shattered fragments reflect nothing of him, only Oyxon's melancholy face...

———

Or was it his father's story that tempted him?

'I was trying to cross a square where a celebration was going on, and so I jumped over a clay wall. The square was as bright as daylight, with lanterns hanging from the tree branches and silk carpets on the ground. On one side there were big brass samovars, and opposite them enormous cauldrons of food, still bubbling and seething. In the middle of the square about a hundred men of various ages were sitting in a circle, feasting and making merry, while musicians were playing lutes, viols, side-drums and kettle-drums.

'Right then a man runs up and shouts to the merrymakers, 'Brother O'sar has just come!'

'All the merrymakers looked at me. "You've come, you've come, brother O'sar, have you got rid of the stakes?" they asked.

'I can't remember now how I answered: I was so badly taken aback.

'They dragged me against my will, and made me sit in

the place of honour. Usually, when someone new joins a group of men sitting together, prayers are said. But nobody thought of prayers, it was nothing but questions and greetings. When I had gathered my wits, I passed an eye over the people assembled there. I seemed to have seen some of them somewhere. Yet, when I looked closer, they seemed to be strangers that I had never seen or known in my life. Yet they treated me as if they knew me, called me by my name, asked what I was doing, and they even knew I had been going to cut reeds that day: all that astounded me.

'One of them, I don't know who, evidently the host, said, "Serve some food to brother O'sar!"

'Someone objected: "First let's have our party, then we can all start eating." Then he looked me in the face and asked, "You must be longing for a song and dance. Shall we have our party first?"

'I had an empty stomach, but being a guest, all I could do was to go along with their wishes.

'The lute-players were beginning to tune up. I recognised most of the instruments – lutes, viols, fiddles, mandolins, cymbals, trumpets, tambourines – but there were some I'd never seen or heard of. Once the lutes were tuned, they started playing a restrained, solemn sort of music.

'That music was bewitching; I was rooted to the spot, ecstatic, crushed, captivated to such a degree that I began to sigh with all my heart for reasons I didn't know. The musicians played on, very gently reaching a climax. Finally, I could hold out no longer. I started sobbing. I wept for a long time. The music finally ended. It finished, but it had nearly finished me off, too. I was crippled, like a man crushed between two millstones. I didn't have the strength to move. I opened my eyes. The entire gathering was watching me with the same sarcastic look on their faces.

Prostrate, I looked down at the ground.

'The lutes were about to start a second piece of music. But, just as before, I couldn't endure to listen. My heart was pounding. If I were to listen to any more of this music, I would collapse in mortal agony.

'The second piece began. As it began, the water of life raced into my entire being. I felt such bliss. The music was extremely joyful. I couldn't put a name to it.

'A girl of about fifteen or sixteen then appeared, wearing a light, straight, green velvet gown. She took a few steps into the middle, and the bells on her ankles jingled. The girl began to dance to the rhythm of the music.

'The music continued, the subtle waves of sound from the lute seemed to urge the dancer on to further efforts. A joy and a spirit was descending to this world, as if to resurrect the dead, to make the earth quake, to move mountains and rocks, to send the stars flying and make the tops of the trees shake.

'My joy went straight to my heart. Some force raised me up from where I was sitting. Whatever happened, I badly wanted to dance with the girl. The girl danced with me for a short while, and then moved away. But I couldn't stop dancing, I couldn't even think of stopping. People were standing there applauding; they seemed to be making fun of me, pulling faces at me, but I didn't care, I went on dancing.

'After a time I tripped and fell down. I recovered, and made a move to start dancing again, when I collapsed again, completely.

'Quite a lot of time passed before I recovered; when I opened my eyes I looked all round me.

'There was nobody there, no lutes or anything else: nothing and nobody! The square was in total darkness, and I was up to my waist in a ditch.'

Wasn't Abdulla's present situation like his father O'sar's, sinking into the filthy ooze?

—

When he was a young man, Abdulla used to write down his dreams. Later, perhaps because he slept too deeply after spells of hard work, he stopped dreaming, or, if he dreamt, he couldn't remember the dreams. Today his dreams were chaotic as before, but lately... wait, wait: what had he dreamt of? The dream began with nothing that was clear: it seemed to be happening in water, like a fish flashing past, as you glance at the current. But however hard Abdulla tried to trace that smooth current back, there was no getting to its source. There were vague thoughts about his Moscow life, for some reason, those who came later into his life, his neighbours in the dormitory, Sergei Berezhnoy and Serik Saktaganov appearing for no good reason, and, wearing vest and shorts, doing acrobatics with them in an enormous stadium. Abdulla stood on the bare ground of the courtyard, and the two of them stood on his broad shoulders, lifting up a blood-red flag with a star and sickle. Abdulla couldn't imagine how these two burly men could climb onto his shoulders. But they jumped down before Abdulla collapsed onto the ground, and before Abdulla's eyes they were smashing the star, one with a hammer, the other writing something in the grass with the sickle... Abdulla was trying to make sense of this, when the man holding the hammer turned into Vinokurov, and the man with the sickle into Trigulov, who began questioning Abdulla in front of a thousand spectators.

'Are you a writer?'

'Yes...'

'Do you consider yourself a creative person?'

'Yes...'

'Do you invent lives of people who don't exist?'

'Yes…'

'Do you yourself believe in your inventions?'

'Yes…'

'Do you know that nothing in this world disappears without a trace?'

'Yes…'

'Do you believe in the Day of Judgement?'

'Yes…'

'Do you know what temptation is?'

'Yes…'

'Are you not afraid that on the Day of Judgement all your invented characters will go for your throat?'

No reply.

'Do you compare yourself to God?'

No reply.

'Do you know what the punishment for that is?'

No reply.

'Then let us show you!' And on that Day of Judgement his head is cut off, like a sickle mowing the first grass, and the head, as it rolls off his body, is knocked into the bare ground with blows of a hammer. That must be Munkar and Nakir, who question the dead in their graves…

As he lies in his vest, prostrate on the rough ground, a beautiful Uzbek woman descends, utterly inappropriately, from somewhere in a Moscow sky. She can't be a stranger; her movements seem familiar. Abdulla doesn't recognise her, but the woman knows him well.

'I've come to say goodbye to you,' she says. There is a charming quality in her words, which one only ever comes across in books. Abdulla feels ashamed to be in this situation, but thinks, 'This is how my heroines Kumush and

Ra'no might be.'

'Where are you going?' Abdulla asks, conscious of his own awkwardness and ineptitude.

'I'm being separated from you...' The woman's soft speech betrayed bitterness and suffering, rather than teasing or reproach: certainly not flirtatiousness.

'Will you remember me?' she asked.

For what? Abdulla meant to ask, but once again he was silent, ashamed to be so coarse and uncouth, lying there in just a vest in the presence of a woman.

'Well then, I'm off, I suppose,' she said hesitantly, fiddling with the fringes of her silk headband. She pulled a folded piece of paper from a bundle, and offered it to Abdulla. For a moment Abdulla was at a loss, not knowing what to say or to do. Then someone tapped him Abdulla on the shoulder. He shuddered and turned round: it was his wife Rahbar.

'Are you going away?' she said with something between desire and pain, putting all her feelings into one word as only women can, and pointing into empty space.

Abdulla stretched out in that direction, then woke up.

He lay there for a long time thinking about the sense and meaning of this dream. Cho'lpon's verses came to mind:

> Leave now, Satan; I am afraid.
> Go! My sword's smashed, my shield holed.
> Don't you see? I am lying underneath
> A mountain of troubles, crushed and cold?
>
> Oh angel, one last breath, the last of all:
> One last look, then may the skies fall!

Who was the beautiful woman in his dream? What had her words implied, so ordinary, so enchanting? Was she leaving something for him? He looked down at his hand and saw he was holding half a sheet of Kokand paper. Trembling, he examined the paper, his lips moving as he whispered, and read a poem written in a familiar, beautiful Arabic script:

> Shame on me I never found my beloved nor love of any kind
> My heart is hard, my spirit thrown, and vengeance fills my mind.
>
> I have no strength to journey, my shadow's lost in the night
> Like a shadow of disgrace, I at once disperse in light.
>
> For those parted by love, there is the hope of meeting,
> But my chains of despair deny any hope so fleeting.
>
> No friend can hear me now, even my rival's blind,
> And the bowl's turned upside down by the unforgiving wind.
>
> I am the martyr Hassan bereft of his Husain.
>
> Coming to this spectacle unbidden as nonentity Oyxon,
> Should I cry aloud, 'What did you promise everyone?'

———

From that day on, Abdulla's thoughts were no longer troubled by any temptation, or inspiration, no superfluous images. The hottest forty days of summer had come, the days when antelopes piss in the water, after which the summer passes its peak and the year begins rolling towards winter. Something had been interrupted in Abdulla's heart. It seemed as if autumn, as it entered the world, had also come to his soul, and yellow leaves were falling onto the clear water.

That day Oyxon woke earlier than usual. She had dreamt something which made her heart beat with pleasure, made her long to slip back in to sleep, but the memory had already slipped away from her, and however hard she tried she could not bring it back. Still in bed, she searched her thoughts, seeking the identity of its protagonist: her father G'ozi-xo'ja, her late mother, her children? Her life in the palace of Kokand, her journey to Bukhara? But none of that could have made her heart ache so. What was it about, that bitter-sweet dream?

She got up, threw on a quilted gown of striped silk, and went out into the courtyard. Nobody else was yet awake, and all around was dark and silent. She took a brass ewer of water from the veranda and went to a privy under the vines. Just then, as if to be contrary, brazen moonlight shone unveiled from behind the clouds. Oyxon lifted her eyes to the heavens, and a cluster of stars dripped their light onto her lashes. No, these were drops of water falling on her face, glittering like stars in the moonlight. Her head began to spin, and instantly it was clear in her mind what she had dreamt of that night.

She had seen the last bunch of grapes poking out from under the vine's turning leaves: its bright red fruit had made her heart miss a beat. Trying to reach it, she had put her foot on the first cross-support, then on the next one up, climbing higher until the wood under her feet cracked and she dropped from the sky to the black earth below.

Lying on the ground, she heard a voice calling her: 'Oyxon, Oyxon!' Opening her eyes, she saw bending over her a handsome young man. This was not Qosim, nor her friend Gulxaniy. A young man with black eyebrows, black eyes, and a well-trimmed moustache was wiping the sweat from her brow with a handkerchief that smelled of attar of roses.

At first, Oyxon trembled, thinking: who was this stranger? Then, looking more carefully, she saw nothing ominous about his behaviour, no impropriety or violence;

on the contrary, there was calmness and grace in the set of his features, and in every movement he made. Oyxon found herself struck by the urge to confide in him, to be rid of the dirt and blood that overlay her life like layers of slime. The youth was taciturn, still wiping her forehead and cheeks with his perfumed handkerchief, as if to say, don't be afraid, I'm here with you. His melancholy eyes never left hers.

'Do you know me?' Oyxon whispered.

'I do,' said the young man. 'I know everything about you.'

'Where am I? Am I in Bukhara?'

The young man nodded.

'What's happened to me? Did I fall?'

He said nothing, but went on wiping Oyxon's cheeks and chin.

'If the Emir sees you he'll have you hacked to pieces.'

The young man shook his head.

'Kenagas, his senior wife, can see a snake even under the ground.'

The young man shook his head.

Such laconic persistence, such gravity and dignity: might this be an angel come down from heaven? It was a worrying thought. But Oxyon felt then a warmth on her lips: his fingers had brushed them accidentally as he wiped the sweat from her chin.

He seemed concerned simply that she not distress herself, but in his face Oyxon saw her entire life reflected. This youth really must know everything. Why then was he silent? Here she was, a woman prostrate on the ground: why wasn't he crushing her, bullying her, trampling her, as other men would?

Tears welled up in Oyxon's eyes. Neither wiping them away nor trying to comfort her, the man only sighed as if to say, weep, poor woman, get it off your mind... Her blurred eyes looked up at the sky beyond him. All the wrongs and hurts now rose to the surface. Never in her whole life had anyone pitied the broken clay vessel that she was, nobody had asked, 'What's happened to you, slave?' Not when she was a little girl, bare-foot in the snow; when she lay bruised and dishevelled after having been raped; when she was passed from hand to hand, an object for amusement and debauchery – what else could this wretched woman remember, what feelings could she pour out to this young man?

Oyxon could not hold back her tears; curling up, she turned her head towards the youth's knees. Her face touched him, and she was struck by a warm breath she had not known since her distant childhood, immediately awakening in her feelings of safety and peace.

'What's happening to me?' Oyxon asked.

Should he tell her or not? What good to shatter an already broken heart? The young man heaved a sigh. One thought after another was passing through his mind.

It was a June day. A pitch-black sun had reached its zenith, and the disgruntled Kenagas, whose jaws were age-less, had ordered her junior wife Oyxon to appear before the Emir. Oyxon dragged her fragile shadow after her as she went outside to get into the royal carriage. Would God bestow upon Nasrullo some measure of mercy and make him give her back her sons? The sun was hammering itself like a nail into the ground, burning through Oyxon's thick veil and burrowing into her brains, giving her an unbear-able headache. She had trouble climbing into the carriage and was too weak even to respond to the young driver's greeting. Half-suffocated, she cast off her veil and flung it aside, then unbuttoned her stiff collar. It didn't help. There was no air. The carriage rattled down the road from the fortress, and at every jolt Oyxon's heart beat more anxiously. Why hadn't she got hold of some arsenic when she was still in Kokand? Because she didn't want to lose sight of her children? Did she still think she could save those two infants, when the other princes had been martyred? Might death not be the kindest fate for them? She fought for breath, there was no air…

The carriage moved out into the square and turned left towards the city. Aren't we going to the country estates? Oyxon wondered. Although the sun was at its height, the streets were filled with the sound of people shouting and calling. What were people doing outside at this time? In the distance, someone was shouting the praises of his cold yoghurt drink, clearly anxious to sell it quickly. Oyxon's lips were cracked: should she stop the carriage? Would the young driver listen? She hadn't even greeted him: perhaps he would resent that? No, he was more likely to fear Nasrullo's wrath.

She was still desperate for air, and gasping to breathe. Or was it thirst, or anxiety? Women's laughter could be heard in the street. Did children's giggling bode ill at this hour?

The carriage passed down streets and lanes, leaving clouds of dust in its wake. The dust got into her dry throat, and she began to gasp for air. Her face and neck were covered in sweat. A dog barked, but the carriage rushed on. The dog running alongside the carriage suddenly screamed, a drawn-out sound that receded into the distance as the carriage rushed on. Had its wheels crushed the wretched animal? Or had the shriek and helpless howl come from Oyxon's confused mind?

This was enough. Whether she is to be knifed, strangled or suffocated, let Oyxon spend her life rushing on in this carriage. Under no circumstances would she enter that devil Nasrullo's country estate. Under no circumstances would she meet the face of her tormentor, neither in the shade of vines nor in the baking heat of the open courtyard. Let him not give his guards the signal to bring Oyxon's little sons out of the house. Let her not throw herself in the dust at his boots, to beg in her crazed state for mercy when they pushed one of the boys forwards and Nasrullo pronounced the dreaded words: 'Sentence! Exterminate the whole tribe!' Under no circumstances, absolutely not.

Why should the young man talk about such things to this unhappy woman, why should he dig the knife in further? He had trouble swallowing the lump in his throat; he bent down and kissed her on the forehead.

'You won't abandon me, will you?' Oyxon pleaded. Wiping the tears from her face, the young man shook his head.

'I have nobody left in this world,' she whispered.

'Neither have I,' Abdulla said in a strangled voice.

No, he didn't believe this. One hot summer day, Oyxon had been sitting in Nasrullo's harem and weeping over her unhappy life when her old maidservant Gulsum came from the city and told her that two English spies had just been beheaded at the fortress. Afterwards, as Hakim-to'ra had written, Emir Nasrullo returned again to Kokand and had Oyxon, her sons Muzaffar and Mansur, and the servant Gulsum, executed. Hadn't Cho'lpon said:

> She listened, constantly toying with her hair,
> And then declared, 'Legends are false and vile.'
> The words the angel spoke have stayed in my ear:
> 'I'm swimming,' she said, 'in streams of blood and bile.'

Life is nothing but a swim in this bloody, bilious water. You get only a momentary glimmer of the moon's face, the literal meaning of Oyxon.

'But it's not evening yet... They still don't know who they're dealing with,' Trigulov continued in full flow, standing up: as if divining Abdulla's thoughts, he approached and whispered in his ear: 'Come on, let me show you your final scene. You'll remember it for the rest of your life.' He stepped out into the corridor, dismissed the guard by the door and gestured to Abdulla to follow him. Abdulla got up. Trigulov led him past three cells to No. 38, peered inside, and opened the spyhole.

'Take a look,' he said. Abdulla set his eye to the spyhole. In the middle of the cell – he couldn't believe his eyes – was the mighty elder Jur'at, stroking his red beard; next to him was the squat, potbellied Muborak; listening to them were Kosoniy and Professor Zasypkin; while Laziz and the frail Mulla Shibirg'oniy staggered about in the background. In the centre of this devils' dance was Abdulla's best friend, the wretched poet Abdulhamid Cho'lpon, whose tear-filled eyes shone through the lenses of his spectacles. Or were these the wax figures Muborak had told him about? Abdulla bit his lips until they bled.

> Leave now, Satan; I am afraid.
> Go! My sword's smashed, my shield holed.
> Don't you see? I am lying underneath
> A mountain of troubles, crushed and cold?

> Oh angel, one last breath, the last of all:
> One last look, then may the skies fall!

—

Early autumn had come to the region. As Cho'lpon said:

> In the autumn... when the soil is dead –
> When the soils are pale in the falling time.
> For the last time, when the leaf turns red –
> When the leaves are red for the last time.

Crows croak in empty gardens but
Whose fate are they bewailing?
They fiercely clutch the fallen nut.
Yet whose final hope is failing?

You ice-clad folk from lands that freeze:
Leave your foul dreams there in the snow.
You stole the fruit from my orchard trees:
May your black heads be buried below!

Who knows whose hopes have now been lost
In the falling time when the leaves turn red?
Whose destiny's withered with the frost
In the autumn… when the soil is dead.

As Abdulla whispered these verses to himself, new meanings emerged each time; red leaves, bare earth, cawing
crows made his head spin, a nostalgia for vanished hopes
and broken fates.

On one such autumn days, he was taken yet again to
Trigulov.

'Let me show you something,' the interrogator said.
'Something you'll remember it for the rest of your life!'

But he there was to be no tour of the prison's cells this
time. Trigulov stayed seated, pulled out a document from
a thick criminal case file and passed it to Abdulla. Abdulla
read silently, translating the Russian in his head:

'Ever since 1932, he has been engaged in spying for
Japan and giving secret information about the Council of
People's Commissars of the USSR through an agent known
as 'S'. He used the same agent to pass on information
about the situation in counter-revolutionary and nationalist organisations in the national republics.'

Abdulla was lost for words.

'Do you know whose case file this is?' Trigulov asked.

Abdulla shook his head.

'Your friend Cho'lpon's. Those rogues were the devil's apprentices when they fabricated cases. Here, read this, and see the state they reduced him to.' He proffered another document.

Abdulla looked hard at the neat handwriting he had known since his youth:

'To close this statement I wish to affirm that there have been plenty of mistakes in my life. These have to be struggled against, they are not my mistakes alone, and in general there is no need to search for them in places where they are not to be found. Where they truly exist, they should be easy enough to find; otherwise, all that will be unmasked is the level of deception to which the 'unmaskers' have themselves fallen victim; the deception, and the deceit...'

They couldn't crack Cho'lpon if they died trying, Abdulla thought.

'Now read this,' said Trigulov, handing Abdulla yet another sheet of Kokand paper. Again it was the same familiar Arabic calligraphy.

'A savage wind blew into the harem, a number of golden vases were knocked over, tea cups were smashed... wine was spilt, water containers broke, chalices were cracked... there is as much pleasure in defeat as in victory.

'Rise up from defeat and head for victory! Our wings have been broken, our light has gone out, our woes are shattered; we walk forwards in the darkness, ignorant of our destination...'

There was more: 'To forget your bright face, the white-faced beauty has to put on a black veil. The waters of the yellow river swallow the blood of the fish that have been hacked to pieces...

For Abdulla, at least, these words were an epilogue; an epilogue to a novel that had long been finished.

EPILOGUE

Autumn that year was unusually miserable. On the fourth of October, while it was still dark, Abdulla was awoken by a familiar voice; he opened his eyes and saw Sunnat standing there.

'What is it? What's happened?' asked Abdulla, who hadn't yet washed his face: he didn't wish Sunnat good morning.

'You're expected,' said Sunnat. The boy had gone to the old town, which was why he hadn't been seen here for some time.

'Who by?' asked Abdulla, getting up and throwing his violet Uzbek kaftan over his shoulders.

'You've been summoned,' said Sunnat, squirming awkwardly. Abdulla swallowed.

'What's the time?' he asked.

'I'm not sure... maybe four or five.' Sunnat would not meet Abdulla's eye. Abdulla felt his legs give way.

'So they sent you to fetch me, did they?' he whispered.

'It's my job, boss,' the soldier replied, seeming apologetic.

'And if they tell you to fire, you'll shoot, will you?' Abdulla pointed to the rifle slung over Sunnat's shoulder.

Sunnat said nothing.

'May I go and get washed?'

'No, they're waiting, boss, you need to get a move on.'

'Aren't we even allowed to relieve ourselves, then?

'I don't know. Let's be quick about it.'

They filed out into the prison entrance hall. Four soldiers, with nervous dogs, guarded the outer doors to the
prison. Now prisoners' silhouettes could be seen in other
cells. The smoking paraffin lamp revealed a magnificent
shiny forehead: it could only be Fitrat. Some distance away,
a pair of round spectacles seemed to flash in the distance:
Cho'lpon? Abdulla thought he saw the hunched figure of
G'ozi Yunus, and Anqaboy's long neck. The dogs were
barking, the soldiers holding their leads were yelling, and
the Black Marias in the NKVD yard had their engines racing as they warmed up. All these sounds merged into one
single roar.

When Uzbeks have their early morning plov the first
guests appear and the hosts, taken aback, bustle about not
knowing what to serve first: someone runs to fetch water
to wash the guests' hands, someone else to get a towel,
another to warn the cook, another person to put the sam-
ovar on. But what sort of feast were they preparing now?

When Abdulla came out into the yard, he looked up
at the heavens. The October sky was covered with black
clouds, but gusts of wind off the Caiman mountains were
tearing through the layers of cloud and in the gaps that
opened up he could see a little cluster of stars, like a bunch
of grapes peering out when you part the thick foliage.
Abdulla's eyes stung with frustration when he recalled his
vineyards, the late-season grapes, as golden and warm as
these stars, hiding underneath palm-shaped leaves.

'Hurry up, get into the van,' Sunnat yelled in Russian.
Abdulla took a deep breath of the autumnal air before
climbing into the zinc-lined cabin. Fitrat, Cho'lpon,
Beregin and Anqaboy were already sitting on the Black
Maria's metal seats. Old Moshe was immediately noticea-

ble, because he was wearing his white gown. Are we really going to have a haircut and a shave before we're shot? Abdulla couldn't help wondering. But a closer look told him that the barber was also handcuffed. Moshe wasn't panting, snuffling or rasping any more: he sat in silent misery. As he made his way towards Cho'lpon, Abdulla accidentally jogged Moshe's knee: he looked up at him gloomily and said, 'We've been fooled, too.' Abdulla gave his shoulder an encouraging squeeze before moving to hug Cho'lpon, awkwardly, because of the handcuffs. Behind the pebble-lensed spectacles, tears were streaming from Cho'lpon's eyes.

'My weeping poet,' said Abdulla, embracing Cho'lpon tightly.

'My pride, my brave hero,' said Cho'lpon, unable to control himself.

The Black Maria's doors were slammed shut. All the prisoners sat down. The van moved off. They sat clinging tightly to one another's arms, as tight as their handcuffs would allow. Abdulla turned to Fitrat:

'Professor, they...' he began to say before Fitrat interrupted him:

'I know, I know, but I never did trust them. They've played that trick on all of us.' Abdulla relaxed. The van turned out of the gates onto the road: it raced down the asphalt streets of the new town. They all knew where they were being taken. For a long time, silence reigned in the van.

Then Abdulla leaned over to speak to Cho'lpon. 'For some reason,' he whispered, 'I remembered my vineyards today: the stakes, the leaves, the bunches of grapes.'

Cho'lpon's response was a heavy, pensive sigh. His lips began to move:

Softly, dawn breeze steals from the sky

> To kiss the blooms of the apricot flower.
> But the peach blossom turns her head away, shy:
> 'Go rot, you shan't kiss me at this early hour!'

> Old mother vine creeps from the frame
> To wake her tender, green leaf girl
> And, as the day begins, she will
> Bestow on her the utmost skill –
> And with the sweetest tendrils' curl,
> Mother entwines each passerby
> To fall in love with her girl and sigh…

At this point Abdulla joined in, and they began reciting in chorus:

> But now she's been rudely plucked, this young maid;
> Just wrapped around mince and tossed in the pot.
> Lovers of *dolmas* demand their mince hot –
> But think how old mother vine feels then!

Now Fitrat and Anqaboy added their voices:

> And when the wedding march is played
> And the bridegroom is led into view,
> Please remember the girl who's deep in the stew:
> No, don't forget, unbelievers, again!

Their voices were now so loud that they were ordered to shut up: a rifle butt was banged against the metal of the speeding van. But still the poem rose towards its climax.

> As nightingales kiss the sweet gentle breeze
> They are thinking of nothing but flowers.
> And though they sing with such wondrous ease,
> Blooms alone fill their warbling hours.

Fitrat and Cho'lpon leaned their heads on Abdulla's shoulders; the tears flowing from their eyes were like bunches of late autumn grapes. But these tears came not from fear of death, but joy of life.

> And the breeze that caresses one leaf today
> Doffs his cap to others tomorrow,
> And flirts with never a hint of sorrow;
> That's the only way he can play.

The noise coming from the depths of the Black Maria was like the cries of migrating birds, swirling into the air and then swelling again for a final uproar. What seemed to be a simple poem had become the language of birds, the song of a nation, the sorrow of their land. The van braked sharply and stopped. Like winged birds, the prisoners tumbled off their perches. Outside, dogs started barking, chains rattled, soldiers yelled. But Cho'lpon, however hoarse, did not stop reciting:

> "It is a leaf's destiny to fall;
> That is how it must be," they say.
> But mighty Life, which makes rules for all,
> Makes thousands more every day.

As he got out of the Black Maria and drew the fresh air into his lungs, Abdulla had time for one final thought: what a pity: only one of my stories has an ending.

TRANSLATORS' AFTERWORDS

This Uzbek novel gives the reader two for the price of one. The 'frame' novel is documentary fiction, a reconstruction of the last months of its main protagonist, the writer Abdulla Qodiriy, as he spend most of 1938 in an NKVD prison during Stalin's Great Terror, in which three quarters of a million innocent citizens were shot, and several million sent to be worked to death in the Gulags. In Uzbekistan, as in other republics of the USSR, the terror was even worse than in Moscow, for it virtually eliminated, on spurious charges of spying and counter-revolution, not just the Communist Party and local government elite, but much of the country's intelligentsia and trained professionals.

Abdulla Qodiriy was twentiethth-century Uzbekistan's most popular novelist. His *Past Days* of 1921–5 – the first modern full-length novel in Uzbek – was so popular that it was recited to gatherings in tea-houses: legend has it that a shepherd drove a flock of sheep 200 miles to exchange each one for a copy of the novel. His *The Scorpion Under the Altar* was equally loved: parents named their daughters after Qodiriy's heroines.

Born in 1894, Qodiriy was formed by the Pan-Turkic modernising movement of jadidism, and his efforts in the early 1930s to write works of socialist realism could not save him from Stalin's repressions. The son of the fourth wife of an elderly illiterate gardener, Qodiriy had a breath-takingly wide experience of life in Tashkent, working for a wood merchant, then as a Russian-language secretary. Like many Uzbeks, he was fluent in both Farsi and Russian; he was educated at a secular Russian school and at a madrasa (where he perfected his Arabic). He established himself as a writer in a country where literacy was still low (for a twentieth-century Uzbek, reading did not come easily, as the population went through five changes of alphabet – from standard to simplified Arabic, then to Soviet Latin, then Stalin's Cyrillic and, most recently, a new Latin alphabet). Qodiriy's love of satire (his article 'A Collection of Rumours') had him arrested in 1926, but his popularity and the patronage of the Communist leader Akmal Ikromov gave him one more decade of freedom.

The title of this novel comes from an early short story by Qodiriy, which Ismailov has integrated into his text. But it is Qodiriy's third and non-existent novel, *Emir Umar's Slave Girl*, that forms the core of Ismailov's *Devils' Dance*. *Emir Umar's Slave Girl* is rumoured to have been completed in the mid-1930s, but disappeared without trace, presumably burnt by the NKVD. Here it is re-imagined, along lines similar to Qodiriy's earlier work (which could be characterised as modernised Walter Scott) – the conflict of private love and public tyranny a century earlier, in an Uzbekistan that then consisted of antagonistic Khanates and Emirates, while the British and Russian empires watched, like hungry hyenas, for a pretext to intervene. What unites the core and frame novels becomes steadily clearer, as striking parallels emerge between Qodiriy awaiting his fate in prison and the beautiful Oyxon forced to marry the Khan of Kokand and then the Khan's doomed heir.

—

Poetry, unlike prose fiction, has been the mainstay of Uzbek culture for six hundred years; in the structure and tone of this novel it plays a key role. Qodiriy often recalls the lyrics of Cho'lpon, Uzbekistan's great poet, a man of the same stature as Europe's best twentieth-century poets. Cho'lpon (who also appears in the novel) shared the same fate as Qodiriy, but his later poetry showed that he foresaw their common tragedy.

In a similar way, a hundred years earlier, poetry flourished at the courts – and particularly in the harems – of Uzbek khans and emirs. Here, women found their voice, and it is the poetry of Uvaysiy, a close friend of the Khan of Kokand's first wife Nodira (who was herself a poet) that expresses, sometime with the modernity of a Marina Tsvetaeva, the frustrations and despair of a woman under a ruthless Islamic tyranny.

—

As an academic, primarily qualified in Russian and Georgian, I should explain why, with little Turkish and less Farsi, I have translated this novel from its original Uzbek. I first encountered the novel in Russian translation; it was clear that, in the worst old Soviet Orientalist traditions, the verse quotations had been travestied, not translated, and would have to be re-translated from the Uzbek. (In any case, I believe that bridge translation, no matter how competent the translators, is a game of Chinese whispers which exsanguinates or even cripples the original author's work.) After studying the Russian version of this novel, I found whole pages of the original Uzbek missing, and many passages glossed over, while pithy, even fruity Uzbek phrases were replaced by bland cliches.

Fortunately, the resources available to me – the Akobirov *Uzbek-Russian Dictionary*, the internet corpus of

Uzbek, Redhouse's Ottoman, and Steingass's Persian dictionaries, but above all the patience of Hamid Ismailov himself in answering questions and correcting errors – have, I hope, been sufficient to mitigate the arrogance of my translating the novel from an initial position of deplorable incompetence.

Oddly enough, in some ways Uzbek is closer to English than to Russian. Just as English is a hybrid of Germanic Anglo-Saxon with Romance Norman French, so Uzbek is a hybrid of Central Asian Turkic with Farsi. Both languages, unlike, say, French, have the luxury of choice between 'low' or 'high' synonyms and styles. Uzbek, like English, has a wide range of verb tenses, aided by an extensive range of auxiliary verbs, all of which facilitates the translator's work. But Uzbek, even more so than English, has a wide range of dialects. In Ismailov's original, particularly in the dialogues that take place in a crowded cell, where men from all over the country exchange views and informations, we meet every variety of Uzbek, from Jewish Bukhara to Afghan Uzbek. No translator can reproduce these variations in another language. All I could do was to enforce a standard language on the prisoners – allowing some local colour just in the proverbs that the cell elder comes out with.

In spelling the names of persons and places, I have tried to follow a principle: nearly all countries using the Latin script (the exceptions are Latvia and Croatia) reproduce letter-for-letter the spelling of foreign languages that also use the Latin script. Since Uzbek has, since 1995, had a stable and sensible Latin script, I have kept to the original spelling of Uzbek names. The pronunciation is self evident (even 'sh' and 'ch' have the same value as English). But there are two peculiarities the reader should note. One is that the letter [x] is pronounced as a Scottish or German [ch]

– the heroine Oyxon is pronounced more like 'Oyhon', but not 'Oykson'. The other quirk in Uzbek is the odd use of the apostrophe. A [g'] is the voiced form of [x], i.e. it is pronounced a little like a guttural French [r]; an [o'] is usually pronounced like the [u] in southern English 'put'. In all other cases, the apostrophe is just a transliteration of an Arabic glottal stop [*'ayn*] and is not usually pronounced. As is usual, however, where the spelling of an international place name is established, we keep that spelling: so Bukhara, not Buxoro; Kokand, not Qo'qon; Fergana, not Farg'ona, and so on. Utter consistency is elusive: for example, Ghazi is the international term for a fighter for Islam, but we use the Uzbek spelling G'ozi when it is a person's name.

Donald Rayfield

The Devils' Dance is filled with the poetry of Uzbekistan, including the work of Cho'lpon, one of the nation's most revered poets. Rhythm and metre are hugely important to Uzbek poetry, and to give any sense of what the original is like, it is crucial for an English translator to try and replicate this. That's of course quite a challenge, since Uzbek verse forms don't always sit comfortably with English words.

You might think that replicating metre and rhyme would tempt the translator to stray from the original. In fact, I found the opposite to be true since in order to phrase with clarity in English, rather than poetic obfuscation, I needed to work hard to get to the heart of the precise meaning and the way the original worked. It involved cross-referencing multiple translations again and again, with the help of Hamid Ismailov, Donald Rayfield and T. Mansurjon, all of whose help was invaluable. My versions, of course, are but shadows of the originals, but I hope that, at very least, they give a clear impression of them.

John Farndon